P9-AGI-750

This extraordinary novel,
by Greece's foremost young novelist, is both
an act of political daring and a work of art.

Needle sharp and harsh as a documentary,
Z is based on an actual murder—the political
assassination of a celebrated Greek patriot
and pacifist, and the subsequent investigation
by an extremely courageous young attorney
who followed the trail of responsibility and
guilt to the highest levels of a ruthless military regime.

Delving into the lives of dozens of people
—a carpenter, a fruit seller, a truck driver, a
reporter—Z shows how each played a role
either to toady to the regime or to bring the
crime to light. A beautiful elegiac passage,
"A Train Whistles in the Night," rises to
heights of lyric power as Vassilikos describes
the slow passage of the funeral train bearing
the shattered body of Z back to Athens.

Although Z is officially banned in Greece
and Vassilikos, for daring to write this book,
is now an exile from his native land, Z has
been a best seller throughout Europe and the
motion picture of the book, soon to be released
in America, was the official entry of France
at the 1969 Cannes Film Festival where it
won the coveted Jury Prize.

CINEMA V DISTRIBUTING, INC.

Presents

YVES MONTAND   IRENE PAPAS
JEAN-LOUIS TRINTIGNANT

DIRECTED BY COSTA-GAVRAS

FROM THE NOVEL "Z" BY VASSILI VASSILIKOS

MUSIC BY MIKIS THEODORAKIS

PHOTOGRAPHED BY RAOUL COUTARD

WITH

CHARLES DENNER, GEORGES GERET, JACQUES
PERRIN, FRANCOIS PERIER, PIERRE DUX, BER-
NARD FRESSON, JULIEN GUIOMAR, MARCEL
BOZZUFI, MAGALI NOEL & RENATO SALVATORI

American Premiere, Cinema I in New York
August 4, 1969

Z

VASSILIS VASSILIKOS

Translated from the Greek

by

Marilyn Calmann

BALLANTINE BOOKS   •   NEW YORK

English translation copyright © 1968 by Farrar, Straus and Giroux, Inc.

Library of Congress catalog card number: 68-19010

All rights reserved

Translated from the Greek original Z, published by Editions Themelio, Athens

Copyright © 1966 by Vassilis Vassilikos

This edition published by arrangement with Farrar, Straus and Giroux, Inc.

First Printing: September, 1969

Printed in Canada

Ballantine Books, Inc.
101 Fifth Avenue, New York, New York 10003

to Mimi

Acknowledgments

I would like to thank Mary Manheim
for inestimable help with the English version of my book.
I would also like to thank
Mary McCarthy, James Merrill,
Professor Joseph Frank of Princeton University,
and Ralph Manheim.
Also the Ingram Merrill Foundation,
whose generosity left me free to
work on the Greek text in Greece and
on its translation now in exile

Part 1

AN EVENING IN MAY,
FROM 7:30 TO 10:30

Chapter 1

The General looked at his watch as the speaker of the evening, the Assistant Minister of Agriculture, was winding up his address on the methods of fighting downy mildew:

"In summation, I recapitulate: the outbreak of the Peronosporaceae, or downy mildew, is prevented by spraying the grapevines with a solution of copper salts and especially copper sulphate. The classic solutions are the bordigalian and the burgundian fungicides; and it is called burgundian because it was first concocted in French Burgundy, from whence originate, believe me, the truly superb wines of the same name. The first, the bordigalian, is composed of a one-to-two percent solution of copper sulphate in water, the acidity whereof is neutralized by the addition of lime. The latter differs from the former insofar as use is made of Solvay soda instead of lime. These classic concoctions are modified by adding highly viscous substances to prevent the mixture from being washed away easily by the rain."

The General shifted his legs, setting the right one over the left, impatient with the length of the Assistant Minister's peroration.

"Also," the Minister continued, taking a swig of water from the murky glass the Secretary General had had the usher bring (it was May 22, 1963, for a whole week the heat had been stifling, and if the Minister's tongue were dry, his words might stick to each other), "powders with copper salts as a base are used because they are easier to work with. Three sprayings per year are carried out by means of special instruments called sprayers: the first spraying when the shoots attain a length of twelve to fifteen centimeters; the second slightly before, or slightly after, the blossoms appear; and the third a month later. However, when it is a damp year, and if the locale is damp, spraying must occur more frequently."

The rest of them, prefects and commissioners of the police department, had begun to feel sleepy. A good fellow, the Assistant Minister, but he spoke as if testing his forensic skill for the first time. He spoke in an overly scientific way, and besides, what did these officials care about downy mildew! The Assistant Minister, who did care, failed to realize that in Macedonia and especially in Salonika, where he was presently speaking, the vineyards were not as important as in his home territory, the Peloponnese, his electoral district. Here they had tobacco, and he still hadn't said the first word about that. On their level, they had managed things well: without knowing a thing about the subject, they had spread it about in their villages, districts, and prefectures that downy mildew was a disease brought directly from Eastern countries—thus enormously contributing to the anti-Communist movement in the area, because many villagers believed the rumor. Alas, not all. But the irresistible argument remained that the downy mildew oppressing their fields and withering their tobacco plants had appeared for the first time with Communism. They were of the same age. And in the pamphlets scattered from planes (which should have been spraying the tobacco fields instead) they had written in big red letters that Peronosporaceae was the disease of Communism.

Only the Directors of the Agricultural Bureaus of Northern Greece listened with attention, almost with reverence, to the flawless scientific analysis of their Assistant Minister. He continued:

"During the spraying process, the entire foliage of the vine must be well covered. The effect of the spraying is merely preventive and for this reason must never be neglected. Another genus of the Peronosporaceae family is the *Plasmopara nivea,* causing the Peronosporaceae of the shade plants. This too is controlled by being lightly sprayed with the bordigalian mixture. In concluding my present analysis of the methods of fighting downy mildew, I wish to thank you warmly for the attentiveness you have shown during this talk."

A bit of faint-hearted applause was heard and the Assistant Minister got down from the rostrum.

Then the General rose. He waited for the Assistant Minister to pass into the auditorium, and then, turning his back to the rostrum and facing the middle-aged, fattish, bald prefects and those officers of the police department inferior to himself in rank, indifferent perhaps only to the Directors of the Agricultural Bureaus, he said:

"I too wish to take the opportunity to add a few supplementary remarks to what the Assistant Minister has so elegantly expounded to you. Of course I am going to speak about our own downy mildew, Communism. And it is a rare opportunity for me, who am in charge of the supreme administration of the police department of Northern Greece, at this moment when the highest officers of the government are before me, to say a few words about the ideological mildew scourging our land.

"Personally, I myself have nothing against the Communists. From the very beginning, from time immemorial, they have roused in me only pity. I have regarded them as lambs strayed from the right path of our Hellenic-Christian civilization. And I have always been ready to help them, guide them, bring them back to the straight and narrow path of national consciousness. For, as we all know, Greece and Communism are irreconcilable by their very nature.

"However, like downy mildew, Communism must be fought at least preventively. With Communism as with mildew, we have to treat conditions caused by a variety of parasitical toadstools. And just as the spraying of the grapevine in three stages may keep it from being attacked by downy mildew, just so the spraying of human beings with mixtures appropriate to the circumstances becomes indispensable. The schools are the first stage for this kind of spraying. The shoots—to use the Assistant Minister's metaphor—have not yet acquired a length of more than twelve to fifteen centimeters. The second spraying—and my long-range experience at the head of the force can tell you that it is the most critical—takes place just before or shortly after the blossoms appear. Here, of course, I refer to the universities, to the workers, to the young people with problems. If this spraying is successful, it is very difficult, not to say impossible, for the sickness of Communist mildew to spread and by its corrosive influence wither the sacred tree of Greek freedom. The third spraying must occur a month thereafter, as the worthy Assistant Minister has emphasized. For this month substitute a period of five years and you will see that the same holds true here too.

"Conclusion: in this manner, the fertile fields of the Greek earth will nourish only good fruit, and the illnesses of our time—Communism and mildew—will vanish finally and forever. This is what I had to say to you to encourage you all in the difficult task of fighting both downy mildew and Communism."

Tumultuous applause drowned the finale of his speech. The assembly was over. Prefects, commissioners, and directors got up, lit cigarettes, stretched themselves, and, following their superiors, prepared to leave.

At the exit the Secretary General approached the General with a spineless, fluid movement and shook his hand. "And now, where to?" he asked him.

"To the theater, the Bolshoi Ballet," replied the General. "I have an invitation and I've got to go. Though I must stop first to pick up the Chief of Police, who . . ."

"They didn't send me an invitation," the Secretary General said suddenly, stopping in the middle of the long corridor that led to the broad marble staircase covered in red Persian carpeting.

"What an omission!" exclaimed the General, though he had little interest in the Secretary General. Secretaries general came and went, depending on what party happened to be in power. In the course of his long career he'd known dozens of them.

"But what can the State Theater have against the Ministry of Northern Greece?" the Secretary General exclaimed as he walked down the steps.

"Obviously it was carelessness or an oversight on the part of Personnel," said the General. "In any case, I'd be very happy to give you my invitation."

"But I wouldn't think of it!"

"I insist. The fact is—between ourselves—I have no intention of going. I only said so because I thought that ex-Communist—you know the one, the present manager of the Salonika rice fields—was listening."

"He was listening? The ex—?"

"The late leftist. In my files I have his statement denouncing Communism and all its fruits."

"I understand, I understand." The Secretary General was sticking with the General as far as the Ministry exit. "Even in ballet, you can't stand anything of Red Fascist origin."

"That's not it. At my age, I've learned to distinguish art from life. It's something else."

He lowered his voice as the guard at the door gave the military salute.

"Tonight," he said conspiratorially, "some so-called Friends of Peace are having a rally. I'm going to attend as an ordinary spectator and study the new slogans. Because, you must not forget, my friend—we who have been entrusted with the supreme task of protecting the state from infectious fungi are duty-bound to be omnipresent. That is why I am giving you my invitation to the Bolshoi Ballet with pleasure."

"Don't insist, General. It's impossible for me to accept this from you, truly impossible. I'll send my complaint through official channels to the director of the theater."

Meanwhile the General had unlocked the door of his

car. Protocol entitled him to a chauffeur, but he adored driving. He was getting in when the Assistant Minister and company appeared, hastily descending the staircase of the General Administration Building, in which the Ministry of Northern Greece was now located. They accosted the General just as he was turning on the ignition.

"May I give you a lift?" he asked, rolling down the window.

"I'm rushing to the airport," the Assistant Minister told him.

"My favorite drive," said the General. "Come on."

Who would have dared to turn down such a flattering proposal from the General? Generals, especially police-department ones, were always needed. They set out for the airport.

As they crossed the city, the General noticed that the evening lights were just beginning to glimmer faintly. The neon signs showed hardly at all in the darkness. The night, a beautiful, hot May night, was descending, ready to envelop all the strictly confidential secrets awaiting that evening. The General felt a profound delight. The plan had worked out to perfection; he himself was creating an alibi right now. So, chatting with the Assistant Minister about irrelevant matters, he drove him to the airport. On their arrival the first propeller of the plane, a D.C. Dakota, slowly started to revolve, the hulk still motionless. All the passengers were aboard; only the door remained to be closed. From his car the General watched the Assistant Minister and his retinue enter the plane. Then the flight of steps was removed. The other propeller was set in motion and the airplane taxied toward the runway.

The General turned back to the city just as things were starting to happen.

Chapter 2

From his open seat on his three-wheel pickup truck, Yango caught sight of the General's bony, retiring, cavernous features and took courage. He was running low on courage. The closer the moment came and the fiercer things around him got, the more clearly he heard a voice telling him: "Yango, don't do it." It was the first time he'd ever heard such a voice inside himself, indissolubly blended with the rattling cough of his machine, which still—where could he find the dough?—lacked mufflers.

Yes, because he liked beating up Reds. He got a profound kick out of it. The last time had been three weeks ago, at their May Day get-together. He'd broken into the group along with the other guys in the organization and given them a little lesson. Especially that tall one with the glasses who didn't know what it was all about and kept asking: "Why are you hitting me?" "Because I enjoy it, Four Eyes," Yango had answered and kept on punching him in the head. This was what he called a real beating: with the club an extension of the hand, the hand an extension of the soul, the soul an extension of the teachings of Autocratosaur, Autocratosaur an extension of Hitler—the only man, as Autocratosaur said, who had really tried to save the world from the Communists.

Only tonight, on the saddle of his pickup truck, he felt dependent like a rider on his horse. He knew his Benver; adored its every valve, its every pipe. From the starter to the speedometer, he knew its caprices. And the Volkswagen engine he'd installed in it had turned out to be a champion. He wasn't afraid the axle might break, or the pistons get banged up. He trusted it completely. What bothered him was having no slugging to do, not being free to use his hands. And besides, why was he doing this except for his poor little truck, his livelihood, his faithful companion in the daily struggle to earn his crust of bread and feed the five mouths—five counting his own—which had fallen to his lot in this dog's life?

He still needed ten thousand to pay off Aristidis, his partner. They'd bought it together, but he was doing the work and giving Aristidis his share. Little by little he had seen the unfairness of it. Why should Aristo—a good guy—but why should he get money for nothing? Who faced danger every second, in the midst of trucks, buses, military vehicles—those killers? Who lived on the razor's edge? He did. His partner didn't do a thing but pocket the dough. That's why he had decided to buy out Aristo and have the pickup truck and its revenue all to himself.

But where was he going to get that damned ten thousand? Ten grand in one pile. The last time he'd seen *one* grand was more than three months ago. The time he'd smacked his wife because she'd given a cup of coffee to that dirty Communist who'd been installing a pipe outside his house. He himself hadn't been there. He learned about it when he got back. He'd gone on a delivery job with some coffins. He took it hard, this being called by Nikitas, the varnisher, to take some coffins to a funeral parlor. They'd been sent to Nikitas for finishing. "Listen to that. I mean, polishing coffins!" Nikitas had sent his apprentice to call him from Vasileos Irakliou Street, at his regular pickup stand, to take them back. Not having any change himself, Nikitas gave Yango a thousand. Yango had changed it at the undertaker's and then come back to Nikitas with the money, keeping only thirty drachmas for himself, the price agreed on for the haul. At noon he went home gloomy. The funeral parlor had turned his stomach. His wife was doing the laundry. The kids were out playing on the street, in the ditches dug by the workmen. And just at that point, as he was gulping down his boiling-hot bean soup, she told him that she'd offered coffee to the Commie.

"He was working outside the house," she told him, "and we know him, don't we, Yango? So when he stopped to light a cigarette I invited him in for a coffee."

"And who do you think you are, you bloody bitch? Letting people into our house who don't want our King. You've stunk up the whole house, you damned whore. I've been feeding you and keeping you all these years and you go and fix coffee for the . . ."

And then one good slap—and another. He grabbed her by the hair. She started screaming. The children came running in. They got their share too. Just as she was, all wet from the laundry, she ran to the police sergeant, bawling and screeching hysterically that the brute had beaten her again, that she wanted a divorce, and the rest of it . . .

Every time he thought of that scene his chest swelled with pride. A feeling like just now when the General had greeted him with a nod, as though telling him "Everything's O.K." Well, the police sergeant had summoned him and in the presence of his wife had told him severely that he shouldn't do such things. They came under code regulations and as a representative of the law he would be forced to punish him. What punishment?—well, the two of them would discuss it after the woman left. Marigo went off, wiping her wet eyes with her wet housedress. Then Dimis (that was the police sergeant's name) got up and gave him a friendly punch on the back. "That's the way, Yango. That's what it means to be national-minded. Keeping the social parasites from even entering your house. Serves Marigo right, what you did. Next time she'll know who to fix coffee for and who not to. These women—all women, Yango—have their brains between their thighs. They won the vote and upset the balance of the country. The Reds have increased. Would you like some coffee?"

Ever since then, he and Dimis had been close friends. When they went for an evening stroll through the slum neighborhood—which, although it was in the center of the city, still had about it the misery and stench of a frontier village—Dimis would take his arm. That's right, arm in arm. Yango had the three stripes leaning on his arm, and his soul felt chevroned all over. The tenderest female hand had never given him as much pleasure. As they walked together, the neighbors would greet him with respect—those neighbors, what hadn't they called him? Louse. Lazy, good-for-nothing bum. Hooligan. Now, seeing him with the cop, they bobbed their heads as he passed. It gave Yango ineffable delight.

Around that time he met Autocratosaur. And Autocratosaur started his indoctrination. In the course of this morning's visit, he'd promised to pay the fine they'd slapped on him for the First of May disturbance. And to find the ten thousand to pay off his partner, so that in the future Yango could have the kamikazi—his pet name for the three-wheeler, because it was a Japanese make—all to himself. In return, Yango had only to take on the "transfer job."

That is to say, Autocratosaur put a lot of pressure on him. But slugging a guy was one thing; a traffic accident was another. Yango would do anything; he didn't draw the line. Yet in this case he felt hesitant. A voice kept telling him: "Yango, don't do it." But Autocratosaur was a clever one, a real snake. This morning he had led him to the café under the arcades and explained things to him man to man.

"Listen here, Yango," he had said, "I'd never ask you to do anything unless I knew in advance that you weren't going to come to any harm. The transfer job must be done. This VIP who's coming here tonight is a VIP who must be out of circulation for a little while. Because he's gotten very much under our skin. In London he stirred up that trouble for the Queen. At Marathon he made a peace march all by himself. In the Chamber he punched one of our deputies in the eye. And today he's coming here to play the tough guy. We have to give him a little lesson we Macedonians. The VIP must understand what Macedonia means."

"What's the VIP's job?"

"Deputy."

"Communist?"

"Yes, Yango. A fresh fruit, all shiny on the branch. And he's gotten too full of himself. We have to trim his wings a bit. Otherwise he'll fly too high and if they come to power they'll slaughter us—you and me first and foremost—with a tin-can top."

"Well—must I use the kamikazi?"

"Use the kamikazi."

"When does the VIP get here?"

"This noon, by air. From the capital."

"This calls for thought," said Yango, slurping his coffee down to the dregs.

"It calls for immediate action. You must give me a yes or no right now. After all, don't you belong to the death branch of the organization? What sort of a commando are you?"

These words from Autocratosaur hurt Yango deeply. He stared absentmindedly at the coffee dregs, as though trying to read his luck in them. Then, taking a deep breath, he said: "For this transfer job—he's a deputy, he's no ordinary little man—they will have to pay off my pickup truck and pay my fine, both."

"So be it," said Autocratosaur and got up. "We'd better go, because your colleagues are outside watching us. We mustn't incur suspicion. Tonight's the big night."

He paid for the coffees and they emerged from the arcade. It was sprinkling. A sudden springtime shower wetting the parked three-wheelers.

"Just one question before we separate," said Yango. "Today's Wednesday. The stores are closed in the afternoon. What's the excuse for the kamikazi being at the stand?"

"Don't you worry. You'll get more specific instructions elsewhere."

And he went, leaving Yango to his fellow drivers.

They had gathered under the marquee of the movie house to keep dry. Yango told them he was going to a tavern up the street for some retsina. Mastro-Kostas remarked that he too was thirsty. As they walked, Mastro-Kostas accidentally bumped against Yango and felt the club hidden on him.

"What's that?"

"A club," Yango said.

"And what do you need it for?" asked Mastro-Kostas.

"I've got it for a job this evening."

"Hey there, Yango, you've got a family. Just cool it."

"Somebody that's coming today—we've got to give him a little lesson, we Macedonians."

Mastro-Kostas didn't understand and Yango explained in a few words.

"If it's found out, it will be through you. Watch it!"

Mastro-Kostas left. Yango went on drinking. Ever since he had woken up that morning, something had been bothering him. He had reached the stand at 7:30, and still not one pickup. He was champing at the bit; he wanted to let off steam somewhere. Then he caught sight of the Commissioner approaching in plain clothes: yes, Mastodontosaur himself.

This was somebody he didn't know very well. He'd seen him twice, at most three times, always wearing his uniform, the white strap and the insignia. Now in plain clothes he looked different. From a nod in his direction, a cop's nod, he understood that the Commissioner wanted to talk to him in private. He threw down his cigarette butt and ground it out with his foot, then heavily —for the retsina had thickened his mood—went over toward him.

Mastodontosaur was standing under the big posters of an American Western that was playing at the movie house that week. Turning around, Yango saw that two or three of the boys from the stand were watching him. As soon as he got close, the Commissioner ran his hand over his thick mustache: "Let's go."

"Where?" asked Yango, feeling the club under his armpit to make sure it didn't show.

Mastodontosaur caught on immediately.

"I fixed a cord around the top to make it easier to hold," Yango explained.

They were now moving toward the tavern where a few minutes ago he had been drinking murky retsina with Mastro-Kostas.

"Can I get you a little drink, Mr. Commissioner?"

"No drinks for you today. You've got work, heavy work, and your brain has to be clear."

They sat down in a *bougatsa* pastry shop. A great honor for Yango, sitting at the same table with the Commissioner. For himself he ordered a cream *bougatsa* with lots of cinnamon. It was hot. When he saw it on the baking pan, his mouth watered. The shopkeeper sliced a piece, weighed it, then took down the scales and cut it into smaller squares. With the wax paper underneath, he put it on a plate and sprinkled it liberally with cinnamon and confectioners' sugar; then the waiter brought it with glasses of ice water. The Commissioner had ordered a cheese *bougatsa* and hot milk. Since the baking pan was now empty, he had to wait a bit till the next one came out of the oven. Before Yango had finished his *bougatsa*, the Commissioner's arrived with the hot milk.

"Be careful, it's boiling hot," the waiter warned. The Commissioner asked Yango if he'd like something more, but Yango said no.

"Their meeting was scheduled for the Catacomb, but they won't get that hall. However, they'll gather there, until they find another one. You'll go there too, early in the evening, without the kamikazi, and throw your weight around."

"Do I go into action on the spot?" asked Yango, shaking the powdered sugar off his lapel.

"No. You'll go there only to spread a little terror. You're for the big VIP tonight. You mustn't show your hand too soon. The rest don't interest us."

"And if it rains?"

"If it rains, it rains. What do you mean?"

"The tires might slip and I might not be able to . . ."

"It won't rain."

"And where are they going to hold their meeting?"

"That you'll find out at the police station. After the Catacomb you'll go by there to get final instructions about time, place, etc. Do you understand? And something else. When de Gaulle was here, you left your post, I hear, and went off to a barbecue. I don't want anything like that today. I know you're a good man. Don't mess things up for us. The orders are strict. I'll be there too, and I'll have my eye on you. And all the higher-ups will be there. It's an honor they chose you. Understand? The VIP is strongly built. You may have to wrestle with him. Though that's rather unlikely, because the kamikazi will do the job."

"I can handle them all with my little finger. They knocked off my father, so . . ."

"Bravo. Your little *koumbaros*, your buddy, will be with you—Vango. He'll get into your kamikazi by then. He knows."

"Where will I find him?"

"He'll find you. But you tell him what I've been telling you because I don't have time to see him again. And today you haven't seen me, and I haven't seen you. Understand?"

"Yes sir, Mr. Commissioner."

"I want a good transfer job. Now beat it back to the stand, and button your lip."

This last hint Yango ignored, however, once on his own. He felt the club strong in his armpit and calmed down. He had the happy feeling that the entire police force, which tracks down thieves and cheap crooks, drug pushers and pimps, had concentrated its attention on him. So, back at the stand, he couldn't restrain himself. He peacocked to his boys there.

"That man you saw is the Commissioner. He treated me to a *bougatsa*. A real full-grade Commissioner."

"Which Commissioner?"

"Mastodontosaur."

"You're playing the big shot these days, Yango."

"And what's he after, Yango?"

"He's after me because he needs me. Did any Commissioner ever treat you to a *bougatsa*?"

"When you don't eat *bougatsa*, you don't care if it's burning in the oven."

"I'm indispensable to them."

"You're an honor to the porter's profession."

"We're not porters. We're transport men."

"You wangle things for yourself. You do jobs outside the city too. If they catch us, they take away our license."

"If you get caught for any violations, I'll wangle things for you."

"And just how, Mr. Yango?"

"I've sweated to have a good name with the police force. I've got privileges."

"I'd rather croak without a cent than have a good name with the police. You never know when they'll do you dirt."

"What're you saying, you scum?"

"Your mother's ass. That's what I'm saying."

"Your own mother's, you piece of fairy tail!"

"Go get screwed, you dirty stool pigeon . . ."

In a rage he pulled out the club.

"Calm down, boys," said Mastro-Kostas, stepping between them. "Stop the brawl. All this time here and not a single job yet. Are we going to earn some bread or just eat each other?"

At that moment two men appeared, calling out from the sidewalk across the way for Yango Gazgouridis.

It was the first time Yango had seen them. They were mysterious types, whom he immediately sized up as shady characters. One of them crossed the street in his direction.

"Are you Yango?"

"I am."

"We want you for a job."

Yango understood and went toward him.

"Let's go and I'll explain it to you."

"Looks like a lot of chasing about today, Yango. Watch it!" the oldest of the porters shouted after him.

The other shady character was waiting behind the columns of the Agricultural Bank. They put Yango between them—one on his left, the other on his right.

"Guarantors of the King."

"What's that mean?"

"Members of the League of Guarantors of the Constitutional King of the Hellenes. Fatherland—Religion—Family." And simultaneously taking out their membership cards, they stuck them under his nose. Though Yango didn't know how to read, he understood from the shape of the card and the skull and crossbones that they must belong to some organization affiliated to his.

"Pleased to meet you," he said.

"Tonight our league is going to participate too. And we're rather insulted that they chose you for the GC."

"What GC?" asked Yango. He certainly didn't like these shady characters at all.

"This baby here's a fine one," said the second one sarcastically.

"He's playing the virgin. Doesn't know what GC means! What do they teach you in your league?"

"I do delivery work, big boy—pickup runs, as we call it."

"GC—as you call it—means Gorilla Communist. Get it?"

"I get it."

"Well, we came first of all to make your acquaintance —look you over because we're guarantors of the King— and then we'll make our report to the leader."

"Which leader?"

"Ours. He sent us a message last night to come and meet you. You better know we'll have an eye on you tonight. It's a tough assignment. Evidently you don't know. But we do, we're in the underground network. Our outfit isn't recognized officially and our membership cards aren't stamped by the police department. We'd have liked to do the job, but since we're undergound . . . Well then, good fishing."

He gave Yango a kidney punch, but his hand hit the hidden club and he pulled it back, making a face.

"He looks good," said the first to the second.

"Armed to the teeth," said the second to the first.

"Now go back to your little truck and shut up," said both together to Yango.

With relief he watched them out of sight, then went back, walking glumly under the arcade. Though it had stopped raining, the pickup trucks were still covered with burlap, parked one behind the other. "Not a single hauling job all day, not one single hauling job." As he passed the kiosk, Yango heard the voice of the kiosk owner, like an answer to his complaints: "Yango! Nikitas sent his apprentice with a message for you to stop by. He needs you for a transport job."

He turned and looked at the old man in his kiosk, all covered with scaly newspapers and gaudy magazines. This job was what he wanted. He'd got dizzy tramping around all morning. Time to get down to the grind. Besides, Nikitas owed him twenty drachmas: he had gone by yesterday to collect but hadn't found him.

On his way to the varnisher now, he glanced at the big town clock. Twelve o'clock sharp. Very little traffic in the center of town. He thought of going into a tavern to have a drop, but he preferred to wait till he had concluded the job with the furniture man.

The shop had that familiar smell left by soot and turpentine. FURNITURE—WALLPAPER—POLISH—VENETIAN BLINDS —UPHOLSTERY. Bent over a small table, Nikitas was rubbing away. In the back the apprentice, who had a way of always looking dumbstruck because he was deaf-mute, was puttying an armchair.

"I got the message from the kiosk and came," Yango announced.

Nikitas wiped his hands on his white smock and extended his little finger by way of a handshake.

"I've got two bureaus, one bed, and this table I'm varnishing; they have to be delivered to the merchant this evening."

"It's Wednesday. The stores are closed after noon."

"That doesn't matter. He'll be expecting them. Take them around to the back door. Here's the address."

"This afternoon I can't. I've got work."

"Come later this evening. Seven, seven-thirty."

"I can't."

"They have to go tonight. The merchant is a good customer and I've promised him. Then I'll give you the twenty drachmas I owe you. I'll be here till nine."

"Tonight I've got work," said Yango with a sigh. "Tonight I'm going to do something big—really nutty. It may come to killing a man . . ."

"Quarreling with somebody again?"

"Don't bother about it. You'll find out tomorrow."

"Why tomorrow?"

"Because it'll happen tonight and you'll find out about it tomorrow."

"I don't get it. What's up?"

"What's it to you?"

"Yango, you get worked up too easily. You're a good man, watch out you don't get involved."

"I thought you had a job for me right now. If I'd known it was for later, I wouldn't have come."

In the background the apprentice was smiling, dumbstruck, uncomprehending.

"You think what I'm saying is funny, kid?" Yango said, ready to take offense.

"Let the poor kid alone," Nikitas begged him. "I took him in for my father's soul."

Yango went back to the stand.

Now it wasn't just the General who greeted him. Other familiar faces nodded as he passed. Astride his kamikaze, he couldn't make them out clearly. Night had fallen and the area was now jammed with people. There were very few neon signs and the lighted store windows were hidden by the passers-by. He kept thinking of the ten thousand drachmas he'd get to buy out Aristidis and of the fine that was going to be paid to buy off the law. He felt proud of being the only mounted person among so many pedestrians.

Yes! Now he was getting hot. He was getting angry. He was boiling inside, all over, looking for an excuse to blow his lid. An hour ago he'd been at the Catacomb. Mastodontosaur was there and told him to go tear down the announcement put up by the peace-meeting people.

Yango didn't understand why he had to tear it down.
"So they won't know where to go," the Commissioner
growled. The hell with it, was Yango's opinion. What
did he care? He knew the place well. With a resolute
step he pushed through the waiting crowd and reached
the big poster put up there in the traffic island, where a
little grass relieved the expanse of asphalt. With one big
hand he grabbed the poster from up top and tore it off
the way he would undress a whore—a violent movement
which aroused general anger all around him. "You, if
you've got the guts, come back here!" someone shouted
at him. That did it. The blood went to his head, but he
had his instructions: steer clear of these people. He—
Yango Gazgouridis—was assigned to the VIP. On the
other hand no bastard had ever dared say to him: "You,
if you've got the guts, come back here." He turned and
eyed them as they gestured threateningly. He could
have taken care of them easily. But he had to hold back.
And he moved along down to where the Panorama bus
station used to be. Outside the Petinos Café.

And right there he saw her. "You here too, you bloody
bitch?" It was the female community councillor in his
neighborhood, the one the leftists had supported. Seething inside from the insults he had had to put up with, he
had to let off steam. He gave her two kicks in the belly.
The first one missed, but the second landed right in the
meat. She doubled up. He was ready to pull out his
club, but she ran. She was hiding in the shop next door,
where there were antiques, icons, candlesticks, and other
junk in the window. "She got away," he thought, en-
raged, and in his blind fury he grabbed a chair from the
café and hurled it into the bric-a-brac shop. The chair
went through the door, hitting a little girl, but missed
the dirty bitch he was after. The café owner and his customers got up; they were coming at him menacingly.
The shopkeeper, a fat bald man, came out with a pole.
Yango realized he would have to put the brakes on
again so as not to show his hand too soon. If Autocratosaur heard about it, he might refuse to pay up. So, even

though all these dead ducks were no problem for him, he hopped a taxi—it was almost time—and went straight to the police station.

The taxi driver, who had witnessed the scene, made no comment. "Those son of a bitches," said Yango, "think they're somebody." The station was close by. He told the taxi driver to wait: he'd go upstairs for two minutes and be right down.

Inside, the smell calmed him, his fever passed as though he'd taken a cold shower. He had a buddy with him when he took the taxi back to the Catacomb. By now the crowd had dispersed. The stand at Vasileos Irakliou was only a step away; he went there and got in his pickup, and now for an hour he'd been doing chariot races by himself on the pavement, which was gradually emptying of traffic and filling with people, outside the new hall found for the meeting, at the corner of Ermou and Venizelou Streets. He greeted the General and took courage. "You, if you have the guts, come back here." The voice refused to subside. "I've got the guts and here I am," he told himself. Just so long as they weren't late for the transfer job. Now was the time to strike, while the iron was hot.

Chapter 3

Mastro-Kostas couldn't stomach Yango. And tonight he'd dropped by there—corner of Ermou and Venizelou—just to have a look. He saw the fierce expression on the faces of the counterdemonstrators. He saw the policemen, some in uniform, some in plain clothes, unmoving; he saw stones being thrown at the

Labor Union Club windows, heard shouts: "Bulgar Z., you'll die!" "You dirty nances, you'll all die!" And he saw some of the true believers who were heading for the meeting being seized abruptly and beaten in dark corners. He veered sharply and took the bus back to his little house. What he had suspected ever since that morning, what he'd "squealed" in fact, he now saw with his own eyes actually happening tonight. And who knows, he thought, what is still to come.

In his mind he relived the black days of the underground, deportation, torture. To someone else, what he had just seen would have been inexplicable. But not to Mastro-Kostas, whose whole life had been taken up with fighting for the same ideals. In the end he'd gotten tired; he'd bowed down. Eh, he wasn't made of granite. Others he knew, more established than himself, with better connections, had nevertheless signed their "declaration of repentance" even earlier. He had been out of action only for the past six years, and he'd sworn in the name of his children never to get involved in politics again. Because, as he got older, his arms got weaker. He could not lift heavy weights any more. He was a porter at the same stand as Yango.

But he couldn't bear Yango; he reminded him of the torturers he'd known on the barren islands. Those brutes, who had no soul yet tried to tear souls out by the roots, who dipped men in the sea tied up in sackfuls of cats till they'd abjured Communism, who beat them raw, who degraded them. That was the kind of scoundrel Yango was. And if they took it upon themselves to build a New Parthenon,* Yango would have been among the first to be drafted.

But Mastro-Kostas had learned to keep his mouth shut. He himself had been shaken. His faith in the Idea had crumbled. So much struggle, so much sacrifice, so much blood; and once again the traitors, the collabora-

---

* New Parthenon: the name given to the island of Makronissos, where political prisoners were deported during the civil war of 1947–1949.

tors, the men who'd sold out to the Germans, were in power. Those who had "repented" earlier, he realized, had been paid off, were more or less in clover. And he was still here, with two kids who never stopped growing; with a wife who never stopped doing other people's wash; with his back, which never stopped lugging other people's wares. Well, what for? The time comes when a man cracks. It had happened to him just six years ago.

But that Yango, he couldn't stomach him. He knew about his life and habits. They would talk it over with the other fellows at the stand, whenever Yango was off on a job. A pet of the police, Yango could operate as he pleased. They all had licenses for delivery jobs in the city only. Yango had a license to take the stuff anywhere he wanted. If any of them stepped over the line, they had to pay for it down to the last cent. Yango always fixed things up—how? in what way?—and even groused into the bargain. He was so sure of his power he didn't even bother to keep it secret. He blurted out everything like someone who'd never learned to be afraid.

Exactly like this morning. When Mastro-Kostas saw him glum and sullen, he asked what was wrong. Instead of answering, Yango suggested they have a drink of retsina. Mastro-Kostas also liked a drop. And so they went to the tavern across from the Modiano Market. While they were walking side by side, his hand had involuntarily brushed against the brute and hit something hard, heavy, something he didn't recognize.

"What're you hiding, Yango? A whip?"

He said it was a club.

"And what do you need it for? You've got strong arms."

"Tonight arms aren't enough. Forget it. Better not ask. I've got obligations."

They had sat down at a little table and ordered half a kilo of wine.

"Well, here's to you!"

"Here's to you," replied Mastro-Kostas, who had noticed something funny in Yango's mood and wanted to get to the bottom of it.

"Eh, how'll you do it? How're you going to get hold of those ten thousand drachs?"

Yango explained, told him everything down to the tiniest detail.

"Don't get involved in such things, Yango. You're poor, a nobody, a nothing. The poor always get it in the neck. The big ones stay on top. The big fish eats the little one . . ."

"Are you giving me a lecture to wake me up, Mr. Kostas?"

"You have kids, a family, Yango."

"Anyway, if it's leaked, it'll have come from you. Watch out!"

That Z.—Mastro-Kostas didn't know him. He must have been one of the deputies who'd come up with the left after withdrawing from the party. His brain, still murky from sleep and retsina, began turning swiftly. He hadn't tried to find out more; he hadn't wanted the brute's suspicions aroused. Deep inside, a feeling of solidarity began to stir, a feeling for whatever had once formed the core of his life. In front of him he had an enemy, someone aiming, if he could, to mangle a deputy on his side. Every time an election came around, though he steered clear of the parties, for once Mastro-Kostas would feel at one with the others, when he secretly gave his vote *there*.

"Let's drink another half," Yango suggested and banged the half-kilo can on the table.

"No. I have to get some radios in a shop."

He had been in a hurry to get away. Mrs. Soula, in the shop where he went for these jobs, was the wife of the director of the EDA * offices of Salonika. He wanted to tell her at once what he had heard.

He walked along in anguish. It was his first political act after he had sworn he would never touch politics again. And his joy, surging from a source he was surprised to find in himself, only increased his anguish.

Yango, who had not known him very long and to

* EDA: United Democratic Left.

whom nobody talked much at the stand, was ignorant of his past. If he'd known that Mastro-Kostas had once been a devoted party man, perhaps he wouldn't have opened his mouth.

In every man—especially in a porter—there are smoldering embers from a life never lived, a house never built, a pickup license never obtained. At the slightest breath, the embers flare up and the past comes to life.

He had reached the Electroniki shop and walked in through the glass door. The manager, seeing him enter in a hurry, shook his head no; he didn't want him to deliver anything today. But Mastro-Kostas signaled he was not there for business and skipped behind the partition to find Mrs. Soula, who worked there as a bookkeeper.

She was surprised to see him. Maybe he even smelled of wine. He told her it was absolutely urgent that they go outside and talk. On the sidewalk, once he'd made sure that no one was listening, he said: "Someone's supposed to come who's called Z. They'd better look after him; a trap's been set."

"And where did *you* find out about it?"

"They were talking about it somewhere. I was there and I heard. Don't say I told you; I've been threatened. They said: 'If it's found out, it could only have come from you.'"

"Who are they? Where's the somewhere? Who threatened you?"

"I can't tell you any more, Mrs. Soula. I'm only a poor guy, try to understand. I've started building a house without a permit. I've been after a license for my three-wheeler for two years now and I haven't got it yet. And then I'm afraid of their gang. They're brutes, don't stop at anything. I've got three broken ribs from Makronissos."

"I won't say anything."

"Not even to your husband. No one told you about it. Otherwise I'm lost."

"I won't even tell my husband."

"I know what they're like. I know what foul trash they

are. You live somewhere else. We're with them every single day and have to be careful. Look out for Z.! They'll eat him alive!"

On this note he had left. Now, home and falling asleep, he no longer had any doubts—after the counter-demonstrators he'd seen outside the building where Z. was to speak, and the worked-up crowd—that trouble was brewing for everyone this night. "It was the same then, too!" he said aloud. "The very same! They put the women in black outside the law courts and shouted: 'Death to the murderers!' Nothing's changed. Seventeen years have gone by; it's all the same again. Again! Ah, where are you, youth—you who mirrored the man I betrayed."

"Stop raving," his wife called out from the kitchen. "It rained today and the ceiling's leaking. A rotten house built on the sly is all I deserve and all I've got for a lifetime with Mr. Kostas."

He turned over on his good side and went to sleep.

Chapter 4

She'd been right. That's the only thing he could say now as he looked through the Labor Union Club window at the commotion outside. "They'll kill him: they'll consume him, just the way they tossed the first Christians to the hungry lions." And these hungry lions howling down below—skinny, ill-dressed, sickly—how could they clamor for hunger and misery and against peace? But this was no time for philosophy. It was a seething, dangerous time. He was waiting for Z. and his entourage to emerge from the hotel.

He had done his duty. When his wife phoned in the morning, saying, "I want to meet you right away," Z. and this evening's assembly hadn't crossed his mind. Soula's voice was alarming. He thought: something serious has happened to her, an error in the account books, a threat. "What is it? What is it?" he asked her anxiously. "You start out at once from your office, and I'll start out from mine. Come down the right-hand sidewalk." When they'd parted this morning, everything had been fine. It wasn't yet ten o'clock. What could have happened in an hour and a half? He knew his wife. She wasn't easily upset. It took a great deal to shatter her splendidly cool nerve. So what had happened? He stumbled down the stairs. On the street he was almost running.

"Someone came," she told him once they had met as agreed, outside a perfume shop. "Someone who begged me not to tell who he was—not even you—and he told me they're going to assassinate Z. tonight. I didn't know you expected Z. tonight."

He was silent. His wife's ignorance of Z.'s coming lent greater urgency to her message.

"And the one who gave me the information, he doesn't even know who Z. is."

"How did he find out about it?"

"Is this a cross-examination, or will you believe what I'm telling you? You've got to act at once."

She was ready to leave.

"Just a moment, Soula," he said. "One moment."

"I can't. The boss looked at me suspiciously as I left. You know very well he may fire me any time on account of you."

Then he, returning to the EDA offices, immediately called the lawyer Matsas, without revealing that the information had come from his wife. And Matsas said he would report it right away to the Public Prosecutor and ask for protection.

"What kind of protection?" he reflected now in front of the Club window. "They'll kill him. They'll eat him alive!" Till a stone, accompanied by a cry of "Bulgar, you'll die tonight!", came through the window and hit him on the nose.

Chapter 5

The lawyer, Georgios Matsas, son of Jannis, member of the Salonika branch of the Greek Committee for International Détente and Peace, was waiting below at the iron gate of the building on whose third floor Z.'s speech was scheduled to take place in a hall next to the Labor Union Club. He himself was greeting the audience, to give them courage.

The Friends of Peace, like the first Christians, arrived with reverence, with that deeper certainty of people who believe in something, in an idea, in a God. They believed in peace, a badly worn word to be sure, which in our own days has acquired a new meaning. Peace could no longer be conceived as the apathetic preference of human beings for concord and love among nations. Peace required support, participation, a struggle against whatever threatened to disrupt it. So they were not afraid of the howls of the pterodactyls or the swooping birds of prey—bearded vultures, sparrow hawks, turkey buzzards—or the menacing movements of the carnivores —jackals, coyotes, wolves—which had gathered on the surrounding sidewalks and were choking the entrance, beneath the almost paternal gaze of the police and the security agents.

Many of them streamed in right from the Catacomb, where, according to the newspapers, tonight's meeting was to take place. There they had read the torn an-

nouncement about the change of hall and without a fuss
walked on: it was just two blocks away. And when they
saw the "outraged citizens" arm in arm with the police,
hurling curses and denunciations, jeering, aiming
punches at them, they realized how essential the meeting was.

And Matsas at the entrance was keeping up their
courage, welcoming them. He was trying to counteract
at least the fright caused by the policemen, who were
loudly shouting their names, as though they—the friends
of peace—were princes and counts whom some old ma-
jor-domo was announcing at a reception held by two
deaf kings. Other policemen, in plain clothes, threatened
them in furtive whispers: "Remember the hospital!" or
"Ten years in prison and you still haven't come to your
senses." Matsas's presence was one familiar element in
an unknown quarter of the moon. Because this quite
friendly part of the city, with its closed shops and old
buildings, its commodious intersections and small alleys
radiating from the Modiano Market like little streams,
had metamorphosed into a bloodthirsty arena, a clandes-
tine crossroads of the anomalous, a danger zone planted
with mines left over from the Occupation.

Who else indeed, Matsas thought, was here in this
place tonight except the impenitent murderers of the
Occupation? There's Autocratosaur, for example, an important Nazi hireling, acquitted after the Civil War.
There's Dougros, from the Hitlerite Militia of Poulos,
carrying a life sentence for collaboration with the Germans; Leandros, an old member of the Greek Nazis. Too
many others to count.

Every so often he would leave his post near the door
and go over to the kiosk to phone either the Public Prosecutor or the Chief of Police. What unheard-of things
were happening tonight! The darker it became, the fiercer were the faces all around. Neither the security
agents nor the policemen were lifting a finger to help
those being knocked about by the counterdemonstrators.

"Where's the Prosecutor?"

"I don't know."

"Who's speaking?"

"Who are *you?*"

"I want his home number."

"Look it up in the directory."

"The directory doesn't list it."

"I don't know it."

And then: "Mr. Chief of Police?"

"He's not here."

"Where is he?"

"Where the trouble is."

"But I'm phoning you from there."

"He'll be coming along, he's on his way. Phone the station." He phoned the station and some officer put him on to the Emergency Squad. Did they take him for a fool? He saw baboons in the distance, approaching with baskets of stones. These were not chance occurrences.

He knew very well they were not. Ever since the meeting had been announced in the press, they'd begun following him and the other lawyers of the committee. He himself had had two shadows. Wherever he went, they tagged behind him. Suddenly his actions were no longer private. His freedom had been cut off. As if he were smuggling dope and the bloodhounds of the Security Police wanted to catch him in the act. Once he caught one of them off guard—the short one with the checked jacket. "I'm on duty, Mr. Matsas," was the answer. Then he turned to his friend, the Secretary General of the Ministry of Northern Greece. The latter pretended surprise. "If you don't believe me, come and look." And he drew him to the window and pointed out his shadows at the Ministry exit. It let up for a day or two—he thought his complaints had worked. Later he learned that during those days all the detectives had been mobilized for the security of an eminent visitor, General de Gaulle. After that a black limousine would park at the corner, by his house, and remain until late at night, when all the lights had been turned off. He watched it from behind the blinds. At that point he went, with the president of the legal society, to the Chief of Police. "Unfortunately, that's an order from the Ministry of the Interior, Mr. Matsas. We have to follow all members of the Peace Committee. I cannot do otherwise, no matter how much I respect you personally."

This was one thing that convinced him nothing was happening by chance tonight. The other was the strange attitude of Zoumbos, proprietor of the Catacomb. He had agreed to lend his place for the Friends of Peace meeting and had pocketed the full rent—three thousand drachmas. Then yesterday afternoon, out of the blue, Zoumbos said he couldn't let them have it unless they brought a permit from the police. In vain Matsas tried to explain that a permit was required for outdoor meetings only, not for meetings in an enclosed area.

"I don't want to get mixed up in anything. Either you bring me the permit or I won't let you have the place."

"But, Mr. Zoumbos, you're being unreasonable."

"I know exactly what I'm saying."

"Unless there's something you're not saying."

"There's nothing I'm not saying, and I'm very reasonable. You lawyers can make up whatever you like out of your heads."

"If you'd told us this several days ago, we'd have had time to look for another hall. We'd have had time to inform people through the newspaper. Now you're really making trouble for us! They'll come here from all over the city, and what will they see? An announcement telling them to go somewhere else! And where else, Mr. Zoumbos? At the last minute you tell me! Where'll we find another hall?"

"That's your affair. I'm returning the rent you paid me in advance. I'll also give you the forfeit that's due because of the cancellation of the agreement. Now . . . leave me alone!"

"But this isn't the way to behave, a big cabaret-owner like you!"

"What do you want, Mr. Matsas? I have to make a living."

"I'm not saying you don't."

"Then leave me alone."

"Did they put so much pressure on you?"

"Who put pressure on me?"

"You know very well who."

"I don't know anything."

"Why are you stuttering all of a sudden?"

"You're not getting anywhere, Mr. Matsas. Nowhere at all. Goodbye." And Zoumbos got up to leave.

"One minute," the lawyer called after him. But Zoumbos had already disappeared.

"It started him thinking. Not only was he being followed, there was now Zoumbos's refusal. Had someone perhaps overheard their conversation? Turning around, he saw a character who at that precise moment lifted his newspaper to cover his face. Had he been planted there? Or was Matsas overly suspicious? Then he got another idea. He remembered Prodomidis, of the Rotunda Theater. He had let them have the theater on a previous occasion for the same kind of meeting. Matsas telephoned him, but he too beat around the bush.

"Just now, a little while ago, Mr. Matsas, they paid me a visit here . . ."

"Who?"

"Inspectors from the Department of Public Entertainment. They prohibited the renting of the hall until it's fit for the public."

"What's wrong with the hall?"

"The seats aren't set up."

"Our meeting won't take place until tomorrow."

"We're short of staff because the summer season hasn't started yet. And it's not as easy as you think to set up the seats. I'm very sorry. Truly, I'm sorry."

"I understand."

"You remember how pleased I was in the past to let you have the theater. I also happen to be a pacifist. But now . . ."

As he hung up, he thought: No, Zoumbos couldn't get away with it. He had to find him again, talk to him, persuade him. He phoned Zoumbos's home and his wife gave him all the phone numbers where he might be found. He went through them one by one but couldn't locate him anywhere. He got home about 11:30 exhausted but in spite of everything woke at dawn. From behind the blind he saw the black limousine; this time it had been there all night.

Early in the morning he went to the Prosecutor and demanded his intervention for the hall. The Prosecutor actually sent a written message to the Chief of Police requesting that he "persuade the owner to make his hall available after all." About eleven o'clock Matsas had to return to the Prosecutor on another, more serious matter. He now had been informed that they were planning to murder Z. Who? How? He didn't know. Someone got wind of it and passed it on to someone else. Finally it had reached him. He didn't find the same prosecutor. Another man sat in the armchair, shaking his head gravely.

"With such vague charges, all I can do is relay the matter to the police force. While you are here I'm going to phone the Chief of Police and pass the information on to him."

He phoned, but the Chief was out. He then asked the officer on duty to have the charges communicated to the Chief.

"All right?"

"All right."

The Prosecutor actually looked sleepy. He was probably thinking that lawyers these days (perhaps because of lack of work) spent a lot of time on extracurricular affairs.

"At any rate," concluded the Prosecutor, "rumors of this nature often circulate. It is not wise to pay too much attention to them."

Still in search of a hall, Matsas left the Prosecutor. The only possible site was the Catacomb. But Zoumbos had disappeared. At 2:30 Z. and Spathopoulos arrived. Along with the others, Matsas met them at the airport. He didn't know Z. But when he saw him coming down the steps off the airplane, a feeling of certainty flooded him. Z. was a real man, powerful, with a high forehead, a leader, a true champion of the Balkan Games. He was holding a raincoat in one hand, and a briefcase with the other. Matsas recognized him from photographs in the newspapers when he'd walked alone from Marathon to Athens, the month before. Then he'd looked tormented, harried. Close up, he was something else. As they all walked toward the car, Z. turned and asked him suddenly: "Is everything ready for this evening?"

"Nothing's ready, unfortunately. We don't have a hall, and the public hasn't heard about it. They'll come, and we won't know where to put them."

They didn't stop to eat. After dropping their suitcases at the hotel, they all went to the Chief of Police. He received them coldly though not hostilely, as representatives from the other shore. He had the air of a movie American negotiating with Russians, carefully observing his adversaries' every gesture and movement as though fraught with meaning, when in reality it meant nothing at all.

"Well, gentlemen," he told them, "to be brief, the hall isn't in good shape. I have here"—and he drew a sheet of paper from his drawer—"the report of the committee of public entertainment. It says that the hall needs certain improvements, which Zoumbos hasn't taken care of."

"But it was in use as a music hall right up to April, Chief. How can it be unsuitable now, less than a month later?"

The Chief turned a steady gaze on them, hoping by the serenity of his countenance to prove his sincerity. "By far the most important thing," he went on, "is that the hall lacks an emergency exit."

"Then it shouldn't have been used as a music hall."

"Music halls don't have emergencies; in meetings such as yours there is always the risk of stirring people up."

"The report, if I'm not mistaken, mentions an exit not an emergency. No emergency will be created by our side."

The Chief assumed a professionally patronizing manner. "Listen, boys, I have nothing against your renting the hall; and you have nothing against me. I'll call Zoumbos and try to persuade him. Though I very much doubt if I'll succeed."

"When you want to, Chief, you can manage anything."

"I respect you personally, Mr. Matsas, and I hope that you, especially, won't overestimate my power. I am only a humble cog in the government machine."

Z. had said nothing, Matsas recalled. He was too proud to mention the rumors of an assassination. He merely stared over the Chief's head at the portraits of Paul and Frederika, examining the frames.

Only later in the afternoon did Matsas learn definitely from the officer on duty that Zoumbos had refused, giving unlikely excuses such as that he'd thought he was renting the hall to the lawyers' association; that if he'd known it was for the so-called Friends of Peace, he'd never have signed the contract.

"But it says on the receipt who's renting it. He's talking nonsense!"

"That's what he said, Mr. Matsas," the officer told him. "Just what I'm telling you."

He was in his office. The telephone had begun to sweat against his ear. He hung up. Before he could wipe off the perspiration, he picked up the phone again. This time it was Zoumbos himself.

"Well, I won't give you the key." He was all excited. "I won't give it to you. Go somewhere else; go wherever you like. From me there's no key. We made no agreement—nothing at all. There's no key."

"But what's the matter with you, Mr. Zoumbos? We're the ones who should be angry, not you. You've left us in a fine jam, without a roof over our heads. And you have the gall to shout at me!"

"That's all I have to say. I can't stand it any more. I can't sleep. My father died today. Goodbye."

How strange, Matsas thought at the time. But now it didn't seem at all strange. Now everything was converging on the same point, like so many radiating roads leading to the same neuralgic center: this hall on the third floor, found at the last minute by a "process of elimination." The shadowing; Zoumbos's reneging; the anonymous tip that Z. was in danger—all these unrelated events of the past days now, at five minutes to eight on the twenty-second of May, 1963, in Salonika, were falling into place, like the parts of a child's puzzle finally fitted together: a menagerie in full array—vultures, jackals, pterodactyls—monsters shrieking, striking out, snarling, under the very eyes of the police, who suddenly seemed blinded. Why don't they maintain order?

Someone came downstairs to say that the hall was full and that he should get the speakers. Their hotel was directly opposite. But to get there he would have to cross this storm-tossed sea, with mines broken loose from the depths and floating like jellyfish on the surface. He set someone else to watch, took a deep breath, and headed for the hotel.

He walked with his heart in his mouth. Presently he found himself exposed in the center of the little square formed by the deltas of the streets. He hurried his steps, dodged a blow aimed at him from behind, and reached the opposite sidewalk, like a drowning man who unexpectedly gets hold of a board. "Not even in Mau-Mau land do such things happen. Where are we? What sort of cannibals are we? What's happening?"

At last he reached the hotel. He found Z. and Spathopoulos sitting there, upset by the delay and prepared to go into the arena with the lions.

Chapter 6

The dead do not speak. Clothed in the beauty of death, they have carried off those innumerable secrets that no April profusion will ever bring to light. Earth pregnant with revelations never made; with stifled confessions, memoranda, apologias, petitions for exemption, statutes, interpretations, all deposited among the frozen bones, like salt.

The dead do not know how history is made. They have fed it with their blood; what comes after, they never learn. They are unaware of their sacrifice and this makes them still more beautiful. The early Christians knew why they were being sacrificed; they went to conscious martyrdoms. But in our day why should anyone talk of being sacrificed when what he believes is simply common sense—just common sense? Who ever said that justice and injustice should go hand in hand? Poverty and wealth? Peace and war? Nonetheless, though no one has ever said it, many people—a great many people— seem to uphold it every day in their words and actions.

He had no missionary impulse. It was merely that he had known poverty and illness at first hand. That was his work. He knew that better hospitals lessen pain. He knew that, in another order of things, many intractable problems of our time would become clarified. If a bullet costs as much as a bottle of milk and if a Polaris submarine costs enough to feed a whole people for one week— and feed it well—what was the difficulty?

Common, very common sense; and out there, the dark. Thick darkness, without flashes of lightning or even the schizophrenic's lucid intervals. This was how he saw things, and why he wanted to talk. He wasn't a Communist. If he'd run for deputy as a candidate of the left-wing party, he'd done so because their views were the only ones that somewhat accorded with his own. They stuck together, like twin shadows. He wasn't a Marxist theoretician, a person enclosed in a theory. Open on all sides, he felt the currents passing through him unobstructed. He naturally preferred the ones that warmed him.

He'd come to believe that human pain could not be cured by attention to individual cases. He was able to take a certain number of patients free of charge at his clinic, every Tuesday and Thursday afternoon. To no avail. When he compared the number of patients he cured with the number of human beings the world over who could not buy even the most ordinary medicines, it was enough to make him shudder. The same with begging. What was the good of giving money to the poor? The balance of poverty on the planet remained unaltered. For the world to change, the system had to change.

Knowing this, he could remain, in a tense situation like today's, unperturbed and beautiful in his serenity. It had nothing to do with apathy. Only impassioned people sink into apathy, and he was not impassioned. He believed merely that sense, common sense, must triumph once again; that a certain few words must regain their meaning, a certain few actions their original urgency.

It didn't matter whether you agreed or disagreed. It mattered only that you *saw*. Saw how the world is weighed down by the pressure of a threat. How military rulers are always wrongheaded idiots. How monopolies are obliged to defend monopolies for the good of monopolies.

He didn't care about becoming a professional politician because he was a professional doctor—one of the best. University professor, when the country had only two universities. In his youth an athlete, a champion of the Balkan Games. Now that his body had grown heavy with years, thought darted up and stole the body's shape, becoming sword-like, supple, daring, broke records in high-jumping and long-distance running.

He was not self-deceived. He knew he couldn't go it alone. Like it or not, he would need to channel himself to arrive at the sea. How many good wells ran dry because there was no one around to exploit them! And exploitation was a proper course of action. There was metal —iron, copper, gold—in the bowels of the earth, congealed by planetary frost. Needing it, people came and dug it out. There was no evil in exploitation, so long as the metal existed and people wanted it.

A man alone can have whatever he wants and it is of

no interest to anyone except himself. But the moment you aspire to reach the many, the anonymous masses, you choose whatever means of mass communication is nearest to hand. Then begins the problem of choice, which is no problem at all, because things speak for themselves.

Unless you are alienated to the marrow of your bones; unless you are stone-blind—like so many people in this world; unless you are one of those who live in fear of change, of any change, tell me, what other position (not to speak of party) stands for the progress of the whole rather than of the individual? Or aims to deliver us from hunger, poverty, misery, to help us evolve into a nobler animal and leave behind the old familiar ways that have tormented us over the years and the centuries, glued to us like leeches to the dull-eyed fish in the tank.

And how beautiful life becomes when you believe in others! How womanly the women seem, how manly the men—thinking for the moment just in terms of the two fundamental poles of self-perpetuation. Never again those weak and pitiful creatures forever multiplying and forever lost, submerged in obscure abysses where no light falls, these Giuliettas of the Spirits, these moons in eclipse. How beautiful life is when you say to me: "Your hand in mine . . ."

The dead have never spoken; this great accusation weighs upon them. They have forgotten once and for all the precious uses of the voice. It is we, then, who must speak in their name. We must plead the cause in their absence.

One is afraid of being insignificant; of lacking horizons to roam in, sand to stretch out on, women to caress, and the chance to extract from falsehood the seeds of the great truth. One is afraid of being small, one's head not reaching the foliage of the tree, the almond grove of the stars. One is afraid when one has grown used to the law of gravity, a law as intimately related to our planet as the hen to her egg. On another planet, with another law of gravity, one would have to learn all over again how to live.

And when your soul has not rusted, love is always love. Bodies, the vessels of love, may change. Alas, if they didn't! But love remains always the same, behind every face, behind every pair of transparent eyes. It is the thirst for water, the thirst for something transcending us. Rejecting these walls that hem us in, these easy chairs, it demands something else. Your voice within my voice, two voices, no voice; you and I, without our being you and I, but we, who to the rhythm of drums from a prehistoric era perform an act as sure of itself as sunlight.

He loved his wife. When she complained, weeping, of his unfaithfulness, those blue veins in her neck, swollen with sobs, became roots that led him deep into creation. Its very source was this alabaster neck of hers, the human form, the light of the soul, the voice repeating "Come!" And her eyes, her large eyes fixed magnetically upon him, with all the intensity of seas that have never been sailed or that have been much sailed (it comes to the same thing), her eyes, light-bearing, earthy, struck a chord within him, vibrations that woke the chord of the whole world. "I love you," he told her, and with these words a thousand times uttered, "the world became beautiful once more according to the measure of the heart." And it was as it had always been, every evening, at the time when he scarcely knew her. The same agony: "Will she come? Won't she come?" The same pounding in his chest until she did come and draw near, infinitely dead in her vitality, infinitely dark in her whiteness. And her hands had a taste of loam.

With her he recaptured his lost youth. With her the world grew wide again. The studies, his military service had made him small. "You're always drunk," she had told him. "What's to be done with you?" Until he slept with her and then married her. And then he knew other women and he went on loving her always. Now, in this unfamiliar city, he missed her incredibly.

Life is beautiful when you trust in the sun! You stare and everybody stares. You love, and everybody loves. You eat and it is just you eating, and not the person next to you.

This was why he sought the organization, why he ran for deputy. All his deputy's salary he turned over to the party. He didn't mind. Knowing that in order to admire the sunrise you must first have a full stomach, that in order to enjoy love you must have a strong body, he knew also the necessity of working with means that were perhaps not so pleasant. Otherwise the danger was that one would always settle for substitutes; live by illusions; hope for illusions; see the half-used lipstick and dream of her lips; notice how the edge of the stick got blunted in its passage over her large, ideal mouth, those lips so intensely desired, without ever being able to kiss them.

Suppose they did murder him, what would it mean? Ever since first hearing of threats against his life, he had not only felt free of anxiety—he had felt happy. He was sure of just one thing: that he would never in any way hinder them. Exactly as he had never lifted his hand against a policeman even while being pursued by one, because he knew the strength of his fist. One good blow and the other might sink to the bottom, men and all, like a foundered ship, on the spot. All he knew was how to caress; it is the way of the very strong.

He had risen and was preparing to go out with the rest of them. Mastas seemed upset. "You've got no idea what's happening out there," he had said. "We'll have to collect some of our own people to form a protective ring around you."

"It's not necessary," he heard himself say. "If they're men, let them come on alone, each man by himself."

The others, however, disagreed. They weren't playing with fire. The entire police force was out there, virtually assisting the counterdemonstrators in their task. Practical steps were necessary. In our era, there was no place for heroics.

"Who said anything about heroics? Those people are such cowards underneath, they won't dare even come near us."

"They're beating others up without any restraint. No one's stopping them."

"Let's go."

He went ahead. He glanced at the hotel manager, who greeted him from behind the desk. Then he stepped out on the sidewalk. Night had settled on Salonika. Across the way, a neon sign flashed on and off at the pace of a feverish pulse. His own pulse was calm. For the speech ahead, he'd merely made some notes. When you have something to say, it's not difficult to say it. The difficulty comes when you have nothing to say and must talk anyway.

The others followed him. At his nod they all started out. They crossed the little square without incident. Then, near the entrance to the building, three young men in black turtlenecks jumped on him from behind. They struck for his head, the blow fell above the eyebrow. He heard a voice: "For shame! What sort of behavior's this? We have guests here. We're civilized human beings." And falling back on the shoulders of the people hurrying forward alongside him, he went in. A great wave surged forward at that point, intent on passing through the open door, violating the immunity of the meeting. But, with an immense effort, those inside managed to bar the outer, iron entrance. In the midst of the butchery, however, Spathopoulos was left outside—and for a long time after, it seemed to those within that he had fallen among sharks and was being torn to pieces.

Chapter 7

"This is only the appetizer!" said Autocratosaur to the General, alluding to the blow Z. had received. "The main course is still to come."

The General agreed in silence and assuming an air of indifference moved a few steps away. Even though he had no respect whatsoever for this worm, this larva desperate for wings, he was indispensable all the same: he was his eye in the mud, where dozens of protozoa swarmed. He had known him from the Occupation, in the squads of Poulos. As much as he detested him, he was obliged, every time Autocratosaur came to visit him in his office, to make him feel welcome, talk with him, offer him coffee. Every New Year's Eve he attended the cake-cutting ceremony with his organization at Ano Toumba.

This organization had turned out to be the salvation of Autocratosaur. He had left Greece with the Germans and, with a fake Greek government, had become, in Vienna, self-appointed Minister of Propaganda. He returned, expecting to go scot-free; but they caught him and tried him as a traitor and collaborator; he was given a life sentence, only to be released shortly after, his legs rotted by the dampness of the prison. He remembered his chilblains in the Partisan War, when he and poor Poulos exterminated the Red bastards. This time he had little courage to appear anywhere or to embark upon any career, until he founded the organization of the Combatants and Victims of the National Resistance of Northern Greece, thus emerging from disgraced oblivion to fame and recognition. The police force—a good mother—welcomed back her prodigal son, especially since the aim of his organization was "the reinforcement of the security units for as long as they continue to be needed for preservation of order and tranquillity in our land, for protection of Greek rights and interests by every legal means, for combating all anti-nationalistic activity and plots wherever they may originate, and, finally, for defense to the last breath of our Hellenic-Christian civilization."

It was this final item—"our Hellenic-Christian civilization"—that had won the General over and led him, despite his personal antipathy to the quisling, to bestow his approval on the organization. From the General's point of view, ever since the reconstitution of Israel, the sunspots had been multiplying, because the sun refused to shine upon the Jews. "We are terminating a very brief period," the General used to say, "from whose depths is emerging a Hellenic-Christian world hegemony. The significant disturbance on the solar mass and the crisis of the nations are due as much to the Jewish conspiracy as to the expansion of Communism."

Autocratosaur was no fool. The police force was one thing, the state another. It was necessary to arouse the latter's interest. So he began publishing a small bulletin called *Expansion of the Hellenes!* (of a "truly infuriating pro-German character," as the General admitted), which, though supposed to appear every month, had in fact been published three times in two years. But that was of no importance. With this small bulletin, Autocratosaur burrowed like a rodent into the secret funds of the ministry supporting the anti-Communist struggle, nibbling on whatever cash the official anti-Soviet experts left behind. It made him furious to be told he was doing this for his own profit. In answer he would point to two newspapers he'd brought out in the past: a weekly, *The Olympus News,* in 1928, in Katerine (where the Communists had butchered his nephew and his wife's brother); and *The Agricultural Flag,* in 1935. Perhaps he wasn't a professional journalist—one had to live—but he could always pass as one, and tonight he was at the scene along with the other reporters.

There were other outfits similar to his: for example, the incredible Organization of National Security—Guarantors of the Constitutional King of the Hellenes—Might of God—Divine Faith—Greek Immortality, whose leader, a retired major from Kilkis, had been removed from office because of congenital idiocy. But these outfits weren't recognized by the big shots. They were fly-by-night subversives without any character. For that reason they had been approved neither by the courts nor by the police. Autocratosaur's, on the other hand, was a well-disciplined organization. Every Thursday evening he assembled its members in Ano Toumba at The Six Little Pigs, a tavern owned by one Gonos (now deceased). Gonos would close the door, posting his son to make sure no one else entered. Here Autocratosaur instructed his disciples.

It was his greatest joy. He talked to them about the Communists. About the fatherland. Religion. The family. The members, a fantastic assortment of ne'er-do-wells, would listen open-mouthed. He recalled their last meeting, just before de Gaulle's visit, when his theme had been "Communism as Infuriating Arrogance." What he hadn't told them!

"Don't be idiots. In Russia, the self-styled working-class paradise, the worker doesn't own a thing. He works not for the boss, who might appreciate what he does and give him a raise, but for someone he doesn't know, doesn't see, and never will see. Because the people in power over there aren't like our leaders, who walk about in plain sight and show themselves on their balconies. Over there they live in houses full of mirrors. They can see the others behind the mirrors. But those who talk with them can't see them. The worker gives his blood for them. The farmer doesn't own even a tiny field where he can plant a few onions or his little tomatoes. He doesn't own one little olive that he can press for oil.

You need coupons for everything. The way it was here during the Occupation. You don't know, because you were too young. The Germans gave the people something to eat. But the Communists came along and gobbled it up. That's why the people were starving. Well, then—you over there, when the leader's talking, listen to him, so you can get a little sense pumped into your brain—and you, Yango, that's enough retsina . . ."

The now-defunct Gonos kept bringing cans of wine which Yango drank down like water. Yango was a loafer, a bum, but he was a good man in a brawl. That's why he had been assigned to the organization's death squad.

"Well then, I repeat, it's hell over there. Here we can make a paradise, if we all get together. If you're good at your job and you've got a good boss, what else do you need?"

"It's not always the way you say, chief," an apprentice member dared to comment.

"Shut up. Read a few books before you open your mouth, you uneducated blockhead. Read Hitler's *Mein Kampf*. Who was Hitler?" He addressed this last question to everyone.

"The one who promised to save the world," someone answered from the back of the tavern.

"Excellent! I'm glad you remember everything I've told you. Yes, Hitler was the one who wanted to get rid of the Jews and the Communists. To wipe them off the face of the earth. The former he succeeded in exterminating. Take this city as an example. Salonika. Before the war, Jews made up half the population. Now how many Jews are left?"

"The grocer on the corner."

"All right. Let's say one. What happened to the others? They became little bars of soap. The same thing would have happened to the Communists, but he didn't have time. That year the earth took a sudden shift and the ice melted the flame. You know, Hitler believed the earth wasn't round but dug out on the inside like a quarry. We're living on the bottom. We're the flame that burns and soars toward the upper regions, trying to rise above the ice. Well, the steppes of Russia froze over without warning and Hitler lost his foothold. His soldiers' legs were caught in the layers of ice. At that point the Communists advanced on their sledges and slaughtered them with tin-can tops. They didn't take them prisoner as they should have. They were massacred, helpless, alone, unable to move. I myself knew the Germans. I fought with them against the Communists, who were plotting against the unity and integrity of the Greek nation."

"You've plunged off into theory again, chief! I need a license to sell eggs," said someone who was not a regular member. "I've been waiting for it for months and all you do is make beautiful speeches. I'm going to quit the organization. I'll join a soccer club."

"I'm taking care of it, I'm taking care of it," said Autocratosaur.

"And me—where am I going to find the money to pay off Aristidis?" sighed Yango. "Oh, society, you old whore! It's your fault we were born poor! Gonos, bring in another pint!"

"My wife's sick and she can't get on the welfare list."

"You bastards, you bums!" shouted Autocratosaur. Now he was angry. "I'm trying to make human beings out of you, and you won't stop begging. What do you do in return?"

"Beat people up," said Yango.

"You, yes. The others don't even do that. If you said 'Boo!' to them, they'd faint."

"It's because we're so hungry, boss. Little by little we collect our drachmas, like dandelion greens. But at least we know where the dandelion greens are."

"The day we take over, you'll live like kings."

"Since we're in power, isn't that what you mean?"

"We're not, unfortunately, we're not at all. The people who rule have sold out. Hitler lost his hold for the same reason: his associates were no good."

"What am I going to do with all these eggs? My chickens keep laying eggs. Can't I set up a stall somewhere and sell the eggs for a good price?"

"In a few days you're going to have work. We're going to break up a meeting. You'll get hold of clubs, stones, and poles and you'll go to it. Afterward each one will be rewarded according to what he contributed. I'll be right there, with my eye on you."

Which is exactly what happened this evening. He saw Yango, the best of his men, astride the kamikazi, plunging fearlessly through the streets. And when they struck Z. on the head, a wave of physical pleasure swept over him.

"Before you hook the big fish, you have to knock them out," he told the General, who this time pretended not to hear.

Chapter 8

Hit but not bleeding, he climbed the stairs. He put his hand to the spot. The dizziness crept over him stealthily, like frost. Then all at once the staircase began to toss, a stormy sea; expanding, contracting; a rubber stairway. Two or three men supported him. On the second floor, when it seemed that he was ascending his Golgotha, they hoisted him on their arms. They were powerful young men, the kind to whom the world belongs.

His assailants had struck him before the very eyes of the police captain, there in uniform indifferently observing the spectacle. Z. hadn't even turned around to look at them. Nor had he condescended to make any self-protective movement whatsoever, cheapening them further by treating them as nonentities. They were holding something hard in their hands. This is what he had felt striking him: a stone perhaps, or an iron bar.

He didn't immediately go into the hall, where the audience had been waiting for him quite a while. Instead he went to an adjacent room, fitted out with a frayed couch, and lay down for a bit. The blow had caused a slight concussion; he wanted to calm down. Stationing someone at the door to keep others away, he surrendered briefly to lethargy.

Then the swarming shapes in his head gradually thinned out and assumed coherence. The square he'd crossed after emerging from his hotel was full of lowering tangerine trees. A little square that had the scent of burnt wood. It was cared for by an old gardener with an ancient hoe. "My child, don't neglect your garden . . ." Life took on again the beauty it had worn in childhood. And how, later on, did our garden fill with brambles? Our trees get covered with scale? What made our hearts go on strike?

In the blind dark—his temples bursting—the square changed shape. It became an egg. Queer shapes hovering over it, fluid threads enmeshing it, its inner complexity made plain. Suddenly the egg, this huge egg, was dyed red. But Easter had just passed. How could it still be Holy Thursday?

A little boy on his mother's knees. A mother whose face was that of earth itself, deep-lined, suffering, earth of the village where he went at Easter, home from his studies in the capital. A mother, head of the household, proud within her own kingdom. A sweet mother, all "my child, my little son"; no complaint ever crossing her lips. Mother Earth, Holy Thursday, red eggs, red eggs, red like blood, his hands grasping them.

The concussion made him feel as though underpinnings had been suddenly removed; at any moment everything might crumble. A flaw deep in the foundations. He sank his face into the couch and pressed his fingers against his eyes to keep from seeing those red, swarming sands.

And now what? What was it now? What crazy, chilling ideas? Look, if his eyes were made of glass he wouldn't be able to dig his fingers into them this way to keep from seeing. Suppose he'd sold one eye to the blind Negro singer for ten thousand dollars—those were the terms offered in the advertisement—then he wouldn't . . . A farmer had done it, yes. Outside Volos. He said it was like winning a lottery. Undreamed-of luck. And besides, what did he need two eyes for? He could get alone fine with one. He'd see less of the ugliness around him.

But what kind of people were these who sold their hair and their eyes to live? Hair to be turned into a rich woman's wig, like hers, the American who several months ago had come to his office for an abortion. She'd taken off her blonde wig; underneath was short black hair like a boy's. He had picked up the wig and begun to daydream about whose hair it might be. What peasant girl, blonde, beautiful, plump, from what village in southern Italy, had sold it, perhaps as a vow to the Madonna?

Once again, the square. He knew anatomy. He knew that the last image received by the eyes is engraved forever in the memory of the dead man. Through this last image he begins to contemplate the other world. In his retina, in his brain cells, the image survives, beyond death. Well then, what image would he himself take with him as he left life? Would it perhaps be the image of this square?

O-o-o beautiful Thessaloniki! Old fortresses, the kind that provide walls for a camping ground of the poor. Children flying kites. Mothers spreading jam and margarine on slices of bread. O-o-o beautiful Thessaloniki! A sea, your own sea, now a bay. At bay. Your coast, horseshoe, shaped for luck. Nights and nights without your love. Those diamond metamorphoses of your lights. The fields at Diavata have been appropriated for the Esso-Pappa's refineries. When will the farmers, on tractors, arise and invade the city? Concussion? Rubbish! Why must a high rate of illiteracy go hand in hand with violence? Why does it all go backwards? O-o-o beautiful Thessaloniki!

Three silent young men, up to their necks in black, three young men had hit him. For a moment he'd seen thousands of little stars and then a black incision in the darkness, a door opening upon further darkness, blacker, sootier. Now, little by little, things were solidifying again. The room was regaining its own shape. He was lying on a couch. The dizziness was passing. More quickly than he'd expected, he thought with relief. And he could get up on his feet. He was all right; he could speak. He opened the door and entered the hall amid a storm of applause, while down below, the jackals and the flying lemurs had gone wild and were shrieking appallingly.

Now he had ascended the rostrum. He looked down at the faces—faces full of intensity—whose gazes were fixed upon him. The eyes looked thirsty for a few drops of rain to soothe their smarting.

And he said: "They struck me here!" He pointed to the place above his eyebrow.

"For shame!"

"What were the police doing?"

"What're the authorities up to?"

"It's only us they're after!"

"The others can go where they please!"

"Come on in, wolves, the sheep are waiting for you!"

"Shouts don't mean anything. Better close the blinds."

Two or three got up and started to carry out his order. As they opened the windows to reach the blinds, the roar of the raging sea outside burst into the room. It had grown fiercer. Anything could happen now. The building be set on fire, themselves burned like rats!

"Bulgars back to Bulgaria!"

"Z., you're going to die!"

Pressing the button that hooked up the instrument in the hall with the megaphones on the third-floor balcony,

Z. spoke into the microphone: "I demand from the Chief of Police the protection of colleague Spathopoulos's life. Spathopoulos is in danger. They've kidnapped him."

Then he turned back to the audience in the hall and counseled them: "Calm. You must be calm. Otherwise we won't be able to accomplish anything."

He opened his briefcase and took out some papers. He had no written text to speak from, just some notes, the skeleton of what he had to say.

"Thank you for inviting me here tonight. We are not isolated. At this very moment the eyes of the world are upon us. The world is expecting a great deal from this meeting. Those of you who have come have done so because you don't let anyone interfere with you. There are other people who would have liked to come but did not, for reasons that . . ."

A stone from outside hit the closed blinds.

"Let them throw stones. They'll rebound on their own heads. They'll get hit themselves. As you can see for yourselves, peace incenses them; they find it intolerable. But why?"

"Disarmament!"

"Down with the death bases!"

"Down with NATO!"

"Don't interrupt me. As you understand, we must give ourselves with all our souls if we are to achieve anything. Peace is not an idea. It's a practice. It needs human hands to support it. The world becomes habitable only when human beings live together in peace."

"Democracy! De-moc-ra-cy!"

"Dis-ar-ma-ment!"

"No more Cypruses!"

"No more blood!"

"One bullet costs as much as a bottle of milk."

"Peace! Peace! P-e-a-c-e!"

He felt dizzy. The concussion returned like a wave. It struck upon the breakwater of his forehead and retreated backward into the labyrinth of the cerebrum. He heard the rhythmic chants around him; he heard from outside the chants of hatred louder now through the broken windowpanes. The two mingled, it was chaos. The audience before him now seemed like molten metal not yet cast into steel columns. It was a fluid mass, and he was its fluid leader.

He couldn't speak calmly in such an atmosphere. And his listeners had become inflamed. Hearing the wolves outside, they could hardly sit penned-up and sheepish. And then the moon emerged from behind the tallest building; he saw it through the crack between the blinds.

The night, he thought to himself, the black night pierced by your smile, death pierced by Beloyannis's red carnation. The night, and such desolation within me; why I don't know. It's the first time that such a sweetness paralyzes my limbs, a sweet dimness undoes me. Before the blow on my head, I believed in common, very common sense. Now all of a sudden I am drugged, undone, as if by a sweet voice calling me to a world of visions. Like yesterday, in my room, listening to poetry on records . . .

But you must talk, he told himself. You must talk. These people are waiting. They've left the quiet of their own homes and come here to listen to you. You must talk, say something, address them. But what to say? Where to begin? I have so much to say that I can't say anything, can't venture a single phrase.

Wild beasts—ravenous beasts of a desert which is not a desert, love for all and for no one in particular: these are the emotions flooding me. I am alone and the panic is mounting. In the end we are all alone. However much we deceive ourselves, however much we think otherwise, each of us suffers in private.

"I bring you a word of greeting from Aldermaston, from Betty Ambatielou, whose husband is still in prison. I bring you greetings from all the friends of peace the world over, who at this moment follow our meeting in spirit. Nowadays peace is a new faith. We know that whoever does not believe in peace is, to say the least, a madman. The dead do not speak, but if they were to speak, they would have much to say about the people who killed them. They would rise from their graves and ask 'Why?' But they cannot say anything, ever. And that is why we must speak on their behalf. We must defend the right in their absence. Why? Why? A bullet, for whom? We are all brothers. Brothers must stand together on this tiny earth of ours. Think of the other planets. For the sake of a nobler kind of human being, for the sake of a life that does not end in violent death, I call on you to join the great Peace March!"

"P—e—a—c—e! P—e—a—c—e!"

"Down with NATO!"

"Fascism can't get away with it!"

"Or terrorism!"

From outside, through the blinds, came the slogans of the counterdemonstrators:

"Bulgars back to Bulgaria!"

"You dirty dogs, you'll all die tonight!"

"Z., you're going to die!"

"Commies, your end has come!"

They're shouting, but they don't have anything to say, he thought to himself. Aloud he said:

"Bulgars? What Bulgars? The ones who fought us, tyrannized over us, stole our lands are not the same Bulgars as are living today. Men change with the system. Now they too believe in peace. So why are you shouting out there?"

Without my desiring you, he thought to himself, I want you unbearably. I want you the way water dreams of its source. The way life itself, in your eyes at night, unlids its mystery. I want you because you are a gallant woman, a bloodstained sword, a sheath of lightnings. I want you the way the child seeks its mother. I, a child, seek protection, seek rebirth so as not to die. At your womb's gate, immortality begins. From your hearth streams warmth alone—never that fearful cold which envelops and preserves those who have crashed into snowy peaks and died. I want you because without you I am small, insignificant: even my madness scatters elsewhere, a seed flung where it does not belong, since all things must be measured good, correct, intact. But what am I thinking? Where am I? They're still waiting for my talk!

"Disarmament!"

"No Polaris!"

"Down with the bases!"

And from outside:

"Down with the Bulgars!"

"What are the Bulgars after in Macedonia?"

"Dirty dogs, you'll all die when you come down!"

Inside: "No more Hiroshima!"

Outside: "We want war!"

"Mr. Prosecutor, Mr. Prefect, General, Chief of Police, all of you who are outside, I demand your protection. I am sounding the alarm!"

No response. The night had wound its noose about his neck. Any tighter and it would choke him. Only the night, only an effect of the earth's revolution upon its axis, and here were the consequences. "There is no water, only light. The road is lost in light, and the shadow of the wall is iron."

O night, so infinite, so gentle. O stars, stones of the midnight sea . . . Who is tired? Who is drowsy?

"Long live peace!"

"Down with NATO!"

Chapter 9

The slogans issuing from the megaphones and spreading out over the city aroused the General's wrath to the point where he felt like going up to the meeting alone and exterminating them all with a machine gun. At the same time they provided a perfect justification for the gathering down below. Actually the "outraged citizens" down there—the subproletariat from the poorest districts of the city—had been assembled by order of the Head of Security Police. This the General knew very well, because everything that concerned the left wing in this eternal struggle between spirit and matter had first to receive his approval. It was his passion, his vice. And with the blaring megaphones there was the magnificent excuse that these counterdemonstrators—otherwise peaceable, nationalistic-minded individuals—had just chanced to be passing through this central section of the city and had found themselves unexpectedly confronted by the incendiary slogans of the Communists and that they had considered it their supreme patriotic duty to retaliate with slogans of their own. In this way a counterdemonstration had come about.

The Chief of Police, who had just arrived on the scene, had a different opinion. He insisted that a policeman go up and order the loudspeakers turned off. But the General advised him to wait a bit. Though the Chief of Police didn't catch on immediately, he kept quiet, for he was inferior to the General in rank and had learned to yield in all matters involving national security. Knowing the General's passion for this kind of problem, he had come, over the years, to confine himself strictly to his duties as a policeman, leaving complicated matters of this sort for the old fox to handle. "Watch out that no photographs are taken," the General told him as he moved over to the sidewalk on the right. The Chief of Police lit a cigarette.

Chapter 10

In the back of the pickup, Vango the pederast—hidden treasure of an hour destined to leave its
mark on history—was smoking nervously. Holding the
club tight between his thighs, he waited for Yango to
knock on the window back of the driver's seat. It was
the signal for him to jump out and start slugging.
He neither heard the slogans nor saw the faces; he
had no interest in what was happening. He felt he was
protected, and for a shady character like Vango this
feeling was a vital matter: it gave him a kind of immunity. They'd never catch him, they'd never put him behind bars. In his imagination, the police had acquired
mythical dimensions. He had a bicycle shop in his
neighborhood and he spent much of his time with small
boys. Sometimes he would loan them bicycles so he
could fondle them afterward. Or he would blow up their
balloons or slip them some money. He'd gone to prison
twice, but each time his protectors had got him off after
twenty-four hours. But then, he went to a lot of trouble
for his protectors.
At the Liberation, sensing that the left would come to
power, he thought of joining the party's youth organization, even at that late date, so as to be with them if they
won. But the moment it became clear to him where the
scales were dipping, he ran to the right, begging to be
accepted as a true son. The main thing was to have the
agents of law and order on his side. And so for a time he
had been president of the right-wing youth branch in
Ano Toumba, his neighborhood. However, when someone ratted on him for making indecent propositions to

the boys, they had thrown him out. Next he was made a counselor at a boys' camp, but again his enemies managed to oust him. In the end nothing was left but the police. He took good care to remain on good terms with them.

The crowning of his efforts had been a brief appointment to the Queen's bodyguard. A photograph showing him not far from the Queen had been God's greatest gift to him. It was no small privilege to tread the ground her royal heels had just stepped on, to breathe the fragrance of her perfume. Even if he wasn't interested in women, a Queen was something different, something higher. She was a symbol of virtue. Ah, how he had prayed that some incident might occur on that tour. But, as usual, nothing happened. The peasants drew back, bowing to the ground as she strode haughtily past. Wherever she went, she was greeted by women in folk costume, the ringing of bells, a speech by the mayor, little girls with bows in their hair offering a poem and an armful of flowers from the Greek countryside. That day stuck in his memory as the high point in his life. It was a diploma conferred after assiduous training in the courting of authority. It's one thing to be protected by authority, another to be called upon to guard and protect it. Nothing else in life counted for Vango. It had happened again when big-nose de Gaulle came for a visit. That time they'd promoted him to section head. And today, along with his friend Yango—a good kid, even if he was kind of wild—they had chosen him among so many others.

He had lit another cigarette when he was seized with an uncontrollable desire to masturbate. What with the jouncing of the vehicle and his anxiety over the impending transfer job, he sought relief in the act which often appeased him when a coveted boy was not to be had. Usually he did it in the darkness of an anonymous neighborhood movie. Now there was the same darkness inside the pickup. Scenes from the summer camp floated through his mind, the nights when he had made the rounds of the dormitories, going mad with the bittersweet smell of unripe boys. Or when he saw his little pigeons washing themselves in the morning, almost naked, at the outdoor faucets. He had sauntered about among them on the pretext of asking who didn't have soap or a towel. With these images he surrendered himself to his orgasm. But before he had time to finish, the signal on the windowpane pulled him abruptly from his trance. He sprang up, made sure of the revolver in his pocket, picked up the club, and was ready for action. He felt the three-wheeler braking to a stop. Before jumping down, he saw the piercing light of an ambulance approaching as if bent on crashing into them. Then he saw it stop a couple of yards beyond the kamikazi. Meanwhile Yango had got out and was there beside him.

"Who are we clobbering?"

"The wounded man in the ambulance."

"To death?"

"Till he's unconscious."

Looking about him, Vango noted that they were on Ion Dragoumis Street, near Nea Megalou Alexandrou Street. He recognized the shops, and for a moment he thought it was a risky business showing themselves in this part of town. But presently others of the gang gathered around the ambulance—among them Baronissimo and Jimmie the Boxer—and formed a protective wall with their big bodies, hiding the ambulance and its contents from the passers-by.

He and Yango went directly to the rear of the ambulance, yanked open the door, and disappeared inside. A man of medium size lay on the stretcher, his head bleeding; the light that filtered through the door of the ambulance gave his face a greenish tinge. He made feeble efforts to resist, like an ant that's been turned upside down. Yango grabbed him by the legs and Vango hit him on the head with the club, but he apparently missed his target; the man still struggled. Again Vango raised the club, this time striking the ceiling of the ambulance, which resounded with a hollow thud. "Help! Help!" cried the wounded man. To keep him quiet, Vango tried to close his mouth with his hand—the same hand he'd been masturbating with—but the wounded man bit him and Vango howled with pain. "You dirty dog, die and be done with it!" he roared. Behind the windowpane he glimpsed the staring, terror-stricken face of the driver. He became aware of the hospital orderly making feeble efforts to tear Yango away from the victim. The wounded man lay as if glued to the stretcher. After a mighty effort they finally managed to get him outside.

"Give him some more, the Bulgar!"

"Give it to him, the traitor!"

"Let him have it!"

Their job was done. Now it was up to Baronissimo and Jimmie the Boxer to take over. Vango saw them approaching, fists clenched, ready for action. The victim, half unconscious, lay on the street.

"Move along," he ordered the driver.

The hospital attendant closed the door from inside and the ambulance drove off. Yango went back to his pickup, followed by Vango, who jumped in the rear. From there he saw the whole scene. Spurred on by the rhythmic chants of the impassioned onlookers, the two toughs finished their work and ran off, leaving their victim on the pavement. Yango then started the motor of the pickup. Just before they turned the corner, Vango had time to see two passers-by bending over and trying to lift the motionless body. He did not, for the moment, know if they succeeded.

Chapter 11

This man who, supported by the two passers-by, was now stumbling toward the first-aid station, having miraculously escaped the assassination attempt on Ion Dragoumis Street, was the EDA deputy, Georgios Pirouchas, son of Vassilis. He had been traveling through Salonika that day.

He had no particular reason for being here, and no reason at all for going this evening to the meeting of the Friends of Peace. But last night at Z.'s house in Athens, when the two were alone, after they had listened to some poetry on the record player, Z. suddenly remarked: "Tomorrow I'm going to Salonika to make a speech."

Pirouchas responded with a grimace.

"Why?" Z. asked.

"Go, but be careful. I'm from there and I don't trust them. Let me give you a last bit of advice. If they hit you, use your fist."

"Georgio," Z. said, "if I were to punch someone, I'd knock him out for good. And I'd rather not."

That night Pirouchas took the train, without mentioning it to Z., and arrived in Salonika the next morning. He soon knew all about the difficulties with the hall, the plot against Z.'s life, the first incidents in front of the Catacomb. Although he was supposed to leave for Kavalla by evening, he postponed it to be near his friend.

He admired Z. He admired his courage, his generosity. When Pirouchas had become ill six months before and was hospitalized in Athens, Z. had been like a brother to him. Everyone held him in great esteem. Pirouchas's admiration for this man who so far transcended the commonplace but who sometimes betrayed a childish unworldliness took on a paternal aspect; he wished to protect him.

Since they'd struck Z. on the way to the hall, his friend reasoned that they would lay an ugly ambush for him on his way back. Knowing how proud and brave he was, Pirouchas felt impelled to go to him, to keep him from leaving the hall without a group of strapping young bodyguards. If Z. refused, Pirouchas was ready to use force.

Pirouchas set out from the EDA offices where he had

been waiting for news. Accompanied by Tokatlidis, the only person he could find at that hour, he headed for the meeting. He had heart trouble, he was still convalescent, but it didn't matter. His instinct told him to go. With his deputy's badge pinned to his lapel, he hoped they would let him through.

It was only a short distance from the EDA headquarters to the meeting hall. No sooner had he entered Ermou Street than he began to hear the muffled clamor of the angry night. A chill went through him. This time, he thought, they've thrown poisoned bait to the lions. As he went on, the cries grew more distinct. He never expected such savagery. On every corner he observed little groups, provocateurs freely circulating among them. In spite of his wretched physical condition, Pirouchas plunged ahead, intent on reaching the entrance. At first no one paid any attention. He crossed the territory with its hidden explosives like a mine detector who knew his job. He felt degraded, humiliated by the disgraceful scene. He stared intently at the faces around him, the better to stamp them on his memory, for tonight's vile acts would certainly become, thanks to him, a major topic of discussion in the House. In his official role as deputy, he demanded to speak to the Chief of Police. A policeman answered that the Chief must be somewhere about, but by now it was too dark to locate him. Then, slipping past the crowds of police and demonstrators, he managed to get to the door. There a lieutenant of the police force, a police sergeant, and a policeman, all strangers to him, were guarding—guarding what? They assured him that it was safe to go inside. The loudspeakers on the balcony were silent. In front of the entrance he saw a litter of stones, sticks, iron, which had been thrown against the building.

Then a blow struck him squarely on the head, he felt the world spinning. Turning around, he saw a solidly built young thug, an iron bar in his hands, preparing to strike again. The blood began trickling down Pirouchas's dry, wrinkled cheeks. Before fainting, he was astonished to see the lieutenant, the sergeant, and the policeman, silent witnesses to the assault, standing there as motionless as statues in a public park.

"Why don't you arrest him?" he cried out.

"Be calm!" was the lieutenant's answer.

"Be calm? They've split open my head. I'm a deputy! Deputy!"

With these words, he felt his strength forsaking him. Tokatlidis was just in time to grab him under the arms and drag him behind the iron gate. As he was trying to wipe the blood with his handkerchief, he spied a taxi parked nearby, and decided it would be the simplest means of reaching the first-aid station. But before he could get to it two or three hoodlums had chased the driver off with menacing gestures. Again, no interference from the police.

In the midst of his vertigo, blood flowing, heart faltering, Pirouchas heard himself say: "Someone must warn Z. not to come out alone. These are cannibals. They'll eat him."

An ambulance appeared. From the doorway Tokatlidis signaled it and ordered them to pick up the wounded deputy. Some twenty dinosaurs now encircled the vehicle to prevent his getting through. A man carrying an umbrella shouted, "It's for humans, not filth like this," and with the tip of his umbrella indicated the wounded man. He looked like an English lord. Impeccably dressed, glossy-haired, he had the airs of a maestro.

Two people standing near the iron gate helped Tokatlidis lift Pirouchas to the ambulance, the umbrella hovering threateningly over him. A police captain wearing glasses had appeared, and the deputy cried out to him, "Are you blind? Don't you see they're going to start again?" And the bespectacled captain condescended to speak to the man with the umbrella. "Move along, move along," he said. But he made no move to arrest or penalize him. The elegant man walked away, still muttering threats and curses.

They hoisted Pirouchas inside, laying him out on the

stretcher; he was covered with blood and only half conscious. Tokatlidis and his two assistants were determined to get in too. It was not allowed.

"But we must," they protested. "They'll kill him! Can't you see? They're ready to jump on him."

"There's an attendant to look after him," the captain answered.

The ambulance drove away, turning on its siren to disperse the carnivorous throng; but it appeared to excite them all the more. The whole band began to chase the ambulance, hammering on the hood, the windowpanes, thirsting for blood.

The General on the sidewalk sighed with satisfaction. He and Pirouchas had an old score to settle. During the Occupation they had both taken part in the Resistance, as members of rival units, each bent on getting rid of the other. This evening justice had triumphed. He, the General, had delivered the deputy to the savages.

When Tokatlidis saw the ambulance surrounded by the wild pack of hoodlums, he rushed out to try to wrench Pirouchas from their claws. He was greeted by an avalanche of blows. Stones poured from the sky like rain, paving the street with stumbling blocks, and he was forced to retreat behind the iron gate.

Alone, in the back of the ambulance with its broken windows, Pirouchas was conscious of blows reverberating on the hood and realized that the siren had stopped. Now the real bombardment had begun. He saw, silhouetted in the revolving red light on top of the vehicle, towering figures outside, felt his end approaching. It all happened too fast to take in.

He had just been released from the hospital; now this ambulance was taking him back. This time he was not sure of getting there. There was still a chance for Z. If only they might expend their wrath on him and leave Z. alone! Z. was more useful than he. Whatever Pirouchas

had to give, he had already given. Since 1935 he had devoted himself to the struggle. He had been imprisoned,
he had taken part in the Resistance, he had fought the
Germans and their Greek collaborators. He had been
wounded and exiled. He had come out alive and for the
past five years had been deputy from a region where
year after year more and more tobacco fields were being
withdrawn from cultivation and where the working people in the city were emigrating in a steady stream. Although he had done his best, he did not regard himself
as indispensable. Someone else could do his job. But Z.
could not be replaced. He had come into the struggle
fresh, sound, intact. With his gallantry and his culture, he
had much to give. "If only I had fallen in his stead!"
passed through his mind.

Images, also, of Negro lynchings: he had read about
such things in newspapers. The hunted black animal accused of raping a white woman. Pure lies! They encircle
him, isolate him in a field or a construction yard, turn
him over to the fury of the mob.

Touching his face, he felt the blood, now dry. Now an
image of his daughter—a student of agronomy. If she
only knew where her father was now! Tomorrow she
would read about it and weep. He'd be lucky to be able
to read newspapers tomorrow.

He sensed, rather than saw, that a wall had been
formed around the ambulance. All of a sudden it felt
abandoned like those trucks that, set wheelless upon
hard cement, house the paupers of a city slum, a gypsy
caravan on either side. The ambulance was no longer
moving. They had walled it in, the way people block up
windows with bricks, to shut out the sun.

He had no strength to resist. "My hour has come," he
murmured. Then he saw the double door open and two
fiends from the Apocalypse break in. After that he knew
nothing. When he found himself at the first-aid station,
his wounds being bandaged, he wondered that he was
still alive.

Chapter 12

Baronissimo, alias Baronaros, or simply Baron, had done a fine job; he'd had his fill, he was satisfied. He wiped his hands on his trousers, then stepped back to settle accounts with a few others. Noticing the two men who were lifting up Pirouchas, he called out: "Why do you bother with this Bulgar?" But he wasn't in the mood to insist.

"We gave him a good lesson, we Macedonians," someone near him said. He recognized Jimmie the Boxer. Baronissimo nodded his approval, but added: "You call that a man? He's nothing but a turnip!"

"Whatever he is, he's one of their deputies."

Baronissimo was silent. He didn't know what "deputy" meant. And by the Holy Cross, he didn't want to know! Today being Wednesday and the stores being closed, he'd come home early. He had intended to go down to his shop that evening to take delivery of some figs that Georgios, the commission agent, was bringing him from Michaniona. Unripe figs that he would cover with moistened sacking so they would stay fresh and cool until morning; after that he'd go back to his canaries and chaffinches and nightingales. In the court in back of his house he had songbirds. He spent endless hours with them. But about seven o'clock, while he was resting, Leandros came. He couldn't stand Leandros. He told him to come in.

"The Commissioner wants you."

"What's he want me for?" asked Baronissimo. "I've got work to do."

"I tell you he wants you, damn it. Do you think I came down here at this hour to look at your mug?"

"I have to go to my shop. Georgios is bringing me figs from Michaniona."

"Go tell that to the Commissioner."

"Go back and tell him you couldn't find me."

"As if a guy like you could get lost!"

"Tell him I wasn't home."

"Why should we do all the dirty work?"

"Cool it. What's it all about this time?"

"It looks like something urgent."

With a heavy heart, Baronissimo followed Leandros to the station. Mastodontosaur's invitations made his flesh crawl. Always, or almost always, they had to do with slugging. He'd be sent somewhere to beat someone up, or to start a riot. And the Baron had the good nature of fat people. It was easy for him to do a good clobbering job, but it didn't thrill him to the bone.

"Welcome, Goliath! Sit down." The Commissioner, in plain clothes, was smoking nervously behind his desk. Baronaros sat down, half of him spilling out of the chair.

"Tonight I'm taking you to a meeting. We'll go right now, in my car. The others will be there too."

"Mr. Commissioner," Baron said. "Tonight I'm expecting some figs from Michaniona and I have to be at my stall."

"The place I'm going to drop you is only a hundred yards from your stall."

"But I can't do a job for you and be at my stall at the same time. Figs are delicate like. If you don't take care of them, they rot and stink like fish. I paid for them in advance and the guy who's bringing them . . ."

"Listen, Baronaros," the Commissioner interrupted. "In order to sell figs, you have to have a stall."

"I've got one, Mr. Commissioner."

"I know you've got a stall, Baronaros, the widow's stall. But having a stall means having a license. Catch on?"

"The widow's got a license."

"I know that, idiot! But who issued her license? Who signed it?"

"You did, Mr. Commissioner."

"Right! You've got a drop of common sense, you must know that I can also take it back again, or refuse to renew it, for whatever reason I choose."

Baronaros began to see the light.

"Well—are you coming along?"

"What else can I do?"

"Tonight I want you to put your heart into it."

"I wish I didn't have to, Mr. Commissioner. I don't feel like fighting."

"Listen, Baron, it'll be a great party if you just let yourself go. Yango and Vango are already there." He paused and looked Baronaros straight in the eye. "And besides," he went on, "I heard you've been palling around with a Communist who comes and buys at your place. You haven't gone over to the other side, by any chance?"

"By the Holy Cross, no! no! Every time he comes I tell him to go do his buying somewhere else. But he won't. How can I chase a customer away? The customer's always right. I never say a word to him. I always tell him I'm in a hurry."

The Commissioner smiled. "It sounds to me as if you're hiding something. Let's get going—we don't want to be late."

The three of them left the station and got in the car, Baron in front, Leandros in back. Baron admired the Commissioner's limousine. The little bear hanging on the windshield jumped up and down every time they hit a bump, until finally they left the badly paved roads of the slum neighborhood and came out on the main highway.

"Who are we beating up tonight?" Baron asked.

"A VIP is coming from Athens to talk about peace. The Commies are planning a beautiful reception. We're going to beat the hell out of them, because this VIP deserves it."

"How come, Commissioner?"

"He's no weakling and he's not afraid to fight. That's why we need tough guys to give him a lesson."

Baronaros was enjoying the little bear's dance.

"And this VIP has the gall to send a female comrade to London to rip our Queen's dress."

Baronaros scratched his crotch.

"He had the nerve to lay a hand on our Queen?"

"He didn't do it himself, idiot. He got someone else to do it. And in the House, he gave one of our deputies a black eye."

At that moment Baron was thinking about his figs. The bus usually arrived from Michaniona at 8:10. It took the guy a good quarter of an hour to get to the stall with the baskets. That would make it 8:30. If he could sneak away and get back to the stall to spread the figs out and dampen them!

"What time is it?" he asked.

"Quarter to eight. Why?"

"I just asked."

"Are you thinking about the figs?"

"No."

"If you want me to renew the widow's license, you'd better be on the ball tonight."

He put on the brakes and they got out of the car.

"I'll be coming back along the other street," he said. "I'm going to park the car. I've got my eye on you."

And so Baron slipped into the frenzied crowd of counterdemonstrators. He was the only one who wasn't shouting. He didn't do anything, until someone said to him: "There's Pirouchas. Go clobber him."

The idiot supposed this was the man the Commissioner was talking about in the car. He gaped in bewilderment. Where was this so-called tough guy? Was it this runt?

It was only when his work was finished that he found out from Jimmie the Boxer that the VIP was still in the hall. He'd come out shortly.

"When?" Baron asked.

"How should I know?"

Baron calculated that he would have time to hop over to his stall. Giving Jimmie the slip, he cut down a side street.

The Modiano Market, after hours, was like a big cemetery. Smells of fish and meat. Display windows with frozen goods, crates of vegetables. He greeted the caretaker of the arcade, who was washing the pavement. When he reached his stall, he saw the baskets of figs. The commission agent had left them for him; they had been paid for in advance. Quickly he ripped off the covering and looked at them: big, fresh, egg-sized figs from Michaniona, with layers of fig leaves between the rows to keep them from getting crushed during the trip. He took a fig and ate it, skin and all. Then, fig by fig, he emptied the basket on the ground. Without removing the leaves in between, which would have taken time, he quickly spread them out as best he could, eating a few more as he went— the biggest and sweetest. Large, fresh figs, which tomorrow he'd sell for a handsome price to the people who fancied them. Then he spread sacking over them, took the rubber hose from the arcade caretaker, and wet them thoroughly. He lowered the iron stall front, locked up, and, in terror that the Commissioner might have noticed his absence, furtively rejoined the ranks of the dinosaurs.

After Baronissimo had left him, Jimmie the Boxer went back alone to the demonstration. He too felt dissatisfied with his evening's work. He was a boxer—that's how he got his name—and for him a good fistfight was a sport. But to clobber the first person who came along, especially if he didn't have the vaguest notion about boxing—there was no fun in that, there wasn't any point to it.

But what else could he do? He worked on the docks, and there wasn't always work. Every morning he'd take his gear and stand outside with the others waiting for a call to do some unloading. The harbor of Salonika was dead. Ships turned up once in a blue moon. There was a surplus of workmen. And whenever a job did present it-

self, a union man in the pay of the police came and
called for the person he wanted. At first Jimmie couldn't
understand why they never called him. He would get
angry, curse a blue streak, and walk off the dock. Next
day, rain or shine, he'd be back, waiting for God knows
what . . . One day a fellow worker named Vlamis,
who'd been working in the harbor longer than anybody
else and had his finger in every pie, let him into the secret.

"You were born in Russia?"

"Yes."

"In Batum?"

"Yes."

"Well then, Jimmie, my boy, for them you're a Communist. That's why you never get any work."

"Is it my fault I was born in Batum?"

"Nobody says it's your fault. But they're suspicious of
you. If you want, I can tell them that you said O.K., and
then, you'll see, everything will change. You'll get plenty
of work."

"Said O.K. to what?"

"Never mind. Rush jobs."

"Say I said O.K. I've got strong arms, I like to work. I
want all the work I can get."

A few days after, a stranger from the free port approached him and talked to him about the Communist
danger threatening the country, about the Reds who
slaughter people with tin-can tops. He also told him that
here in Salonika the menace was especially serious, for
with the first crack of a gun the Bulgarians would pitch
into them and wipe them out, because they wanted a
passage to the sea. "You're a dock worker; you understand the value of ships. Therefore," he concluded,
"since you're a boxer and since we need men with strong
arms, we'll give you a call the first chance we get . . ."

Jimmie accepted eagerly. Though he hadn't understood much of what had been said, the very next day he
began to see the difference as far as work was concerned. When there was work, he was always the first to

be called. He was soon working five or six days a week. They also gave him a code number—seven. And invited him to a few meetings, like tonight's, and he'd throw a few punches, even if, deep down, he still looked on boxing as a sport and didn't like this kind of roughing up.

Now, once again at the scene of the demonstration, which he'd left in pursuit of the ambulance, he greeted two or three fellow workers from the docks. They were throwing stones and shouting, while eating roasted chick-peas.

Chapter 13

Someone told Z. that Pirouchas had been wounded on his way to the meeting, that they'd beaten him up and were now taking him to the first-aid station. He knew about Pirouchas's weak heart, having cared for him for two months in the hospital. Spathopoulos had disappeared; Pirouchas was finished. His own turn was coming. He had no reason to fear.

Now more than ever, on the rostrum, he felt the need to talk about peace. All he'd been saying—figures, statistics, quotations from great men, from leaders—was well and good, but it failed to express what he felt. He was not an eloquent man. He had difficulty finding the right words, but tonight something was suffocating him, strangling him—a lump in his throat, a protest he wanted to send beyond city, nation, world, to reach all the way to another planet.

Because life was worth living. He didn't want to die, not at all. He did not accept biological death, often as he faced it in his daily work. An imperceptible melan-

choly pervaded him. Penned in this hall with the blinds
closed, with these people squeezed together listening,
his vertigo recurring in waves; alone and bruised, another Stephen stoned by the unbelievers, among them
first and foremost the centurion Saul, who later on, when
he saw the vision on the road to Damascus, repented in
anguish and became Paul, herald and apostle of the new
religion that abolished idols; without her eyes, which he
had never truly made his own, without her voice, which
the children would now be listening to, safe at home;
what nostalgia, what pebbles lost forever on the shores
of his childhood, in the ancestral haunts, the village sunk
in the slope, a little jaw whose houses poked through
one by one like teeth, abandoned now to scarecrows and
empty courtyards in whose ovens no one baked country
bread any more; at six o'clock the goats to be milked,
evenings at the coffee place, the peasants, he a little
child, discussing the boats no longer manned by oars, little childlike river, cradle of my first love, how we grew
up without ever meeting and how you ran dry, white
stones in your little bed, dead men's bones, how I became what I became, without her eyes, without anyone's
ever learning how much I loved her, and she went away
just like that, married, had children, and was not to return but as an old woman, a little old woman, to the soil
of her fathers; what nights when gliding forth on secret
streams we were taught what we must now forget in
order to learn what we were never taught, about this
poverty heaped on poverty, I a little child before the
great beggar of humanity, "a penny, please, because it's
raining"; a gardenia in gold tinfoil at the tavern, the
woman pinning it to her bosom, and afterwards the balloons exploding, the holiday cannons of Lycabettos, exploding and scattering noise till the air was full of it, the
balloons tugging to ascend while her fragile hand, the
vendor's, pulled them down to earth for the customers to
burst with lighted cigarettes; everything, the music, your
gaze roving unrepelled over the past decade, when you
were almost a girl still and I loved you and admired you

and wanted to make you my own. What has caused your face to wrinkle now? my hair to fall out? both of us to put on all this weight? That absolute of having you near me, with no one and nothing to disturb us: that absolute I now rediscover as an idea, containing everything and everyone, and I am above a sea of clouds, because I do not want to die.

Ever since morning, when he'd first wakened, he'd had this troubled feeling. When he left home, he kissed his wife and children and took their pictures along to show his friends up here. But in the plane he kept looking at them himself, sentimental about something for the first time—about the family, that necessary evil. Beyond this world, life was not enclosed in predefined social molds. Beyond this world lay another infinite embrace. His motions, his actions were not those of a politician. He lacked the cold logic that makes for compromise, so that in the end everyone survives except the gallant. In him, violent emotions induced violent actions, not negative ones like striking and hurting, but positive ones like persuading and touching and guiding.

No, he could not be alone. Thousands of men now dead hadn't even conceived the things he was at present pondering, weaving together the images of a life before its being filed away for good in the archives of eternity. As a little boy, he had loved decalcomanias; later on those transferred images had become reality. He had dreamed dreams. He'd wanted to board ship and see the world. A month ago he'd climbed the Tymbos at Marathon all alone, had walked alone, yes, marched forty-two kilometers, decked in a Greek flag. Peace March. Friends of Peace. Peace on earth. No more Vietnams. No more Hiroshimas. Peace written in letters made from loaves of bread. And that Sunday excursion on the good ship *Joy* to Aegina, the island now in the throes of a second Occupation by German tourists. The mothers of the Resistance waiting to see their sons in the prison parlor. Twenty years behind bars those boys, while the Germans, all shorts and cameras now instead of boots and machine guns, reveled in the last rays of a sun taking to its bed exhausted by the sight of so much injustice. That old woman in black from Kalamata had recognized him: "Ah, Doctor, my tortures are many and my sufferings great," she had said. "I come here to see my boy. How was he to blame? Sixteen years old then, what did he know?" "Sprechen sie Deutsch? Sehr gut! Nescafé! Temple of Aphaia!" And the return trip on a *Joy* which was utter sorrow—how could he accept all that?

"Blessed be the peacemakers, for they shall be called the children of God," he said.

Meanwhile two policemen had come up to tell them to turn off the loudspeakers.

"They struck me, here," Z. informed them, pointing to his forehead.

"We'll see that you leave the building without being molested," they promised. "A ring of policemen will be formed to protect you. Don't worry about it."

"I'm not worried for myself. I'm worried for all these people you see in the hall."

"The proper measures will be taken. Anyway, it's an order, to shut off the loudspeakers."

"The loudspeakers cannot be shut off. A great many people who came have been left outside and now they can't enter because the rabble would break in along with them. They must hear what we're saying."

"The counterdemonstrators are getting excited."

"It's the duty of the police to disperse them. We're the ones holding a meeting, not they. What are the police doing? Have they come to protect us or betray us?"

"But, Mr. Deputy . . ."

"For the last time I call upon the Public Prosecutor, the General, the Chief of Police, the Prefect, the Minister to protect the life of my colleague Spathopoulos. We do not know what has become of him."

Chapter 14

The Chief of Police strode into the hotel like a gust of wind. He found him in the hall, terrified.

"Since your friends, Mr. Spathopoulos, are afraid that you've been kidnapped and are being tortured somewhere, the way it happens in gangster films, I beg you to accept my escort. Let's go to the meeting together, because Mr. Z. keeps on making appeals over the loudspeaker."

"This is a disgrace," Spathopoulos protested. "Where are we? In Katanga?"

"The loudspeaker's getting them excited."

"Why don't you disperse them? Why don't you make them go away?"

"The operation of dispersal is already under way."

As they moved along, Spathopoulos heard some policemen saying: "Go on, boys, tomorrow you can kill them. Move back."

Then, as they entered the building, he heard:

"Is there some other exit maybe, so they could get away from us?"

"Bulgars, you're going to die!"

"Z., you're going to die!"

"But this is a disgrace," Spathopoulos repeated more insistently. "Can't you hear what they're saying? Can't you arrest them? What sort of a government is this?"

Then he passed through the iron gate and climbed to the third floor, where Z. was still speaking.

Chapter 15

He's come, thought Z. as he saw Spathopoulos walk into the hall. He's returned like Lazarus
from the other world. I'd thought he'd vanished forever.
He's come back. But what about those who have never
come back, who've abandoned us without transmitting
their message? All the dead who circulate in our blood
and never put to us the questions we put to them? The
night without mysteries: a big rectangular blackness like
a door. And those two who ordered us to cut the loudspeakers did so because the loudspeakers were opening
holes in the night.

I must speak. The faces in front of me require that I
speak. But when Lazarus came back from the other
world, all he found to say was: "I'm hungry." I'm hungry
means I'm beginning life again from the beginning, I'm
asking for food again. Once again, I want justice, equal-
ity, peace.

A little stream in which two cows stand hoof-deep. A
sun at its zenith, a glare that scourges me. What else to
say? I don't know. When the telephone stops ringing,
you think no one remembers you. And nevertheless you
are lullabied—not you but your image—in the sheets of
women and in the dreams of youth. If they kill me, I
shall become that kind of image. A disembodied face
seeking its justification upon a stranger's retina.

The present day has filtered drop by drop through my
brain, which can no longer follow sequences. A situation
rears itself by degrees alongside us, we see it suddenly
matured and are terrified.

Love is sweet, but sweeter still, myself inside you. The hour of your surrender, nerves of your neck atremble. The hour when you lose yourself in me and I control your yielding. You, a passive and passionate sea, by nature both eternal and ephemeral, a rivulet, a ravine where red-clawed partridges are calling, you and I, peace.

The policemen came up and polluted our hall, demanding—what? They checked on things and left. But the breach was widened, that's what frightens me. Instinctive fear of turning into a photograph. When everything impells me that way. Why?

One photograph clashing with another in the armory of the dead. Traversing time as ships traverse the sea. But the sea is eternal and the ships fleeting.

What was I saying? To these people, nothing. I was talking to myself. Life is, yes it is, beautiful. When there are no telephones, your hand in mine, the nerves of your neck responding to my lips, life is, yes it is, beautiful, when no one dies of leukemia.

I have difficulty speaking in public. I cannot give words to the cataclysm within me. Words are symbols too. Feelings alone are genuine. I can't find the words to say I love you, I cannot live without you, peace.

Stockings and underclothes hung up on a wire line to dry, fastened with decrepit, rusty clothespins. Who are you?

I'm a man shut up in this hall, who cannot speak. People came here to listen, and how little I've said. People nowadays distrust words. Their faith is in images, in just such a photograph as I shall become, for them. Disguised as a photograph, I shall insinuate myself into their houses.

A progress not unrelated to technology. Whoever believes that the spirit exists independently of scientific developments makes a huge mistake. But the pain in my head returns and I see: a big red egg, big as a public square, red as Red Square in Moscow. It cracks and breaks and out comes a bird; even though my mother boiled it, out comes a bird which begins to fly. It flies through the atmosphere, the stratosphere, the ionosphere. Tell me, what do you feel now? The mind is narrowing, the heart is narrowing. Everything depends on a telephone call I shall make this evening when my parody of a speech has come to an end. The planes are taking off. And we take vengeance on everything we could not be. Failure.

Come, come back, I must speak to you. Don't hesitate to come. I have no hesitation about speaking to you. I miss you. Life is beautiful when everyone has enough to eat and drink, when everyone can get drunk.

"But this is a disgrace!"

"What do you want us to do?"

"Disperse them."

"Don't be afraid."

"That's not the point."

"Well then?"

"They must be dispersed."

"We will guarantee your safe departure by bus."

"That is unacceptable."

"Why?"

"Because the buses are traps. The crowd could stone us more easily once we're inside a bus. In our position we've learned to be wary of everything."

My skin perspires; afterwards, the queers take over the world. Whole armies of men who can no longer be men. Undelivered letters for him who became legend. The earth shouts. Injustice shouts. Don't turn me into a photograph.

They're taking a long time; they struck the other without mercy for his weak heart. "O-o-o beautiful Thessaloniki!" And now nothing. Good night. The world is shrinking, the heart is shrinking. Worse, I haven't grown used to being afraid.

"Orderly departure!"

"We're not under siege at Missolonghi."

"No danger."

"And the stones?"

"The crowd's been dispersed."

"To where?"

"To a point beyond your hotel."

And now, my love, farewell. Love is what did not happen, what did not exist. Elsewhere are you, elsewhere am I. For us two there will always be some justification.

Chapter 16

Yango bent down from his seat and peered through the iron lattice protecting the window of a watchmaker's shop, to see the exact time. But that didn't help any, because each clock there had its own time. So he moved on, till he came to a shop that flaunted its advertisement clock before him, like the switch button that jerks automatically when there's a short circuit. Twenty-five past nine. The time he'd been told to be at the appointed place. He was already three minutes late. He tapped on the rear window and Vango's face appeared.

"Let's get going, *koumbaros*," Yango shouted.

Stepping on the gas, he made for the demonstration. He decided to take a different route from the one he'd come by, so as not to attract attention. He would go the long way around by Nea Megalou Alexandrou Street, up Aristotelous Street, keeping in the right-hand lane, turn into Egnatia Street, and from there disappear into the narrow byways of the market, so familiar to him, until he arrived at his appointed post on Spandoni Street, which gave like a secret artery into the very midst of the fray.

All along the way the city seemed relatively calm. Not

many people out, not many cars; and despite the numerous illuminated shop windows, the streets were dark, though not dark enough for him to turn on his own lights. It all seemed very remote from what was going on only a couple of blocks away. Even though driving very fast, he noticed a couple walking arm in arm, a group of young strollers loitering in front of the big Lambropoulos stores, one or two American sailors from the torpedo boat that had just dropped anchor in the harbor. As he waited for the traffic light to turn green, he saw a little boy with a pan of fresh *koulouria* stacked up like a pyramid. He wanted one; his mouth was dry. But he was afraid of missing the next light. The city was breathing in its usual quiet, neutral rhythm, near the sea, which tonight was scarcely breathing at all. He turned left and entered Aristotelous Street.

The sudden swerve tossed Vango to the other side of the pickup. Vango cursed loudly, certain that Yango, who was driving without a thought for him, hadn't heard him. Then, grabbing the railing of the pickup, he amused himself by watching the white arrows on the pavement flashing by behind the vehicle. They reminded him of the furrow made by a submarine torpedo, heading straight for the flagship of the enemy fleet. He'd seen such a thing in the movies.

Yango was now in the neighborhood of the Petinos Café , where he'd beaten up the woman this afternoon. A bit farther on, the Catacomb, where he'd torn down the announcement. In the green traffic island, the empty frame where the announcement had been was still visible. It hung there like the skeleton of a kite caught on wires.

Turning his head abruptly as if saluting officials on the platform at a parade, he caught a glimpse of his own stand at Vasileos Irakliou Street deserted and drowned in darkness. The huge block of the tobacco factory dominating everything. Only the Electra movie house had lights, and they were too weak to pierce the surrounding darkness. At this hour not a pickup truck was to be seen.

Instead, there were piles of crates, sacks of cement, and barrels, which tomorrow morning would provide his friends with delivery jobs. As he drove up the street, he suddenly realized the full significance of his mission tonight. This evening's transfer job was the one that would make all the other transfer jobs secure.

Now he was racing past the stone foundation of the buildings on either side of Aristotelous Street. Columns and arches which, to his swift glance, seemed to melt into each other, forming one continuous, uniform wall. At the intersection of Aristotelous and Ermou he looked to his left and saw menacing figures outlined in the distance. Dimly he heard a voice from the loudspeaker, without being able to distinguish what it was saying. He could have entered Spandoni Street directly from here, but he risked being spotted by some troublesome witness. And so, following Autocratosaur's instructions, he continued toward Egnatia Street. In front of the EDA offices something was going on, but he didn't slow down for a second. He should worry. He had his own job to do.

At the point where Aristotelous Street meets Egnatia Street, he held out his left arm and the traffic cop signaled him to go ahead. Exactly to the right was the police station, where he'd gone that afternoon after the incidents in front of the Catacomb. Grazing the traffic cop's wooden stand, he turned left again and then right, into the market, with its labyrinth of narrow, slate-paved streets. He knew them like the lines of his own palm.

From the way the pickup was bouncing around, Vango could tell they'd entered Modiano Market.

The market was closed. The merchandise was covered with big pieces of canvas. Hardly any light. Not a single human being. Eyeing the window of a butcher shop, Yango felt a craving for pork chops. The smell of olives, oil, of fresh strawberries now in season, of tomatoes he didn't dare look at—he only ate tomatoes in July, when the price dropped to a drachma a pound—of fresh cucumbers as expensive as a leg of lamb, went to his head.

Shifting into second gear and veering skillfully to left
and right, he spied the shop that sold women's purses,
suitcases, and hats and he knew he'd arrived at Spandoni Street. He shut off the motor and coasted along,
stopping three or four yards from the square. Three men
who seemed to have been waiting for him a long time
rushed out to meet him. He jumped out and with a
piece of burlap covered his license plate. He didn't have
enough string to tie the burlap with, but he did the best
he could. In the end, it was completely covered.

"You're late," said one of the three.

"We had another one to polish off on the way," Yango
explained.

"Luckily the guy hasn't finished his spiel yet. All right.
Get ready. Get back on your seat and don't budge. Keep
your foot on the pedal. Got it?"

Yango, who hated to be ordered around, obeyed as
meekly as a child. There were now about ten men in
front of him; he didn't recognize any of them, they
weren't in uniform and had their backs turned. They
formed a wall, like the wall soccer players form when the
opponent is about to kick a goal from the penalty line.
Even though higher up than the others, he could barely
make out what was happening. The cries reached him in
indistinct waves.

It was no coincidence, he thought, that everything
was taking place within one compact space: the police
station, the Catacomb, his stand, the meeting, the hotel
where the VIP was staying right over there, the EDA offices, and all the streets in this space intersected each
other at right angles. Only one ran diagonally—the little
asphalt street where he was now parked. And he, like
the bishop in chess, moving diagonally from this point,
would lunge into the square among the pawns, rooks,
and knights, to check their king.

Chapter 17

Joseph had no interest in politics. His shop was beside the Ministry of Northern Greece, and there he worked peaceably as a carpenter, without bothering anyone. That evening, although the shops were closed, he had stayed on to finish a kidney-shaped table, so that he could deliver it the next day to the woman who owned the neighborhood grocery. She had become rich because of the apartment buildings recently constructed on the corner and wished, as she explained, to replace all the old junk she owned with beautiful modern furniture. This would be added to the dowry of her daughter, who would soon be old enough to marry. She had contracted for the job on terms favorable to herself.

At about 8:30 he decided to stop. The smell of the wood aggravated his asthma. He decided to take a walk as far as the water's edge and get a breath of sea air. He strolled along, absorbed in his own thoughts, passed the Caravanserai, and then turned up Venizelou Street. Noticing a crowd of people in the distance, he thought first of an accident. He stood on the corner waiting for the light to change.

"What's going on?" he asked a man standing next to him.

"I don't know."

"Is it a demonstration?"

"That remains to be seen," said the other.

The green light flashed and they crossed the street together, separating without a word, on the opposite side, Joseph going to the left and the other man to the right.

As he approached, he began to see what was happening. People were fighting among themselves and throwing rocks at a building. Why? He went on, out of curiosity. Outside the Adams Department Store, his attention was caught by a nude mannequin in the window; her nudity contrasted strangely with the opulent richness which surrounded her. He saw reflected in the shop window two men trying to grab a third, who was running away; they tripped him, laid him out, and began kicking him. The victim grasped him by the leg and, with a sudden spurt of energy, managed to topple him down; but the larger of the two aggressors intervened. Taking a thick sailor's belt ornamented with a heavy metal buckle, he began thrashing him.

Joseph looked around: he could see people in other places engaged in precisely the same actions. It was as if one scene were being reproduced in a series of mirrors. Then he felt someone tearing at the frayed lapel of his jacket. Forced to turn around, he found himself facing a character with the eyes of a drug addict, who pulled at his lapel as if he wanted to tear it off.

"Where's your pin?" he demanded. Joseph felt the heavy, foul breath on his face.

"What pin?"

"So you're not one of ours?"

Letting go of his lapel, he punched him in the stomach. Joseph doubled up. He had a chronic ulcer.

"Why are you hitting me? What have I done?"

Meanwhile other people had collected. Somebody tickled him in the ribs to make him turn around; and when he did, an elbow struck him straight in the face. He started to bleed. What was happening?

"Police!" he shouted. "Police!"

A policeman not far away pretended not to hear. One last kick in the back cracked against his spine. He fell to the ground and watched as someone smashed a chair and distributed the pieces to the circle of outstretched hands, which a moment later were armed with improvised clubs. He fainted.

When he came to at the first-aid station, they were sewing up the wound over his eyebrow. He was in horrible pain. Who had brought him here? How? He didn't know, he didn't remember. His bones hurt to the very marrow. When his wound was bandaged, he hurried home.

The hours slipped past and he couldn't sleep. The idea that he wouldn't be able to finish the little kidney-shaped table for the grocery woman worried him. Black thoughts buzzed in his brain. At the first-aid station he'd heard talk of someone named Z.—a stranger to him—and about pacifists: who wasn't a pacifist? The good Joseph himself was unable to believe in the Crucifixion. Around midnight a rooster crowed; someone knocked at the door. Joseph lived alone, his wife had died three years before. His daughters were married, his son worked in a factory in Germany.

"Who's there?" he asked, before opening the door.

"Police."

Trembling with fear, he opened the door.

"Come with us."

"Where?"

"To the police station."

"Just a minute, I'll go get dressed."

"No. Come as you are, in your pajamas. Put on a coat, the car's waiting."

He did as he was told. He was in horrible pain. At the station they sent him directly to the office of the Chief of Police. The Chief asked him to sit down. He seemed very affable.

"Joseph Zaimis, son of Leontos?"

"That's right."

"Occupation, cabinetmaker?"

"That's right."

"Your papers are in order, Zaimis. There's no reason to get them dirty. Do you understand what I mean?"

"Not exactly."

"I mean it's better for you to avoid preferring charges against unknown parties. You're a good fellow and the police have a good opinion of you. You realize that there's been a misunderstanding. They took you for someone else. If you will forget the incident, it will make our position easier. If I can ever do anything for you, just let me know."

It was the first time a full-fledged police chief had ever spoken to him. In a certain way he felt flattered. His work permit, everything, depended on these people.

"You can leave now. Forgive us for bothering you at such an hour and in your condition. But tomorrow would have been too late. The others would have got to you before us. Tomorrow, when you read the newspapers, you'll understand why I made you come. Good night."

He went home, more confused than ever. Now all the roosters in the neighborhood were crowing. He waited until dawn, then hurried out to get the early edition of the papers and find out what it was all about.

The man who, leaving Zaimis at the intersection, had started down Venizelou Street on the right-hand sidewalk saw a man with bushy eyebrows approach from the opposite direction and stop in front of the Singer sewing-machine store. Zacharias—that was his name— had no idea who was beating up whom or why rocks were being thrown and chair legs distributed like sacramental bread to the faithful. As he was standing there looking on, he saw a crowd forming around the bushy-browed man and heard someone say: "Chief, we're going to hang around here till morning and then we'll polish off the whole bunch of them."

The "chief" tapped the man protectively on the shoulder. "Relax," said the "chief." "I know more about it than you."

And the man with the bushy eyebrows, whom the other had called chief, left, escorted by two or three members of the group.

Zacharias was bewildered. True, he had no business being here; he was simply on his way back from the scrap-iron market near the church of the Madonna of Chalkaion, where he went every Wednesday afternoon when the stores were closed, to buy copper and iron wholesale. The mysterious conversation he had just heard aroused his curiosity to such a point that he approached a young man with a neatly clipped mustache who was standing nearby.

"Who's the guy with the bushy eyebrows?" he asked.

The young man stared at him in astonishment. "Don't you know the Chief of Police?"

"Oh!" said Zacharias.

"What are you doing around here anyway?"

"I was just passing by."

"Listen, mister, if you don't want your skull cracked open I'd advise you to keep your nose out of other people's business."

With a menacing gesture, the young man with the mustache turned and left. Zacharias walked a few steps farther. In front of him a crowd of men were fighting and hurling stones. Then he saw one of them approach another and whisper something in his ear. The latter made a sign to a third, and all three hurled themselves on a fourth person who was standing there motionless, looking on. Who were all these people? What was the meaning of this pantomime? Who was beating up whom? And why?

"Your identity card."

Zacharias displayed his identity card with alacrity.

"Not this one," the man said, "the other one."

"Which other one?" Zacharias was bewildered.

"Listen, buddy, if you don't want any trouble for yourself, get the hell out of here—and fast!"

"What's going on anyway?"

"What business is it of yours?"

Zacharias went on his way. Continuing along Venizelou Street, he ran into Vangelis, a friend from his village, whom he hadn't seen in years.

"How's the house going?"

"I've added a second story. Thank God! Have you been back to the village at all?"

"I'm thinking of going this year when I have my vacation. For the grape harvest. Will you be going?"

"It's out of the question. It's too far away, our Crete. I haven't been there in twelve years."

"How's your wife? And the kids?"

"They're okay. And yours?"

"They're fine. My oldest is almost through school."

"Listen, do you know what's going on here tonight?"

"How should I know? It's a madhouse. I was just going to ask you the same thing."

"I don't know any more than you. Let's beat it before we get into trouble."

They were attempting to bypass a group of counterdemonstrators, when two of them seized Vangelis and began beating him. When Zacharias intervened, they attacked him.

"Who told you to stick your nose in?"

"This man hasn't done anything!"

Someone kicked him in the stomach. Vangelis's pockets were ripped. Several coins spilled out, but he didn't dare pick them up.

Zacharias's immediate thought was to go to the Public Prosecutor. He left Venizelou Street and set off in that direction. It was about 9:30. He was revolted to see how completely the law of the jungle had taken over. The Public Prosecutor's office was closed. Brimming over with indignation, he raced to the offices of the newspaper *Macedonia*, slung open the glass door, climbed up the steps, and found himself in the editorial room. A few members of the staff were dozing in their glass compartments. In another room the teletype clicked away. Absolute calm reigned. He approached one of the older men.

"All hell is breaking loose on the corner of Ermou and Venizelou," he said. "Toughs and policemen in plain clothes are beating everybody up without mercy."

"Unfortunately we know about it," the reporter answered him sleepily, gripping his indelible pencil.

"Something's got to be done before things get worse!"

"Unfortunately nothing can be done."

"As a Greek citizen, I protest."

"What would you like me to do?"

"Look here, they beat me up for no reason at all."

"Lodge a complaint at police headquarters. This is a newspaper."

And bending over his metal desk, the reporter began to write. Zacharias went home by a different route.

Chapter 18

"The history of the peace movement in Greece, from the time of its birth in 1955," Z. continued, "is a cruel story. At the first meeting of the Friends of Peace in Piraeus, the police looked the other way while hirelings burst into the theater and threw spittoons at the speakers, shouted, hissed, and threatened, without any interference from the Chief of Police, who was present in the first row of the orchestra. A participant in a disarmament meeting in Lesbos was killed for reasons that have remained mysterious to this day. In Athens a young soldier who took part in another peace meeting was court-martialed and sent to Triethnes, a remote post near the Albania–Yugoslav borders, where he died shortly afterwards, succumbing, to quote the official statement issued by the High Command, 'to the effects of an accident on the rifle range.'"

"Why is peace so intolerable to them? Why don't they attack other organizations and movements, such as the Society for Political Exiles and Prisoners, the League for the Rights of Man, the EDA youth groups, the various trade-union organizations? Why do they vent their wrath on our movement alone, which aims at peace and

international détente, which draws support from all over
the world and includes leaders of all parties? The reason
is simple: the other movements are Greek, local, ori-
ented toward internal affairs. Consequently they don't
interest our Allies—those great protectors of ours, who to
our faces always play the friend and behind our backs
doublecross us right down the line. Think of Asia Minor
in 1922, and now today Cyprus . . ."

"Cyprus! Enosis!"

"Self-determination!"

"Cyprus is Greek!"

"Our Western allies, I say, and their Greek flunkies,
who show the excessive zeal of the slave eager to curry
favor with his master, so excessive indeed, so blatantly
cruel that even their master is often compelled to disa-
vow them—well, our Western allies and their local flunkies look upon peace as a threat leveled directly against
themselves. Because peace in the world would sound the
knell of the big monopolies whose power and growth
depend on the armaments race. Throughout the eighteen years of peace since the end of the Second World
War, some eighteen localized wars have taken place,
and if they remained localized it is only because the fear
of universal devastation serves as a counterweight to the
warlike tendencies of the Great Powers."

"Down with NA-TO!"

"No more Hi-ro-shi-mas!"

"Bre-e-ad! Bre-e-ad!"

"In one of his speeches President Kennedy addressed
his audience as 'My fellow inhabitants of this planet.'
And he was right. At a time when the gates of space are
opening, it is folly for us to keep our own doors closed,
as though we were still living in the past century. Sci-
ence is forging ahead by prodigious leaps and bounds,
we must all try to keep pace with it in our thinking. The
world today is no longer divided into East and West. All
ideas based on the opposition between antithetical extremes are outmoded. Today, the electronic microscope
discloses a world very different from what we were

taught. The electronic microscope shows us that if we make two holes, A and B, in a sheet of paper, and if we have a substance capable of passing through these holes, it will not pass through A before B, or through B before A, but will pass through both holes simultaneously. In order to adapt themselves to the modern world, our minds, accustomed to thinking in the old traditional grooves, must assimilate these discoveries and apply them to life in the world. The anti-Communist struggle is the application of the old method of opposing extremes, in its most primitive and obsolete form.

"I am speaking to you at this moment primarily as a physician. Every day I am brought face to face with the deplorable condition of our country. There are not enough doctors. The mountain villages are isolated. The land that gave birth to Hippocrates lacks so much as a public health system worthy of the name, and it claims to be living in the twentieth century. And when these elementary essentials are absent, how can civilization exist? How can people live under such conditions? If instead of half the government's budget going for military expenditures, it went into education, athletic fields, medical care, and industrial investment, wouldn't we live better? Wouldn't we escape the curse of emigration, which is decimating our towns and villages? That is what peace would mean, and that is why this evening's meeting, and I in particular, are so odious to them that they have hired hoodlums to jeer at us.

"But if these hoodlums were able to read two lines and understand them, they would realize that they are attacking their own interests. Because they are all poor, ragged, wage slaves without wages. And they are condemned to remain so for the rest of their lives because the powers that be have an interest in the existence of this ragged subproletariat, out of which, as occasion arises, they can choose the hoodlums they require, offering them a pittance or some small favor, and so having them always available, as they are tonight.

"My friends, these people who are shouting at us tonight are much to be pitied, because they will never know that we are fighting for them too. To tell you the truth, they don't bother me. I let them strike me, because they weren't out for me personally, but for somebody who had been pointed out to them by the hidden masters on whom the poor wretches depend. They themselves don't even know who I am, who you are. Whatever they do, they do to curry favor with the higher-ups. All of them have children who can't go to school, sick wives, decaying teeth, ulcers, phobias, diseased lungs. They are, I repeat, to be pitied. Therefore, don't listen to their shouts. History is marching on, they will catch up some day. Blessèd be the peacemakers, for they shall be called the children of God."

Chapter 19

Every word Z. uttered was a slap in the General's thin, cavernous face. He stood rooted to the spot, every now and then shifting to left or right, his gaze pinned on the loudspeaker, which reminded him of the funnel-shaped horns used by the Resistance during the Occupation to blast out incendiary slogans. He was waiting patiently for the end of the meeting. But with the phrase "Blessèd be the peacemakers . . ." a chill ran down his spine. How could the words of the son of God, flesh of Mary, Mater Dolorosa, dare come out of the filthy disbeliever's mouth? "The significant turbulence on the solar mass," he reflected, "produces the melting of ice at the poles and the probable deviation of the earth's axis." Such phrases gave him relief and diverted his attention from the loudspeaker.

The Chief of Police, on the other hand, was growing more and more anxious. All the responsibility for the counterdemonstration fell on him. And the thieves, gangsters, hoodlums, dregs of society assembled here tonight to jeer at Z. were carrying things too far. "Give them an inch, they'll take a mile," he thought. He could see the results. After they'd been pushed back to create an empty space in front of the entrance to the building, their fury, far from subsiding, had mounted to a new high. They were completely out of hand and he did not know what to do to restrain them. The General had no responsibility, anything might happen when the Communists came out; he was not in charge of preserving law and order. It was the Chief of Police who would inevitably be blamed for any untoward incidents. He racked his narrow but practical brain to recall some police regulation to invoke. He thought of buses: he might send an officer or two, to requisition some buses from the depots of Vardariou Square and at the Administration Building, so that the Friends of Peace could board them. Knowing the kind of men who made up the crowd, he felt apprehension. Cement-workers, scrap-iron workers, stevedores. If they decided to battle it out, there would be real bloodshed. And it wasn't the wage earners they were after.

"Dirty Bulgar, you'll pay for Papadopoulos!"

"Go back to Bulgaria!"

"Down with Z.!"

Chapter 20

The police lieutenant's jeep started off at breakneck speed and within three minutes had reached Vardariou Square. It stopped in front of the dispatcher's booth at the bus terminal, which looked out upon the statue of Constantine I on horseback. The dispatcher was bent over his timetables, checking arrivals and departures of buses.

"There's an emergency and we need all the buses at your disposal," the lieutenant said to him as he jumped out of the jeep.

The dispatcher looked at him dully. "We have no buses at our disposal."

"I see at least two."

"The first one is leaving in two seconds." And putting his whistle to his lips, he gave the signal for departure.

The driver, who was sitting on a bench with the ticket taker, consulted his watch in bewilderment.

"You're ahead of time, Mitso," he shouted.

"Get going, I tell you." And he motioned him off with his hand.

"Give me your papers," ordered the lieutenant. "Refusal to obey an officer on duty isn't going to get you very far."

"But, lieutenant, it's not in my power to give you a bus. We'll telephone the general superintendent of the lines. He's the one in charge."

"Do you understand the meaning of an order? War has been declared."

The dispatcher adjusted his eyeglasses and looked at

the officer with curiosity. "He must be off his nut!" he said to himself.

Meanwhile the driver, discarding his cigarette, scrambled up through the side door, took his place behind the wheel, pressed the button which automatically closed the doors, and started the motor. In a rage the lieutenant signaled him to stop. He ordered his own driver to move the jeep in front of the bus. The passengers began protesting: "We've got to get home. It's nine o'clock."

In his booth the dispatcher was talking to the superintendent on the phone. "Boss," he said. "There's a police officer here who wants to requisition all the available buses. And there are only two, and one of those is all set to leave."

"Let him have them, Mitso," was the answer. "A police captain came here and took four. They seem to want them for some kind of emergency."

"All right. I can give one. But I can't give him the other one."

"Order the passengers off and give him the bus. You can space out the next departures so as to fill the gap."

The dispatcher hung up and came out of his glass booth. Signaling to the driver to open the front door, he climbed aboard. He asked the passengers to get off, "because of an unforeseen emergency," and to keep their tickets for the next bus. Two or three grumbled, complaining that this was no way to do business, and muttering about "the good old days when they had streetcars," but they got off. A blind and deaf beggar with an accordion began playing "I Dream of Your Beautiful Hair" and took off his cap to collect coins.

"Come on, Barba-Kosta, get off," the dispatcher urged. "You're the last one. Get off."

"Your credentials," the lieutenant said, addressing the dispatcher.

"I don't have them with me. Come by tomorrow. I'm always here."

Drivers and ticket takers climbed aboard the buses while the lieutenant got into the jeep and, signaling the buses to follow him, started off in the direction of the demonstration. The empty buses, with their lights off, resembled those that crossed the city at midnight on their way to the terminal—big, hollow Easter eggs, which the passengers, shivering at the stop and watching them pass, could only regard as dead visions of disappointed hopes. That is how the ejected passengers felt now when they found themselves waiting once again at the terminal.

With the police jeep leading the procession, they arrived at the square. Then the two buses took their places behind the other four, which had already arrived, blocking the Ano Toumba stop; six buses all in a line, silent and deserted factories. The drivers and ticket takers got off to see what was happening. And what they saw made them shudder.

The lieutenant reported to the Chief of Police that the order had been executed to the letter.

Chapter 21

It would soon be over. Nine-thirty had passed. The audience had been in the hall since 7:30. They too had homes, jobs the next morning, Thursday. The masons had to rise before sun-up. Tired faces, beautiful ones, carved by life, ploughed by its ploughshare. Poor people, but aware of it. The people outside, poor but unaware.

Ah, how beautiful life is when you touch it with a virgin hand, before it is blackened by smoke and dimmed by exhaust fumes! How beautiful life is when it goes on a massive strike, all the arms refusing to work, like the hundred arms of Buddha attached to one body! What new dimension is acquired when the body proliferates into thousands of other bodies! How immortal it becomes! Alas for those who die without ever having realized that they form the interchangeable cells on the skin of an idea; that when they vanish, other cells will replace them, so the skin can breathe through open pores. Alas for those who go to die like animals in their lairs, unready to give themselves with all their souls, wherever they may be—on a sidewalk, in a public square, at a demonstration, in a depot.

Death may be waiting for us everywhere, he told himself. The essential thing is for us not to be waiting for it everywhere. Doing so, we should be no more than the oil that lubricates the machine of fear. Death may be waiting in ambush like a motorcycle on a side lane. The essential thing is not to think about the motorcycle, about the side lane, because if we did we should not be able to walk alone, at our own gait. We should have to support ourselves on other people's shoulders, like cripples, in annihilating dependence.

And the sun rises each morning fresh over a fresh world. This sun which we watch for every dawn and which fails us every twilight is the value of life. I measure the molecules of time, I count them, they are mine, not other people's. No estrangement. Once and for all, the workers must understand that providing them with brighter homes does not put an end to exploitation. They must understand once and for all that they can be emancipated only by . . .

Ever since I was little, I wanted to become a pilot, to soar high into the clouds, to live near the sun. Then I became a doctor, because my people wanted it. One brother stayed in the village. Another went abroad. The family must produce one educated man, and the lot fell to me. But the dizzy heights have always fascinated me. The myth of Icarus is my favorite myth.

(On the island of Icaria, where he had done his military service, he had looked closely at people's wounds.

Big wounds, windows onto life, with pure air passing through, despite all the pus that collected on the sills.)

And when I married, I came to know the veins of her neck as she smothered her sobs in my arms after I cheated on her or lied to her. Life is beautiful when you are ready at every moment to die. When the roots of the night descend into you and lustily drink your blood. No one can say that I was weak, that I tried to remove my bodily presence which so disturbed them. Writers can write what they please, for the spirit is free in underdeveloped countries. In underdeveloped countries, what is persecuted is the body, the bodily presence that displaces a certain volume of air. That's why they hounded me when I made my solitary march. So many, many people write about peace. For those others, it's all just vapor. For those pigs nothing exists but the body. My own, though—and I know it well, down to the slightest tremor of its least fiber—has a protective covering: that of parliamentary immunity. No wonder they didn't strike as hard as they might, why they didn't dare finish me off.

O-o-o beautiful Thessaloniki! Some perfume of Byzantine mysticism still clings to you. In the Hippodrome, now overgrown with apartment buildings, the Yellows were forever battling it out with the Greens in the old days, and here tonight, we the Reds and the lizards outside, the Greens, are shouting in a hippodrome where all the horses have been drugged and race on injections.

I must let my colleague Spathopoulos say something too. They took him away, he is back. I can't go on speaking. These people must go home. That's how it is. Now the problem will be to get out. How to do it? I hope the police will be sensible and prevent incidents—I don't want any of us to come to harm.

The rostrum was an outlet for me. I'm glad they listened. I don't know what else to say. Peace, I want to say, is practice. It's refusing to pay your taxes when the money goes for armaments. It's acting crazy to avoid military service. Peace is not an ikon of the Virgin appearing on the front to inspire the soldiers. It's an ikon of statistics, figures, tangible truths. It is not—above all, it is not an idea.

Your hand in mine. A microphone working on electricity. Then the light goes dim: "the shadow of the wall is iron." Black Greekness. Incessantly there are new victims, which, thanks to our progressive municipalities, give their names to streets and squares. Black Greekness which never saw a day's justice.

The lights are flickering. They must be cutting the wires to plunge us into darkness, to spread confusion among us. The lights are fluttering, eyelids of drowsy children who want more than anything to sleep.

And even if you were a whore in your youth, you've acquired wisdom enough by now, I hope, not to change any more. To say that life is beautiful, that whoever thinks justly is beautiful. To say that if you get sick I shall come to keep you company; that if you weep I shall be the pillow that drinks your tears. Yes, it is beautiful, life is beautiful when your hand is in my hand, when our two life lines become one, fused as on the palms of lepers, and can no longer separate.

Chapter 22

He had gone to the meeting early, and now that Z. had finished his speech, he was determined not to leave him for an instant. When he had seen him enter the hall after being hit, and heard him declare: "This is what they've done to me for coming to you," his eyes had filled with tears.

He, Hatzis—or the Tiger, as they called him—had no

definite occupation. He had worked as blacksmith, mason, plasterer, iceman—he had even shined shoes. A slight, wiry, bald man, he lived in his own way, and he was always on hand at meetings like this. When there were clashes, he took part—not because anyone told him to but because he felt it as an obligation.

An obligation to whom? And why? He didn't know. He was obliged to no one. He moved in an orbit of his own and took advice from no one. Today, for instance, he'd come all the way from Ano Toumba on foot. He didn't have enough money to buy a bus ticket. Along the way he saw the automobiles, the shop windows, the sweets, all the riches of a civilization he couldn't begin to approach, much less enjoy. He didn't care. He wasn't jealous of anyone. He practiced a private brand of asceticism.

Tonight he'd been supposed to call on a contractor who he'd been told was a left-winger and who might give him a week's work. But instinctively he decided instead to come to the meeting of the Friends of Peace. He didn't know Z. But he admired him for the march he'd made last month all alone, and for punching in the eye that deputy in the Chamber. And he felt that Z. was vulnerable, especially because the others would not hesitate to plot against a man who laughed off all efforts to protect him.

Now that Z. had finished his speech and was proceeding without any hesitation to plunge once more into the inferno in the street, Hatzis resolved to appoint himself Z.'s anonymous bodyguard. He went over and posted himself near the door through which Z. would be passing on his way downstairs.

He had scarcely begun his watch when he saw Z. in the corridor, and workmen's hands in dense concentrations turning suddenly to sprigs of oleander which grazed his passing body. They all wanted to get close, to snatch one of his buttons, touch his skin while he wended his difficult way through the thousand-handed

fireworks, greeting them, smiling, from time to time
dropping some remark.

As Z. approached the door where Hatzis was waiting,
the crowd in his wake straightened up, like a field of
grass after the wind has passed over it. Their faces were
pressed tightly together. A wall of faces. Hatzis the day-
dreamer saw it all in images. He had the lyricism of the
true lyre player, who transforms his instrument into a
bow in order to confront his enemies, but who retains all
his virtuosity. Now, as he watched Z. moving toward
him, he thought of a battleship coming out of the road-
stead to enter the storm-tossed sea. He, Hatzis, was the
tugboat that would pilot him safely, for even though the
battleship was covered with armor, there were still the
reefs and the torpedoes.

Behind Z. came the members of the Committee for International Détente and Peace. The banners and em-
blems on the platform were already being pulled down
so that the hall could be turned back to the Labor
Union employees tomorrow in the same condition as it
had been found.

An old woman approached Z., crying, "Doctor, my
child is ill. What can I do? I have no money for a doctor."

Z. stopped, looked at her, and said: "Bring him to my
hotel tomorrow morning and I'll examine him. I won't be
leaving before noon."

"Aren't you ashamed, old woman?" someone in back
of her chided. "Talking like that to our leader. What
have we come here for, anyway?" But the old woman
wasn't ashamed. She had many other things to confide to
him, and ills of her own for him to cure as well.

Hatzis saw him now, scarcely a yard away. The
wound above his eye had become discolored, as though
death had planted on his forehead its first poisonous
fungus.

Someone in the entourage—the members of the committee, behind Z. in a group, were mostly lawyers—said to

him: "Mr. Deputy, it would be better if a few of us got ahead of you, to avoid any repetition of the incidents."

"Let them come back, if they dare!" Z. was angry.

He started down the staircase. Hatzis slipped behind him. Someone tried to shove him away, but with his slight build and cat-like suppleness he was able to make a place for himself directly in front of his charge. Z. noticed him and the Tiger felt a trident spring up in his blue eyes. He no longer had any doubt that Z. was a born leader, the leader for whom he'd been searching all these years, ever since the heroes of the Resistance had been killed and only the politicians and theoreticians were left, none of whom, it seemed to him, had the makings of a true leader.

The crowd of people who hadn't been able to enter the hall had now swarmed into the building and were blocking the staircases. They were sitting on the steps, frightened, penned in: at times the iron gate, pressed on from outside by the tidal waves of "outraged citizens," seemed about to give way. Sometimes it would open to admit a police officer with eyes like the lenses of a camera and a little roll of film in his brain, recording their faces for the inquisitions, hearings, or tortures to come; at other times nothing could be heard but the cry: "Come on out and you'll be roasted alive!" while fragments of stone flew about like a shower of foam when a wave breaks against the rocks and sprays the people on shore. Seeing that the entire police force of Salonika was unable to disperse some two hundred hoodlums, the Friends of Peace held back on the steps. But as Z. came toward them, and they pressed against the wall or the banister to make way for him, they regained confidence. Like leaves singed by sulphur, then washed clean by the spring rain, they could again breathe freely, and their assurance returned.

"What a great man!" thought Hatzis, intent on keeping the crowd from separating them. "His body must fascinate women, his mind must speak straight to the heart, his skillful hands must reassure his patients."

By now Hatzis had reached the iron gate. From there he could see outside. The hoodlums had backed away. Two or three police caps could be glimpsed circulating behind the heavy iron grille. With a steady hand, Z. drew the bolt and the gate opened with a grinding noise.

The opening of the gate brought the two hostile worlds into communication. Z. walked through the gate, handsome, proud, alone. When he appeared, there was no clamor, for the simple reason that he was unknown to the people outside. To none of the hirelings who were threatening him with death was Z. more than a name. The name had been whispered to them, an initial, nothing more. They would have behaved the same way if some other name had been whispered to them. They were hammering at a stranger's door.

Hatzis now slipped over to Z.'s left. He could see the General and the Chief of Police on the sidewalk opposite. Apparently Z. had also seen them; he immediately headed straight for them. With his athletic tread, Z. crossed the street in six steps, according to Hatzis's count, who himself had to take ten. Hatzis saw Z. beside him, illuminated by the red light of the Melissa Shop window.

"Mr. Police Inspector!" he called out in a piercing voice.

Hearing these words, the General turned abruptly away, like a comic-opera phantom, as if he were the ghost of himself, visible only to Z. The General's sudden turning away struck Hatzis as very strange. He'd acted as though Z. had some contagious disease, as though, by breathing the same air, he might catch a fatal illness.

"Mr. Police Inspector," Z. repeated.

But the General had already reached the corner of Ermou and Venizelou Streets and was gazing emptily at the sea.

Z. turned toward the Chief of Police.

"Mr. Chief of Police," he said, "this is a scandal. I protest vigorously. This is an open violation of the law."

"If you hadn't installed the loudspeakers, Mr. Z., this crowd would not have gathered. You could have held your meeting quite peacefully, and we should not have had to be present in such force."

"Your men are lending support to the counterdemonstrators instead of dispersing and arresting them. I'm afraid of what might happen when the Friends of Peace come out."

"It's exactly for that reason," the Chief replied, "that I took the precaution of bringing these buses in"—and he pointed to the six dimmed buses. "Your friends need only board them to leave the premises without any trouble."

Hatzis saw Z. stiffen. He turned around and whispered to the members of the committee; they nodded their heads in complete agreement. Z. turned back to the Chief.

"The Friends of Peace," he said firmly, "came as free citizens and will leave as free citizens. They do not find it acceptable to be evacuated in coaches."

Hatzis had immediately figured out what the Chief had in mind. Once bundled into the buses, the pacifists would have been unable to defend themselves and would have been completely at the mercy of the counterdemonstrators. The same thing had happened once before, he remembered. Even assuming that the Chief of Police was acting in good faith and not setting a trap, it would be the same. Hatzis was relieved to hear his leader reply as he did.

The gate of the building, acting like a safety valve, allowed the people inside to emerge only a few at a time, in small groups. These small groups, spaced out as they were, started homeward. The cordon of police was trying to reduce the flow of the valve to a minimum and to hold up the exodus, for reasons only too obvious.

Z. and the people escorting him went in the direction of the Kosmopolit Hotel, which was diagonally across the way from the sidewalk where they had been standing. Down Ermou Street they could see the dimly lit

Ayia Sophia Church, looking like a wedding cake at some royal marriage ceremony. A lawyer held Z. by the arm. Hatzis followed on Z.'s left side. Suddenly he saw three young men in black pullovers advancing toward them menacingly. Z. saw them too and, at once disengaging his arm from the lawyer's, turned his back on the hotel and shouted to some invisible person: "Here they are! They're here again! Why don't you arrest them? What are the police doing?"

At that precise moment, from the opposite corner, on the hotel side of the square, a pickup van swooped in like a rocket. A man crouched in the rear hit him on the head with an iron bar. He wavered, he fell; the wheels of the vehicle passed over him, dragging him a foot or two in the process; a pool of blood began to form on the street.

"For shame!"

"Stop them!"

"Get the number!"

"They've killed Z.!"

"Shame! Shame!"

"Death to the assassins!"

Chapter 23

He was coming from the tailor's, where he was an apprentice, right across the way from the Caravanserai. Bits of thread still clinging to his trousers, he walked toward Nea Megalou Alexandrou Street to catch the bus for Phoenix, the suburb where he lived. Eight months ago he had managed, by a simple political maneuver, to get a roof over his head. Although not right-

wing, he had said he was, in order to get on the preferred list of applicants for housing in a new working-
class settlement outside Salonika, near the airport, "on
either side of the highway." The highway was a menace
to children; nevertheless, the low-income apartments
were clean and uniform, with a row of trees around
them. And so he was on his way home, having just finished cuffing a pair of trousers for a customer, when a
policeman politely asked him to turn back.

"But I'm on my way to get my bus!"

"There's an EDA demonstration and I'm asking you
not to go any farther. I've got strict orders not to let anyone through."

The tailor obeyed. He was a nationalist. He was well
acquainted with the area and knew there was another
street he could take to get to the bus stop. He went by
way of Solomos Street and came out on Spandoni Street.
As he walked along, he noticed at the far end of the
street a parked three-wheeled pickup truck with a man
on the driver's seat. Five or six people standing in front
of it formed a kind of living barrier, and a few yards to
the side were a police lieutenant and two gendarmes.
He went along paying no attention to anybody, when he
heard someone behind him issue a command: "Get
going! What are you waiting for? They're coming!"

He turned around sharply. The voice must have been
the lieutenant's because he was the person nearest him.
He saw the driver of the pickup settle his weight on the
pedals as he raised himself on his saddle. The motor
roared. The men in front moved aside and the pickup
raced toward the intersection at such an incredible
speed that the tailor thought the vehicle was being
driven by a motorcycle acrobat from the circus. He
heard a noise, a thud. Then: "For shame!" "Catch them!"
He saw the police lieutenant clutching his head with his
hands in horror and he heard him cry to the person next
to him: "What happened? I never imagined such a terrible thing could happen." And the other replied sarcastically: "Aren't you ashamed? A man like you!"

The tailor couldn't understand. Many of his customers were police officers. He repaired their uniforms. He was fond of them. All he could figure out was that the pickup must have run over someone. But who? He had no idea. Acting on the saying that no mouse can prove itself not an elephant if arrested as one, he took to his heels. Not until the next day, when he learned from the newspapers whom they'd killed, did he go testify what he'd heard: "Get going! What are you waiting for? They're coming!" He added that immediately after, someone had pointed Z. out to the driver of the pickup as the person he was meant to hit.

Chapter 24

He didn't understand how it had happened. Undoubtedly he never would. These moments are like shooting stars. They pass before us, leaving only a luminous trail impossible to decipher. Where do they come from? What do they plunge toward?

O dark night, night of evil, night of Satan. He held him firmly by the arm, because he knew what Z. was capable of, and led him toward his hotel. He felt the muscles of Z.'s arm twitching with restrained rage. He held him tight so he couldn't escape. After his exchange with the Chief of Police, Z. seemed furious. The indifference, the apathy in the Chief's face, when all around them injustice had run rampant, filled him with horror. To keep Z. from making some gesture that he might later regret, the lawyer held him firmly, accompanied him toward the hotel.

They walked to the middle of the square strewn with

the stones that a few hours before had been hurled at the windows; the stripes of their jackets merged, giving the impression of an enormous hand. They were walking along, the lawyer trying to calculate how many steps they must still take before reaching the hotel on the opposite sidewalk, when he saw them returning—the same three envoys from hell in their black pullovers, who, before the meeting, had struck Z. on the brow. Now that it was darker, they looked even more menacing. Z. saw them too and seethed with indignation. No, he must not let them begin again. He yanked his arm away, despite the lawyer's efforts to restrain him, turned around, shouted: "What are the police doing? Here they are! They're here again!"

And then? A deafening uproar, something like the explosion of a mine in a peaceful meadow where ordinarily nothing was heard but the cows mooing at pasture, and no one would have suspected the mines still buried from the days of the Occupation—mines and men, committing crimes they hadn't had time to finish during the war, now, twenty years later, when the world was preparing to celebrate the defeat of Hitler's Germany, everywhere except in Greece, where the leading collaborators survive and prosper omnipotent—ichthyosaurs, shoebills, swamp dwellers, Siphonophora, pterodactyls, Anopheles mosquitoes—where there were still kings with German blood. Though he couldn't have described it, he saw it. Four men suddenly moved apart and revealed the monstrous pickup van, headlights turned off, descending upon them in terrifying fury. He barely managed to get out of the way himself. Had he still been holding Z. by the arm, he could have saved him. But Z. had turned toward the opposite sidewalk, where, only a moment before, he had been talking with the Chief of Police. Then a man armed with a club rose up in the rear of the van and hit Z. No, he wasn't certain of that—his eyes had been so filled with terror that he hadn't made things out clearly. He imagined himself in Z.'s place, lying on the pavement in a pool of blood. When you get hit by a bullet, you feel nothing at first but a gentle warmth pervading your body. He thought it must be like that when you fall: for some seconds you think you are standing up and someone else is lying on the ground in your place. The lawyer regained his presence of mind sufficiently to try to see the license number of the pickup, this monster that like Achilles' horses was dragging the dead body of Hector. But the number was covered over.

He heard a multitude of voices shouting all around him. For a moment they drowned out the backfire of the van as it vanished, like a black shooting star, up Venizelou Street, in the wrong direction.

"Murderers!"

"Shame!"

"You've killed Z.!"

He saw several people running after the pickup van in an attempt to stop it. But in vain. The three-wheeler continued its insane race. They had to give up. O dark night, night of evil, night of Satan.

And then—all this took place within a few seconds, he later realized—raising his eyes from Z.'s body on the street, he saw the same three young thugs, or three others resembling them—how could he tell, he was so confused—coming back to attack Spathopoulos. Telling himself that his duty was to protect those who were still alive, and also—he wasn't ashamed to admit this—from an instinct of self-preservation, he grabbed Spathopoulos and pushed him into the hotel. Two minutes later the other lawyers arrived, panting, alive, guilty and innocent, thankful that they had escaped the slaughter—at least for tonight.

Chapter 25

But for him, Z.'s self-appointed bodyguard,
it was different. Not for a second did Hatzis's courage
desert him. Before he heard the roar of the motor, he
saw a hand pointing in Z.'s direction. Too short to see
the van racing toward them, he couldn't pull Z. out of
the way and save him. He watched him collapse at his
side, the man who a little while before had planted a trident in his own blue eyes. He heard the muffled sound
of the wheels as they ran over the former Balkan champion, and his whole being turned into a vessel of foam-
ing wrath, bent on catching the assassins.

Two men who had succeeded in getting a grip on the
pickup were shouting, gesturing. But the vehicle moved
so fast they had to let go. The Tiger realized that if he
tried to grab hold he risked having his fingers broken by
the shadow skulking in the rear. He decided to jump on
the vehicle. Either he'd fall on the street and get hurt or
else he'd be able to hang on . . . Luck was with him. He
managed to land on the pickup. It was an insane plan
but it worked. Now there were three persons on the van.

Vango threw himself at him. Still reeling from the
wild jump, Hatzis lost his balance and received a volley
of blows full in the face. But the image of his dead
leader intensified his rage. His adversary was better acquainted with the inside of the van and didn't knock
against things as he lunged about. Despite the disadvan-
tage, Hatzis quickly got used to it.

While Vango had him flat on the floor, Hatzis kept
kicking him from below. Every time Vango bent to

strike him, Hatzis would kick him in the face. Keeping Hatzis pinned down, Vango pulled out his pistol. But the pickup, still pursuing its mad course, made a savage turn, and Vango fell over. Hatzis got up and grabbed the hand holding the pistol. He twisted it so hard Vango let the pistol drop, howling with pain. It fell out of the van onto the busy avenue.

With renewed courage, Hatzis butted him in the stomach. Vango had already picked up his club but dropped it when kicked in the groin. The desperate battle went on in silence, except for the cries for help that Hatzis addressed to passing cars.

At the beginning they had been moving against the traffic, but after a sudden turn they were now going in its direction. Not a single driver seemed aware of the desperate struggle in the van. Hatzis could shout himself hoarse; no one paid any attention. He was aware of their impassive expressions; how could they know that at this moment he, a blacksmith, was on the trail of a dastardly political crime—he no longer had any doubt of it—and was in danger of paying for his daring with his life. Even in the frenzy of the struggle he was aware of the people in the passing cars. A blonde beside a fat driver, head resting on his shoulder as she stroked the nape of his neck. A society woman with a petrified smile reminiscent of toothpaste ads, at the wheel of her latest car; every so often she would peer at herself in the rear-view mirror and smooth her eyebrows or adjust a hair that had rebelled against the hairdresser's tyranny. A priest seated next to a sailor, who drove with a cigarette hanging out of his mouth, had placed his plump clerical hand between the sailor's thighs while gazing attentively at some invisible point ahead. A malicious-looking taxi driver, elbow protruding from the open window, was trying to pass the pickup, radio blaring out deafening bouzouki. In one car sat a stodgy bourgeois couple, the wife driving, the man obviously delighted with his wife's modern ways; they saw the fierce battle in the van and roared with laughter, thinking it an acrobatic stunt.

Hatzis had no time to dwell on the scenes that flashed by. But later, on his hospital bed, where he lay recuperating from his wounds, he was able to recall at leisure those masks belonging to a neutral and indifferent universe in which each being was isolated in a world totally different from his own.

He didn't owe his wounds to the little shrimp, for much sooner than Hatzis had expected, thanks to his knowledge of judo, he'd put him out of commission. No, his wounds were inflicted by the driver of the van. This is how it happened.

When he disarmed Vango and knocked him out, Hatzis tossed him like a useless sack out on the street. Vango turned two or three somersaults and then crawled to the sidewalk; the pickup roared from the scene. Without losing a second, the Tiger—even though he rarely went to the movies—drove his fist through the window behind the driver and with one hand held Yango's head while with the other, already blood-smeared, he broke off a piece of glass to sink into Yango's neck. Yango braked violently, Hatzis lost his hold, and the pickup skidded toward the right-hand sidewalk. Yango jumped off the seat, leaving Hatzis with his arm caught in the broken window, his sleeve torn, and slivers of glass in his elbow. He painfully wrested his arm free, but it was too late. With a club that reflected the neon signs of the Titania Cinema, where the pickup had stopped, Yango struck him a powerful blow on the head. Before passing out, Hatzis heard: "He's a Communist criminal. He killed several people."

"It must be me they're talking about," he thought.

Another blow followed. He'd fallen from the van and was lying on the road, face against the pavement. He saw boots approaching, resembling policemen's, then some high, laced shoes which might have been a soldier's. As he rolled over on his back, he saw a fireman in uniform and helmet bending over him. Then he lost consciousness.

Chapter 26

The red light stopped him just as he was ready to go. In his profession—he was a policeman as well as chauffeur to the Secretary General at the Ministry of Northern Greece—he'd learned to be scrupulous about obeying the law. Any other driver would have gone ahead on the yellow, but not he. He, *deus ex machina,* stopped at the red and looked about him. Only a few people passing by; the jeep belonging to Branchiosaur, which he knew well because he often saw it in the front courtyard of the Ministry, was parked before the Kosmopolit Hotel. The jeep's driver, in plain clothes, noticed him and signaled him over. When the policeman lowered his window, the jeep's driver ordered: "Get moving."

At that moment he heard a shrill female voice shouting: "For shame!" A pickup van raced past him and he saw two shadowy figures struggling inside. A traffic cop blew his whistle, but the van only increased its speed, hurtling up Venizelou Street the wrong way. The square, which a moment before had seemed empty, was now full of people. He started off, rolling along slowly, taking care not to hit anyone. He heard shouting around him; people were pounding the hood of his car with their fists. He lowered the window once more.

"Please, mister," said a stranger. "Take Z. He's badly hurt. It's a question of life or death."

He got out, calmly opened the door, pushed the front seat back to make more room, and let the men lay the critically wounded man down. Two men got in and sat in the rear; a third one tried to join them but couldn't squeeze in. The front seat was soaked in blood. The sight of the giant, half prone at his side, gasping and bleeding from the mouth, unnerved him so that instead of pressing the starter he turned on the windshield wipers. The world in front of him misted over.

"Who is it?" he asked the two men in the back.

"Z. Get to the hospital as fast as you can. His life's hanging by a thread."

"What happened to him?"

"The bastards got him. Get going! Faster!"

"What bastards?"

"The thugs and the police."

"I'm a member of the police," he turned around to say. "And I'm doing everything I can for you, as you see."

The two were silent. The only sound was the groaning of the wounded man and the blood trickling on the seat.

"Use your horn! Faster!"

"The horn doesn't work."

"Damn!"

"The car's not mine. It's rented."

He had rented it for two hours from an agency he knew. He had a date with Kitsa, a "friend of a friend," whose telephone number he had gotten by chance. He had rented the Volkswagen for two hours so they could be alone. He'd come within a hair of missing the date. The Assistant Minister's lecture on downy mildew had lasted longer than expected, and then the General had delivered a lecture on the Communist peril. But, luckily, he hadn't had to drive the Assistant Minister to the airport himself. The General had offered to take him in his own car. And so he'd been able to meet Kitsa at the appointed time.

"But this isn't the way to the hospital!"

"It's better to make this detour; we'll avoid heavy traffic."

"Step on it!"

Then he collided with another car. He stopped; it was his fault.

"Don't stop!" shouted one of the men behind him. "Let the guy take your license number. This man must not die! He must not die!"

"You see what happens when you speed?" he replied. "Now I'm going to have to pay a fine."

The driver of the other car, after examining the damage and seeing that it was nothing serious—a dent in the rear door—came over to jot down the particulars.

"There's a man on the point of death inside," the policeman told him.

The other man glanced inside the car and nodded. He took out a pencil and wrote down the Volkswagen's license number on his package of cigarettes.

The evening had been one unexpected thing after another. Kitsa and he had gone to a vacant lot near Kavtanzoglio Stadium; he parked the car and they began to make love softly, gently, when suddenly she put a stop to it. "That's enough for the first time," she announced. She wanted to get married and she had no wish to get involved in a love affair that had no future.

"Why no future?" he asked.

"Because you're a student," she said.

"But any minute now I'll be getting my diploma," he replied. "And I've already done my military service."

He hadn't told her he was a policeman: too many girls were scared off by that occupation, though some liked the security it offered. He didn't know Kitsa well enough to be able to decide whether to tell her the truth or not. They went to a tavern in the neighborhood and had some beer. After nine o'clock he began to get nervous. He wanted to leave and gave the excuse that he had to return the car on time. He told her he'd phone her the next day.

"Don't you have a phone?" she asked him.

"No."

She took out her lipstick and with it scrawled on a

scrap of paper a telephone number where he could reach her during office hours. She left in a hurry—he noticed for the first time that she was bowlegged. As she went, she was playing with the shoulder strap of her bag.

The wounded man was breathing with increasing difficulty. His two companions listened anxiously, keeping his head still. The road to the hospital was smooth. When the car arrived, two attendants took Z. in on a stretcher, the news having already reached the hospital, so that everything was in readiness. The policeman heard a doctor giving orders to someone to take down the license number of the car, and in a panic he rushed back to the Volkswagen and started off at top speed. He spent some time looking for an open-air water tap to clean the bloodstains from the upholstery so he could return the car to the rental agency as he'd been given it.

Chapter 27

Immediately after the wounded man—or the dead man—had been placed in the Volkswagen, Dinos turned to the police inspector who was standing beside him, pipe in mouth.

"What happened? Who was hurt?" he asked.

"They hit a seventeen-year-old boy," the inspector replied.

"But it was the same van that was parked here a little while ago. Didn't you notice?"

The inspector made no answer.

"It was the same one," Dinos insisted. "It shot past like a rocket and disappeared. It was the same."

The inspector moved away a few steps. Till now the two of them had been amicably chatting about a police officer they both knew who'd been transferred a month ago to Preveza. Why, suddenly, after the accident, had he stopped talking? Why was he pretending to ignore him?

Dinos had known the inspector since his student days. He had often seen him at student conferences or when preparations were being made for demonstrations for Cyprus: on these occasions the inspector would turn up as a quiet observer, always smoking his pipe. At that time Dinos had been an active member of the student body. But afterwards—he had never graduated, because his studies were interrupted by his military service—when he opened his own shop, a branch of a firm that sold agricultural products, he no longer had time for such matters. Besides, for the sake of his shop's good name, he couldn't. Everything depended on the police. If they wanted to close your shop, they could find a thousand excuses. And the city was small, everybody knew everybody else. So small that this evening he recognized, despite his civilian clothes, the inspector of police from his own neighborhood.

He had seen him anxiously pacing back and forth. At one point he had an argument with somebody on a motorcycle when the motorcycle, along with a pickup van, had blocked two inter-city buses that were trying to cross the square with their lights off. Until then the motorcycle and the van had been maneuvering up and down the street, getting in the way of every other vehicle and in effect tying up the whole square—and the inspector had not seemed to notice. Later Dinos ran into the inspector as the inspector came from across the square, and he greeted him for the second time today (the first had been in the morning when Dinos opened his shop). The inspector was heading for the pickup van, which had now been parked for half an hour outside the Kosmopolit Hotel. He had a talk with the driver of the van. Dinos couldn't hear what they said, and wasn't interested anyway. However, he did observe that a few moments afterwards the van moved off and parked in a side street behind the hotel. If he hadn't recognized the inspector, he wouldn't even have been aware of its movements. Suddenly, about two minutes later, he saw the van again. This time, moving with lightning speed, it ran over someone right in the middle of the square, then disappeared up Venizelou Street, and none of the policemen and detectives there had made the slightest move to pursue it.

Dinos was especially shocked by the inspector's indifference. He stood in front of Branchiosaur's jeep. Not a gesture, no reaction at all of surprise. On the contrary, when Dinos asked who had been hit, he answered with no feeling whatever, almost cynically: "A seventeen-year-old boy." And then, when Dinos remarked that it was the same van that had been parked near them a little while before, the inspector had simply turned his back. What was going on? Or was he an idiot for prying into some plot that already involved the police themselves? But why? What? How?

Crossing the square on the way to a friend's house to listen to some new jazz records, he had heard the loudspeaker: "Attention! Attention! Z. is going to speak in a few minutes."

He had stayed out of curiosity to hear the first words of the speech. He was standing in front of the Kosmopolit Hotel, along with the hotel proprietor, who was a business acquaintance, and the owner of a nearby pastry shop, who had left the doughnuts he was frying and come out to watch also; they looked on in amazement as the angry crowd howled its chants of "Bulgars, get out!" and "Death to Z.!" Dinos was thunderstruck when he heard the deputy's first words: it was an appeal to the Prefect, the General, the Chief of Police, and other authorities to protect the life of Spathopoulos, who was in danger. He was bowled over by it. All this maneuvering of the counterdemonstrators suddenly acquired meaning. It was reassuring that almost the entire police force was on hand and could intervene at any moment. But the longer it was, the more clearly he could see that the police were doing absolutely nothing. They were not restraining the thugs. They were not arresting anyone. Once in a while they would ask the noisiest demonstrators to step back. That was all.

He couldn't hear Z.'s speech. All he could hear over the loudspeaker was the thunderous applause and the peace slogans. He decided to stay. To hell with jazz! These events were like none he had ever witnessed, even during his student years.

When he saw the pickup van start off, a man crumple and fall, some others get a grip on the vehicle without being able to stop it, and three panic-stricken lawyers run for refuge into the hotel as though seeking shelter from a bomb raid, his face twitched painfully. And then the strange attitude of the man with the pipe bothered him profoundly. He went home. Under such circumstances it was better not to be present. A wedding was coming next month; he was marrying off his sister. His own youth had long since been buried beneath the agricultural machines.

His apartment was on the same street, two blocks down, directly in front of Ayia Sophia Church. He went home, had some stuffed eggplant his mother had prepared yesterday, and then went out again. He was consumed with curiosity to find out who had been hit by the van. By now the square was almost empty; a few people wandered about like movie extras on a set after the stars have gone. He approached a group.

"What happened here a little while ago?"

"The gentleman's interested in what happened," said a thug to someone who seemed to be the leader.

"What does the gentleman want?" asked the leader.

"Excuse me . . ."

"Go screw yourself!"

"Why don't you go home?" said another.

At that point the thug Dinos had talked to first spoke up. "Nothing very interesting happened," he said.

"We've killed a Communist." He puffed up like a peacock. Then he and the others burst out laughing.

"We've canonized him in style!"

"We made another Athanasios Diakos out of him!"

"We Macedonians, we gave him a little lesson."

Dinos stood still while the group slowly walked away. "The bastards," he said to himself, "they haven't any God." The next instant—his brain was working fast—he started out for the first-aid station. There he encountered the same hostility. The guard wouldn't let him in.

"What's happened? Who was brought here?"

"Who are you? A newspaper reporter?"

"No, a citizen. A simple Greek citizen, who wants some information."

"Nothing happened. Nothing serious anyway. A young man was wounded."

Disappointed, he was about to leave when he saw a man at the admissions office, shirt torn, blood all over him, asking to have his wounds bandaged. On getting a better look, Dinos saw with astonishment that it was the same man he had observed in the rear of the van when it was parked before the Kosmopolit Hotel and the police inspector had come up to speak with the driver. But he could see no connection between these facts.

His way back home took him past the square, now completely empty. A few pople were prowling around in the darkness of the side streets. At the spot where the pickup van had run over whoever it was lay two bouquets of red carnations. "Thus untouched you go unto death," he reflected, sure that a seventeen-year-old youth had been killed.

Chapter 28

He had twenty minutes to go before his shift would end, and he'd written only five traffic tickets. A very poor harvest for a whole evening in the heart of Salonika, the traffic cop considered, as with his right hand he signaled away a little Fiat parked illegally in front of the Agapitou Pastry Shop. It was dangerous to direct traffic among so many cars. And the new head of the traffic department was very strict. He considered it a failing on the policeman's part not to issue a great number of tickets. Unhappily, he hadn't found many people violating the law today. If this Fiat would only stay parked five more seconds . . . But it started off just as he pulled out his pad.

In his uniform he was a great success with female drivers. One of them was smiling at him right now through the window of her car. Following her with his eyes, he caught sight of something a block away, in Karolou Deel Street, across from the Titania Cinema: people coming together from all directions. Thinking that some accident must have occurred, he ran toward the movie house, blowing his whistle. Approaching the wall of onlookers, he saw a bald man wriggling out from between their legs, on all fours like a rat. He was small in stature and was clutching his head as he screamed over and over like a child: "I've been hit, I've been hit."

Thinking there must have been a collision and this man must be one of the injured, the policeman left him to his fate and began to think of the report he would make. He went through the dense crowd of people, forc-

ing them to scatter, and finally he saw a pickup van
parked on the curb, with its motor turned off. Astride
the seat a husky individual, who seemed to be a transport man, was engaged in a violent argument with the
bystanders.

"He was the one who started it."

"You hit him on the head. People saw you."

"The bastard. Too bad he didn't get knocked out."

"You're the b—"

"Shut up, or I'll sock you in the mouth."

"What's going on here?" said the traffic cop, stepping
between them.

"Nothing, sergeant."

"What do you mean, nothing?"

"My buddy and I had an argument. I slugged him.
Then he slugged me back." And he made as though to
leave.

"Stay where you are," said the traffic cop, advancing
toward him menacingly. "Show me your driver's license
and all your papers."

"With pleasure," said Yango, taking a plastic case out
of his inner pocket.

The traffic cop took the papers, examined them carefully, and was about to give them back when a fireman
in uniform and helmet and holding his wife by the arm
broke into the circle.

"Excuse me, sir," he said, "but I witnessed the whole
scene. This guy, without any excuse as far as I could see,
took a club from under his arm and began to beat the
other man on the head and ribs—a bald man, who fell,
half conscious."

He looked around for the injured man, turning his
head with some difficulty because of the helmet. The
traffic cop took the opportunity to order the crowd to
move away.

"What are you doing here? Come on, move back,
move back so we can do our job. Get going! Don't block
traffic."

The crowd dispersed.

"He's got a club on him," the fireman went on.

The traffic cop was about to search Yango, but Yango handed him the club. It was a new club—as new as those just delivered to the police force.

Yango could see that things weren't going well. The fireman's uniform had at first given him a feeling of security. But the nut of a fireman, he thought, didn't seem to know much; didn't seem to know that it was for the good of the country that he'd knocked out the dirty Communist, the leech that had almost spoiled everything. The traffic cop seemed to be a jerk too. He didn't know anything either. If he could only get to the police station! How their eyes would pop if they came there to ask for him. At one point, while the traffic cop was talking with the fireman, he got down from his seat, expaining that his back hurt from staying in one position, and was all set to beat it up Karolou Deel Street, cut through Kapani, and wind up at the police station. But the traffic cop got wind of his intention and grabbed him by the arm.

"Come on across the street," he said.

"And my van?"

"Never mind. No one's going to disturb it."

Across the way was the police canteen. A good place, thought Yango. If he had the luck to run into some policeman he knew, this comedy would soon be over. But the canteen was closed. They had to stand in the corridor.

The traffic cop asked the fireman to go out and phone the emergency patrol from a kiosk and ask them to come pick up the fellow. "For willful bludgeoning and inflicting of wounds, as well as for traffic violations," he said.

The people in the street had moved along. At the canteen there was nobody but the cop, Yango, the fireman's wife, and two friends of his, who had come too. Every other minute a switch closed the circuit, plunging the building into darkness. Each time, the traffic cop had to press the button so the lights would go on and he could check on his prisoner.

"Pst!" Yango whispered to him in a confidential tone. "I'm going to tell you . . ."

"What do you want?"

"I have to tell you . . . to tell you . . ."

"I don't want you to tell me anything. You can say what you have to say at the police station."

"What a nerve he's got," he thought. At the same time Yango was thinking: "What a moron—if you only knew your boss was a friend of mine!" The light went off again and the cop pressed the button.

"I'm leaving," Yango said to the cop. "Just pretend you didn't see me."

"What's that you're saying?"

"I say I'm leaving," Yango repeated. "I can't tell you any more. You just play dumb."

"Don't you budge, or I'll lay you flat, you bum!"

"Who are you calling a bum? You're going to be mighty sorry for this. Show me your papers."

". . ."

"With the pull I've got, I'll see to it that you get transferred."

"Who *are* you?" asked the traffic cop in amazement.

In the street, the sword-sharp light of the patrol car foretold the end.

Chapter 29

Vango was scarcely pleased when the man he had noticed outside the Kosmopolit Hotel emerged from the first-aid station just as he was going in. From the rear of the van he had watched him for more than half an hour standing motionless, eyes fixed on the loudspeaker, straining to hear what Z. was saying, turning slightly sideways so that the sound could reach his ear more clearly. What was he doing here? Who was he looking for? But for the moment Vango had other fish to fry.

He had come to the first-aid station on the advice of his friend, the newspaper reporter. Though his wounds required no special attention, the reporter had urged him to go to the hospital and get himself on the list of the wounded, so that it wouldn't be only the Reds who had something to complain about. He was a court reporter for the *Macedonian Battle*. Vango had a passion for trials. He boasted of never missing an important case. He would rather watch a good, spectacular trial than a movie any day. He and the reporter had met each other in the crowded corridors of the criminal law courts. Vango secretly hoped that if he ever got caught in a nasty case the reporter would keep his name out of the papers, so that he wouldn't have the neighborhood poking fun at him. The newspaper was right-wing, and all the people with whom Vango had relations were right-wing also.

He suddenly remembered the reporter when he found himself lying on the pavement outside the newspaper office. A crowd circled the pickup van, which, as Vango could see, had stopped farther down the street. A few inquisitive people collected around him, wanting to know what had happened. He was afraid that the pacifists might notice him and come around later to settle accounts. Complications might develop before he had time to receive further instructions from Mastodontosaur. They'd foreseen everything, except that someone would jump into his van. "I hope Yango will polish him off," he said to himself, though, seeing the van parked fifty yards away, beneath the lights of the Titania Cinema, he didn't have much hope.

Unable to think of anything better to do while waiting for the crowd to thin out, he decided to seek refuge in the newspaper office. The doorway of the building was garishly illuminated. Huge cylinders of paper, lined up like steam rollers, ready, at the crack of dawn, to pave the way for a new day. Over the main entrance, a wide ribbon dotted with tiny lightbulbs that connected with the teletype was flashing the latest news. Vango pushed through the crowd watching the news evolve. Straightening his disordered clothes as best he could, he went up the stairs.

The reporter was sitting behind his desk, hard at work, as were several editors at adjacent desks. Vango's friend, dizzy from writing, did not recognize him at first. The face seemed dimly familiar. Then Vango came to his rescue.

"Aren't you the reporter from the courthouse?" he asked.

"Why, yes. Ahh! Now I remember you! But you're a sight. What's happened?"

"Happened?" Vango sighed. "We had some trouble tonight."

"What kind of trouble?"

"With the Communists. They were holding a meeting for peace. Z. came from Athens. Do you think we nationalists were just going to stand there with our hands folded? We beat them up good. They got in a few licks themselves. Finally a pickup went past and in the midst of the hullabaloo ran over Z. by mistake."

"By mistake?"

"What? Do you think the guy did it on purpose? He must have been on a delivery job. It happened where Ermou and Venizelou Streets cross. Z. was wounded. Nothing serious. They took him to the first-aid station. Serves him right."

"Well, what can I do for you?" the reporter asked. Political reporting wasn't his job. "You want to make a formal complaint? I'm at your service."

"I want you to write in the newspaper that I was one of the guys who beat Z. up when he came to the meeting. So the boys won't think I'm a coward."

"The boys?"

"You know, the guys who make the trouble."

The reporter stared at him, amazed.

"In any case," he said to get rid of him, "my advice to you is to go to the first-aid station and have yourself put on the list of the wounded so it won't be just the Reds who have something to complain about. And buy tomorrow's paper. Your name will be first on the list."

He must have been in the office of the *Macedonian Battle* about ten minutes. He took a taxi to the first-aid station. At the entrance he ran into Dinos. That seemed odd; but when he came out, his face bandaged and some iodine on his elbow, it seemed odder still to find a patrol jeep waiting for him.

Before he had time to ask any questions, they nabbed him and started off.

"You're wanted urgently. Where'd you disappear to, you louse?" was the sergeant's greeting. "So? We do the job and then we blow, do we? Things are beginning to look tough. And it's your fault for not polishing off that guy who jumped into the van. Yellow windbag! All you know how to do is go make statements to the papers about what a big hero you are. Jackass! Do you want to get us all killed? Huh?"

Out of that flood of words, only one thing struck Vango: how did they know he'd gone to the newspaper?

Chapter 30

After handing Yango over to the patrol car, the traffic cop left the canteen and dispersed the last stragglers. He notified the head of the Traffic Department to come and collect a pickup from Karolou Deel

Street and then returned to his post on Nea Megalou Alexandrou Street, opposite Ayia Sophia Church. The next-to-the-last movie shows were ending and the traffic was somewhat heavier. However, before he had time to make a single signal, he saw his replacement approaching. It was exactly 10:30. He went back home quietly, took off his uniform, sat down to eat, and about a quarter past eleven lay down to sleep. Within fifteen minutes somebody arrived with the news that he was urgently wanted by the Chief of Police. So he dressed again and, cursing every god in creation, left the house.

Chapter 31

Yango, finding himself inside the patrol car on the way to the police station, felt infinitely relieved. He was finally going to get in touch with his own crowd again. He'd been exposed long enough to all those imbeciles. The only thing he worried about was having abandoned his van on Karolou Street. Hadn't it been for the sake of the pickup van that he'd done the job? How could he leave it unprotected in the middle of the street! Even though the traffic cop had assured him that he'd be able to get it back tomorrow, it pained him to think of it abandoned and neglected, like a horse that pines away without its rider.

"Sergeant, is it possible for us to go back so that one of your men could take the van?" he asked the head of the patrol before they turned into Ermou Street. "I'll be needing it when I'm finished at the station."

The sergeant said that was not his affair, and then, making radio contact with his department, he announced that the guilty party had been arrested and was being taken to the police station. The words "guilty party" offended Yango. He wasn't the kind to take a joke like that. How was it possible that the police had not been informed that tonight he, Yango Gazgouridis, was going to render a distinguished service to the nation? And how could they behave so insultingly, treating him like a common criminal?

But nothing offended him as much as having to leave his van in somebody else's hands for the night. He had no sentiment about human beings. But he loved his kamikazi. He decorated it with little flags, polished it to a shine, he couldn't have looked after a woman with more care. And tonight . . . tonight . . . He'd broken so many laws in the past and it had never been taken from him—even for an hour. Yet tonight, when he was serving their own cause, they were going to haul it away! That's what they call a good government? It was a disgrace!

As soon as he reached the door of the police station, he breathed more calmly. The head of the patrol led him upstairs and handed him over to the officer on duty, delivering both his driver's license and his club at the same time. Then he saluted and left.

In the station Yango found all his pals. They were all there: Kotsos, Manendas, Baïraktaris, and even Zissis, whom he hadn't laid eyes on for months. But there were three characters he didn't recognize sitting on the bench. They might have been burglars, he thought, though actually they didn't look like it. He was clever enough to avoid showing too much friendliness with the police in front of the strangers. Then he went to the office of the sergeant on duty and turned over his identity card for the records. From there he was led to another office on the door of which were the words: ASSISTANT COMMISSIONER.

When he opened the door, he saw Mastodontosaur himself, frowning.

"Mr. Commissioner," he began. But Mastodontosaur stopped him with a gesture and signaled to him to close the door. His somber manner made Yango feel ill at ease.

"What's up?" Yango asked anxiously.

"Sit down first," the Commissioner told him.

He sat down and lit the cigarette the Commissioner offered him.

"Things aren't going too well, Yango," Mastodontosaur said, getting up and pacing nervously around; "It's not working out as we planned."

"Didn't I do the transfer job all right?"

"You did it all right. If that slimy devil hadn't jumped into the van, the whole thing would have been just fine. You and Vango would have disappeared completely. We could have made it look like an ordinary traffic accident and we'd still be looking for you. Now everything's fouled up. We can't do that now. You were apprehended by an agent of the law who lacked indoctrination."

"What doctor's station?"

"Indoctrination, Yango. We have families to feed. Now we have to get ourselves out of the mess as painlessly as possible."

"I understand," said Yango, greatly worried by his chief's dejected air.

"It isn't just me, you know. There are others over me. And over them, there are still others."

"For me you're the highest, Mr. Commissioner."

"That's not the point. I'm trying to let you in on things and there's not much time. It won't be long before the prosecutors come to get a statement from you. Then you'll say what I'm going to tell you. Take some paper and a pencil and write it down."

"I can't read or write."

"Hell, I forgot."

He paused, staring at the ceiling light vacantly.

"If only Vango had gotten rid of that scoundrel who jumped into the van, we wouldn't be in this fix now. What a jerk he is! Coward! Imbecile!"

He struck the table angrily.

"I'd have done him in with a twist of my wrist," said Yango. "I clobbered him with the club and the son of a bitch had a hard time getting up again. If it hadn't been right in the center of town, I'd have laid him out on the pavement. But there you are, a crowd gathered and a fireman in uniform kept me there."

"And where's Vango now? What's he doing with himself? Unless your statements agree in every detail, we'll be in trouble. Where's the pig dawdling now? Just on the chance, I sent a jeep to the first-aid station to pick him up if he's there. If the prosecutors get to him before we do, we're done for."

"Maybe he went to the Little Refugees."

"What little refugees?"

"The tavern. It's got good retsina."

"Surely not. God only knows where he is. Anyway, he's sure to turn up any minute."

Yango had never seen the Commissioner so upset. Mastodontosaur kept lighting and stubbing out cigarettes. He paced the floor. His eyes were haggard.

"And my wife will be waiting for me at her Institute," he sighed. "I'm supposed to pick her up. If she only knew!"

Yango himself was calm. He couldn't see beyond the end of his nose. Had he realized that his chief was in danger, he might have been afraid. But to his way of thinking the police were invulnerable. The law couldn't be used against them; it was they who imposed the law. He didn't know that those who make the laws and those who put them into effect are different sets of people. The police station seemed to him as inviolable as Gonos's tavern when Autocratosaur was holding forth. No one could crash the gates.

"And who're those three characters on the bench outside?" asked Yango.

Mastodontosaur was nonplussed.

"What three characters?"

Opening the door a crack, he saw the three lawyers

seated on the bench, taking in everything that was going on in the station. "But this is an outrage!" he thought indignantly. "Spies on our own doorstep."

He went out and spoke to them: "The disturbances are at an end. You may leave."

"We're waiting for the police captain," said the lawyer in the middle, whom Mastodontosaur knew to be a Red.

"Now we're in worse trouble than I thought," he murmured to himself as he reentered his office. "Did they see you come in here?" he asked Yango.

"How should I know? Yes, they must have seen me."

"But they don't know you?"

"No."

"That's all right then," he sighed. "But suppose your photograph gets into tomorrow's newspaper and they recognize you."

"It's a good thing I was suspicious of them," said Yango, "and clammed up in front of them. But who are they?"

"Three lawyers who took part in the meeting and know everything. We're done for, Yango, we're done for! I can see no way out. Let's get in my car and beat it to Germany."

"If I had a passport," said Yango, "I'd have gone a long time ago."

Chapter 32

They were like three pigeons in a flock of crows. They kept their eyes open and they remembered what they saw. The three lawyers were unaware that Z. had been mortally wounded. They had been among the first to leave the meeting. Heading for home, as they reached Egnatia Street, they were accosted by some toughs.

"Bulgar Hatzisavva, drop dead! Go back to Bulgaria, baldy!"

Hatzisavva prudently dived into the first hotel he saw, the Strymonikon, and waited for the storm to pass. The other two quickened their steps, still tagged by the hoodlums. At a shoe store on Egnatia Street they were joined by a colleague as terrified as they. He took the place of Hatzisavva in the group, and the trio went on, trying to shake off their pursuers.

But the owl monkeys and the anthropoids kept on their trail like seagulls following fishing boats. They glided over the sidewalk with incredible agility, sometimes in front of them, brandishing their fists; sometimes in back, shouting: "We're going to knock you off, dirty Bulgars! We're going to follow you right to bed!"

The lawyers couldn't in all decency start a fistfight with these wretches. Fortunately, they met a police patrol returning to the station.

"Officer," one of the lawyers addressed the officer in charge, "we would like your protection. These scoundrels are following us."

Immediately the thugs began to play the innocent strollers taking an evening walk.

"Who is following you?"

"These hoodlums!"

"Come along with us," the officer said, and made a sign to his men to form a protective ring around the three men. But while they were waiting for the green light at Egnatia and Aristotelous Streets, one of the thugs slipped nimbly between the policemen and struck one of the lawyers on the head.

"Did you see that? They've got the nerve to do that in front of you!" And taking a two-drachma piece, the lawyer pressed it on the spot where he'd been hit, to avoid a lump.

"Come on, let's move along," said the officer. "Follow

us to the police station. Nobody will bother you there."

And in actual fact, once inside the station, no one did bother them. No one paid any attention to them at all. They sat there on the bench and waited. A quarter of an hour later they saw the same officer come down the steps and issue a command: "Everybody to the EDA headquarters."

The policemen stubbed out their cigarettes hastily in the ashtrays, adjusted their belts, and tramped down the stairs in a body toward the exit.

"Must be a fight over there," said the first lawyer apprehensively.

"Z. must have got excited and blasted them all to smithereens," said the second one.

"Lucky we're here," said the third. "The only place you're safe from the wolf is in his den."

"What a lousy night!"

"Tomorrow I'll file a complaint."

"Did you see the fellow who punched me? The officer didn't bat an eye, didn't even say anything to him."

The first lawyer noticed Mastodontosaur, in plain clothes, coming in. In a low voice he informed the other two, who didn't know him, who he was. The Commissioner whirled into the station without paying any attention to them and headed straight for a door marked ASSISTANT COMMISSIONER. He didn't come back. A few minutes later they saw a mustached individual come swaggering in, escorted by the head of the Emergency Patrol. He seemed to be much at home in the place, greeting everybody as if he'd already seen them in the course of the day. He looked rather like the hoodlums who had followed them in the street. The following morning, when they saw a picture of Yango Gazgouridis in the papers, and recognized him, they regretted not having watched him more closely in the police station. He too went into the office of the Assistant Commissioner. Somewhat later another man came in; he walked unsteadily, his face was bandaged and there was iodine on his elbow. He made straight for the same inner office. What was going on in there?

There was something sinister about the building. The gray mold on the walls stank of police.

Chapter 33

"At last!" exclaimed the Commissioner when he saw Vango. "Where have you been?"

"At the first-aid station."

"I was just telling Yango, I don't like the way things are going. One way or another, we've got to cover this business up."

Vango turned pale.

"The two of you will have to agree what you're going to say."

"And Z.?" asked the pederast.

"He's about ready to croak."

Vango rubbed his hands in satisfaction.

"Now listen. This is what you're going to say. You were together, you and Yango, and you were doing some drinking. Let's get the name of the tavern right, so you won't contradict each other."

"Pahni's."

"The Little Refugees."

"No, One-Armed Koulou's. If we say the Refugees, someone might say we weren't there. At Koulou's they're all our own boys."

"Fine," said the Commissioner. "You were at One-Armed Koulou's drinking retsina."

"No, ouzo. Their retsina's no good. It's muddy; it stinks."

"Ouzo, then. Along about a quarter to ten, you started for home, blind drunk. You, Yango, were driving and you, Vango, were behind in the van. A traffic cop stopped you from going down Venizelou Street, saying there was a political meeting going on. And so you decided to make a detour through the market, where there weren't any people. You came out on Spandoni Street, expecting to find the road ahead just as clear. And you were speeding—you hear, Yango?—you were speeding because when you're loaded you always speed; all of a sudden, before you had time to put on your brakes, you heard the noise of breaking glass. You didn't know you'd run over someone. You came to a stop on Karolou Deel Street—you don't know how, you were tight and only half conscious. There was a crowd of people and you saw a traffic cop coming toward you and you gave yourself up. He handed you over to the patrol car which brought you to the station."

"And me?" asked Vango.

"You, a little while before, in the middle of the hullabaloo, jumped out of the van because you were afraid you might be killed by that demented guy who fell on top of you, without your knowing much of anything because you were dead drunk. This way you won't be accused of anything but illegal driving: first, for going the wrong way on Venizelou Street, and second, for driving when intoxicated—a minor traffic offense."

"Will they take my license away?" asked Yango.

"Don't worry about that. You'll have the van along with all the papers tomorrow," the Commissioner replied reassuringly. "Tonight you're going to stay right here in the bosom of your family and tomorrow you'll go back home. And you," he said, turning to Vango, "get going. Supposedly, we haven't caught you yet. You're going to be kept out of the picture as long as possible."

"Only one question, Mr. Commissioner," said Vango.

"The character who jumped into the pickup will spill everything. Him we ought to get rid of."

"That's somebody else's job," said the Commissioner. "I've told you what you have to do. So beat it. And above all, don't tell anybody you were here tonight."

"And what about those three outside?"

"I've got a better idea," said Vango.

And from his pocket he pulled a pair of glasses with no lenses. He put them on, shrank into his clothes, and, thus disguised, walked out of the office. As he left, he affectionately thumped the shoulder of his *koumbaros,* who was laughing heartily at the sight.

Chapter 34

The three lawyers saw Yango coming cheerfully out of the Assistant Commissioner's office. He'd gone in sullen and gloomy and now seemed lively as a sparrow. He caught a policeman by the nape of the neck and slapped him one. Recognizing his friend, the policeman burst out laughing. Then Yango disappeared down a corridor. They didn't see him again during the time they remained at the station.

Finally the captain who had brought them and who by now had returned from the EDA headquarters, where apparently nothing was happening, suggested that he escort them to their homes. The three lawyers left the station. The fresh air did them good. The night, the great night, spread about them, as round as the domes of the Turkish baths across the street. Each went back to his own home.

Chapter 35

In this same great, stealthy night, Hatzis sought refuge. When he left the first-aid station, he immediately realized that he was being followed. He was the only witness of an abominable crime and assuredly they would want him out of the way. He used his head. Eluding them by climbing a wall, he slipped down deserted lanes and found himself near the old railroad station. There he fell asleep in an empty coach, his head aching horribly from the clubbing administered by the driver of the van. It would have taken a handful of aspirin to ease the pain, but where could he get any? The nearest pharmacy open at that hour must be miles away. Besides, they must be looking for him everywhere. He fell fast asleep. When he felt the coach moving, he thought at first it was a dream. He stood up; he ached more than ever, it was like waking up after a dreadful binge. He saw he'd arrived at Plati, a half hour out of Salonika. He got out of the coach and went to look for the stationmaster. He didn't have a single drachma in his pocket.

Chapter 36

Vango, instead of heading home, went straight to the newspaper office. When his reporter acquaintance saw him come in, looking like a shriveled old monkey in his disguise, he was flabbergasted.

"What's up?" he asked.

"Z.'s going to die."

"What have you got those glasses on for?"

"So nobody can recognize me. I've come to ask you not to write anything about me. I don't want them to involve me in the case. Z.'s going to die."

"And what's your connection with that?"

"Me? None. But if they see my name in the *Macedonian Battle* and if you write that I was one of the people who hit him when he went to the meeting, the investigations and all that crap will start, and it won't do me any good."

"All right, I won't mention your name. But don't come back here again tonight, because I won't be here."

Vango said good night and left. He went back to his neighborhood, passing by Yango's house to tell his wife that the *koumbaros* wouldn't be coming tonight because he had a job. From there he walked through the little woods, but there were no couples for him to spy upon, the early-morning drizzle must have discouraged them. Vango felt sprightly in his new skin, a stranger in the darkness. He ran into Stratos, one of his neighbors. Vango said he was on his way back from the center of town and that there had been some trouble. Stratos scrutinized him closely but asked no questions. And then Vango went home, rumpled up his bed so he would not have to explain to his folks the next day, and went off again into the night, looking for a trick.

Chapter 37

There was great activity in the Chief of Police's office when the traffic cop arrived. The Chief himself was in a state of feverish excitement. The telephone would ring, he would grab it and converse in a muffled voice with the person at the other end. Then he would be interrupted by a call from the Ministry of the Interior in Athens, wanting to know the latest developments. Then the orderly would come in to announce a new visitor.

"The reason I called you in," he said to the traffic cop, "was to set you right about the whole situation. The man you handed over to the patrol car wasn't just a chance offender caught in a brawl on the public thoroughfare. The man you arrested is one of our own boys. The other fellow is a notorious Communist."

"But . . ."

"There's no need for you to look for excuses. You did your duty and I congratulate you for it. But that's beside the point. Tomorrow you'll probably be summoned to testify about the circumstances under which you arrested him. You understand of course that whatever you say must be favorable to the department that you serve. That's all."

The General, ensconced in an easy chair and listening silently, shook his head. "Listen, my boy," he said to the traffic cop when the Chief of Police had finished, "where are you from?"

"Arnea."

"Are your father and mother still living?"

"Yes."

"Any brothers and sisters?"

"One sister, unmarried."

"Well then, about the club, it's better that you keep quiet about it."

"But I've already mentioned it in my report."

"Listen, I am the General."

The traffic cop sprang to attention.

"At ease! Think over what the Chief just told you. We are all of us subject to the Jewish-Communist menace. The great disturbance on the solar mass . . ."

The telephone interrupted him. It was Athens again.

"There's a bit of light on the horizon," the traffic cop heard the Chief of Police saying. "Everything's shaping up. No, they haven't arrived yet. They're probably still at the ballet. Yes, immediately. Goodbye, sir."

The traffic cop saluted and departed. In the corridor a man was waiting in pajamas, with a coat tossed over his shoulders.

Chapter 38

Yangò ate a helping of lamb stew in the canteen, at the end of the long corridor. He was hungry as a wolf. When he emerged, he saw that the three strangers were gone. On the bench where they had been sitting was a little boy. He was crying because the police had confiscated the tray he used to sell *koulouria*. A policeman had chased him, thrown his *koulouria* to the ground, grabbed him by the collar, and dragged him to the police station along with the empty tray. Then they had taken his tray and thrown it into the room where they kept all the trays of unlicensed peddlers. Wiping his runny nose, he pointed to a closed door. He had been at the meeting, but he hadn't sold much there, so he went over to the theater, where he expected to sell all the *koulouria* he had. Instead, that policeman had pinched him. Why? He was still crying. Yango's fingers slipped gently through the child's blond hair. For a long while he caressed his head.

Chapter 39

The performance was almost over. Romeo, thinking Juliet dead, takes the poison and collapses on the floor of the stage, after two unsteady pirouettes. The superlative artistry, the grace of the Russian dancer, conveys all the shuddering horror of a man poisoned by love. He lies full length; his hand, undulating like the neck of a swan, floats in the air for a moment. And here she is now, thrice-beautiful in her flowing tunic, throbbing back into a world she thought forever lost. She lifts herself on her toes and with utter grace spins around in a hymn of joy, though it is not to last for long—because she sees him. With nervous leaps on tiptoe she approaches him, bends down as a branch bends, then springs back, like the branch when it is suddenly let go. She covers her face with both hands. The music—deep, pained, muffled—accompanies her writhing. In the orchestra pit the Maestro's baton is lifted into the air, starkly, solitary, alert, like a submarine antenna. Ah, why did she awake? Why arise? Why not lie forever in her dreamless sleep? The Russian ballerina, despite her strict, disciplined technique, communicates chills of primitive feeling to the audience. And here she is now, preparing to put an end to her own life. She sees no light. A shadow has come over the sun. There is no joy. How high-spirited, ebullient she had been a moment before! Who would have guessed their love would end like this? Her last moments she dances round the dead body of her beloved, enfolding it in invisible circles of tenderness, as the spotlight tries to keep up with her, abandon-

ing Romeo to the darkness. (If there had been one more
rehearsal, the technician in charge of the lights would
have been able to remember her movements better and
would have had less difficulty keeping her in the center
of the spotlight. But the ballet had arrived the day before and they had had no time for a second rehearsal.)
And now Juliet is flying, dancing to her death. The
music deepens. She grasps the poison and swallows it.
She reels, storm-buffeted in her turn, ethereally graceful
as she yields to inexorable gravity, which as a dancer
she has been fighting all her life. But now it is not the
dancer who sinks and falls: it is Juliet herself kneeling,
lightly stroking his brow with one hand, his head cra-
dled against her breast. And while the audience holds its
breath, she dances in that spot until the thread breaks
and she falls upon him, lifeless.

The last bars of music mix with the mounting applause. The lights go on gradually beneath their cake-
shaped frames. The red velvet curtain falls. The lights
get stronger, as though the cheers of the audience were
rousing them from sleep. The curtain swings open in
jerks, like a pair of fleshy red lips stuck together by too
much lipstick, and here is the whole Bolshoi Ballet ap-
plauding, as is the Russian custom, the audience. In
their costumes—Doges, Infantas, Counts, plebeians—they
make their bows, the third couple coming on to the
proscenium first, and then the second. And when finally
Romeo and Juliet step forward, the spectators, on their
feet, cry "Bravo"; roses are showered on the stage; Juliet
and Romeo stoop to pick them up; two enormous baskets of flowers are brought in from the wings. They are
called back at least seven times. And then the curtain
falls definitively and the crowd begins to move toward
the exits.

Ladies in the most expensive gowns, embroidered
with jewels, from the best dressmakers in Athens, sigh:

"How marvelous!"

"I liked *him* the best."

Gentlemen in tuxedos jostle one another in the corridors. All the top society of Salonika is present.

"I can't see Deppy!"

"She left during the intermission. You know she's expecting a baby, and she gets nauseous."

They greet each other. They light cigarettes after the long deprivation. The Prefect, the Mayor, the Minister of Northern Greece, the Chief of the Army Corps. Only the Archbishop and the General are missing. All very well about the former, but the latter? Oh, look, there's the Secretary General; he's managed to get here, though heaven knows how he got an invitation! The city's artists. The aged painter who makes portraits of the tobacco manufacturers' wives. The ex-ballerina, who has now opened a ballet school.

"I'm ashamed to say that I too used to dance."

Big-time merchants. Importers of tractors. The Director of the Esso-Pappas factories. Estate owners. Speculators. People who divide their lives between this city and central Europe. They take their coats from the cloakroom, handing back the check number and a small tip, and descend the marble stairs leading to the brilliantly illuminated exit of the theater. A few do not resist the temptation to go to the toilet.

"Where did you have that dress made?"

"At Kiouka's. And yours?"

"In Athens, at Thalia's."

"It's a dream!"

"Thank you."

They are keeping their programs as souvenirs. The gentlemen help the ladies down the arduous stairs.

"I didn't like the second part."

"I liked the death of the swan."

"It wasn't the death of the swan, dear. It was Prokop's *Romeo and Juliet.*"

"Anyhow, he was as graceful as a swan."

"Romeo, the swan."

"Adorable . . ."

Look look look! There are the two faded countesses who write the society news for the Salonika papers. All the ladies want to greet them.

"What a marvelous tradition that counry has in the dance!"

"So what if it has changed its system and gone socialist? Dancing's in their blood."

"The system has nothing to do with that."

"Then why did Nureyev run away?"

Groups of friends greet one another. They kiss hands. The society that finances the arts is all there.

"This was an evening I shall never forget."

"I wasn't able to get tickets till the last moment. They've been sold out for two weeks."

"I got mine on the black market."

"And just think, this was only the second troupe of the Bolshoi Ballet. What if we'd seen the first?"

Now some get into their private cars. Others take taxis. Others buy hot *koulouria*, or go next door to the terrace of the Do-Re Club. And they're still coming out of the theater. The musicians, carrying their instruments in their cases, are swallowed up in the throng of spectators.

"The Maestro used his baton like a drinking-straw."

"She was like a piece of chiffon in his arms."

"The psychiatrist told her she'd work out her troubles with Vallium."

"You know, I'm on a new diet. I've lost six pounds in a week."

"Impossible!"

"And Alexandros?"

"He's getting married next week. I'm going to his wedding. You know who he's marrying?"

"I am proud to say he met her at my home."

"She's a pretty girl. A simple person, even with all that money."

"They're suited to each other. You know the only thing they disagree about?"

"No."

"About hunting. He wants to go every Sunday."

The inside lights go off; the last of the crowd has reached the bottom steps of the marble staircase. The theater and the White Tower confront each other, all flooded in light.

"Shall we play canasta tomorrow? Come along, you'll be the fourth."

"I'll come. I've been wanting to play. I haven't played for three days."

A group of young people go off in an MG. They're going dancing at the Swings. Two bankers are discussing the slump in the market. The Minister is leaving in his official limousine, bowing to his acquaintances. And the two public prosecutors, holding their wives by the arm, move on in the direction of the old city. When a jeep stops, they rush to get into it, leaving their wives on the sidewalk and dashing to police headquarters.

Chapter 40

There they found the General and the Chief of Police.

"How was the ballet?" the General asked.

"Why didn't you notify us earlier?"

"We couldn't locate you."

"What happened?"

"A traffic accident," said the Chief of Police. "The EDA deputy, Mr. Z., got hurt."

"Was the culprit arrested?"

The Chief of Police started to speak, but the General interrupted him.

"He hasn't been arrested yet, but, no matter where he goes, he'll be caught."

The Chief's face turned ashen. How could the General tell such a crude lie? Why did he do it? The workings of the General's mind had always baffled him.

"Is Z.'s condition serious?"

"I don't know."

The prosecutors rose and went immediately to the AHEPAN Hospital, where the wounded man had been taken. They didn't know how serious the accident had been. They thought they'd be able to get a statement from the victim. But when they arrived, they were shown a mutilated face. Clinically speaking, Z. was dead.

When they returned to police headquarters, Yango was brought before them; he told them what he'd been told to say by the Commissioner.

"Therefore," the first prosecutor said to the General, very excited, "when we came here the first time, you knew that the culprit had been arrested and you concealed it from us."

The General protested violently. "By no means! I did not know it!"

"But is it possible that your subordinates would not have informed you? And you, my boy, where have you been since ten-thirty?"

"At the police station."

"In the station lockup, you mean?"

"Lockup, nothing. I was eating lamb stew in the canteen."

"There you are! I regret to say, General, that you are going to be accused of protecting the guilty party and obstructing the course of justice. Z. is breathing his last and you didn't even lock up his murderer. You didn't even handcuff him."

The police captain intervened.

"Mr. Prosecutor," he said, "the cell at the station can't be used. It's full of *koulouria* trays and junk that has been taken from the unlicensed peddlers. Besides, the lights don't work. But what better cell do you need than the police station itself?"

"And you, Chief, were you also ignorant that the culprit had been arrested?"

"Inasmuch as the General has answered in my place, I think it best if I keep silent. But in the interests of the truth I should like to add that I had not yet had time to inform the General of the circumstances of the culprit's arrest, not being myself quite certain that the person in question was in fact the culprit and not some individual whom the policeman on duty had taken into custody, presuming him to be the guilty party."

It was 3:30 when they took down Yango's statement in writing. The first prosecutor told him to open his mouth and say "A-a-a-h." He noted down in the official report: "When the suspect exhaled at our request, his breath did not disclose a perceptible consumption of alcohol." Thus collapsed the argument that he was drunk when he hit Z. Then the prosecutors signed a warrant for the arrest of the person who had been in the van with Yango. The warrant was transmitted to the police station in Vango's neighborhood. The policeman on duty awakened the Commissioner, the Commissioner went to Vango's house to "arrest" him. He failed to find him there, but a few hours later Vango came by the station on his own. The agreement was that he should come back next morning and turn himself in "voluntarily," as the newspapers said he had done.

Chapter 41

Hatzis knew he should be getting back. He was the only witness, the only person who could help the reporters and the judges. The Athens–Salonika train would stop at Plati at 5:30 in the morning. It was 3:30 now. He slept for a while on the one bench in the deserted station. It was daylight when he opened his eyes. The broad plain was a baking sheet in the universal oven. Under the still-glowing embers of the stars, the yeast of dawn began to work. Soon the day's loaf would be ready and the early workmen would buy it as it came out of the oven, to eat at lunch, with a few olives and some cheese. When such images as these occurred to him, Hatzis knew he was hungry.

For some time he had been hiding behind the tank that supplied the trains with water, its huge hose hanging from it like an elephant's trunk. He was watching for the train, having made up his mind to scramble aboard and stow away to Salonika. Finally he saw it coming, twenty minutes late, a monster whose head alone gave signs of life. It stood still a long time, waiting for the signal to leave. Hatzis fixed his eyes on the play of red and green lights and listened to the whistles. When the train began its jerky puffing, he scrambled up to the footboard of the last compartment and stayed there during the whole trip, holding on to the door and leaning out into the void. It wasn't much of a feat. If he could jump into a van racing seventy miles an hour, why should he have any trouble when he had a whole train at his disposal and it was moving at a snail's pace?

Along the way he watched the plain waking up, the first oxen on their way to the fields, the plows, the black-garbed peasant women. The mist hanging over the plain had crystallized into hoarfrost on the acres of clover. Later the scene changed, the odor of industry filled his nostrils. He saw the workmen on their bicycles, the nervous crowds, the gray suburbs, the central station. The sooty air irritated his throat. His hands were trembling as he let go of the train.

In the railroad station, over somebody's shoulder, he read about his leader in the headlines of the *Macedonian Battle*.

He didn't want to admit that Z. could die.

Part 2
A TRAIN WHISTLES
IN THE NIGHT

A train, the train, non-stop, engine out-of-breath, coach with lights dimmed, and then Car Z-4383, in which he was traveling the same route traveled by air three days before, one hundred May hours before, as many hours as the agony of his soul had lasted, as many hours following his fall as his soul needed to prepare her departure, the eviction having struck her so brutally that at first she could scarcely credit it; in another coach his wife, veins swollen in her neck, a brother, the one who hadn't studied, and his mother, her face a carved image of the earth, thinking of earth, which soon was to receive her beloved son; and in the last coach, filled with their rough stench, a squad of policemen, weapons between thighs, terror-stricken on this death train, prepared to intervene in any incident, however trivial, gaping at countrysides which could not penetrate the sealed door of his coach, whose coffined body descended from North to South while his soul, following above the coach like a helicopter, hovered, dawdled, careful not to leave the train behind, a lepidopter spraying the fields against mildew, its fleet shadow setting foliage aquiver, refreshing the parched soil for an instant only, and the earth, thirsting for rain these hundreds of years, vibrated at its mere caress, this shadow's light as if one hand had lightly grazed another, the fingers not intertwining, because that would mean brotherhood, signal for blood and revolution, no, only an imperceptible plume stroke,

157

waking the blood in the veins, and the earth (fields of Thessaly, plains of Macedonia, Bralos, Pinios, Saranda-poron, Thebes, Levadia) knew that it would soon receive his body, the "forty-first brave lad" of the song, the earth (so the winged soul reflected) whose blood, her eaters, seeking their own level, in their own sweet time, undermine foundations, prepare the great, tidal revolution, in view of which the engineer's orders were explicit: "No stop anywhere," from the Communications Bureau of the Presidency of the Council in Athens, where an entire general staff was following the route of the train by radio, conferring with local police and regulating the trip accordingly, in touch by telephone with the engineer, all scheduled runs canceled, no trains approaching, none following behind, all postponed in order to clear the way for this one, in order that it not be sidetracked into some backwater whose sailors and whores and stevedores would rise up in revolt; these authorities panic-stricken, exposed, could not cover their shame, a child having shouted as in the fairy tale, "The King is naked!", causing utter dismay after countless ceremonies had persuaded him of his rich clothing, of his own beauty, of his power rooted in the people's enduring love, and then, at this one cry, havoc, whereupon, seeing no other way, they chose to remove the child, find peace once and for all, remove the witness to their deception, for it had not sufficed to cry "The King is naked!" but he had dared to strip the Queen as well, that time in London, a hired hand ripping her dress at the shoulder; and now the train was racing through a world suddenly stilled by his thunderbolt, a world wanting only the signal to rise up, but in the end everything would be orderly, there were to be no incidents even at the funeral, the slogans disseminated were soothing ones, appeals to avoid further bloodshed at all costs, the times not being ripe, and politics, its eye on final victory, must prudently, if temporarily, forfeit the great opportunity his death afforded, while the other side, all during

his soul's long agony, tried with vain words to cover
their nakedness:

"The true facts concerning the sanguinary incidents
incited by the Communists in Salonika.—Deputy Z. accidentally injured by a motorcycle while he was leading
an illegal Communistic demonstration.—The Police had
offered to transport the Communists from the scene by
buses, but the Communists refused in order to organize
a march upon the EDA headquarters.—A police captain
was gravely wounded when he attempted to protect
Deputy Pirouchas from being molested.—Such has been
the solicitude manifested by the government in this
affair that it even provided a military aircraft to transport a great surgeon to the bedside of the accident-in-
jured deputy, Z."

And the train whistled before entering the tunnel,
emerging presently with the darkness for its trail, while
the helicopter soul had started to tremble during the few
seconds she had lost sight of the body and one of her
great colored wings had begun to flutter as though a
valve had loosened, soul the *Papilio cresphontes*, soul
the *Argynnis cybele,* soul the *Neonympha eurytus,* soul
the *Satyrodes canthus*, soul the *Vanessa atalanta,* a butterfly emerging on schedule from its cocoon woven of
the strong threads by which men attach their dreams,
like balloons, like anchors dropped on fine cord into the
bosom of the deep, but the soul grew calm as she saw
the diesel engine's nostrils reappear from the tunnel, followed by the dimmed coach, his own sealed coach,
tear-stained windows of the relatives' coach, and finally
that tent of green caterpillars, plague of the pine tree,
the coach full of policemen, which, if it were to burst,
would have drowned the world in slobber; and he, un-
seeing, saw nevertheless everything from his lepidopter,
this earth, his earth, earth of his fatherland, mother
earth, sagely fashioned by the aeons, an ever-living land-

scape, and of a beauty for which human beings ought always to suffer, always wallow in blood to defend from the barbarian hordes, from the neo-Fascist gangs, always, with no justification other than the safety of the mountains beneath the blessed, blessing sun; he saw the trees, little prayers, resting on the sea's doorstep like old women spinning on thresholds; he saw a sea gull veer in fright as the train brushed against the sea by the Moschofs' villa where the locomotive leaves the tunnel; he saw villages imprisoned forever in mountain ravines, no human eye to see them, villages emptied clean by emigration; soon he saw Olympus too, snow-covered in the glory of May, and Mount Kissavos opposite, the two still unreconciled, like the rival Resistance camps during the Occupation; the Venetian fortress above Platamon, a fortress abandoned centuries ago, now the redoubt of crows keeping watch over the sea, if no longer for pirates, then for the mine-sweepers of the Sixth Fleet, and just here the soul, wishing to rest a moment, entered a cranny in the wall, displaced a green lizard; she saw the marble, wind-veined sea, hoped for a sail, a sea temple facing Olympus; she welcomed the breeze, because it is said that the soul, so long as the body remains unburied, wanders insouciant, but once the body has returned to its dark womb, her self returns to air, dissolves into molecules which then become oxygen for the living to breathe; and the soul knew that on this last journey she was seeing the fortress for the last time, how she had loved it once, crown of the little mountain turning and turning beyond the windshield as on a revolving stage, only it was in fact the road itself winding and winding, memories for whose sake she had lingered a moment today until the train whistled her back to Tempe, the propeller started to whirl, the butterfly soared off the ground, leaving no trace of its momentary presence in the fortress, carving no date, returning the cranny to a green lizard much put out by the whole affair, and hastening off in the wake of her body—a stranger to all this —a body terribly damaged, appallingly mutilated, which would have chosen for its own crown the very tar of the streets, though perhaps not, after all, because:

"The fracture found on the skullcap of the aforesaid Z. could not have been caused by a fall on the macadam pavement of the street and the ensuing blow; it can only have resulted from a blow dealt when the victim was standing with his head erect, for it is only in such circumstances that one finds symmetrical lesions of the brain in the underlying region and in the region opposite to the wound. In the autopsy of the said Z., such lesions of the brain were in fact found, accompanied by a cerebral hemorrhage of the left hemisphere, while the fracture occasioned by the blow was located in the right temporal bone, and had it resulted from a fall onto a hard surface such as the pavement of a street, these typical symmetrical lesions would not have been found."

And the train raced on, whistling in a paralyzed world, on a day when only stationmasters and switchmen gave way to panic, "Never before in a lifetime spent in the service of the railroads," thought the master of the little station at Papapouli, "have I seen such a thing," telephones buzzing with reports that the funeral train had passed this or that station "without incident," only here at Papapouli, whose stationmaster had just eaten a chicken decapitated by the previous day's express, and could not manipulate the switch, so that the train got onto another track and all but collided with some freight cars seen fortunately by the engineer in time to put on his brakes, and slid two hundred yards before coming to a stop, the coffin, fastened down, though it was rocked in its bolted enclosure, the relatives glued their masks to the windowpanes, a suitcase fell from above, and the caterpillars, the policemen, into a tangle from which it seemed doubtful they would ever extricate themselves; for a moment the officer in charge suspected sabotage, feared that the corpse was going to be stolen, signaled, as soon as the train stopped, for his men to jump down from the coach and spread out like sharpshooters along the tracks, until of course they saw the train backing up and the engineer's gesture of reassurance and realized that no hostile force was threatening them. The soul, watching the confusion from on high, came to rest on an elm tree at whose roots a young Thessalian shepherd was playing the flute, charming a snake or two thereabouts, while the stationmaster, once the train had got back onto the right track, breathed with relief and duly made his telephone call, adding yet another buzz to the telephone wires crossing the Pinios, that sweet green river indifferent to the rest of the plain, flowing in inchanging servitude ever since its Liberation; only the river, reflected the soul, dream of the plain-dwellers, which alone bore their dreams seaward to liberation, only the river, soul of the leveled life, its banks embroidered with willows, deep-rooted plane trees wading in its waters, would give way to the tremors and gooseflesh of adolescence before disappearing into the sea, just as she—his soul—before disappearing into cloud, could look beyond his dead body upon the world she was soon to lose. Now she descended, passed the vale of Tempe, passed the National Highway, the sugar factory with trucks full of sugar-beets lined up in front of it, reached the station at Larissa, through which the train shot like an arrow, leaving the little yoghurt vendor, hand in air, unable to understand why the peasants were brandishing rakes with red handkerchiefs tied on top, he thought it must be some Minister, one of the big landholders of the plain who often became Ministers in order to defend their interests, and so all the more expected the train to stop, but it shot past like a rocket, leaving behind only a veil of smoke and a bundle of newspapers thrown from a window to burst at his feet like a grenade. Morning newspapers, which said:

"But, from whatever angle one surveys the incidents at Salonika, no one can entertain any doubt that they were a consequence of truly unendurable provocation on the part of Communistic elements. Unless the populace of Salonika had felt this provocation, why would anyone have bothered the assembled Communists? Had there been no loudspeakers broadcasting incendiary slogans, what law-abiding inhabitant of Salonika, happening on the vicinity, would have thought it necessary to take action? Wasn't it precisely because of the provocation emanating from the Red orators that they felt such a need? And if, after this provocation, the Communists had not attempted to organize a protest march headed by the Communist deputy who was to meet with a fatal accident, would any of these events have occurred?

"From the instant that the Communist organizers decided to conduct this march, in defiance of an order not to do so, the subsequent events became inevitable. At that point in the demonstration the motor vehicle of Gazgouridis appeared. He was coming out of Spandoni Street—conceivably not by chance, just as the Communist and the Center parties claim—and he lunged intentionally upon the column of demonstrators. But here questions arise. How could Yango know that the Communists were organizing a march, how could he arrive with his pickup at just the right moment and get into just the right position to cause an unavoidable accident? Might he not have feared that the Communist demonstrators would attack him, lynch him? Even granting that the act may in fact have been premeditated—as has been brought out, the Communists murdered Yango's father—once he had decided to assault the line of marchers with his vehicle, how would he have recognized the EDA deputy among so many demonstrators, and aimed for him, even if he was marching in front?

"Communism, the bloody Communism which rages in our land and which has already in the recent past shed whole rivers of Greek blood, is attempting to exploit these incidents for the purpose of casting our country into disrepute abroad and of creating internal upheavals. We believe that the state is duty-bound at this juncture to take a decisive stand, and that it must begin with the

IMMEDIATE DISSOLUTION of the subversive Bertrand Russell League and of the swindlers of 'peace,' who today are serving as the spearhead of revolutionary Communism."

The body imprisoned in the train saw nothing. The body was without memory. Memory had abandoned it at two minutes to ten on Wednesday evening. Clinically speaking, Z. was dead. From that moment on, no organ, no sense functioned. The body, the beautiful athletic body, lived inanimate, like wheels of a capsized car which—all contact lost with brakes and gears, everything smashed in the disaster—nevertheless keep spinning in the void. So it was with the body, the deep rattle in its throat serving as a kind of basso ostinato to the doctors' efforts. There were many doctors. Some had come from abroad: Hungary, Germany, Belgium. They could do nothing. They marveled that an organism was still alive when all its centers had been paralyzed. The organism refused its death. It was too early for it to die. The headless body clung to an existence of its own. But now at last it had surrendered. And it was journeying in peace toward the grave. What bothered the soul was not so much having been evicted and forced to watch the autopsy. (Of course, it is disagreeable to discard a costume because they've botched it, to see it ripped to shreds before your very eyes. This part, however, she could bear.) What bothered her was a coroner, who had insisted from the outset—before the autopsy, as indeed after it, with all that it had brought to light—that the fracture could not have been caused by a blow dealt while Z. was standing upright. The sole cause, he said, was the "violent collison of the head with a stable, hard surface, such as the pavement": in other words, the fall onto the asphalt. A coroner's profession is a gruesome one. But death has not room for politics. Professional detachment is one thing, reflected the soul, and quite another to indulge in low politics over a corpse. Leave low politics to the living. For the dead, let there be only high politics. And this coroner, after returning to Athens —whence he had come uninvited—dispatched a report to be countersigned by his opposite number in Salonika. Backed up by two other doctors, however, the Salonika coroner maintained a contrary opinion. He believed the fracture to have been caused by a blow on the head, and he refused to sign. At that point the doctor from Athens was obliged to draw up another report which admitted as "probable" the contingency of a blow caused "by some contusive instrument, but without personally sharing this view." All this sickened the soul through and through.

The train raced demoniacally on, passing mountains and plains, a zipper drawn upon this great affair. But it was a broken zipper, one of those that reopen in back what they have closed in front. For no affair could be closed by a drugged train stopping nowhere. The case remained wide open like doors in the dog days. The train blew its whistle and raced on, panicked and guilty. The relatives feared the worst. The wife looked out the window, seeing nothing. Her mind was in the next car, where her husband was shut alone, as if in a dungeon, while the policemen ate their meal. She got up. On the one hand, he was dead. On the other, those who had killed him slept on. She could not stir, could not go anywhere. The train became a prison on wheels. She could stand no more. She was stifling. The alarm signal? Not to be left with this last image of him: under the oxygen tank, gasping for breath, pulsebeats getting feebler and feebler, surrounded by doctors no longer hoping for the miracle. One mountain followed another, one plain followed another. She saw nothing.

Only at some point so high that the air was rarefied, they stopped to wait for a local connection, apparently a scheduled run there had been no time to cancel. There, high in the mountains, the policemen got down and stood guard around the train. There on the mountains, the high mountains, the soul perched herself on a post and waited for the klephts to come and steal the body.

Waited for the brave men of the Resistance, for Ares Velouchiotis, to come out of their hideouts and fall upon the policemen and take possession of the body. For them to carry it to the peak, adorn it, roast many lambs and drink much wine, and then bury it up there among the eagles. All night long to dance—old Dimos with Leventoyannis—and when they were good and drunk, to start firing shots into the air, the way the cannons on Lycabettos boom out for royal funerals. Thus would the body find its place in Greekland, and be honored in keeping with ancestral tradition, though today the brave men of the Resistance were not on the mountains but in the cities. A whistle summoned the policemen from their thicket-urinals and they climbed back aboard the train. The connection had passed, they could start up again. The body was aware neither of the stop nor of the starting up, nor did it smell the mountain thyme. The body was like those third assistant engineers, who spend their lives deep in the bowels of ships, who, if the engine breaks down, never see a port or breathe the salt air of the open sea.

At one station, somewhere after the train had returned to flat country, a steam engine replaced its diesel. And now the butterfly soul—the *Papilio cresphontes*, the *Argynnis cybele*, the *Neonympha eurytus*—must fly through smoke. Her beautiful iridescent colors blackened. Her wings grew heavy. And she grieved, needed protection, wanted to reenter a skin where nothing could touch her. Night was falling and the soul had always been afraid of darkness. These three nights without a roof over her head had been harrowing. But the body received no message from her, and she despaired. His batteries had broken down, his antennae, everything. A crippled typewriter in the junkshops of Monastiraki; a deaf-and-dumb machine. That's how the soul felt when the sun's fires began to dim.

The train passed through level fields where the grain took courage from the setting sun. The ears of grain straightened as the light diminished. And in the breeze that came in the great benefactor's wake they all rustled together, the ripe ears rise up, my love, let us dance till dawn! Formless waves, like those of the ocean, lapped the breakwater of the railway line. The deep breathing of a woman surrendered to the stars. And this beauty grieved the soul still more.

An old woman drew the chain at the intersection. A tractor crossed the tracks. Now the sparse villages with their sparse lights glittered in the foothills. Night had fallen. The stations were projected upon the darkness like colored slides. The train did not pause at any of them. It raced and whistled demoniacally. A train whistling in the night, a train, the train, compartment Z-4383, engineer Kostas Konstantopoulos, assistant engineer Savas Polychronidis, a train, the train, and the body mute, a door closed at nightfall, the body, a tree uprooted in a thunderstorm, the body deprived of the caresses which once restored it, in a walnut coffin, a good coffin, but how desolate in there, without its soul!

"Greece—we shall never weary of proclaiming it— needs to silence its discords and quarrels. Our enemies are jealous of our progress, and a number of foreign states would like to see us plunged into the abyss of anarchy. It has become customary for people to excuse Mr. Papandreou's insane mistakes by suggesting that they are a consequence of his passion for power. But however violent this passion may be, the leader of the Center Union Party cannot possibly be unaware that it is not the knight's steed of Democracy he has mounted, but the rebellious bull of Communist anarchy."

The train tore the fabric of night, and the lady watched her little Pekingese trying to cover up its "misbehavior," unsuccessfully, because there was parquet underfoot, not dirt. However, the mess did have to be concealed because it spoiled the aesthetics of the floor. She pressed the button on her desk, summoning the maid, and ordered her to clean it up. And then, taking her little dog in her arms, she went on writing:

"The nationalists in this country are sincerely grieved about the death of Z., because respect for human life is one of their fundamental guiding principles. And it is these citizens who are today being shamelessly accused of responsibility for Z.'s death. The truth is that, in accusing the nationalists, the extreme left wing and all the dark forces standing behind it mean to undermine the foundations of the entire edifice of our national, civic, and religious way of life: our Church, our educational system, our Armed Forces, our police system, our judicial system . . . Mr. Papandreou and the people on his side are gravely deluded if they think that, by outdoing the extreme left with their slanderous charges . . ."

The little dog was squirming in her arms. The lady broke off writing to soothe it. Then the maid came back with a plastic dustpan, bent down, picked up the droppings, and sprayed the area with deodorant. The lady got up, still holding her Pekingese in her arms, went over to the spot, and rubbed his little snout in it. In protest the Pekingese tried to sink its teeth into her wrist, but the lady, who knew all about little dogs, let him go in time. Then she returned to her desk and continued, just as the train was passing the royal residence at Tatoï:

"If we examine candidly the attitude of the extreme left in this matter, it would not be difficult to show that it is by no means grieved by what has happened. If the respect due a dead man permitted, we might say that, on the contrary, its members rejoice. For now they have their Person, their Victim, their Hero. And, indeed, precisely he whom they wanted: a brilliant scientist, a top athlete, a good husband and affectionate father; not a Communist Party member, a young, enthusiastic politician recently celebrated for his strivings for peace rather than for his efforts on behalf of the politics of the Kremlin. Their exploitation of the funeral bier, the free rein given to naïve emotionalism, the laments and the weeping women, the petitions from the seamstresses and the construction workers, all show clearly how the extreme left seeks to profit from the tragedy . . ."

The soul sighed above Tatoï, where the royal estates are carefully fenced in to keep the pheasants from running away. She saw the palace where the train whistle crept in like a snake, chilling to whoever noticed it; she saw the pine trees weeping tears of resin, and she too wept because of the fenced-in woods. Gliders from the airport at Tatoï approached, reminding her of the great flight she herself would soon be making. But now Athens came into distant view, a meadow of lights tremulously playing, candles lit to welcome his body, behind the smoke curtain of Eleusis, whose mysteries would remain mysteries forever (for the initiates disappeared without leaving texts or bas-reliefs or ikons), under the protective smokestack and the blue flame of the oil refineries, huge metal tanks, like silver dollars seen under a magnifying glass; sweet Athens, across from ancient Salamis, where the cargoless ships were moored, alongside the dockyards of Scaramanga, where starvation wages no less than its layers of polluted air after so many hours in the open country caused the lepidopter soul to tremble. The lies were over and she had reached her destination. At a moment like this she wanted to be like the body: to understand nothing, to suffer nothing.

However, she had no reason to complain, she reflected, as she spied in the distance the skeleton of the Acropolis, all lit up (if only for the Sound and Light performance), since so very many had died before her without having given the least bit of what they carried within them. She at least had been able, had given something that would outlast her dissolution: she would become a symbol. Old streets, beloved streets, neighborhoods where every tree stood sentinel, little houses built on the sly, whole households inhabiting the remains of trucks, without water, without light, though everything around them was lit with electricity.

"It's mad of Z.'s relatives and friends to insist on displaying the body in the Chapel of St. Eleutherios, by the Metropolis Cathedral."

"Tako, did you phone the Archbishop again?"

"I did phone."

"And what did he say? Will he give in to them?"

"He talked out of both sides of his mouth. I don't like that at all. They phoned him from the Palace too, but apparently he did the same with them."

"Phone him again. He has to give a clear answer. Tell him there'll be disturbances; tell him that blood will be shed, that they'll burn down the church, that . . . Tell him whatever comes into your head, only convince him! I'd phone him myself, but I'm afraid of losing control and telling him where to go. Phone him again."

These hands will never again touch human hands. These hands will return to water. They will become rich earth to nourish the flowers. These hands that held the lancet and cured human pain, free of charge. This face will never plunge into the sea again. These lips will not kiss again. A body enclosed, and returned to its sender; a letter stamped "Departed without a forwarding address." Body with blood frozen in the veins, like a photograph on the screen, frozen at the moment of greatest movement in the street, in the shops. Now, at this very moment, everything comes to an end.

"A secretary entered from the next room and whispered something in his ear. The Archbishop shook his head. 'I'll take it in the next room,' he said. And addressing the relatives and friends of Z., he added: 'More telephone calls.'

"He left the room and in a few minutes returned. As he sat down with a sigh, he murmured: 'It was about this matter again. They communicated to me the wishes of a very high personage whom I would not like to displease. And I put a question to myself: if all these eminent people in responsible positions are so anxious, mustn't there be something to it? Mightn't trouble indeed occur? In this new telephone call they mentioned bloodshed and the danger that hundreds of people might be killed. My responsibility is great. I'm in a most difficult position, my children.'

"'Your Holiness,' said a cousin of Z.'s then, 'no trouble is going to break out. You may rest assured on that score. But if you did refuse us the chapel, your action would have highly unfavorable repercussions among the people, and you would become a target for criticism abroad. The man in question died with Christ's message on his lips, the message of peace and love.'"

May, too, is a cruel month. The earth reabsorbs its fruits. The first flowering and the second are over. Now, heavily, like ears of grain, everything returns to its beginning. Everything is over. Even memory will be lost. To live again perhaps in others, nourished by their blood. His own memory, that of his own soul and body, will wane and be eclipsed. And yet, no, no, reflected the butterfly soul *Satyrodes canthus*. It cannot be, everything must not be over. Where a hero falls, a people is born. It cannot be, it isn't possible for me to die. When? How? I do not know. You too will remember me, sweet, beloved body. You will remember me eternally, because I loved you very much. You will remember me. You who reveled in the sea, you whom the sun wearied, you who wanted to make love even without me, you, body, will remember me. Now that you are going into earth, remember my love for you; it will never let you die. My love, if only at this moment I could take your hand! If you could talk to me, look at me. I am tired. How? Why did everything end like this? Without my enjoying you as you declined, without my learning to lose you little by little. You left me too abruptly, and I have a sharp emptiness in my arms, through which the wind whistles. I am all of me an empty cistern, without you.

"The Archbishop paused a moment in thought. Then he turned to the EDA representative and said: 'Do you guarantee that there will be no trouble?'

"'We give you our word, Your Holiness, that on our side absolute order will be preserved. If there is any breach of order, it will be created deliberately by the government and the police.'

"'Very well, I give you the chapel. God help you.'"

Body beloved, adored in the stadiums and in the fire, body which even the most horrible alterations have left so much my own, if only I might have you near me one single evening more, I'd give you leave to go. My eviction was too sudden. I'd never supposed that anyone else could possess you. And now what? Your hands, just your hands, and that quickening—how I miss it all! I'm so alone! I have literally no place in this world. No place and no pleasure. As for reincarnation—there is none! I shall lose myself too. I shall become vapor, atmosphere for the birds to stir on their migrations. The solitude is unbearable without your nerves to explode with. Your nerves, threads of a warm sweater unraveled stitch by stitch. A warm sweater that I wore, and the world was mine. You held life and the living in your embrace, and I rested easy. Now you are going to leave me. You are leaving me. And I shall remain alone.

"The hour, four minutes before midnight. The special train comes into the station at Athens with a wail that resounds like a funeral chant. It brakes, it stops; the crowd shoves, people trample one another to get up front, nearer the door of the sealed freight car which contains Z.'s remains.

"The door is unsealed. A coffin laden with wreaths of flowers, and now overspread with the Greek flag, is borne to the hearse. And the throng of people instantly divides to make way for the dead deputy.

"A one-minute silence. Then two sobs are heard. And cries:

" Z., our hero, you're not dead!'

" Z., you will live with us forever!'

"A thunderous shout shakes the station and immediately afterwards the National Anthem rises from thousands of throats.

"Outside car Z-4383, an employee affixes a sign: NO ADMITTANCE ALL PERSONS FORBIDDEN TO ENTER TO BE DISINFECTED."

The procession advanced slowly and the soul reveled to see so many bodies protecting her own. From on high, they became one single body, as on Good Friday, with the flag in the middle. The streets ran in new directions. The lights were transformed into candles, which melted as he was carried past. And the policemen escorting the procession might have been those who officiate at the Good Friday ceremonies, armed with rifles.

They were taking him to the chapel by the Metropolis Cathedral. There they would leave him until Sunday. Day of Resurrection. And the crowd tightened further and further around his dead body, as if Roman soldiers might steal it.

The omnipresent Caiaphas radioed instructions to all the police patrol cars. When the body had been deposited in the Chapel of St. Eleutherios—without any incident—he felt relieved; he accompanied Pontius Pilate home. On the way they talked about Sunday.

"Strict measures must be taken, Draconian measures."

"The entire force will be on hand," Caiaphas assured him. "With tear gas, fire hoses, and all the paraphernalia."

"I'm quite anxious," said Pilate.

They took leave of each other at three o'clock in the morning, wishing each other pleasant dreams.

But events belied their fears: no incident occurred, not even on Resurrection Day. The only "incident," reflected the soul, was this extraordinary mass of flowers, the like of which had never been seen. The entire springtime came to the funeral, floating in from all sides, passing first through the suburbs and then for three whole hours occupying the city of Athens, fragrant at her heart of hearts. "There was no flower left in all of Attica."

"Immortal!"

"He lives!"

"No more blood!"

"He lives! He lives!"

With battle cries such as these, the Romans might rest easy. Wars are not waged with carnations, however many, however red. Neither are revolutions. And yet the finger remained on the trigger. And though ineffably bitter, the butterfly soul *Neonympha eurytus* tasted deliverance of a sort. It wasn't that cowds inundated streets and squares around the Cathedral: it was the fact that this crowd constituted a single body. And if one person had been missing, nothing would have been altered. Even if ten, a hundred, a thousand persons had been missing, the body of the people, come to restore their hero to life, would have remained indissoluble. This was the soul's consolation. Her body had served to bring about a sudden, unbreakable union of numberless human molecules. So be it! What she had lost, the others had gained a hundredfold. And the idea of peace, for which the one body had been sacrificed, suddenly became flesh and blood in the rarefied air. The same immortality that flooded the streets flooded also the hearts of men. The sea is inexhaustible; it is full of unexploitable riches. It will not dry up when you lean from your small boat and draw a pail of water. The sea is what never ends.

And so, between two heavens, the soul followed the procession of the Resurrection. She well knew, now, that the body had not died, since a whole people thronged around its coffin. She knew too that immortality is whatever survives in the memory of others. And the cry that reigned throughout the whole journey was "He lives!" No one would admit that death existed in the realm of the idea. Death exists only for the individuals who one day discover with stupefaction that their private little lives come to an abrupt end. At that point they panic. And must shut themselves up in psychiatric hospitals to recover. There is no death when by falling you help a people to rise, when your monument has become the very scale and standard of a people.

"In the foreground came the young people with the wreaths of flowers. Each wreath was held by two boys and two girls, taking turns. The members of the Peace Committee and the Bertrand Russell League followed, holding sprays of roses and carnations. Not far behind came the Philharmonic Municipal Band of Piraeus. An enormous banner with the symbol of disarmament was carried by the young people of the B. Russell–Piraeus branch. Z.'s fellow athletes marched in front of the hearse, displaying the trophies won by the dead Balkan champion. All along the route, people crowded on balconies of apartment houses threw flowers as the procession passed. Citizens of every age and class lined the whole length of Mitropoleos Street, Philhellinon Street, Syngrou Avenue, Anapafseos Avenue. The cries 'Long live Z.' 'No more blood!' 'He lives!' 'Peace—Democracy!' were rebroadcast as though this ceaseless mass of people were an electric cable accompanying the procession along the whole endless way to the cemetery."

When they arrived there, the soul came to rest, in profound anguish, like the kite at its zenith when you see it suddenly halt, a motionless speck in the sun, while on the ground the kite string in the child's hand relaxes, just as above deep waters his fishing line slackens inward without revealing the exact spot where it has touched the sea's floor—so proving once again that up and down are the same; arrived there, the soul came to rest, waiting for them to set the body down so that she could ascend, waiting for the earth to receive him so that she could head high up, up and down, body and soul, making only one; until after having come to a halt above the huge body of the halted world, at one point she had to descend again for a clearer view of an old woman dressed in black who darted through the crowd, pulling her hair hysterically and crying just as they laid him in the grave: "Wake up, Z.! We're waiting for you! Wake up!"

Which sent a shock through the crowd, for this old woman with her simple words had expressed precisely what an entire people was feeling at that moment. And the soul sighed, knowing that what the old woman had said in her simplicity could not be, for the body had plainly not gone to sleep, it had been cleft asunder, disfigured, deprived of its foundations, and the total demolition of the house was being completed.

Big rooms where they had lived together, she and he, with windows open to the sun and wind, spacious rooms without a spider or a figment of mold, this house, his body, was descending into earth. In these rooms they had seen innumerable suns rise through the bodies of neighboring houses, through her thickets who lay all night long at his side. Here the soul had built her heart, her nest, a house adored by her as well as by that other woman, those other women. In its place now remained nothing but wind. The house had displaced a certain volume of air, and now the gap was closing. The house was sinking, in ruins, into the earth from which it had risen. Its raw materials, now mere worthless rubble, were returning to earth. And her grief was boundless as she watched earth reassume this house, her hearth, big rooms with windows open, Thessiou Street, number 7.

At the moment when I'm losing you, she thought in her pain, at this last instant, after which I shall neither see you again nor caress your beloved form, this voice of yours that uttered my everything I felt, your arms linked with the cypresses, your nerves, conductors of a whole world's power and light, at the moment of losing you, do not say that what we lived was a lie. Suddenly this earth which is swallowing you consumes me as well. I rise without wanting to, I am rising higher, higher. We are losing one another.

Ships from the North no echoing trace of your passage, fires that have burned and left no ashes behind, and you, my house, my warmth, who gave me new faith in life, legs on which my world rested, you, now, hands of light, eyes without my image, why, why are you leaving me like this, with so much pain, such anguish and fatigue, a stopped clock in the sky, I keep ascending, ascending without wanting to, as you are descending without wanting to, there is no hope of finding you again, I know there is none, I do not want to leave, let me at least stay near what you loved, when we lived, in our house, with our pictures, the very chinks in the wall, I want to stay near the streets where you lived, but I cannot, I am rising, leaving, vanishing into space and I don't know how to tell you, my house, my love, I miss you, I miss you horribly, there is no wine to drown your memory, I knew you or did not, if I had truly known you, you would not now be escaping from me, me, raving on because I can less and less make out what is happening below, more and more the people, the crowd gathered to see you off, are turning into an inkblot, a black smudge on the map of the world, this world that I am leaving and do not want to leave, for the grain is sweet before the harvest, and your hair sweet shining like grain to the wind's touch and mine, and your large mouth molded for kisses, I miss you now shamelessly, I curse you, hate you, worthless body that they killed, thing, cipher, house that surrendered to the city planner, dumb thing, and defenseless, ridiculous thing too, disappearing like this without a pang of remorse, without the least alarm sounded in the almond grove of the stars, and stupid, don't even feel that you might miss me also, don't even know that I am orphaned by you, I who know you don't know it, ah, why spend so much precious time with you, why not try to slip in somewhere else, form some lasting relationship, don't know how good it is never to have been born and how horrid to die just when you want most to live, I see nothing below me any more, a poor photograph of land and water in some intermediate state, neither city nor Greece; I don't know where I'm going or who cut my string, only that I am going, and tell me why, why don't I have your hand now to caress me, tell me, why don't I have your smile, where are you, what are you doing, I am losing myself as you are, and I need to know how you are faring in that darkness, that dampness riddled with furtive subterranean railways and undermined foundations, I need to know, in that inferno you have entered, what you feel as the fever sears you, for up here, in this intense light hardly different from your own intense darkness, I have lost contact, the Hertzian waves bring me no messages from that world, and yet that world exists, it does, only you and I exist no more, only you and I, my house with curtains and tall palm trees, with all the things that made us one, what will become of me now, I've never been sentimental, I am losing myself but not my feeling for you, it is terrifying, if at least I could forget you, if at least I weren't suffering, I am losing myself, it isn't the sky here, big birds lie sleeping on couches of air, a different kind of transparency, a different depth and density, yet more than anything now I miss your voice, miss more than anything your laugh, your bravado, your strong arms round the whole world. That embrace ended, the world ends as well.

I hate you. I always hated you. I always envied you. Without the olive trees, even the vineyards look like orphans. Without the rocks, even the sea seems unreal. Without your kiss, my lips are two worms. Without you I am nothing. I hate you for betraying me, my beloved house, I hate you tonight for being late to our rendezvous. I shall never believe that you aren't coming back. I shall never believe that you have canceled your trip. Do you know why? Because I am incapable of suicide. I must carry you in me until I become utterly dissolved, voice of a voice that has faded away, chaos of my time,

the sun's rays burn savagely here, high up here. Burn
and are beginning to singe my wings. Now I'm melting. How pleasant it is! Disappearing at last. Forgetting
you. Yes, so suddenly. Who were you? Where was it? I
remember dimly that once . . . No, it can't have been
you. On earth? You mean that planet? Yes! Yes, of
course, yes indeed. Oh, very well, thank you. Yes. Yes. I
don't know. What was that? I don't understand. I don't
know. I never knew you. What pleasure, this losing of
oneself! What a relief! Once, perhaps . . . No. It's you
who betrayed me, you are faithless. You abandoned me
first and left me homeless. And I became a whore and
forgot you in the brothel of the Great Bear. I forgot you.
You deserved to be forgotten. You betrayed me. Betrayed me. I have lost you and myself alike. I do not
know you.

"In the course of the funeral of Deputy Z. yesterday
there were no incidents or clashes with the police. Why?
because the EDA decided to give orders for the funeral
ceremony to be conducted in an orderly fashion. When
the EDA does not want incidents, there are no incidents.
And when entanglements with the police are provoked,
they are provoked because the EDA wants them, organ-
izes them, creates them. These are the conclusions to be
drawn from the funeral of Z."

Part 3
AFTER THE
EARTHQUAKE

Chapter 1

It was hot. People went about their jobs indifferently, except in a district near the AHEPAN Hospital: Syntrivani Square. The stadium had been closed, but the street leading from it to the hospital was full of people. The hearse would soon be passing on its way to the railroad station and the train to Athens. "The hearse of our adolescence," reflected the young student, for it was on this same street, under this same tree, in front of this same bolted stadium gate that he had parted forever from his girl two days before. And now, though he had come to bid farewell to the dead hero, the two funerals were strangely confused in his mind.

A friend who was with him tried to console him by saying that in this day and age there were more important things happening and that anyone wanting to face the problems of his time could not allow himself to succumb so easily to autosuggestion. "Because in one way or another," he said, "you are enjoying your obsession with Maria. You love your legend. Maria is an excuse. Even if you hadn't broken with her, you'd have found some other reason to suffer."

He listened, relieved to hear his friend talking this way. Yet on that particular morning he was inconsolable at having lost her. Spring with its leaden weights sank, into his sea, nets utterly lost in the deep blue waters, a darkness on the floor of the sea. That's how he felt since parting from her. It was so senseless! And all this in front of the cold, ugly, forbidding gate of a football field! A cry behind him made him turn abruptly.

"I've been hit!"

He saw a man lying in the middle of the street, unconscious. In the dense traffic of Syntrivani Square—cars seem to spin around it like tops—he couldn't make out who had hit the man. In a second all his personal obsessions vanished. He ran to the nearest telephone, the one from which he used to phone Maria after class, and called for an ambulance. It arrived a few minutes later, picked up the injured man, and drove him to the city hospital.

Chapter 2

On his way to the Public Prosecutor he was struck on the head. It was the second time he was going there. The first time he had told the Investigator the whole story. After struggling with himself all day he had weakened. Ever since that accursed Thursday morning when he'd read in the newspaper that Yango had run over the deputy, he was revolted. He was the only person who knew the truth. The day before, Yango had said: "Tonight I'm going to do something big—really wild. It may come to killing a man . . ." And he'd done it. He didn't know if Z. would die, but did it matter? "Clinically, Z. is dead. A body, essentially speaking, without a head. The body is still alive. The brain has undergone necrosis."

He was at his varnishing shop when he read the news. He was stunned. In spite of all the work he had to do (yesterday's order still hadn't gone out and the dealer was waiting for the furniture, the same furniture he had called on Yango to deliver yesterday, but Yango couldn't make the delivery, he had more important things to do, such as "killing a man," and he had not been able to find another three-wheeler; it was Wednesday, the shops were closed, and the pickup trucks had left the stand early), in spite of all the work he had to do, his hands turned to stone. He let the newspaper drop. His smiling deaf-mute apprentice picked it up and handed it to him. Nikitas shoved him aside. For the first time that smile exasperated him. He began pacing nervously. The shop seemed too small. The polished walnut coffins depressed him. No, he had to do something. It wasn't possible to remain silent when he was the only one who knew the truth. Then he would be no different from his apprentice: a deaf-mute wearing an idiotic smile.

He was not a leftist. Or a rightist. Or anything at all. Of course, he read the right-wing papers—to delude his enemies, since he had a shop. Just the day before, someone had tried to open the same kind of shop across the street. Nikitas lost no time in going to the police; the result was the man's chances were destroyed. But what angered him was that the newspaper should refer to "a traffic accident." He knew perfectly well that Yango the night before had been planning in cold blood to kill a man. How could he keep his mouth shut?

That Thursday seemed endless. He felt he had the weight of the world on his shoulders. No one else knew what he knew. At noon he bought the Athens newspapers. All of them were decorated with Yango's mustache. In one night this good-for-nothing braggart, this lazy bum, had become famous all over Greece. He was jealous. If he went to see the Investigator and made a clean breast of it, they'd put his picture in the papers the next day too. An insignificant varnisher suddenly abandons his modest vocation and becomes a celebrity, like . . . certainly not like Yango, who wins fame by committing a crime. He would make a name for himself with a good deed. On his way home at noon, he looked at all those people who took no notice of him, and he imagined the sensation he would create after his revelations, recognized and hailed everywhere, boarding the Forty Churches bus, where everyone would get up to give him a seat.

His mother had cooked rice with spinach for lunch. She noticed that he ate without interest while angrily reading a pile of newspapers.

"What's the matter, Nikitas?" she asked him.

"Nothing," he said, not looking at her.

"Why did you buy all those papers?"

"Because of the crime."

"What crime, Nikitas? A man killed his daughter?"

"No."

"Did some brothers kill each other over a legacy?"

"No."

"A lunatic escaped from the asylum?"

"No."

"Well then, tell me. What crime?"

"Somebody I know killed a deputy yesterday right in the middle of town."

"Heavens! How is it you know him, my son?"

"He had a pickup truck and once in a while he made deliveries for me."

"What party did this deputy belong to?"

"Communist."

"Then he had it coming to him."

"Keep still, Mama. What was this man guilty of? He'd come here to make a speech, and Yango, the guy I know, sneaked up and hit him from behind."

His mother put on her old-fashoned spectacles and leaned over to look at the newspaper. First she studied the photographs and then she spelled out the headline: "Traf-fic ac-ci-dent. EDA dep-u-ty in-jur-ed . . .

"Eat, child, and don't worry about the world. When it's not the *bougatsa* you're eating, you don't have to worry if it's burning in the oven."

Nikitas wiped his mouth and got up from the table.

"I made the kind of cake you like," said his mother. "I'll go get you a piece."

Instead of waiting, he went out. The house was too

small for him. He went back to the shop and worked absentmindedly till evening, speaking to no one. When he got home again, his sister was there. His mother, worried about him, must have asked her to come.

"I don't know what to do," Nikitas said to her. "I'm in a dilemma." He explained the affair to her.

"Are you mad?" his sister said. "Do you want my husband to lose his civil-service job? I suppose it was you who provided my dowry? I got married without anybody's help. We're getting along fine. And now you . . . Forget it. Do you hear me, Nikitas? And besides, it served him right. Don't believe what you read. The ERE * is a great party. It doesn't sponsor crimes."

"Oh, stop it! You bore me."

His sister left sputtering threats. What wounded him most was that she called him an epileptic. He had never been an epileptic. Once when he was a little fellow, he'd had a convulsion because some children in the neighborhood had hit him on the head. He had never been an epileptic. Never.

He lay down to sleep. Though he had done less work than usual today, he was worn out. His mind kept running on and on; he turned off the light so his mother would think he was asleep. He saw the world divided into two hemispheres. On one was written "Go"; on the other, "Don't go." Rotating faster and faster, the two merged and became one. The deputy left a wife and two children. He was a doctor, a professor, a cultivated man. Why did that lout Yango do it! He fell asleep and he saw Yango delivering furniture and killing people with it. Since the furniture belonged to him, then he, Nikitas, was responsible. Then it was noon in his dream and he had stretched out in his shop for a nap, as he often did when he was working too hard. Suddenly the door opened and there stood Yango, threatening him with a pistol. "Choose a coffin that suits you." And he

* The National Radical Union Party, right wing.

pointed to the coffins that Nikitas had been polishing that day. "Traitor!"

"Why, Yango, why?"

"Come on. Step on it! Faster! One, two, three!"

He woke up with a start. He was streaming with sweat. At last it was morning. He shaved, put on his Sunday clothes, and presented himself "voluntarily" to the Investigator, to make his deposition.

From that time on, his shadow appeared to proliferate. No matter where he went, two men followed him. Then a car with no license plates turned up. He deliberately took long walks in the center of town. The car was always twenty or thirty yards behind him. Meanwhile some lawyers, members of the Peace Committee, contacted him. They persuaded him that without his help nothing could be done. His deposition in itself, they told him, had torn the case for the "traffic accident" to shreds; he had to stick to it and not give in. For the good of Greece. For everybody's good.

Yes, he agreed. But how was he going to live? He was afraid to go back to his shop. He walked around all day, as if there were no safe place to sit down. They'd got one deputy, they'd almost got another, and they certainly wouldn't have any qualms about him! It was a question of time. Now he was determined. He wasn't an easy nut to crack.

Then the Public Prosecutor had summoned him. He had an appointment with him this morning. Leaving his house, he made a wide detour through the Old City to shake off whoever might be shadowing him. He had a coffee at the Skopos Café, where he used to play backgammon. As he rose to leave, he looked carefully up and down the street. For the first time the anonymous car was not in sight. He walked the length of Ayiou Dimintriou Street and skirted the Evangelistria Cemetery to reach the avenue leading to the Prosecutor's office. Taking the right-hand sidewalk, he mingled with students and with priests who were also studying theology. Arriving at Syntrivani Square, he was suddenly confronted by a large crowd and an array of police cars crammed with helmeted policemen, the rifles between their thighs resembling enormous Easter candles. He asked what was going on and was told that the deputy's hearse would shortly be passing by. He swelled with pride at having been the first to lift the stone and reveal the vermin swarming underneath. And reassured by the presence of so many policemen, he started to cross the circle of Syntrivani Square.

He was walking rapidly along when suddenly a truck pulled up beside him. Two crab-like hands reached out, grabbed him by the collar of his jacket, and dragged him against the side of the vehicle. The first blow made him scream, "Oh, I've been hit!" The Syntrivani fountain seemed to be spurting jets of scarlet blood, turning green, blue, white, and red, like the Water Ballet at the International Fair. A second blow opened a crack in the earth, and then all was darkness.

He came to in an empty ward with forty beds, himself the only patient. There was a hospital smell. He saw a chart hanging at the foot of his bed; he knew that must be the fever chart. He felt a weight on his head. Cautiously he raised his hands and discovered an ice bag. But what he couldn't figure out was why all the other beds were empty. If he'd had someone to talk to, he would have found out what had happened.

His head ached. Maybe there was a fracture. But if so, wouldn't he be bleeding? No, he'd got off lightly. But for how long? And suppose this was the prison infirmary? Suppose everyone had forgotten him? Suppose everyone was happy to know he was locked up there?

He began to shout. No one came. He tried to stand but he quickly saw this was impossible. He dragged himself on his knees as far as the window, and looked at the hospital garden, which was teeming with policemen. With a great effort he crawled to the bed. As he lay down, the ice bag almost fell off. He ached all over. Now he recalled the two hands which had lashed out of the truck like the tentacles of an octopus. Whose were they? And why hadn't the police interfered? Had the hearse gone by? His bones ached; had he been trampled by the crowd? Perhaps his sister was right, he shouldn't have talked. Nonsense. He was alive, wasn't he? Nobody could shut him up. He might not be a hero but he was very touchy where honor was concerned.

The door creaked open as in a horror movie. He heard authoritative voices. Then a man, followed by his body-guard, entered and, introducing himself as the General, sat down on Nikitas's bed.

"Well, sonny, how did you fall and hurt yourself?"

"Are you kidding, General?"

He saw that the General was looking him over, casting an ironic glance at the turban of ice covering his head. He saw the wrinkles at the corners of his lips, clothespins on a sarcastic line, holding up the dirty laundry that tumbled from his mouth. Nikitas bravely propped himself up higher in the bed.

The General bent over him, pretending to be searching vainly for a serious wound. "You're in fine shape!"

In spite of the ice bag, Nikitas could feel the blood rising to his head. He couldn't believe that the General, the "immune leader," had come expressly to bait him. Here he was, not knowing where, alone in a ward with forty beds, and to make matters worse, people came and made fun of him. No, that was too much. He stared at the General, who stared back with thorny eyes, trying to penetrate his soul. Neither spoke. Finally the General got up, went to the window and opened it, "to let in a little fresh air," accompanying these words with a gesture suggesting that only thus could he clear the fog out of Nikitas's brain.

Then, approaching him with the elastic tread of an old fox, he tapped him condescendingly on the shoulder. "And to think you're one of our boys. How could you do such a thing?"

Nikitas understood. He had a *koumbaros,* an officer on the police force, and the General certainly knew it. But he couldn't help it if all his kith and kin were on Yango's side. He, Nikitas, knew the truth, and he also knew that unless he made it public, it would weigh on him like a stone the rest of his life.

"Well," the General said as he went out, "in good time you'll go back to your work and your little shop. If I were you, I'd forget the whole business. We're even going to find you a better house."

He closed the door, leaving behind a bunch of thistles and a frost of fear because nothing specific had been said. A nurse came in to change the ice, and then the medical examiner—the one who had maintained that Z. had not been wounded by a blow with a club but by his "fall on the pavement"—entered. After taking Nikitas's temperature—100 degrees—he examined the wound on his head, concluding that it was nothing very serious, that in a day or two he'd be able to go back to work, provided, of course, he cooperated.

"Which means?" asked Nikitas.

"You know better than I."

"Which means they didn't hit me?"

"You slipped and fell."

"Then I'll take off this ice bag."

"No, for God's sake, don't take it off!"

"There are only two possibilities, sir. Either they hit me, in which case I need the ice bag, or they didn't hit me, in which case I don't need it."

The doctor too had managed to inject him with the anguish of doubt. "They can't all take me for a lunatic," thought Nikitas. He was dozing off when a third visitor arrived. It was the Public Prosecutor, the one he was going to to testify when he had been struck down in the street.

"How many years have you been in the party?" he asked abruptly.

"What party?"

"The left."

"I was never in the left party, or in any other party. If it's absolutely necessary for me to belong to something, well then, it's the PAOK soccer club."

In the newspapers the next day he read the account of his accident: "The theory of a criminal assault does not stand up. Despite the man's assertions, he fell on the street; he was not attacked. The student who picked him up made a formal statement before the Public Prosecutor: 'I was walking along when I heard a noise. Turning around, I saw a man stretched out on the street . . .' The medical examiner later found him smoking and reading the newspapers. Moreover, his sister, Roxani Koryvopoulou, maintains: 'My brother was not attacked. He must have stumbled, and fallen.' And his mother: 'Ever since he was a little boy, he's been telling tall stories.'"

He clutched his head; he was losing his mind. It was now that he was suffering from delusions. They were all conspiring against him, trying to show him up as a mythomaniac. So no one had struck him? He'd fallen down in a kind of epileptic fit? That was certainly what his sister had intimated. Of course, she hadn't dared to assert it openly because it might have been damaging to herself as well. But Nikitas was sure that was what she meant. His head was whirling. He skimmed through the newspaper again, and among the miscellaneous items on the last page he read the following: "It is alleged that the two doctors who first examined him and reported lesions induced by a blow have been under extreme pressure since yesterday to retract their diagnosis. It should be stressed that certain eminent physicians at the university have cast doubt on the judgment of these doctors, describing them as 'second-rate.'"

Then he saw her. Yes, it was his mother. She'd come, bringing some fruit and other delicacies. She'd made him a spinach pie, his favorite dish.

"Now then, what's all this about, my boy? What a thing to happen! Everyone in the neighborhood sends you greetings. Our house is like a railroad station. Newspaper reporters, photographers, you can't imagine . . . But tell me, my dear son, prop of my old age, what's this they're saying—that someone attacked you? You who wouldn't even hurt a fly! Why did they have to come and tell *me* that? I told them it wasn't possible, that no one could have anything against my Nikitas. Once, while you were a little boy, you slipped and fell—do you remember? You thought you'd been hit on the head. Remember? You thought the kids in the neighborhood had done it because you had a beautiful new ball. They ran after you and you fell down and hurt your head. You came home and cried in my arms. My poor Nikitas! The truth is that nobody hit you, either then or now. You don't want to make us the laughing stock of the neighborhood, do you? Say you slipped! So we can have some peace. Since these are the people who have the power why don't you cooperate? Or are you maybe with the others—the dirty Reds, who butchered my father-in-law in '45? No, it's not possible; you never were. I told them you only cared about two things: your work and the soccer club. They keep coming and asking me about you. They want photographs of you when you were a little boy. And I tell them: 'He didn't have any appetite when he was little. I had to tell him fairy tales to make him eat.' When I told you the story of the wolf and the sheep, your mouth would open wide, and I'd quickly put a mouthful of food in it. 'Ah, so he likes fairy tales?' they said. 'He's always liked them,' I told them. You're all I have, my boy. Think of my rheumatism. And just when I was getting ready to go to Eleftheres with Mrs. Koula for the sand baths! If I don't get there this summer, I'll suffer all winter long. Do you want me to be ill when the rainy season starts? You know it rains all the time in Salonika. Why can't you just say you slipped and fell so we can all have some peace."

"Who sent you here, Mama? My sister?"

"I came of my own accord, my son. I don't want you to go to prison."

"Prison? That's where I'm going to send those culprits. Please, Mama, I beg you, stop talking, I'm dizzy."

"Come, eat a little fruit."

"I don't want any."

"Try to think of me—your poor mother."

"I've had enough. You're all trying to make it look as if I were a nut. I've not had a second's peace since I got here. And now . . ."

The mother went out; the sister came in.

"So we make statements to the press, do we?" he shouted. "We do everything to protect our own little interests."

"What do you want to do? Break up my home?"

She was dressed in a pink printed cotton dress and was carrying a smart handbag. Everything about her bearing and dress made it clear that she was utterly unlike her brother.

"You've always been cheeky," she said to him. "And you've always despised me."

"No, it's you who despise me! You're two years older than I am, and you've always treated me like a kid."

"Tell me, did you ever take me anywhere? You chased after girls, while I stayed home embroidering. And whenever one of your friends asked about me, you'd lose your temper. You were so afraid one of them might get a crush on me. How I used to long for our father! How much more understanding he would have been. He would have allowed me to go to the movies. But you! Well, I got married, I made a home, I'm very happy, and I won't let anyone wreck my life. I'll say again what I've said a thousand times before. You're nothing but a liar. You've let yourself be taken in by those bums!"

"Tell me, Roxani . . . But first calm down. Sit down."

"Why haven't you shaved today? Do you want to make it look like you've been mistreated, that they've tortured you?"

"Sit down," said Nikitas gently. "That's right. And don't, please don't cry."

She took a handkerchief from her purse and wiped her eyes.

"Now tell me: if someone came to you and announced that he was going to commit suicide that very evening, wouldn't you do anything to save him? Wouldn't you notify his family? Wouldn't you notify the police? Well, that's all I did. I told what I knew, to make their task easier for them."

"Whose task? The Reds'?"

"Can't you understand? I mean the police! So they could do their duty. And the judges. All of them."

"The only people you'll help will be those bums, the Communists. Take Nikos the party organizer in our neighborhood. Did you ever see him do any good? He only causes people trouble. Those are the ones who have influenced you, I know. The moment you made your deposition, you fell into their trap. I hate them."

"Roxani, either you don't know me at all or you're raving!"

"You're the one who's raving!"

Just then someone burst into the ward and introduced himself as a newspaper reporter from Athens. He was young, blond, alert.

"I will tell you what happened to my brother," said Roxani, turning to him still upset and tearful. "You reporters put too much nonsense in your papers."

"Were you present at the accident?"

"No, but that doesn't matter. My brother was not the victim of any attack. Any one of three things might have happened: either he stumbled, or he felt dizzy and fell, or else he was attacked by some Reds to stir up trouble."

Nikitas winked at the reporter, to indicate that it was better to let his sister go on talking.

"So that's what you think happened?" the reporter commented.

"I'm absolutely convinced of it," Roxani went on. "The ERE has no criminals. Mr. Karamanlis wants peace, progress, stability. The troublemakers are somewhere else."

"Then, if I'm not mistaken, you're supporting the contention of the police that your brother has gone mad. The police don't have any evidence on which to base their charge. Do you?"

"What kind of evidence?"

"A few witnesses, for instance, who could certify that they saw your brother stumble and fall?"

"No."

"Then how can you claim he's crazy?"

"I'm not claiming he's crazy? On the contrary. I just think he's wicked and wants to drive everybody else crazy with his obstinacy."

"Obstinacy about what?"

"About insisting that someone hit him."

Nikitas, losing patience at this point, broke into the conversation. "Roxani, you haven't told the reporter everything. You haven't told him, for example, that you're a member of the women's branch of the ERE in Forty Churches, and that your husband is in the civil service."

"I certainly do belong to the ERE and I'm proud of it!" she exclaimed, turning beet-red and snatching up her handbag. Without saying another word, she stalked out of the ward, slamming the door.

"I can't take any more," Nikitas said, leaning back against his pillow. "My nerves are going to crack. This has been going on for three days. When people think you're crazy, you end up believing it yourself. But I think they're crazy and I'm the only one who's got any sense. They're trying to convince people that I don't know what I'm saying, that I keep changing my story to suit my interests. But I have no interests. They have. I don't *think* they are crazy, I *know* they are. So I can be at peace. But since I've been cooped up in bed here without being able to stir, my nerves are finally giving out. And then I've these horrible headaches, right here; they come on me like an electric shock. I hate having to stay in bed. I'm pining away in here all by myself. I know the more determined I am, the more determined they're going to be. Would you mind looking in the hall to see if the policeman is still there? The idea that he might leave his post and give the others a chance to come in and murder me gives me nightmares."

The reporter rose and opened the door. There was no one outside.

"You see! He's gone again! And I told them not to leave me alone! By the way, how did you get in?"

"With the yoghurt."

"With the what?"

"I arrived when the yoghurt man was making his delivery. The guard opened the gate for him, and I came in at the same time. 'What do you want?' he asked me. I showed him my press card. 'It's forbidden,' he said sleepily. I pretended I didn't hear him and followed the yoghurt man into the hospital. The guard was too lazy to run after me, and anyway it was dark. I stumbled on a police sergeant sitting in a chair without moving a muscle. When I asked him if I could get through, he didn't answer me. For a minute I thought he'd had a heart attack. I went over to him and tapped him on the shoulder. He hardly moved his head. Here in Salonika I've noticed that people are slow and heavy and wary with their words. In the end, I got through. I wanted to see you; to get first-hand information. I'll be sending a story to my paper this evening."

"Write the truth, please," said Nikitas. "I can't bear it any longer. The last thing I want, write this, is to harm my family—my mother and sister. I was a kid when my father died, and since then I've had full responsibility for the two women. But for the first time I've come to understand what 'conscience' means. It would have been immoral not to go to the Investigator, isn't that so? I didn't sleep the night I made the decision. But once I'd made up my mind, nothing could change it. I'm a mule in such matters. But I feel fear all around me. Especially in the night with the light on, I'm frightened. I'm suspicious of every murmur, every noise. I feel, write this, like a soldier abadoned in some huge barracks, with nobody but the barracks guard for company, while all the other soldiers have been killed in battle. And for their spilled blood I must stay alive, to justify them. The

Public Prosecutor, who was here yesterday, sitting right there where you're sitting now, asked me to describe Yango, because Yango had told him he didn't know me, that he'd never seen me. I only said two words to him and he said: "To think that Yango went on for hours trying to convince me that he didn't know you. In just two words you've persuaded me that you *do* know each other.' You understand what I'm trying to say? Nothing can stop the truth, it will win out in the end. The General can't stand me. What did I ever do to him? Why shouldn't I reveal anything that might be of help in tracking down the guilty parties? Didn't I do right? No. I'm neither a dope addict nor a drug fiend. Twice, as a boy, I was caught stealing. I was hungry. Since then my police record has been spotless. They're trying to foul me up. Well, let them try! There is no retreat. Write that I'm not a Communist. I never was. Or anything else. I've never been mixed up in politics. The proof is that I've been on the voting lists for three months and—I'm ashamed to say—I still haven't voted. That was my mistake—not knowing who governed us. Also, I shouldn't have gone to the headquarters of the party Z. belonged to. That's how they labeled me a Red. But where are we living—in Al Capone's Chicago, as one local paper wrote? They grab you in the middle of the street, knock you out, and then spread the rumor that you did it yourself! I'm a Greek citizen, I have the right to expect police protection. I can't trust the law till the guilty parties are found. . . . No, please don't go. Don't leave me alone. The night will stifle me. And the guard has gone. I'm lonely. Stay. I know you have work, but you did want me to talk. Well, I'm talking. I've grown old in the last few days! Don't leave, I'm talking. Why were they following me? Is there some organized crime syndicate? If there is, I haven't a chance. I knew from the start that I'd end up like Z. The minute I left the Investigator's office, I went straight to the Public Prosecutor to ask for protection. He wasn't in his office, and I left a message with his secretary, who looked at me oddly. Everybody looks at me oddly lately. Except you. You're the only one who seems to think I'm normal. As for the others, I might as well be a leper. Stay a little longer. We could have some coffee. There's a bell for the nurse, but it's out of order. I'm absolutely alone. Do you understand? I hope that tomorrow or the day after I'll be able to get out and get back to my work. I should finish some coffins—how do you like that?—I'm already late on the delivery. How one's life can change from one day to the next! It's strange. The man I was yesterday hasn't any connection with the man I am today. And tomorrow I know I'll be another man still. And I forget. I forget all those stupid little things I used to care about. Well, that's enough. I've worn you out. I understand. It's only my mother I can't understand. How could she? I love her, even though I don't understand her any more. My sister and I never got along. I don't mind. But my mother, how could she?"

The reporter got up, put his pad in his pocket, and opened the door. There was a policeman in the corridor.

"He's back," he told Nikitas. "You needn't be afraid. I'll be going now. Thanks for everything. Get the Athens *Morning News* tomorrow. You're quite a guy."

"I'm so broke I can't even buy a newspaper," Nikitas said.

"Take this."

And he left a bill on the nighttable. Nikitas wanted to protest, but he didn't have the strength. His dizziness suddenly returned and he was sinking. He saw the reporter go off as in a dream.

In two days he was permitted to leave the hospital. On his way out he got confused in the corridors. Opening a door at random, he stumbled on Vango, the pederast, lying in bed with his leg in a cast. He was reading a newspaper. Nikitas had never seen him before, and he did not recognize him from the photographs in the newspapers. He excused himself hastily and closed the door.

But Vango recognized Nikitas. If it hadn't been for his cast, he'd have run after him and eliminated, in some dark dead-end corridor, this second serpent of evil.

Chapter 3

The medical examiner bent down and looked at the cast.

"An old fracture in the heel," Vango told him.

"Take off the cast," he ordered the nurses.

No fracture, either in the heel or in the ankle.

"Let me see his papers," the doctor said.

They brought him the admission slip, which stated that Vango had entered the hospital for a heart ailment. And here he was, being treated for a fractured heel. A nonexistent one at that. It was beginning to look suspicious. A few smiles, a few hints. The medical examiner caught on.

"Fine," he said to Vango. "You've done your time here. Now get over to the Investigator's."

The lawyers had set this in motion. They had sent the medical examiner because Vango had been hospitalized on the sole authority of the police physician. This time the medical examiner could not keep silent or cover up for anyone. He had to send Yango's accomplice to the Investigator; the machinations of the police had kept him hidden all these many days.

The morning after the assassination, Vango, as agreed, went "voluntarily" to the police station. From there he'd been dispatched straight to the city hospital with a fraudulent medical certificate. He was placed in strict isolation. The point was to prevent his giving evidence at the same time as Yango, for the Investigator would have had no trouble getting them to contradict each other. The strategy had in fact succeeded, since only now, after a week had passed and after Yango had already been jailed, was Vango brought to the Investigator's office.

The only trouble was that he didn't have a lawyer. Yango's lawyer, realizing the rottenness of the whole affair, had withdrawn from the case, pleading "overwork." Another lawyer was found, and Vango was closeted with him for hours, getting primed, the Investigator having granted him a forty-eight-hour delay to prepare his defense.

". . . Inasmuch as the said forty-eight-hour period has expired today, May 30, 1963, at 5:30 P.M., the abovementioned accused has appeared before the magistrates, in order to reply to their interrogation, in the presence of his lawyer, and after he has taken cognizance of all items in the file."

"Have you ever been charged before?"

"Yes, I've been convicted for rape, illegal bearing of arms, burglary, and slander. That is to say, four times."

"You are hereby accused of complicity with the accused Yango Gazgouridis, in the premeditated murder of Z. in Salonika on May 22, and in the intentional infliction of contusions and abrasions on the person of Georgios Pirouchas, in such a manner as to cause grave bodily injury and endanger the life of the said person, and in any case to deprive him of the normal use of his faculties for a long period of time; all of which acts evince on your part an exceptionally aggressive and provocative spirit toward society. Have you anything to say in your defense?"

Fortunately his lawyer had told him beforehand what the charges against him were, because Vango would never have understood. This wasn't Greek; it was some language created for the express purpose of bewildering him. First of all, he didn't like the Investigator: he was young, he looked honest and alert. He wasn't the usual corrupt magistrate. That's what worried Vango most. His lawyer had warned him, "He'll get you into a tight spot, and if you want to get out of it, you'll have to be slippery as an eel."

His interrogation lasted nine hours. He told him the story of his life. He was born and bred in Salonika, since 1931 he had been living in Toumba. He'd never left except to go to the army, prison, and camps. He knew every stone in Toumba, and he loved it. The neighborhood was poor, so was he, but the people were wonderful. The government neglected them, but even so, he didn't hate the government, he was a good Greek. The only other times he'd been away from Toumba were when he had to go to the hospital. He had heart trouble. Yes, he had a heart condition. He couldn't stand emotional excitement. He might even collapse during this interrogation. No, he hadn't been to school very much; only as far as the fourth grade. Then he had to go to work because his father was dead and he had younger brothers and sisters. He'd done all kinds of jobs. He'd always been hard-working. Of course, it had been his dream to study. If he'd studied, he wouldn't be in the scrape he was in now, being accused of absolutely imaginary things—as far as he could understand the charges from the reading of the indictment. If he'd studied, he'd know how to distinguish good from evil, and he wouldn't have fallen into all the traps that had been laid for him; these had cost him a lot of his life. And then there was the Occupation. A harsh time, with the hunger and black bread. Two uncles of his had starved to death before his very eyes. They'd spread their legs wide apart and dropped dead just like that in the middle of the street. That year there weren't even any birds in the sky. The Stukas chased them all away. He used to set bird traps hear the brook in Toumba, but there wasn't a wing in the air. So as not to suffer the same fate as his uncles, he joined the German labor squads, just to earn his daily bread. But the work was too heavy and he was too weak, so he had to stop. The Germans arrested him and, without a trial, shut him up for thirteen months in the Pavlos Melas concentration camp, outside Salonika. He stayed there until the last of the Germans departed after blowing up the port, and the Liberation armies arrived. It was only natural for him to join the liberators. First he got mixed up in ELAS *—at the time he had no idea what it meant. Later he was in charge of the National Mutual Aid Society of Toumba, and he wound up as the second administrative secretary of EPON.** He got caught up in the wild unrest of that period, and since he'd come straight from the concentration camp, he hadn't had time to learn who was who. When he began to see more clearly and to suspect their real aims, when he saw with his own eyes that the dirty Commies were planning to sell Greece to the enemy, he resigned. That happened in 1946. After the elections and before the plebiscite on the King's return. He didn't resign out of fear that they were going to lose. He resigned out of a feeling of disgust and hatred. But this didn't prevent them from arresting him when he went for his military service in 1949. He was sent to Makronissos, along with all the Commies. There he found himself among those with whom he'd collaborated in the past and who had never really forgiven him for bolting. How long was he going to be hunted? He was accused of being a Red and subjected to all the tortures inflicted on the Communists—while the Reds charged him with being a traitor and a stoolpigeon, planted with them to denounce them. He was rejected on all sides. Luckily, just at that point the saving declaration-of-repentance forms came along, and by signing that he "disowned and execrated Communism and all its by-products," he was able to escape from the hell. And if anybody wanted proof that he was a good fellow and didn't wish any harm to anyone, all he had to say was this: they'd made

* The military branch of the Partisan front; the equivalent of FLN.
** The youth movement affiliated with the Partisan EAM front.

him a proposition to stay on at Makronissos, be a tor-
turer or political instructor, and he had refused. Yes, he
—Vango—had turned it down, even though he knew that
when he got out he'd be unemployed. He'd turned it
down because he couldn't bear to see other people
suffering. Later on, he was "cleared" and got his honorable discharge from the army. He at last had understood
that it was better not to get involved in parties and political organizations. Enough. He'd mede a vow and kept
it. That's what he meant when he said a little while ago
that if he had had some education he would have known
better. He had wasted ten years of his life and gained
nothing. Had anybody so much as thanked him? His
only decorations were slipped discs, heart ailments,
scars, and weaknesses. And everything they said about
him was lies, such as that he had been president of the
ERE youth organization in Toumba, or again—this was
unheard of—that he belonged to a league—what did you
call it?—Guarantors of the Constitutional King of the
Hellenes?

Yango and he were neighbors and *koumbaros:* Vango's brother had been best man at Yango's sister's marriage. That's how they became friends. Of course, Yango
had faults, but as the proverb goes, "Love your friends,
faults and all." Wasn't that right? Who doesn't? But
Yango was a good guy. And he owned a truck. What did
Vango have? Nothing but a brush. That was how he
earned his livelihood, as a house painter. He went to the
Parthenon Café, where all the house painters gather,
drank coffee and waited till a contractor came along.
With a brush planted in the pail beside him, he waited
for hours on end. Some days he'd eat, others he
wouldn't. Whereas Yango had security. His truck. For
Vango this meant power. One has to face it, the fellow
who gets respect in this world is the one with the where-
withal. If you haven't got it, you get trampled on like a
slug.

Finally he got to the point. Just as in telling his life
story, he began at the very beginning, so now, to tell

about that Wednesday, he had to start all over again
from the beginning. The previous night, he hadn't been
able to sleep. His foot hurt; he'd strained it two weeks
before on a construction job, while painting. It hadn't
bothered him before. But that evening it ached, because
of the dampness. And so, the next morning—Wednesday
morning, it was drizzling if he remembered rightly—he
headed straight for the outpatient clinic of the central
Salonika hospital to find out what was the matter. A
sprain? A cramp? Something more serious? People were
lining up. He'd got there very early but they didn't finish
with him until about 11:30. By then it was too late to go
to work, so he headed for Toumba. They had told him
to come back in a few days to get the results of the X-
rays. That's why he'd stayed in the cast in the hospital
for so long. Yes, he knew now! There was a crack in the
bone. He had taken a nap that afternoon and at 5:10
that evening had gone to the usual café, had taken his
post to see if he couldn't perhaps rustle up some job for
the following day. He couldn't have been there a quarter of an hour when he got the urge—if they'd excuse the
expression—to piss. He'd left the café to go to the public
toilets up the block.

"There is a toilet in the Parthenon. Why didn't you
use it? Why did you decide to go to the public urinals
on Balanou Street?"

Well, he hadn't gone to piss, he now explained to the
Investigator. He suddenly remembered it was Wednesday, the shops were closed and no one was going to turn
up with a job. So he decided to go home, that was why
he left, not expressly to piss. Because of course there
was a toilet in the café too; though it was true that the
proprietor grumbled every time the house painters used
his privy, and always made the same remark: "Don't you
have any crappers at home?" No, that's right, he was on
his way to Dikastirion Square, where the Ano Toumba
bus terminal is.

"When—and please write it down the way I say it—
passing the public urinals, I got the urge to go. It was

probably because of the smell. Also, I have weak kidneys. All right, that's another story. Anyway, when I came out of the urinals—I know the old lady in charge of them, Aunt Ammonia, as we call her in Toumba—who do you think I saw sitting outside a tavern right across Balanou Street? That's right, my *koumbaros*, Yango himself. 'Hi there, Yango,' I say to him, 'couldn't you find somewhere else to sit? A place that smells a little better?' He motioned me to sit down at his table and invited me to drink some retsina with him. He said he often went to that tavern because it had good retsina. His kamikazi was parked nearby; it was Wednesday, you see, and everything was closed in Kapani Market. Then I got the bright idea that when we'd finished our drinks Yango might offer to take me to Toumba in his truck since he didn't have to work, and that way I'd save the price of the bus ticket. 'Yango,' I told him right off, 'I don't have any money.' 'Don't worry about that, Vango,' he said. 'The drinks are on me.' That's the way he is. We stayed quite a while talking about the in-laws, we drank about three quarts of retsina and had bread and hard-boiled eggs. 'Man,' I said to him, 'this retsina's got a kick!' 'Go on,' he says, 'it's like water.' Yango can't hold his liquor, and I'm worse. He paid the bill—sixteen or twenty drachmas about. Then we left, because some gypsies had come in with their noisy brats. I was afraid we might catch some of their fleas. Besides, I can't stand gypsy women. Whenever I see one, I choke.'"

And so from there they'd gone to One-Armed Koulou's tavern around 6:30. And why in the hell did they order ouzo? It's very bad to mix drinks like that. They'd gone through five or six carafes of ouzo and . . .

"Yango began to cry because he couldn't make ends meet to buy out his partner Aristidis's share of the truck, and I began to cry too, and I consoled him. Yango paid sixty-two or sixty-three drachmas and we climbed aboard the three-wheeler to go back home, both of us dead-drunk. Someone at the joint came out and said: 'Listen, guys, you shouldn't be on the road in that condition, you might have an accident.' But we didn't give a damn what he said. Yango got up on the seat, and I lay down in the back, just what I wanted. I put my hands behind my head so I wouldn't feel the jolting, and fell asleep. No, I didn't really fall asleep, I just closed my eyes, out of contentment. I don't know how long it was after we'd started off when I heard a crash that shook the whole truck. At first I thought we'd been knocked into a ditch or something, it was such a violent jolt. Before I had time to get up and see what was happening, two characters jumped into the back of the truck and began punching me. 'Hey, what's going on?' I shouted, keeping my hands in front of my face for protection. I yelled to Yango to stop. But he could not hear me, with all the racket the motor was making. I didn't have any idea what part of town we were in. I took the pommeling with stoic patience—isn't that how you say it? I didn't have any kind of weapon. How could I buy a revolver when I didn't even have the money to buy a water pistol for my nephew? Without knowing how, I found myself under the cart, shaking my head so that the nightmare would go away. When I looked around I recognized the Philipos Pottery Shop, where they sell flowerpots and jugs and things. Then an old man came over, like in a fairy tale, and pointed to the street that gives on Aristotelous Square, where all the outdoor movies are. Since I couldn't understand what he wanted to say, he motioned for me to follow him. Walking along, I felt ashamed of the way I looked and I wanted to cover my face with my hands. By the waterfront, near the Hotel Mediterranée, there were limousines and a crowd of people in evening clothes, all the high society, while we poor buggers—oh well, the kind old man pointed out the red sign of the first-aid station. I went in, a male nurse examined me, put some iodine on my wounds and bandaged them, and by the way here's the slip he gave me—" And Vango laid the slip with the hospital letter-head on the Investigator's table. "I don't have a watch, so I don't know what time it was when I got back home.

I wanted to go and see what had become of Yango, but I was so befuddled with drink and the pain was so bad that I fell asleep on the couch with my clothes on. In the morning I went out and bought the newspaper to see if our adventure was mentioned. And what did I see? Yango's picture spread all over the front page! The story said he'd killed some deputy by the name of Z. with his truck. First time I ever heard the name. I roared with laughter. I didn't know any more about Z. than I knew about the meeting that had taken place the night before in the center of town. The paper was full of a lot of other crap of the same kind, and God only knows what crocked schemes they were trying to cook up. Then and there I decided it was my duty to go to the police station and tell the truth as I knew it. I told it all to the police captain, not leaving out a single thing, and he turned me over to the officer on duty. Ever since then I've been in custody as an accomplice to the crime, that's what they say; and I haven't seen a single human being except my lawyer."

"So you didn't know Z.?"

"No. I didn't know him."

"Had you any grudge against him?"

"No, none."

"Had you any reason to kill Z.?"

"No."

"Not no," intervened Vango's lawyer. "My client means 'No, I did not kill Z.' "

Both answers were noted in the minutes.

Vango noticed the Investigator toying with a metal letter opener, looking at it first on one side, then on the other. After a long silence he raised his head, looked at Vango with a broad, open smile expressing boundless confidence, and said to him: "Everything you've said fits perfectly with what Yango told me, and since you two haven't seen each other since the evening of your excursion, I believe you are telling the truth. Nevertheless, in your statement there was one sentence that has given me much food for thought. If my idea should prove correct, then I must direct my entire investigation along that line. I think you are a Communist."

"For God's sake, Mr. Investigator! After all I've suffered at their hands! And I haven't told you everything about Makronissos!"

"Your past doesn't interest me. In any case, it's easy to check up on it. What interests me is what you think today, and from a single sentence, which probably slipped out unawares, I conclude that you're with the Reds."

"What sentence, Mr. Investigator?"

"I've written it down. Here it is: 'By the waterfront, near the Hotel Mediterranée, there were limousines and a crowd of people in evening clothes, all the high society, while we poor buggers—oh well . . .' At that point you stopped short; you knew you had unintentionally betrayed yourself."

"I swear I hate the Communists."

"Your oaths don't interest me."

"I hate them! I only have to see one in front of me and I'm ready to . . ."

"Don't try to justify yourself. We judge by actions. We want proof. A sentence like the one you allowed to escape couldn't be uttered by anyone but a Communist. No one but a Communist could even conceive such a thought."

Vango was furious. Before his lawyer had time to stop him, he blurted out: "I'm a member of an organization whose aim is to fight Communism in every possible way. It's called the League of Former Combatants and Victims of the National Resistance of Northern Greece. I can show you my card."

"Give it to me," said the Investigator.

"It's home but I can get it for you right away. Its emblem is a skull and crossbones. Autocratosaur . . ."

And so Vango went to keep Yango company in prison. The Investigator had found a trail which could lead to the powers behind the crime.

Chapter 4

He had been profoundly impressed by the confession of the principal witness for the Prosecution, after visiting him in the city hospital. "There's something shattering," the young journalist reflected, "about all these people who've somehow got mixed up in this sinister affair. Unfortunately we journalists can't report everything we see and feel, because our readers don't know all the facts. But if I ever do write up the conversation I had with Nikitas, I'll have plenty to say. An outsider like him suddenly feels his conscience rising up like a sword and striking at the beast of the Apocalypse. Yes, the Apocalypse. For days now I've been hanging around this city with its dead harbor and its anything but White Tower, and I haven't come to a single conclusion. Are the police involved? Of course they are, but to what extent?"

Meanwhile, the investigation, like an icebreaker, was forging a path through the general indifference. A few people had taken the case of the assassinated deputy to heart; the rest were not only indifferent but definitely hostile. "Just why are you Athenians always so ready to criticize us? You don't live in Salonika. You come as tourists, you find the food good and the people horrible. You like the Old City and detest the climate. You ridicule the New Theater and the film festival and then you go away, leaving an even greater void. We don't need people to judge us. We need people to come here and live with us. We want to expand!"

The young journalist understood all this, and up to a

point he found it logical. What he couldn't forgive was the way they were protecting their own class. For, of course, the people who were saying these things were members of the bourgeoisie. The others still had a long way to go before they could afford the luxury of chauvinism. For them, bread was bread, and a drachma was a drachma. The bourgeoisie refused to admit that a murder had taken place, because they were terrorized by the sudden surfacing of all this lumpenproletariat. In the evening at the Do-Re or some other café, the reporter saw people his own age—doctors, lawyers, merchants, bankers, salesmen—clam up as soon as the matter was broached. It amazed him. They refused to take sides. They wouldn't discuss it at all. But why? What was there about it that bothered them? It didn't take him long to figure it out. It was another layer of society that the case of Z. brought to the surface: the stevedores, the dock workers, the Yangos and the Vangos; the section of society that a bourgeois tries to ignore. He makes use of these people, but to him they remain invisible, without substance. Otherwise his own class would be in mortal danger. If he were to recognize that such unfortunates ought not to exist, he would have to question his own existence. The shock of their appearance at the very footlights made him evade all discussion. Z.—or to be more precise, the murder of Z.—was a stigma, a stain on the linen tablecloth. The solution was not to remove the stain but to cover it with a plate, a glass, a fork, to hide it from the lady of the house, to avoid that smile of silent accusation. So elementary.

Notwithstanding, the investigation progressed. Each turned-up card helped him play the game of solitaire. Everything fitted together. Not a discordant note. Bit by bit, the sinister story crystallized. And the credit belonged to one person alone: the inspired young Investigator. As the reporter observed, all the people involved in the case were young. Z. himself had been a tyro, he had been on the political scene no more than two years.

Once it transpired that Autocratosaur, the General,

and the entire police force were the instigators of a bull-
fight in which the sacrificial animal, pierced with deadly
banderillas, fell to its knees beneath the last thrust, the
investigation had reached a crucial point. The young reporter decided it was time for him to take action. Aware
of the dangers involved, but always bearing in mind the
example of Polk—the young American journalist during
the Civil War who had tried to reach Marko's Communist Partisans up in their mountain strongholds and
ended up instead in the muddy Gulf of Thermaique, before he had even digested the crabs (or was it lobster?)
he'd eaten at the seaside restaurant, the Luxembourg—
he threw himself resolutely into the breach. With a
Kodak, from inside his car or from some concealing
niche, he began to take secret photographs of persons
linked to the extremist quasi-governmental organizations
that flourished thanks to police connivance and the secret funds they received from the Ministry. He unearthed
names and addresses in shady dives where his flashbulb
resounded like the kiss of Judas. After all, even Judases
help hasten the catharsis.

And so the photographs piled up, in conspiratorial
darkrooms which kept their secrets (guilty moments of
his life, coins withdrawn from circulation, appreciated
only by collectors, which others would consider terra in-
cognita, moments beyond time and space, so unique we
feel like thieves), rare photographs of an oppressed life
within life, under the terrible pressure of monopolies.
He had collected some sixteen of them when his camera
was ruined. The thugs of Ano Toumba assaulted him
and smashed it to pieces. It was a miracle that he himself escaped. As for the Kodak, it died honorably, having
done its work to perfection. He took all sixteen to the
AHEPAN Hospital and showed them to Georgios Pirouchas, the deputy who had survived the disaster. (Pirouchas was the tragic figure in the story, for he had longed
to be in Z.'s place, holding that Z. had no right to die because his mission had not yet been fulfilled.) The sick

man examined them attentively, until he saw Baronissimo.

"Fine work, my boy! This is more than I dared hope!" he exclaimed. Yes, it was the same man. Pirouchas remembered every detail of that fearful night and had described his assailant to the reporter, who, with only Pirouchas's description to go on, had located the man outside his stall in the Modiano Market—a small shopkeeper with the body of a giant. To avoid being seen by Baron, the reporter had snapped him from below and his legs looked huge, out of all proportion to the rest of his body. Legs like boulders, pylons, and between them, like great swollen testicles, a basket of eggs.

The sick deputy groped for his glasses on the bedside table. He couldn't believe his eyes: there before him in a photograph was the hound who had bitten him. He pressed the reporter's hand. The feeling that he had survived by mistake had tormented Pirouchas horribly since Z.'s death. Strangely enough, he hadn't wanted to get well. Today for the first time he found strength to fight. He was the only person who could speak on behalf of his dead friend. He took his pen from the table and, with a spasm of pain which the gauze bandages around his forehead did not conceal, he began to write for the first time since his injury. On the white margin at the bottom of the photograph, under the executioner's enormous legs, he planted the grenade.

"This is my would-be assassin. I would recognize him anywhere. He attacked me first in the presence of about fifteen policemen and later in an ambulance. I owe my discovery of him to a reporter."

He fell back on his pillow. This trifling activity had completely exhausted him. He took a heart stimulant to revive him. Thus labeled, the photograph would appear on the front page of tomorrow's Athens *Morning News*. The journalists had made up for the deficiencies of the Security Police. They were the cops; the police were the robbers. But the Security Police had its tentacles everywhere. The AHEPAN Hospital, with its narrow corridors and silent separate cells, had been transformed into a labyrinth in which everyone was trying unsuccessfully to reach the lair of the Minotaur. The Security Police had got wind of the photograph. How? It was a mystery. Had they installed microphones in the walls? Had they bribed the nurses? Be that as it may, the Chief of Security Police in person visited the injured deputy only a few hours later, bringing with him photographs of individuals who might possibly have attacked him. Pirouchas examined them one by one: burglars, drug pushers, pimps, who had no connection whatever with the events, for such people defy the law openly and do not ask the protection of the police, whereas the professional thugs are another category, and they were obviously missing among the photographs.

"Unfortunately, I do not recognize any of them," said Pirouchas, handing back the photographs.

Chapter 5

At daybreak they came and routed him out of bed. "They must want to foul me up again, the louts," Baronissimo said to himself, cursing them. This time, however, instead of taking him to Mastodontosaur, they conducted him to another place in the center of town. The Chief of Security Police, who had visited Pirouchas the previous day, was there waiting for him.

"Things are looking difficult for you, Baronissimo," said the Chief. "An Athens newspaper is publishing your photograph today and saying it was you who attacked

Pirouchas. Pirouchas himself has identified you. You've got to strike back. You'll go to the AHEPAN Hospital, where he's recuperating—pavilion 4, room number 32—and you'll tell him straight from the shoulder that he doesn't know what he's talking about, that you weren't involved in any way in Wednesday's events, and whatever else comes into your thick skull."

Baronissimo nodded his head stupidly. He hated being awakened so early.

"Now pay attention," continued the Chief. "Here's the main point. You're not to go immediately. You're going to wait till ten o'clock. That's when the Athens newspapers get here on the first Olympic airplane. Then you'll go to the hospital. This will prove that you didn't know about it before, that no one told you anything. You saw your photograph on the front page; you read, or you got someone else to read you, what was written in the caption, and 'on your own'—pay close attention to that, that's the key phrase—you came to make an indignant protest. Understand?"

Baron was still nodding his head.

He went back home. His wife made him some coffee. She noticed that he was out of sorts. "Where'd you go so bright and early?" she asked.

"Business," he told her laconically.

The political opinions of his wife and his brothers were the opposite of his. But they weren't too hard on him, they knew about his financial difficulties, the trouble he had getting the license for the stall and the money he had to pay to the proprietor's widow.

Around eight o'clock Baronissimo went to the Modiano Market. He kept his eyes glued to the clock across the way and as a result made mistakes in weighing out merchandise and counting out change. At exactly ten o'clock he locked his stall and took a bus to the AHEPAN Hospital. He asked to see the deputy, Georgios Pirouchas, pavilion 4, room number 32, but was told that the doctor was with him and he'd have to wait. Someone else was waiting in the anteroom for the same reason. Not knowing it was the Investigator, Baronissimo paid no attention to him; nor did the Investigator have any idea that the colossus was Baronissimo. The nurse came to tell them they could go in.

Baronissimo made his entrance furiously protesting against the caption of his photograph published in to-day's Athens newspapers.

Pirouchas and the Investigator stared at him in amazement.

"What newspaper?"

"Some newspaper that's just come from Athens. All I know is I look like a gangster with that basket between my legs. I don't know how to read," he went on vehemently. "I never got any further than the second grade and I can just barely make out the headlines. That's why I never buy the papers. But today at ten a newspaper vendor showed me my photograph. 'I didn't know you were one of those hoodlums,' he said to me. 'What are you talking about?' I answered. 'Look at this!' He took one of the papers from the pile he had under his arm, opened it out wide, and showed me my picture. I could hardly recognize myself! First time I ever saw myself looking like such a wreck. This guy, this news vendor, has a stand at the corner of Venizelou and Egnatia Streets: I see him every morning and we say hello. Quick as a flash I rushed to my brother, who knows how to read. He advised me to go to the Security Police to see if they could tell me where to find you. So that's what I did. And here I am. And I can tell you this is the first time I've ever laid eyes on your mug, Mr. Pirouchas. And you have the nerve to say you've seen me before!"

The Investigator could scarcely conceal his agitation. He was dumbfounded by Baron's audacity. In the scene now being played he perceived a hidden, splendidly organized mechanism that functioned with clock-like precision. Except that one little spring had worked loose, which was going to spoil everything. A diabolical coincidence, of the kind that betrays otherwise perfect crimes, had upset the system. The coincidence was that, whereas ordinarily the Athens newspapers appear on the newsstands at ten o'clock, today was an exception. The Olympic plane had been delayed by unforeseen weather conditions, and the Athens papers were not yet in circulation. The Investigator knew this, because he had been asking for the Athens papers himself.

"Well, do you recognize me?" Baron persisted.

"I must have met you *somewhere*," the deputy retorted ironically.

"Take a good look at him," the Investigator counseled the sick man, "because you won't be seeing him again until the trial."

And he ordered the policemen in the corridor, Pirouchas's permanent guards, to arrest Baronissimo and take him away for questioning. The colossus burst into tears. His body shook with sobs. He blubbered like a baby.

"It's me! It's me! He recognized me!" he sobbed.

But at the door of the hospital he found himself surrounded by reporters who wanted to photograph him. He raised his hands to the heavens and arrogantly declared: "No, it's not me! He didn't recognize me. He's got things all balled up. It's not me!"

Then he asked them to give him time to pose, so he'd look his best in the photographs.

The lawyer who was defending Yango and Vango now took him on too, and asked the Investigator for a forty-eight-hour delay to prepare his client's defense. The man who appeared before the Investigator when this "delay was over," was anything but the brash and arrogant Baronissimo charged in the indictment. He seemed miserably penitent, reduced to a passport-size snapshot of himself, pitiful, discouraged.

His past was much less colorful than that of the other two. He was a small-time operator who hadn't even a license for his stall in the Modiano Market, the license was in the name of his partner, Markos Zagorianos, with whom he'd worked eight years. His stall faced Ermou Street, between the central lane and the right-hand entrace. He sold eggs, fruit, and vegetables. Markos and he had shared the profits. Markos had been a good man, he never cheated Baron. Markos—God rest his soul!—sang in the church choir and was always quoting the Bible. He must surely be in heaven. Good people like him God summons to Himself. Nevertheless, Baronissimo longed for a license of his own. He'd applied for one three years ago—at that time the General was chief of police—but his application had been turned down. Two of his cousins were known Commies, and because of that the police probably thought he was a Red too. But no, he didn't belong to any party! And did anyone think he'd asked for a license in order to open another stall? No! He'd merely asked the police for permission to share Markos's license—with the consent of the deceased—so that he could have a little security. It was as if he'd known—again he was on the verge of tears—that poor old Markos would soon be giving up the ghost. The police never told him in so many words that his request had been refused: they simply renewed the license in the name of Markos Zagorianos. And then this year, on Good Friday, Markos had a heart attack right in church, just as he was singing a hymn with all his heart and soul. The license for the stall automatically went to his heirs, his mother and his widow, Zacharo. And that's how it came about that Baronissimo was working for the two women. They were good women, religious, always dressed in black, always off to all-night vigils in the church, but they pocketed half the money. Well, why shouldn't they pocket it? Once again he tried to get the police to straighten it out, and once again the license was renewed in the name of Zagorianos's widow. And he was slaving on the job without having any contract with Zacharo. She had the right —of course she'd never do it, she was too saintly for that —but she had the right to tell him to get the hell out any moment she chose. This was the truth about his life, and how could he be in cahoots with the police when the police kept putting spokes in his wheels?

Autocratosaur? Yes, he knew him, but not very well.

He'd never belonged to Autocratosaur's organization, because it was his principle never to join any organization. They'd got acquainted because he, Autocratosaur, had taken an interest in his wretched financial situation. In what way? Well, one day Autocratosaur had come to his house and had seen what kind of foul hole he lived in, leaky ceiling and all, and said to him, "Baronissimo, I'm going to do everything I can to help you. I'm going to find you a better place to live. The whole trick is to get your name down on the waiting list. Your turn will come one day. Take the fellow who wants to work in another country. Doesn't he first have to go to the emigration service to have his name put on a waiting list? Well, that's what you've got to do, and I'll help you any way I can." Another time Autocratosaur had come and taken him to the office of the Welfare Center. Autocratosaur had a lot of connections; he was respected by the top people in society. Actually he hadn't had to push; he just described Baron's miserable circumstances to the head of the Welfare Center. That's how he was able to get an apartment in the Phoenix, one of the lower-class housing projects in Votsi. He'd never gone to his meetings or for that matter to anyone else's.

Ah, yes. He must be objective. Autocratosaur had come to his help another time. This was going to be a little harder to explain. Baron had one passion: he collected songbirds. Yes, he knew it was hard to believe of anyone with his build. In the little courtyard in back of his house he had cages full of nightingales, chaffinches, thrushes, cardinals, magpies, robins, and sparrows. Some had individual cages. But the ones that went in pairs, he kept together. They warbled and sang, it was always springtime in his court. He trapped them with nets in the woods at Seïch-Sou, where the Ogre used to hang out. He'd had trouble with the police about that. He was also very fond of pigeons. It was a shame that he didn't have enough room in his courtyard to raise them. But his sister had a little plot of land on the same street about five hundred yards away, and he'd built a dovecote there. After he'd built it, the man next door had lodged a complaint against his sister, claiming that his land was being trespassed upon. That was when Autocratosaur helped him again. How or by what means, Baronissimo didn't know; all he knew was that the neighbor stopped complaining and the subject was dropped for good. This was the time of year when his pigeons had their young. You should see them come out of their eggs—completely blind! Their mother feeds them out of her beak, and later on they get special seeds. As for the big ones, you'd never believe how much they can eat, and they drink water until they're ready to burst. My God, can they drink! Maybe the Investigator would do him the honor of passing by sometime to admire them. People say that pigeons are gentle and peace loving. It's not true! They're all out to eat each other! When you give them food, they spread their wings to cover as much space as possible and keep the others from getting near. They're very jealous. They only act sweet to each other, cooing and all that, at mating time. Had he ever killed any? Such a thought would never enter his head! He kept them just for the fun of having them. He'd often let them out of the cages and watched them flying in the blue sky, playing with each other, perching on roofs in the neighborhood, and finally they'd come back to the dovecote, to sleep in their own nests.

Yes, he'd gotten off the subject. Please to excuse him. What had he been doing the evening of Wednesday, May 22? Nothing, because the shops were closed. He had left his stall at 2:30, gone home, taken a nap, and between 7:30 and 8:00 he'd come back to the stall because he was expecting a delivery of figs from Michaniona. The bus arrived at 8:15, that's why he'd got there a little earlier. He'd ordered those figs from the best orchard in Michaniona, and he'd paid an agent to select and deliver them to his stall. He was waiting for this agent when he heard people shouting: "Go back to Bulgaria!" So he left the stall for a couple of minutes and went to see what was happening. The shouts were being drowned out by a loudspeaker, it was a terrible uproar. As he said, since he never read the newspapers he had no idea what all the fracas was about. He didn't care either. Let people knock each other's teeth out; he had better things to do. Returning to his stall, he saw that the figs had been delivered. He spread them out, moistened them, and put a few in a bag to take home. To get back home, he had to catch the Ano Toumba bus, which stopped exactly where the rumpus was. When he reached the stop, he discovered that, because of the trouble, the buses were making a detour. If anyone saw him in the area, it was while he was waiting for the bus. Then he went to Kolomvou Street to catch the bus there. Back in his own neighborhood, he stopped for a drink at Chinky's Café. It was around quarter after nine, and his pals were sitting there, drinking ouzo while the Armed Forces radio station played bouzouki songs. He passed his figs around—they're great with ouzo—and in the end nobody would let him pay for his drinks. What did they talk about? About Sunday's match.

Yango—no, he didn't know him, and he'd only met Vango at the PAOK soccer field; once or twice Vango had let him sneak in without paying when he didn't have money for a ticket. As witnesses he suggested all the people at the tavern that evening listening to the bouzouki. Pirouchas had to see him again, so he'd realize he was confusing him with someone else.

And so Baronissimo went to join Yango and Vango in jail. It was the Sunday of the big match—the first one he'd ever missed in his life. The blind baby birds would be hatching into the light; he was inconsolable not to be at his dovecote now.

Chapter 6

He felt his shoulders gradually weaken under the pressure of the material. He was just starting his career as an investigator eager for truth. But this case, for which he had been made almost wholly responsible, was coming to resemble an avalanche. The labor of investigation grew more difficult with each passing day. He was not faced with one or two guilty parties; there were dozens. Yet he could hardly indict society as a whole. In order to suceed, he must wage the battle in narrowly confined stages, win the field yard by yard, attacking the most vulnerable points first.

He was sure of one thing: the entire city was involved in the crime. Whatever stone he turned, whatever door he knocked on, he would find some thread, some link that in one way or another related to the case. He had never dreamed that so many relatively disconnected persons would converge at the same central point; that underneath this crust of legality existed an illegal mechanism, organized to perfection and functioning according to the laws of darkness.

Every contact made him feel soiled. He didn't know if he could endure it to the end. He did not fear for his life. But he could see the chasm widening between himself and the others. As the case unfolded, its thorns cut into him more and more. Every uniform hid a sleeping viper. How could such rottenness be? He preferred to eschew theoretical questions, but he was compelled to conclude that there must be something very sordid in this society if so many people had become enmeshed in a murder which, after all, might have been carried out far more simply.

It was summertime. The heat was intolerable, and made worse by the humidity of the Gulf of Salonika. He should have been on vacation, but he requested his superiors to cancel it this year; he could not go off leaving so many loose ends. He felt the need to arrive at some conclusion. Why should the illiterates, the jackals, the protozoan scum be the only ones to pay, and not the pachyderms on top?

He knew that everything depended on him. Everyone was waiting for him to snatch the snake from its lair. So enormous was the snake that, once it was out, the hole might devour the ground. The boa constrictor could not be hauled out so easily. The boa had become one with its hole, or perhaps the hole had become one with the boa.

Meanwhile Salonika was closing in, asphyxiating him. He remembered his joy at his appointment; he had imagined it to be a city. Today it seemed the narrowest of provincial towns. People started snubbing him. They found it intolerable that prominent members of society, pillars of the regime, should be branded as suspect by an insignificant young investigator. From him they required support, not accusations. The heat made the investigations unbearable. He had installed two electric fans in his office and at home he worked all night to keep up with the accelerating pace of events; he lived under such tension that he doubted if he would be able to hold out. Only his mother's presence, silently waiting for him at home every night, could renew his courage in his desperate struggle with the jungle, the monsters and mobsters he had vowed to combat to the end.

Chapter 7

The heat did not bother him in the AHEPAN Hospital. He had requested admittance more for refuge than for any medical reason. This was undoubtedly the first time in his life he had ever slept on a soft bed, between such white sheets, or been so pampered. It was like a luxury hotel. From time to time he went to see Pirouchas, who was in the same pavilion, a few doors away. But Hatzis was crushed by sadness. For the moment matters had gotten out of hand. There was nothing he could do. He'd already done all he could by jumping onto the kamikazi. Now it was time for education—which he lacked—to take over.

Yet the sadness lingered. His leader had died before his very eyes. He thought of him constantly. He had lived through Z.'s last moments; he recalled him walking down the stairs and drawing the bolt of the iron gate, a figure full of strength and beauty, with the mark of death upon him. A great wave had snatched him from his arms—arms which might have protected him, saved him. After all that, how could he recapture his taste for life? He followed every detail of the case in the newspapers. But it dragged on. They couldn't find the guiding thread. He could have told them what it was. But he was in no position to say anything.

He missed Z. He was left with a terrible void. And true to his habit of conceiving everything in images, he saw him now as the beautiful stopper on a bottle of noxious gas. The stopper had been blown off and foul odors filled the air. By his sacrifice, Z. had let the abscess burst and drain. He missed his manly gait, his coolness in the face of danger. He missed him as a person. A sword among bent daggers. A fresh breeze in the doldrums. From his window he could see the new university buildings, the dome of the observatory, and the doctors' cars in the hospital courtyard. "What is life?" he asked himself. Nothing, since it can be shattered so easily. Whenever he tried to think, his head ached from the club's blow. Nowhere in the newspaper stories had he seen any mention of Yango's club, the cause of his terrible headaches. Not a word had been said about it during the investigation. Why? Who had taken it? Where was it?

Chapter 8

"I have a carpenter's shop on —— Street, number ——, in this city. I make clubs for the police. If I remember correctly, I have thus far received two orders from the high command of the police force of Central Macedonia, each calling for five hundred clubs. I should also add that sometimes a policeman in uniform comes to my shop to order a club. Then I have to make it for him free of charge. This doesn't happen often, at the most once a month. I've never made any clubs for private individuals, nor has any private individual ever come to order a club from me with the authorization of the police. A month ago, three men in civilian clothes came to my shop and ordered three clubs; since I didn't know who they were, I told them I'd have to have a note signed by the police. They went away, and I've never seen them again. The clubs I make for the police are about sixteen inches long. At one end there is a hole for a strap. The clubs I made for the police high command (the large orders I told you about), I painted a dark walnut color. The ones I gave the policemen free of charge, I did not paint. I left the natural color of the wood."

Chapter 9

His telephone rang. The voice on the other end sounded out of breath. At first the young reporter was on his guard.

"Who is it?"

"You don't know me. My name's Michalis Dimas, I'm a dock worker from Salonika. It's important that I see you."

The reporter thought it might be a trap. Since the arrest of Baronissimo, obscure threats had reached his ears.

"You're the only person who can help me. I've got to see you."

"Come over here to the newspaper office."

"It's the first time I've ever been in Athens. Where is it?"

"Where are you now?"

"In Omonia Square."

"Fine. It's very easy. Take Panepistimiou Street toward Syndagma Square. On your left you'll see the sign with the name of the newspaper. Second floor, room 18."

"I'm on my way."

The reporter went out to tell the doorman that someone would be coming to ask for him shortly, someone who might be dangerous. "Watch out for him and look him over carefully," he said.

Not that he was afraid. But since he had revived the investigation by uncovering Baron, he had reason to believe that efforts were being made to get him out of the way.

A few minutes later the man stood before him: about thirty-five, with deep-set eyes and the air of a hunted animal. He shook hands with the reporter and sat down. The reporter ordered coffee.

"Mr. Andoniou," he began, "I've come all the way from Salonika to see you. I've been following your investigation in the papers, and though I don't have much education, I want to congratulate you for your courage. But you're somebody, I'm nothing. I've been forced to leave my neighborhood—I live in Ano Toumba; I've had to walk out on my wife and child to escape. It's hell there. It's gangland. Since the prize hoods got locked up, the rest are out for blood. No one dares speak. And if you don't do what they tell you, it's too bad for you. You're done for. I can't explain it very well but, you see, at night after I've locked and bolted the door I have to put the wife and kid in the back room and then go stay awake listening in case they raid the place. They did it night before last. I saw them ganged up in Chinky's Café. I went in too, to have a little drink. 'You've been playing the good little boy a little too much lately,' said Hitler, slamming into me. Hitler is what we call Halimoudra, a guy at the dock, because he stops at nothing. 'You finished Z. off,' I said then, losing my temper. 'Don't think you can try it on somebody else.' He jumped out of his chair and came at me. Luckily there were two or three other people around who aren't part of the gang, and they stepped in between us. I didn't want to be the first to leave the café. Why should I, do they own the place? I sat down again and drank down my retsina. Hitler kept looking at me with hate. He was plotting his revenge. He knows I know them all and can

spill the beans. I left the café and went home mad. I
locked and barred the front door and my wife and kid
went to bed. A little later, I don't know exactly
when, I heard someone banging at the door. It was Hitler and he was shouting: 'If you're a man, get out here,
Dimas, and we'll have a talk. Come on out if you've got
the guts.' He must have been drunk. I couldn't call the
police; we don't have a telephone. So I let him rave. My
wife and kid woke up, scared as hell. They huddled up
close to me. My little girl couldn't stop crying, and she
kept asking: 'Who is it, Papa, who is it?' Hitler kept
right on banging. I'd have gone out, Mr. Andoniou, he'd
cast a slur on my honor as a man, but to tell you the
truth, I was afraid he might have his revolver. I've seen
that revolver twice. The first time was at our annual
election for the committee of the AETOU—that's our
soccer club. Hitler was treasurer of the old committee.
He pulled out his revolver and put it on the table, as if
to say: 'If anyone wants me to account for anything,
here I am.' Of course, no one said a word and they re-
elected him treasurer by acclamation. They're all petrified of him. The second time was when he was slugging
Aglaïtsa. She's a woman in our neighborhood who—well,
she's sort of a prostitute. Anyway, Hitler had grabbed
her by the hair and was pounding her with the butt of
his revolver. I made him stop. That was before Z.'s murder, so there wasn't blood between us. You should have
heard Aglaïtsa howling. She's a good woman all the
same. Her husband's a sailor, he turns up once in a blue
moon, and when he does come, he never stays more
than a few days. He brings presents for everybody—last
Christmas he even gave my daughter a little Japanese
boat with lights that turn on and off. O.K., well, Hitler
put his pistol away, he seemed pretty mad that I'd seen
it. Then he shoved Aglaïtsa to the ground and spat on
her. Aglaïtsa got up and said she was going to the police. She told him she'd have him in the clink in no time,
since she had a witness. Hitler burst out laughing. One
thing he sure wasn't afraid of was that. He and Masto-

dontosaur were pals. He told her to go right ahead but she'd better be careful—he happened to have some pull with the vice squad, and if she didn't watch out she'd be classified as a whore because she wasn't married to the sailor. Aglaïtsa was so insulted that she fell into a faint. Hitler went off and I stayed there, trying to bring her to. That's the kind of guy he is, Mr. Andoniou. That's why I didn't go out night before last. I was afraid. I knew that somewhere, in some corner—the streets in Ano Toumba are rat traps, you know, and there aren't many lights—he was going to sneak up on me when I wasn't looking. I haven't wasted any time. I borrowed five hundred drachmas from my father-in-law and took the bus and came to you because you're the only one, as far as I know, who can put them all in their place and keep them there. They're scared because I know them, I was one of them before the crime."

Andoniou smiled. "If I were Public Prosecutor," he said, "I could do what you ask of me. Unfortunately I'm just a reporter and I can only write what I find out, and sometimes not even that."

And he cast a significant glance at him. Dimas relaxed.

"Where's the coffee I ordered?" sighed the reporter. He phoned the corner café. "Did it evaporate on the way?"

He turned back to his visitor, who was looking around the office with curiosity; he was shabbily dressed and kept tapping his fingers nervously on the table.

"Go ahead, tell me the whole story. This gang you mentioned—who are they? From whom do they take their orders? How many are there?"

"I work on the docks by the day. To have a regular, decently paid job, you've got to do a lot of pushing and a lot of ass-licking. The guys who run things at the port are the Bonatsa Brothers, Xanalatos, Yatras, Kyrilov, Jimmie the Boxer, and Hitler. Then there are others, like Yango, Baronissimo, and Vango, who are part of the gang but have different jobs."

"I know about that."

"Well, all these fellows get together in the Commissioner's office, and he sends them out on various jobs. What sort of jobs they are, you know better than I."

The coffees finally arrived. The waiter set them on the desk, took the coin Andoniou gave him, and left.

"If you want the particulars," resumed Dimas, "these are the same fellows that beat up the woman deputy from the Center Union Party in 1961. She'd come to Ano Toumba to give a talk. That's the kind of cowards they are. They even attack women."

"And you—why didn't you inform on them? Why didn't you report them to the police or to a newspaper?" Andoniou asked him.

The dock worker looked him straight in the eye. "Do you think I'm crazy, Mr. Andoniou? Don't you think I could see that whatever was happening it had the blessing of the police? What do you think it meant that Yango's best friend was Dimis, the police sergeant? Wasn't I also invited to the Commissioner's office for instructions? Do you think my job is secure enough that I can fight them in the open? When you work on the docks by the day you can be fired any minute. I've got a wife and kid! They've got you coming and going. But Z.'s assassination was the last straw. I lost my temper and told them off. That's why they put me on the black list. After that it's been practically impossible to find work. It's only because of the spot I'm in now that I got the courage to come and tell you all I know. They all have one thing in common: they're not afraid. And it's not because they're brave. No. They're not afraid because they know the police are on their side. I was in seventh heaven when those guys got locked up. When the rest of them found about it, it was weeks before they believed it. They were certain it had been done to trick the public, and that Yango and Baron and Vango would soon be out again. Do you understand what I'm saying?"

The reporter nodded. "Drink your coffee," he said kindly. "It's going to get cold."

Dimas drank it down in one gulp. Then he took out a cigarette and offered it to the reporter.

"Thank you, I don't smoke," said Andoniou.

"Well then," said Dimas, "I'll go on. The last time we were rounded up was during de Gaulle's visit. Looking back on it now, I can see that that meeting was a sort of general rehearsal for the later incidents. All of them were there at the Ano Toumba branch of the Security Police. The Commissioner divided us into groups of ten; each group had a leader. My group leader happened to be Hitler. Then they handed us little pins with yellow, green, or red plastic heads. We were supposed to stick these into our lapels, to recognize each other by."

"Pins?" asked the reporter, jotting down this detail in his notebook. "We could call it the Affair of the Colored Pins."

"That's an idea. I still have mine," said the dock worker. "I should have brought it with me. Anyway, to get back to the meeting, someone asked why we had to guard de Gaulle. And a cop in plain clothes told him that de Gaulle's life had been threatened by the Communists. He'd played a dirty trick on them during the war and they were looking for a chance to bump him off. Once, he said, they'd peppered his car with machine-gun bullets, but the windows were bullet-proof. The Greek government didn't want any trouble with the Big Powers. Besides, the Bulgars weren't very far away, they could easily slip past the guards at the frontier and join in the hunt. So keep your eyes open, he told us, and above all, watch the windows in the houses. They stationed me in front of the Electric Company, where there weren't any houses at all. I had to stand there from eight in the morning till seven-thirty in the evening, without a bite to eat. When I got back home I took it out on my wife. As if it had been her fault, poor thing! But I swore I'd be smarter next time and find some excuse to get out of it."

"Now tell me something—and this is between you and me: were you there at the incidents that evening?"

"I'm going to speak frankly, Mr. Andoniou, because I like the truth. I'm in a tight spot. If you work at a job and live in a neighborhood where everything depends on the kind of pull you've got, it's pretty hard to keep your hands clean. About six o'clock the night before the incidents just as I was getting off the bus on my way home, one of the hoods came up and told me the Commissioner had ordered us to be outside the Catacomb Club at five the next afternoon, to break up a meeting. I was mad as hell. De Gaulle had barely left town and here they were with another crappy idea! I told him flatly that I wouldn't and that he could tell the Commissioner what I said. 'Michalis,' he said to me, 'don't be a dope. If I tell him that, you're done for. Say that you'll go, let him see you there, and then play it cool. When you get a chance—beat it.' I took his advice. I've been playing the nincompoop too long, I thought. It's time I wised up. Next day I left the dock at two in the afternoon—I hadn't made a drachma. It was one of those bad days—lucky they don't come very often—when being unemployed really gets you down. Maybe that was why I decided to go. My wife was set against the whole business, so to get out of the house at five I had to lie. I told her I was going to get some paper bags from the printing office, I hadn't had time at noon. My wife needed the bags for her job. She works in a fertilizer factory. She reminded me that it was Wednesday and the shops were closed. I told her the printing offices stayed open illegally. And so, with this excuse, I got out of the house. Going along in the bus, I saw the Commissioner's limousine outside the local police station. That seemed funny. And I couldn't have been wrong about it, because there isn't another car like it in the neighborhood. I know that car very well. When I got off the bus, I ambled over toward the Catacomb Club and the first thing I saw was Yango punching a woman. Later I saw him tear down the poster and jump into a taxi, which went down one lane of Aristotelous Street and came up the other. It went past me, but I didn't see where it was going. I went to the printing office and got the paper bags. On the way back I passed the building where the meeting was to be held, and there they were, all of them—Bonatsa, Xanalatos, Baron, Kyrilov, Jimmie the Boxer, Hitler—yelling, throwing stones, clubbing people. The Commissioner saw me and I pretended I was yelling too; and after that I managed to sneak away and went home. There was something appalling about that night. And I wasn't surprised when I learned the news next day. I had seen the mob in action. Not one of them was missing. But once they'd locked up Yango and then that other louse Vango and finally that bird-brain Baronissimo, I took courage and began speaking my mind. It was then that they began making threats about getting rid of me. And when this incident I told you about at the beginning happened, I asked myself what I should do. 'Go to the newspaper reporter who tracked down Baronissimo,' I said to myself, 'and tell him the whole story.' But I'm afraid, Mr. Andoniou. I don't know what's happening in Toumba now."

"In your opinion, it was the Commissioner who gave the order to liquidate Z.?"

"I can't say that. It was the Commissioner who rounded them up. But where the orders came from, I have no idea."

"Good. Now I'm going to tell you what you must do. Tomorrow morning, go to the Public Prosecutor here in Athens and tell him everything you know about this mob. Tomorrow afternoon we'll both leave for Salonika. Is it clear? I'll take you in my car, there's nothing to be afraid of. You'll go to the Investigator, who seems to be a very honest person, and you'll tell him everything. All right? From here on in, you're under my protection."

Michalis smiled. "Yes, but how am I ever going to get any work at the docks again? That's my big worry. They might let a pulley drop on my head and say it was an accident."

"You won't have to work for a while. Consider yourself my employee." And he gave him a friendly pat on the shoulder.

"Thank you, Mr. Andoniou."

"Well, come around tomorrow morning. The Court of the Areopagus is close by. I'll drive you there. And at two-thirty we can be under way."

Dimas left. Andoniou headed for the office of the editor-in-chief. He found him in the middle of a telephone conversation with Salonika.

"It's chaos up there," he said when he hung up.

"We're going to put some order into it," Andoniou replied enigmatically. "I'm on the trail of the instigators. An ex-member has just confessed. I'm going north tomorrow. Keep the front page open Friday. We're going to call it the Affair of the Colored Pins."

"What's that?" the editor-in-chief asked, smelling a scoop.

"You'll see. Just be patient for one day."

"Splendid," the editor said. "But be careful."

"It's only the driving that's dangerous," said the young reporter as he left.

The next day at 2:30 the reporter's Fiat was humming along the National Highway from Athens to Lamia.

Chapter 10

From the reporter's car, Michalis Dimas watched the newly paved road with its white markings like tracer bullets scarring the air race past beneath the wheels. He had never before taken such a long trip in a private car. He loved it. The security of the little car was increased by his friend's presence at the wheel. He was going back with a good escort. He had nothing to fear from anyone.

They talked very little. In Lamia they stopped and had a cheese pie. Then the reporter turned on the radio. At seven there was a news bulletin. "The Court announces that the visit of the royal couple to London will definitely take place . . . Mr. Rallis, the Minister of the Interior, has taken up headquarters at the Ministry for Northern Greece in Salonika to keep in closer touch with the Z. case. Mr. Rallis has stated once again that the government did everything in its power to save the injured man, that it has entrusted the judicial and administrative aspects of the case to high magistrates and taken all calculated measures to facilitate their task. Moreover, Mr. Rallis added, the government has on this occasion laid no restrictions on freedom of the press or freedom of worship, and has even permitted the political exploitation of the affair, whereas the opposition, for partisan purposes, has basely exploited the death of a man, issuing false news reports, distorting events, suborning alleged witnesses, defaming our country in the foreign press, and systematically impeding the course of justice . . . By decree of the Minister of Agriculture the minimum price of green cocoons for the current year has been set at 33 drachmas per kilo . . . Foreign news: At the White House, Preisdent Kennedy received the congratulations of the press corps on his forty-sixth birthday, with his usual good humor. 'Somehow you seem a bit older today!' the President exclaimed, taking the representatives of the press by surprise before they had time to wish him Happy Birthday. Apart from this brief ceremony, President Kennedy observed his usual working day . . . Bulletin: The General Association of Three-Wheeled Public Vehicle Owners of Attica has energetically protested the allegedly unfair tendency of a large part of the press to discredit all three-wheeled vehicles on the ground that Deputy Z. was mortally injured by such a vehicle, whereas the offending vehicle was privately owned and had no connection whatsoever with the peace-loving Association of Three-Wheeled Public Vehicle Owners . . . Weather forecast . . ."

Andoniou turned the dial to another station. Dimas was silent, looking out the window. Night had fallen, and in the blackness the car lights shone yellow. He saw the dark shape of an overturned truck in a ditch. After Larissa, he began feeling a lump in his throat. They were getting near. It was too late to turn back. The closer they came to Salonika, the more his feeling of panic intensified. The radio was playing music. Andoniou at the wheel was fighting off sleep. Once, when they stopped at Tempe to pay the highway toll, Dimas had the impulse to open the door of the car and disappear into the night. To go anywhere at all, as long as he didn't have to return to the misery of Ano Toumba, the poverty, the plumbing, the gutters full of garbage. So long as he'd never again have to walk past Chinky's Café, the mobsters' hangout.

The reporter assured him once again that he had nothing to fear. When at last the city came into sight, its lights reflected in the bay, the dock worker thought it looked like the monstrous claw of a crane. A claw that, no matter how much mud it dredged from the floor of the sea, would never succeed in making the waters of the bay any deeper.

Chapter 11

The Investigator summoned all those whose names had been given him by Dimas. A miserable order of human beings vegetating in a quagmire, like frogs. What was worse, they had no interest in getting out of it, for the simple reason that they had nowhere to go. None of them, according to their statements, had been present at the incidents.

"Me?" said Bonatsa. "I was at Stroumtsa's grocery that day. I sometimes help out there when I don't have work down at the docks. Since the shops are closed on Wednesday afternoon, I stayed with the boss to put the stock in order. We pulled everything off the shelves and cleaned things up. I even scrubbed the floor. Then we put everything back in place, the tubs of olives, the oil, the feta cheese, the dried beans, the canned goods. The grocery store doesn't have any windows, so for two days I'd been trying to make one in the back. Well, that night I saw the hole was big enough to allow some louse to climb in and loot the store, so I put some iron rods across it. After that, I sprinkled rat poison and insecticide around, then I threw the cat out and pulled down the iron shutters. By then it must have been about nine-thirty. I was all in, and I hit the hay as soon as I got home. When I'm tired I snore something awful, and my wife told me next morning she hadn't gotten a wink of sleep all night."

"Me?" said his brother. "As soon as I finished work at the dock, I went and had a good shower in the barracks the company fixed up for us. When you work in cement like I do, you look like a snowman at the end of the day. It must have been about seven o'clock. I took the bus from Egnatia Street and went to Toumba. I didn't take the bus from the Aristotelous Street stop but from the terminal on Venizelou Street, because I was afraid I might not be able to find a seat and I wanted to sit down, I was all in, that night. I'd spent the day loading sacks of cement on a ship that was sailing for Volos. Since the earthquakes they've been doing a lot of building at Volos. When I got to Toumba, I went to Chinky's tavern. There's a jukebox but it wasn't working and I bawled out the proprietor because I couldn't get my coin back. I had a couple of drinks with the guys and about nine-thirty I went home, dead tired."

"Me?" said Xanalatos. "I didn't have anything to do with the incidents. I left home at five o'clock and went to the Mimosa Café and played cards with Vassilis Nicolaïdis till about seven-thirty. I kept winning and he didn't feel like playing any more. Then I got up and went across the street, where my friend the tailor was playing backgammon with the neighborhood dentist outside the tailor shop. The dentist filled five teeth for me last month and I still owed him for two of the fillings. I sat down and watched them play till ten. I get a big kick out of watching them. I bet the dentist the price of one of the two fillings I owed him that he was going to lose. And I won. So now I only owe him for one. At ten o'clock I went home."

"As for me," said Hitler, "I wasn't at the incidents either. I was home, fixing a leak in the water pipe. Toward evening I went to the football field, where the AE-TOU—the team I'm treasurer for life of—was having a practice session. Sunday we were playing the Progress Team of Kalamaria, and I wanted to see what shape our players were in. They're scared of me, and since I didn't want to get in their way I sat up in the bleachers a good distance away. That's when I met Stratos Metsolis. He is divorcing his wife and I'm going to be a witness at the trial that's coming up, and he gave me the latest news about the case. To drown his sorrow—he loves the bitch and she can't stand the sight of him—I took him to Chinky's joint. We sat down and ordered something to drink. After a little while, in came Baron with fresh figs from Michaniona. There were a couple of other guys there too. We left at ten."

"I, Jimmie the Boxer, not only did not hit Pirouchas but, on the contrary, came to his aid, along with a second lieutenant from the army whom I didn't know. We took him to the first-aid station. I spent the whole evening at the Housing Association of Dock Workers, the St. Constantine office, because we also are trying to get a roof over our heads, and I was talking with the labor big-shots. When I came out, I saw someone lying flat on the sidewalk, at the intersection of Ion Dragoumis and Mitropoleos Streets. Not knowing what was up, I tried to get the man to his feet with the help of the second lieutenant—who, like me, just happened to be passing by —and we saved him. It's too bad Pirouchas was out like a light, otherwise he'd remember me and he wouldn't be accusing me of beating him up. 'When you try to help the other guy, you only get it in the neck yourself.' That's what my grandmother from Batum used to tell me when I was a kid."

"I, Mitros, am a baker by trade and I always sleep after lunch, because I get up at three in the morning to bake bread. My job is exhausting, especially in the summer heat. I work when everybody else is sleeping, like a night watchman. So that day I went to sleep at three in the afternoon and woke up at eight-thirty, like I always do. Then I went to the café to meet my friends Phoscolos and Gidopoulos, and we were together till a quarter to ten. I never drink, I'm sorry to say, on account of my liver. And now you come along and tell me I was at the incidents! How do you like that! When you work like I do, you don't have time for anything. Z.? Never heard of him. Never wanted to hear of him."

"I, Kyrilov, am a marked man, no matter what I do. I spent eight years in jail with Autocratosaur for collaborating with the Germans and I'm branded. But that night when I left the dock I remember very well that I went past the old post office on my way to the shoemaker's in the alley. The sole of my shoe had come unglued and I wanted to get it repaired. His shop was closed, and so since I was only a couple of steps away I stopped by to say hello to my brother's widow. She has a newsstand in front of the Strymonikon Hotel on Kolomvou Street. I asked her how business was going. She said business was all right, but she was scared to death of the cars racing by, because the stand was on the edge of the sidewalk; she was sure she'd be smashed to pieces

one day. She said she'd rather rent the stand to somebody else even though it meant sharing the profits. I
said goodbye to her and went off to take the bus for
Votsi, where I live. On the way I saw a crowd and
heard some shouting, but I didn't stop. Politics! Don't
mention that ugly word to me. That stuff's for the crack-
pots who don't know any better. I went home and my
wife and I went over to see a neighbor, Kyria Zoe,
who'd just got out of the hospital, where she had a her-
nia operation. The day before, May 21, was St. Eleni's
day—her little girl's nameday—so we were killing two
birds with one stone. There were some other neighbors
there, and her relatives. We left at ten."

"I, Georgios, the fruit dealer, got off the bus from Michaniona and went straight to Baron's shop in the Modiano Market. Baron wasn't there. I had about 200 pounds
of figs for him and I carried them into his shop myself,
going back and forth five times. I didn't run into him on
any of those trips. I don't know where Baron could have
been that evening."

"I, Nikos, no occupation, did actually see Baron that
evening at Chinky's Café. It was the bouzouki hour on
the Armed Forces station, and they were playing the
song Baron likes: 'Society Has Wronged Me.' I remember, because Baron shouted to Chinky to turn the radio
louder. Baron is my friend. We've both been in the
AETOU ever since it started. He can't play, he's too fat,
but sometimes he acts as referee, to lose some weight."

"I, Petros Paltoglou, member of EDA in Ano Toumba,
heard from Baron's brother that when he asked him:
'Where were you yesterday?' Baron answered: 'They
wanted to foul me up again, the louts . . .' Who the
louts were, or what to foul me up meant, his brother
didn't say."

"I am Baron's younger brother. We don't disagree po-
litically as people say we do. I'm on the left, but my
brother isn't anything, so I don't see how we could disagree. I know he wants a license for his stall, and that
the matter depends entirely on Mastodontosaur, who

calls on him from time to time. I know my brother. He's a coward. He'd never hurt anybody, he'd be too scared. But he's more scared of the cops."

"I, Chinky—they pinned that nickname on me because I took part in the Korean War and the Chinese captured me (but I escaped)—can't remember whether Baron was in my café that evening or not. How do you expect me to remember? My customers come and go. I'm not supposed to check up on them, I'm supposed to wait on them. They come in from the docks dog-tired and they're hard to please. Everybody wants to be the first one served. As far as his credit goes, Baron is in good standing."

"I, Epaminondas Stergiou, a mason, declare that the day following the incidents, Toula, a dressmaker whose brother works at the same stand as Yango, dropped in for a visit. She shouted—my wife Korina being a littlt deaf—that her brother had seen Yango the day before, that is, on Wednesday, at lunchtime, just when the shops were closing. Her brother said he had suggested to Yango that they go back home together, and Yango told him he couldn't because he had a job to do later. And Yango had opened his shirt and showed him a club. He'd actually said, Toula told us, shouting at the top of her lungs, that 'it might come to killing a man.' Then I told Toula, who's a neighbor of ours, to tell her brother to report all this, because it would help the investigation along. But she answered that neither her brother nor she wanted to get into any trouble. 'And besides,' she said to me, 'you saw what happened to that poor furniture varnisher when he talked. Leave the poor to their poverty.'"

"I, Toula the dressmaker, never heard my brother say that Yango had boasted that he was on the point of killing someone. All I said was that he showed my brother a club. Nor did I call Yango a drunkard and a bum. My brother and I don't want any trouble. Korina may be deaf, but Epaminondas hears things that haven't even been said. That's all I have to tell you."

"I, Autocratosaur, condemn crime as a means of political persuasion. At the tavern of the late Gonos, where I was in the habit of meeting with the members of my organization, I used to speak to them about the noblest ideals of humanity: fatherland, religion, family. I was trying to make them more human. Yes, I am an out-and-out anti-Communist. But no member of my organization could take part in any action without first receiving my consent. As far as the membership cards are concerned, there was nothing secret about them. The reason that some of the letters on the membership card are written in black and others in red is that my typewriter has a ribbon in two colors and the lever you use to switch from one to the other doesn't work well. Occasionally it slips and then the key strikes the red ribbon. My review *Expansion of the Hellenes!* is a monthly, except that the last issue came out two years ago. The organization, being recently established, doesn't have any archives. The evening of the incidents, I was present in my capacity as a journalist. I was intending to publish my impressions in the next issue of *Expansion of the Hellenes!*, which was already on press. I believe that it is to the interest of Greece to maintain good relations with West Germany. I am opposed to the English, and in favor of the Americans insofar as they have German blood in their veins. I do not live in the Federal Republic because I love my own land. However, I am preparing to make an extended tour of that country, in order to infuse them with the divine flame of the Hellenic-Christian civilization. Mr. Investigator, I wish to use this occasion to demand that you call a halt to the indignities to which I have been subjected today—not for the first time—and I appeal to your impartial judgment to restore me, cleansed of all suspicion, to the bosom of society and my sorely-tried family."

"I, the widow Gonos, after my late husband's funeral —attended by Autocratosaur, the General, Mastodontosaur, and the cream of society—cleaned up the tavern and threw whatever papers I found into the fireplace and burned them. I don't know whether these were the archives of the leader's organization or not, especially as I can't read. The only things I remember are some skulls and crossbones."

"And I, Apostolos Nikitaras, butcher by trade and brother-in-law of the late Gonos, never had anything to do with Autocratosaur's organization, because my father-in-law warned me that it would ruin our business if I did, since most of the people in Ano Toumba are Reds. On my honor as a butcher, I hereby declare that I am stating the truth."

Chapter 12

They decided to drop in on him in Oraiokastro, a village a few miles outside Salonika. This time the reporter took a colleague along. While the Investigator was opening plank by plank the doorway to the mystery, only to be confronted by an even denser darkness, since all these rotten mobsters were only the façade of the haunted castle and when you opened one door it led to another door and that one in turn to another, till suddenly you found yourself out in the open again, but on the opposite side from where you'd entered—the journalist had scented a new hare, who might prove exceedingly valuable to the investigation. This was a certain Stratos Panayiotidis, member of the ERE in Ano Toumba. He had been described by the neighbors as "the man who knows a lot and, if he wants, can get them all grilled." Andoniou had contacted him first and learned that on the evening of the crime he had met Vango late at night on a street in Toumba. "Where have you been to get in such a shape?" Stratos had asked him. "There's been some trouble in town," Vango had said. "And since when have you been wearing glasses?" Vango had removed them at once. "It's to keep people from recognizing me. How can I go home at such an hour?" This was what Stratos had told Andoniou a couple of days before. Today, when Andoniou went back to find out more, he was told that Stratos had left for Oraiokastro to help his uncle build a house. Andoniou and the other journalist took the Fiat and went off to surprise Stratos in the village. They had no idea what might come of it. But the fact that Stratos had met Vango, "by chance," on the night of the crime looked suspicious. They didn't find Stratos. They were told by his aunt that he had returned to Toumba yesterday to see his mother, who had had a heart attack. The aunt added that Stratos had told her when he was leaving that he intended to go by the office of the Security Police to see what was going on.

At that point the uncle interrupted. "What's this fairy tale you're telling these fellows? What Security Police?"

The two reporters exchanged significant glances.

"You just shut up," retorted the aunt. "Go talk to your friend, the police sergeant of Oraiokastro."

"You go back to your kitchen," the uncle ordered. Then, addressing the reporters, he said: "My nephew Stratos doesn't know anything about all this. He comes here once in a while to give me a hand with the house I'm building."

"Does he know Yango Gazgouridis?" Andoniou asked him.

"Who doesn't know Yango? They grew up together. They're the same age."

"Did he tell you what he and Vango said to each other when they met that night?"

"No. He didn't even tell me he'd met Vango."

Nothing was coming of all this. The reporters prepared to leave. Stratos, they decided, was a sphinx without secrets. Just then they saw him emerging from a thicket, holding his feeble mother by the arm. Even before he noticed the reporters, Stratos was troubled by the sight of the car in front of the house.

"You again?" he said to the reporters.

"Yes, it's us," Andoniou said. "You lied to us. You told us you didn't know Yango. Your uncle just told us you grew up together."

"I didn't tell you that I didn't know him. I told you I *hardly* know him. The fact that we grew up together doesn't mean we're friends." He helped his mother into a chair, in the shade of a tree.

"Why don't you come inside?" suggested the aunt from the door. "That sun's too hot."

They went into the house and sat down in the big, peasant-style room decorated with handwoven hangings.

"Well, where were you a little while ago?"

"I don't have to account for myself to anyone."

"Did you go to the Security Police by any chance?"

Stratos blanched. He looked around him nervously. Had they been talking while he was away? His aunt brought out her walnut preserves.

"No, I didn't," he said. "What business could I have there?"

"Why didn't you tell your uncle that you met Vango the night of the incidents?"

"I did tell you, Uncle. Don't you remember?"

"Absolutely not, Stratos. You didn't tell me any such thing."

"Then I'm mistaken. I must have said it in the café. I don't remember. Anyway, I had no reason to hide it."

"What else did Vango say to you?"

"That the police were looking for him."

"That's something new. According to what you told me day before yesterday, all he said was he was coming back from town and all hell had broken loose. You didn't say anything about the police."

"I guess I forgot."

"And if the police were looking for him, why did he go to the Ano Toumba police station all alone at the crack of dawn?"

"Maybe he had a friend there."

"You seem to be getting things a bit confused, Stratos," said Andoniou.

"Stratos, were you at that wedding too, perhaps?" The questions came from his aunt, who was sitting there, her long braids wreathed around her head.

The reporters looked at each other. By "wedding" she must surely have meant "murder."

Then Stratos's mother, who hadn't said a word, spoke up: "The evening of the incidents, Stratos was at the ballet."

"What ballet? The Bolshoi?" asked the other reporter.

"No. He was at the Turkish ballet at the Pathé movie house."

"Yes," said Stratos, thanking his mother with a glance for getting him out of a tough spot. "I stayed for both performances. I'm very partial to belly dances."

"How did it happen that they allowed you to stay for both performances? Did you buy another ticket?"

This took Stratos off his guard.

"A ballet," Andoniou explained to him, "is not the same as a movie. When the performance is over, the audience has to leave, like at the theater."

"Well, I'm telling you, I stayed to see both performances and nobody kicked me out. Ask the usherettes at the Pathé, they know me. I went back home at twelve, and that's when I met Vango."

"O.K. But don't you think you ought to make a statement about all this to the Investigator?" asked Andoniou.

"I don't think it would be of interest to anyone."

"You're wrong! It's a very important piece of information. We're going back to town. There's room in the car. Do you want to come with us?"

"I don't have anything to hide," Stratos said. "I'll come."

The next day the papers carried a photograph of Stratos Panayiotidis being escorted to the Investigator not by the police but by newspaper reporters.

Chapter 13

On the point of lying down to rest, the Investigator saw all their faces filing past in the darkness. Faces twisted by horror, between two cracked walls, beneath a ceiling ceaselessly dripping, small-change victims while the bankers, the backers, the backgammon players carefully preserved their invisibility. He saw them unwittingly entangled in a web of steel, fish caught in a net of indestructible royal horsehairs; and if he had placed them in custody before the trial, it was less for what they themselves had done than to reach the powers behind them. But would he succeed? Or like mountain climbers who aspire to untrodden peaks, would he succumb to his own passion for heights? Somewhere must be a shelter, he thought. A fire to warm him. He was as sure that in the end they would remove him as he was of his own eventual death.

And if he believed in society, it was precisely to prevent this void, this vortex caused by the abrupt departure of some particular person. Z. had vanished and immediately the whirlpool had begun to rage. How foul the water must be, he reflected, for such chaos to exist! In youthful waters—the expression pleased him—the void fills automatically. The molecules of water, living cells, immediate reflections of the sky, renew themselves as rapidly as the brain cells of the young. Whereas, in swamp water (that of the society he served), you have only to toss a stone to release the stench of prison latrines.

He had started on this case the way one sets out on a cruise, brimming with the hope of enriching his still limited experience. But nausea had overcome him. He already longed for solid ground. Everything from the food to the entertainment, from the captain to the merest mechanic made him want to vomit. The boat was old and rusted, a Liberty ship, now a slave ship for all concerned. There were leaks everywhere. How was he to plug each one?

But he could not give up. He had been sucked into the vortex. He found himself buffeted by the full force of the cyclone even as he tried to keep within its calm eye. The pressure was growing more and more intense. Every day increased the load. He couldn't hold out.

Now he would have to renounce forever the girl whose fresh young face had helped him forget the documents piled on his desk. On the street the other day he'd met an acquaintance from the army. With all the intimate candor one acquires with the khaki and forgets to put aside afterwards, he had offered advice: "Let them fight it out themselves! Do you think that you're going to pull the snake out of its lair? After a hundred and twenty years of slavery, servility, and corruption? Do you think that you, at the very beginning of your career . . ."

Only the faces, he thought during the long night when sleep was impossible, those faces whose common denominator wasn't the fifty-drachma note or the hundred-drachma note (much less the thousand), those faces with the ten-drachma coin for a denominator—what was the answer to that? What was the answer? Where then were the eminent ones? The great ones? The vertebrates who, while the protozoa suffered in their scum, were drinking whisky with ice and soda on some cool veranda, where the hostess, trilling a thousand pardons for being late, was just back from the Athens Festival?

Chapter 14

"I am beginning to forget your face," thought Pirouchas. "Little by little it is being erased from my brain cells, as new faces arise and supplant your beloved features. What will become of me? Little by little you are disappearing. Only your eyes in the enveloping darkness. What will become of me? Your movements I so admired. Merely to see you walk made the world my own. I no longer expect your phone call. Worst of all, one grows accustomed. We haven't time to mourn forever. I forget you and something inside me rebels, twists, a blade, a bayonet that pierces me. It isn't possible. I am inhabiting your last dwelling place, this hospital built with money from Greek emigrants in America. You are sinking and I sink with you. Neither of us has any hope. You are a dead man reborn. I am a live man dying.

"I wish I had you on film. I could look at you and recharge my cells with your battery. Nothing remains except photographs. I shall have to reconstruct your movements from these. I haven't even a tape recording to bring back the warmth of your voice.

"We are being swallowed up, you understand. How many years have I left? It doesn't matter. In earth that received you I place all my love. In black earth, for springtime's sake, for the flowers of May to blossom.

"I am suffering. Nothing can fill the void you left. The pavement weeps, they say, at the spot where you fell. I too am weeping. To what avail? Tears are only salt and water.

"What particles of air have preserved your glance? Into what caverns has your voice descended? My ears are split with the sound of a distant motorcycle. A single unending rattle, as of machine guns or road drills.

"I miss you. I know there is no return. Only in our memory do you go on living. You will live as long as we do. Otherwise I'm in good enough health. You, who used to worry so about me. My heart beats with a different rhythm now.

"How do you feel in this inaudible silence?

"I never imagined that I would be the survivor. Life belonged to you, I'd told you that. There's nothing I can do in the future. It's night. Outside, the heat has dulled the stars. Everything puckers up, like the hide of an elephant. I do not exist. The heat anesthetizes me. No, we aren't water, because we loved you. What one loves cannot die. If only I were in your place now, and had you to think these thoughts about me! No, one doesn't die when thousands of mouths shout 'Immortal!'—or one mouth only, mine."

His meditation was interrupted by the arrival of his daughter, who announced that a warrant had been issued for the arrest of Kareklas. Kareklas was the much-talked-about student member of the EKOF* who had led the attack on him. Pirouchas's daughter had found out about it from a neighbor, a woman who had been at the meeting of the Friends of Peace. On the day after the incidents, while Z. was still in his death throes and her father in a coma, the girl had seen this student hanging about outside the hospital and had called out to him: "Go away! Haven't you done enough! You wanted to kill my father!" He was astounded. "All right! All right!" he replied. "Don't shout! I'm leaving." Then he sent friends to beg her not to file charges against him because his stepfather would be outraged and would not

---

* A student organization of the extreme right wing.

let him go on with his studies. Two other students asserted that Kareklas had not taken part in the demonstration. But someone else heard from the butcher that Kareklas had boasted of being there and even of having got in a few blows himself. One Sunday evening when the girl was alone, a stranger came to her house and told her that Kareklas was the one who had assaulted her father in front of the ambulance. The man left without revealing his identity, not wishing, as he explained, to create difficulties for himself. Finally, the neighbor who had been at the meeting, who had identified Kareklas in the first place, also received an unexpected visit: Kareklas's mother, who came to beg her to say nothing about her son; his stepfather would beat the boy up. She pleaded with the woman not to mention her visit; her son might find out and turn against her. The mother wept and the neighbor said merely that it wasn't the first time Kareklas had made trouble. Since they all lived on the same street—Pirouchas and she and Kareklas—she had had to endure his arrogant backtalk, especially as her husband had been exiled for political reasons. Well, it was time he got a little sense into his head, she told his mother; otherwise there was no telling how he might end up.

Once the assassins had begun to be wrested one by one from their sanctuary and locked up in prison, attention focused on those still at large; among these was that brash EKOF student who was just waiting for more trouble to flare up so he could assault someone else. But the various witnesses produced sufficient evidence to bring about Kareklas's arrest. Kareklas himself, of course, denied everything when he appeared before the Investigator. Specifically, he claimed he had had an affair with Pirouchas's daughter and she, feeling he was betraying her with other women and knowing his extreme right-wing political views, had decided to take revenge. The evening of the incidents he had had a date with another girl and she knew it. Instead of throwing vitriol in his face, he said, she did something much worse. She accused him of having beaten her injured father. "If I understand the situation correctly," Pirouchas said to himself while his daughter sat on the bed changing the compresses on his forehead, "Kareklas has been locked up not only for assault but for slander as well."

Chapter 15

Meanwhile Salonika, "the south wind's bride," had surrendered to the sweet torpor of summer. Its daily routine continued undisturbed. Through the prison bars of Yendi-Koule, Yango watched the somnolent city lulled by the noon breeze off the gulf; it reached him untainted by the New City's raw cement, since the prison stood on a barren hill. From another wing he could even see his neighborhood, below the huge horseshoe of the new stadium. Twice he had attempted suicide. A waste of time. They had forgotten him. He believed he was a scapegoat for the authorities. And he remembered the words of wisdom of Mastro-Kostas that Wednesday morning at the stand on Vasileos Irakleiou Street: "You've got a family, Yango . . . Don't get involved in such things . . . The big fish eats the little one . . ." Life continued without him. Nobody needed him any longer. His silence was the only precious thing for them, and it wouldn't be difficult to obtain. Vango, in prison, found what he had always lacked: sleep. He slept endlessly. He got fat and round; and from time to time, just to practice, he would whitewash a wall. Baron, however, got thin; his heart almost broke every Sunday when he heard the cheers from the football stadium. And later on, when Autocratosaur joined them, he acted like a teacher who had failed the same examinations as his pupils.

And life in Salonika went on. Aristophanes' *The Birds* was being performed at the Park Theater. The new Baxe-Tsifliki beach was inaugurated. At Tagaredes, on the road to Michaniona, the land was being feverishly broken up into plots to be sold to Greek workers coming back from Germany. Esso-Pappas continued expropriating the fields near Diavata to establish his big industrial unit there. People died, got married, went swimming. They danced at Swings and were bored at Do-Re. A patient escaped from the city psychiatric clinic. The sea washed up an unidentified corpse. The Ogre hadn't been arrested yet. The ladies who raised money for the Home for the Blind played cards every afternoon. In the evenings the verandas were hosed down with water which drained onto the sidewalks as though the buildings were urinating. The moon turned moldy over Aretsou. There were relatively few campers this year. And eventually the opinion of the Judge of the Areopagus was made public. It held the police force responsible for a "breach of duty, with criminal intent."

Chapter 16

"If I hear one more word against the Royal Greek Police Corps, I'm going to commit suicide." He drew a .45 from his jacket and, with his plump finger on the trigger, pressed it against his graying temple.

Samidakis was appalled. He couldn't believe that the Generalissimo himself was talking this way.

"All right, I'll sign," he said.

"That's the way! Good lad! Now you're talking like somebody from Crete!"

He had had Samidakis in his office four whole hours, trying to persuade him to retract his testimony about the policeman's shaving of his head. What with the slanderous campaign now raging against the police force, this affair, if it came out into the open, would be the bitter end.

"All you have to say is you shaved it yourself."

"Yes, but for what reason?"

"Because of the heat."

"Like this, without leaving a hair?"

"Well, because you're getting prematurely bald. Where's your barber?"

"Near Kamara."

"We can make him declare that you're losing your hair."

"But, Generalissimo, sir . . ."

"Call me comrade."

"Well then, comrade! . . . When you lose your hair . . ."

Here's what had happened. The previous evening—exactly two months to the day since Z. was killed—Samidakis and some other students had gone to the spot where the hero had fallen, to leave flowers as a memorial. The point where Spandoni Street joins the public square was watched constantly from neighboring houses and shops by plain-clothesmen. Aware of this, the students had planned simply to toss the flowers on the pavement and make a quick getaway. What Samidakis had not foreseen was that one of his loose moccasin-style shoes would get stuck in the tar softened by the heat. He was stooping down to pull it out when a policeman came up from behind, scissors in hand, and clipped a large tuft of hair from the top of his head. This tonsure, which resembled one of the swathes cut in the mountain forests against fires left by careless shepherds, could not be concealed. There was nothing to do but have his head shaved. Then he had gone to the Public Prosecutor and testified that the policeman had cropped his hair for leaving roses at the spot where Z. had been assassinated.

At midnight the police came and got him out of bed. He was wanted immediately at the station. His landlord, who knew all about it, told them he hadn't come home. But they forced their way to his room and took him away.

"Be gentle, the boy has a weak heart," the landlord warned them.

At the station they conducted him straight to a room where the Generalissimo was seated behind a desk, having arrived the same evening from Athens by special plane. It was impossible to let the newspapers print a story about a policeman who cropped the hair of a student. What a scandal! The police force was under enough fire from the libelous Commies. After the verdict rendered by the Judge of the Areopagus, the airing of this case would complete the cycle of shame.

"Welcome! You know who I am?"

"I know you from the newspapers," Samidakis answered.

"All right. Sit down. And now talk to me as if I were your godfather. Tell me everything that happened."

"I've already told everything in my deposition."

"I want to hear it from you."

Samidakis repeated the whole story.

"Impossible!" exclaimed the Generalissimo when he finished.

"Why impossible?"

"It's impossible that what you say took place."

"I don't understand."

"You will." And pressing a button, he asked to be connected with Athens.

The student began to catch on.

"Now you're going to talk with your uncle," said the Generalissimo.

The student did in fact have an uncle who was head secretary in a key ministry.

"Yes, Uncle, this is Samidakis. How's my aunt? Yes,

they cut my hair . . . Impossible? Why impossible? No one forced me to say it . . . No, I don't belong to the Bertrand Russell Society . . . Nor the Z. Youth . . . You want me to tell the truth? But that's what I'm doing . . . The other truth? But there aren't two truths, Uncle!"

Since the cord on the receiver was short, he had to stoop over the desk, and not liking this servile posture, he walked around the desk to a point where he could talk standing up straight. From his new position he could observe the Generalissimo stroking his thick mustache with the air of some great landowner in Czarist Russia. His uncle was speaking to him in the severe tone he had adopted since Samidakis's father died and he assumed the obligations of legal guardian. He had difficulty hearing and was finally cut off.

"How long has it been since you were in Astrachades?" the Generalissimo asked. Astrachades was the village in southern Crete that both of them came from.

"I haven't been back since my father died," Samidakis replied coldly.

"I haven't been back in five years," said the Generalissimo. "But today somebody sent me some magnificent pears from there. They smell like home. Mm!" He opened the desk drawer and took one out. "Have one."

"I don't feel like it."

"Go ahead, eat it, I tell you—you'll have a change of heart."

"Do you think a pear will make me retract my testimony?"

"It's not the pear," the Generalissimo said, puffing up like a turkey. "It's Crete, where this pear comes from and where you and I come from too. We Cretans, Samidakis, aren't like the other Greeks. We're a distinct race. We have a language of our own, a tradition of our own. We produced El Greco."

"And Kazantzakis."

"He was an atheist," said the Generalissimo. "And a Communist. We Cretans are never Communists. It's a disease that never touched our island. Even Venizelos fought the Communists, though . . . Well, to get to the point, we must support each other. The rest of the Greeks are jealous of us. The openly avowed aim of the Communists is to heap calumny upon the prestige of the Royal Greek Police Force. A stupid policeman, who in the middle of the street shaves the head of a student of the National Aristotelian University of Salonika, is of course behaving barbarously—which by extension proves that the entire police force is barbarous. With this Z. affair they threaten to tarnish the reputation of our incorruptible police. But I call the fatherland to witness, they're going too far, I shall commit suicide! We're not letting the Bulgars make our laws!"

The Generalissimo began to weep like a baby. The orderly who was present at the scene played nervously with his wedding ring. Samidakis was in a quandary. And when the Generalissimo drew out the revolver and pressed it against his temple, he looked as if he were saluting someone even higher than he. The student passed his hand over his shaven head, and at the touch all his fury blazed up again.

"Well, if that's the way you want it," he said. "But on one condition."

"Whatever you wish, my boy."

"In a few months I'll be going into the army. I'm ready to say that I willfully shaved my head; but I want your written assurance that when I present myself at the recruiting center at Corinth they won't shave me again, as the regulations require."

The Generalissimo sprang out of his chair gleefully. He wiped his tears with his handkerchief and blew his nose so loudly that the whole police station vibrated. Then they destroyed Samidakis's previous statement. The student signed a new one. That night he slept at the police station to avoid encounters with the press.

Chapter 17

A reporter knocked on her door. She opened it.

"I realize, Mrs. Z., that you have refused to make any statement. I realize the futility of my visit. Still I wonder if you could tell me . . ."

I miss your face terribly, face like the earth, as you used to say of your mother's; I miss your eyes, need them to make me radiant; miss your lips, for without them I cannot love my own. I miss everything about you. Forty days have passed since then, forty-two days since I stood at your bedside in the hospital and you didn't know me, while the doctors worked to revive a dead brain in a body still intact. But only today I realized that little by little you are dissolving within me. I recollect details of your body; I can no longer remember you in your entirety. Even in the old days, there came times when we were apart for months, but deep within me I knew I should see you again, and your absence perfectly corresponded to my shock of joy at our eventual meeting. Now . . .

"How do you explain the fact that you entrusted your case to Communist lawyers?"

I know all this is happening in a region that has ceased to concern you, that no longer has anything to do with you, since you are dead. Otherwise it would be so easy: a movement, a word, a quarrel, a kiss on the floor of a boat, a tremor shaking the body, a cigarette, and everything would become human, quite human. We would understand each other; others would understand us too.

Now no one can understand me because you have left me alone in my grief and become a symbol, a banner for others.

"Are you distressed at the political exploitation of your husband's death?"

I know you always wanted this to happen. I think your ambition was justified. "God helps those who have no goal," you used to say. But it is one thing, believe me, to have such an ambition while living, and quite another to have fulfilled it in death. I was orphaned by you at that very moment when the world made you its own.

"Are you thinking of looking for some kind of work?"

The morning sun through the window is not the same, it does not reveal you at my side. The night's black swathe is poison. Where will our next meeting be? On what dead point of the horizon?

"Have you ever considered writing a book about the tragedy?"

Night descends upon you like a veil, hiding those fine points that were visible only after you had shaved. Details that make a face different from all others. The pores are the first to fade. Then the mole. Then the furrow at the base of the nose. The relief vanishes as in a badly printed map where the green of mountains runs into the blue of the sea.

"Did you ever quarrel with your husband about ideology?"

"I am without you" means "I no longer know what is happening to me and I don't care to know." A heightened lethargy in the depths of my being. The blood thickens in my veins. To be without you is to have nothing left. Light of your street, darkness of my house. To others you mean the rising sun, for me you have darkened the moon.

"How do you spend your time here in your retreat?"

Now I am looking for the particles of air that have preserved traces of your passage. I am looking for the streets that loved you, for the houses touched by your glance. I cannot rise to the occasion, as they say. I am inconsolable. Nothing said about or written about you has any meaning for me, nor does the investigation. I think about these things only when the lawyer calls. Afterwards the abyss opens: a void full of you.

"Was your husband tender with you?"

I miss you terribly. Nothing has any savor. And although you could not possibly be more present—everyone is talking about you, every newspaper I pick up mentions you—still I am hideously alone, because only your human presence could assure me that you haven't become a phantom in the minds of others, a means of relieving their own frustrations.

"Do you intend to remarry?"

Strangest of all, I am no longer jealous of your former mistresses. On the contrary, I seek them out, ask for them, want to know them. I believe that if each of us contributed the part of you she knew, we might all together be able to resurrect you. If each contributed her bit of stolen warmth, we might be able to rekindle your fire. Outside the heat is stifling, but indoors it's cold as ice!

"How long will you wear mourning?"

I talk to myself, to the wall. I have taken down your photograph. Now that Greece is covered with photographs of you, I think I have the right—haven't I?—to imagine you alive, moving, not framed and frozen by the click of the shutter. To others a paradise, for me a wasteland.

"Is your silence your own wish, or imposed by others?"

And your eyes are fixed in time. What troubles me is that last image of you. All the others, strange to say, have dimmed, or return only after an exhausting effort to remember. The morning you left for Salonika, you said something about the coffee, said it would make you miss your plane.

"This tragedy is a trump card for the Communists. Have you anything to say about this, since you are not a Communist?"

The church bells are pealing. It's Sunday. I imagine you on some other island, I've missed the boat and cannot come to you tonight. How will I get through a whole week of waiting for next Sunday's boat? I imagine myself at a railway crossing and the guard has put up the chain between us, an endless train roars over the rails, with as many cars as the years I shall not see you. Only at fleeting moments, through the spaces between the cars, I catch a rare image of you waiting for me on the far side.

"Have you been able to obtain a pension?"

I don't know whether you loved me. My trouble is, I must keep you alive. My whole body is empty without your kisses. Other kisses, other embraces may console me, but they cannot replace what you were to me.

"Thank you, Mrs. Z. Goodbye."

I know you loathed sentimentality. That's why I must stop. I've been interrupted a number of times by a stupid reporter from a right-wing paper. I won't mail this letter because I don't know where you are. I shall read it later, perhaps to our children when they are grown up. It will show me that I once remembered you vividly and was afraid of losing you, and I shall have it when I shall have lost you forever, when you will have become a street, a public square, a novel, a play, a film, an art show, and I an old woman, burdened with the sad duty of being present at openings.

Chapter 18

The "individual whose identity has not been made public" remained for some time unidentified. The only thing known about him was that he had been approached by left-wing militants with a proposition that, for a financial consideration, he kill a right-wing deputy in reprisal for Z.'s death. At last he materialized, a man by the name of Pournaropoulos, from a village outside Kilkis.

"I don't have any money," he told the reporters, "and I don't even own a field. That's why every two or three months I come down to Salonika to sell my blood."

"How do you do that?"

"I stand in front of the main hospital and auction it. I have more blood than I need and less bread than it takes to keep the blood going. Therefore I sell the blood. They know me at the hospital, and if someone with the same blood group happens to be dying, I can sell it at a high price."

"Why don't you volunteer to the Red Cross?"

"Why doesn't someone volunteer to give me something to live on? 'Your death is my life'—isn't that what they say? That's my motto. And when you sell your blood just when the other guy needs it desperately, you get more for it. Like tickets at the football field just before the match begins."

"Black market."

"Red market, mister. So what? A peasant from our village sold one of his eyes and now he has enough to live on for the rest of his life. What's wrong with selling a little blood? Besides, even the tourists do it. They come here without any money, sell their blood, and go to the bouzouki. Well, anyhow, last May 28, while I was waiting outside the hospital—the guard had informed the doctors, and they told me they'd call me because someone with B-type blood who'd been injured was being operated on—a black limousine stopped and a fellow got out. He was wearing dark glasses, so if I were to see him today I wouldn't recognize him."

"Would you recognize the limousine?"

"Not even that."

"Why not?"

"Because I'm only a peasant. I don't know anything about cars. If it was a horse now, I'd recognize it in a million. But all cars look alike, don't they? They've all got four wheels and a steering wheel."

"All right, all right, go on."

"Well, the fellow asked me if I was the one who sold blood. I said yes and my first thought was that he must need me for something mighty urgent and I said to myself, 'Yannis, we've struck it rich!' But not at all! Instead of that, he made me a proposition to drink somebody else's blood."

"He took you for a vampire?"

"I don't know anything about vampires. He told me that if I agreed to do a job I'd make more money than I make selling a hundred quarts of blood. I looked him over good and hard. To tell the truth, I wasn't much taken with him. 'Don't you need money, for heaven's sake?' he asked me. I nodded. 'Well, you'll make a pile out of this.' Then he gave me an idea what the plan was: I was to kill some Karamanlis deputy, that was it. He even told me the name."

"How did he want you to kill him?"

"He didn't tell me. But me, I told him I love Karamanlis, he's one of our own people, a Macedonian, he's a prince. He may not hear very well, but he's got good sharp eyes. He got us a water tap for our village and he told us that next year, if we vote for him again, he'll bring us electricity. So how could I go and kill someone on my own side?"

"Would you have been willing to kill a person on the other side?"

"I never hurt a fly in my life. I sell blood, I'm not a gangster. And I don't read newspapers either. If I could read and if I knew what was going on, I would have understood what this was all about. I'd have caught on at once."

"Caught on to what?"

"Who's stupid—you or me? We'd done one of theirs in, they wanted to do one of ours in. I could have told the guy that he was knocking on the wrong door. But even at the risk of my life, I preferred to clear up the mystery. I pretended to accept the offer."

"So then, even without reading the newspapers, you did catch on."

"I'm no dope. Then the fellow told me to get into his car. I told the hospital guard that I'd come back next day, and we drove to Aristotelous Street and stopped. He told me to wait a minute while he dashed up to the office to let them know I was coming. And he left me there waiting in the car. I started to play with the doorknobs and buttons. I pushed one button and the windowpane began coming down by itself. What a contraption! When that happened, I stuck my head out the window, and I looked up, and I saw a big EDA sign spread across the front of the building. Then I got scared. Why should I look for trouble with the Communists? Two cousins of mine had their throats slit by the Communists. They did it with a can top. I may be poor, but I'm honest. And since I now understood that was the place the guy had meant when he said office, I opened the door and beat it. I went straight to the Security Police."

"How did you know where to find them?"

"If you know enough to ask the way, you can find the North Pole. You think I couldn't find the Security Police?"

"Had you ever gone there before?"

"No. And from there I went to the Public Prosecutor and told him the whole story. But I asked him to keep my name out of it, so I wouldn't get into trouble with those guys."

"Why didn't you get a policeman to follow you and let him catch them in the act, just as they were handing over the money to you?"

"I didn't want to get mixed up in it. I earn my bread with my blood."

"What else did this man say to you? Do you remember?"

"He told me the people on the right are like the downy mildew that's scourging our fields. 'I don't have any fields,' I told him. 'One more reason,' he says to me then, 'for you to do what I'm telling you. When we take power, the land will be distributed equally among all the peasants.'"

"You've only made one gaffe, Mr. Pournaropoulos," said Andoniou. "There's just one person in Salonika who has an automobile with a button that automatically raises and lowers the windows. And that's the well-known rightist terrorist, from your own haunts—Kilkis. You'll be locked up for slander. Because, you understand, blood cannot turn to water."

Chapter 19

An anticlimax by definition follows a climax. How can you have an anticlimax all by itself? Ever since you died, that's what I've been experiencing. I re-

read what I wrote you the other day; and today I feel the need to continue, because I didn't say everything.

The night was sweet when it came down from the mountains and we welcomed it into our house. We opened all the windows to make it feel more at ease and we sent it packing whenever we wished. Love with music, music with love, it all belonged to us, do you remember? Now—this painful now, from which I can't escape—now the night besieges me, stifles me in the widow's weeds provided by your assassins.

A question obsesses me: Why you and not someone else? Why you, who were not a Communist but a humanitarian in the broadest sense, a pacifist like everyone else? Then the other day I read the letter about you written by Pauling to President Kennedy. Among other things—the biographical details were rather funny—he writes that what the Greek right struck out against in you was the spirit of cooperation with the left. The left they know and are not afraid of. But they fear just such men as you who lean more and more in that direction. The intention of the right was to intimidate the others. They succeeded in killing you, concludes Pauling, but they didn't succeed in arresting the movement, which because of you goes on with increased momentum.

Today I started moving. I'm going to my brother's temporarily. I can't live any longer at 7 Thessiou Street. Every time a board creaks I feel a thorn in my flesh. The book you ordered from abroad arrived. Things keep arriving every day, packages, letters, poems addressed to you, and they drive me to despair. I don't have the courage to bear it alone. Today your son came in from play, in a state of panic. They'd been playing with their scooters and some child had threatened, "I'll kill you the way they killed your dad." He thinks you're still in London and he imagined you had had an accident. I reassured him. But in the end my own eyes filled with tears.

The whole house is in disorder, a kind of rectangular disorder—the movers come and go as if this place were a sanctuary. As I leave this nest of our love, my legs tremble and I don't know how I'm going to manage, alone and exposed to the world. I talk to you at night for hours on end.

This letter sounds like *Romance Magazine*. And I know you'd hate it if you read it. But I hate *you* for not writing to me. I've taken two sleeping pills, and I hope that in a little while I'll fall asleep. I miss you unimaginably. The bed is too big for me, your coffin too narrow for you. Isn't there some middle way? Can't we find some compromise that will make your life and my death more bearable? Whoever lays a flower on your grave defiles my heart. Because from this point on I am indissolubly bound to you. That is why I hate you even more.

Chapter 20

The rock had become an obsession. Since the side of a mountain had broken away and blotted out the whole village of Mikro Horio at Karpenissi, Hatzis had felt certain that one day that rock was going to come crashing on his roof. The little house, his wife's dowry, was on the outer edge of Salonika, where the neighborhood ended and the mountain reared itself, a hovering weight, primitive, ominous. An enormous rock hung over his roof like a curse. His wife was forever harping on the danger. But what could he do without money?

It was March this year, during a night storm, that he heard strange cracking noises. At the time of the Mikro Horio disaster he had read in the papers that rainwater sapping away the earth beneath the surface had loosened the crag which crushed the village. He had children; when they grew up, he didn't want them accusing him of being a neglectful father. The next day he started to build three cement columns to prop up the menacing rock.

Not knowing much about building, he enlisted the aid of a cementworker friend. Together they put up frames to hold the cement. When it had set and the frames were removed, the rock had three strong buttresses. The job took two months. Nobody came around to interfere, for everyone knew what a difficult time he had of it. All his neighbors said was, "Bravo, Tiger, you should have done that long ago." This was before Hatzis had become famous.

For the time being the rock was no longer a menace, but presently a new, worse menace appeared. During the interval Hatzis had become a celebrity. He was the man whose jump into the pickup van, the night of the crime, had introduced a thread into the labyrinth. Since then his life had been threatened and he was often followed. It would be very easy, he knew, some evening, in his deserted neighborhood . . .

It happened not at night but in the morning. At nine o'clock, three clerks from the Prefecture, accompanied by two workmen, knocked on his door. Introducing themselves as representatives of the City Planning Bureau, they asked to see Hatzis's permit for building the columns on land he didn't own. Hatzis told them he didn't have a permit, and that he had put up the columns to keep the rock from breaking away and burying him, the way Mikro Horio had been buried.

The gentlemen from the City Planning Bureau appeared unmoved by his pleas. They represented the law and the law said no one could build anything, even a column, without authorization. And so, to their great regret, they must demolish the columns immediately. They ordered the workmen to set to work without delay.

Hatzis was outraged. If they did this, the rock would fall; the extremities of the columns were cemented to it.

Did they want to shatter his little house? Who could possibly be bothered by these columns which no one could see anyway here at the end of town? Who had sent them? They'd come on their own, they said. Then why hadn't they come earlier, why had they waited until now? Was it because they'd just heard about his part in the Z. affair? The three gentlemen weren't going to listen to a word about politics. They were merely employees of the Prefecture, and as employees they were not allowed to express any opinion whatever. Meanwhile the workmen had got out their crowbars and sledgehammers and had begun the demolition. It had taken two months to build the columns; it would take two hours to pull them down.

Hatzis rushed to the neighborhood café and telephoned Matsas the lawyer and told him about his latest difficulty. Matsas promised to take action at once.

Before an hour had passed—the first column had already been torn down and the workmen were hacking away at the second—a limousine stopped in a dust cloud outside Hatzis's door. The chauffeur opened the back door, and out stepped the Prefect himself in all his early-morning magnificence.

"What is going on?" he demanded.

"These columns were erected without a permit," answered the senior clerk of the City Planning Bureau. "We're pulling them down."

"Stop at once."

"But that's the order we were given, Mr. Prefect."

"Well, I'm canceling that order."

The entire neighborhood—old women, little children, housewives, men from the café—stood watching the scene, ready to intervene. Since the Z. affair, the Tiger had become in a sense the pride of the neighborhood. The Prefect turned to consider these people: women with kerchiefs around their heads, old women with their spindles, unemployed men waiting to be called to Germany, an oppressive group of mute and tense human beings. He felt uncomfortable. The chauffeur was busy chasing away youngsters who kept fingering the limousine's gleaming chromium.

"I am ordering you," the Prefect repeated in a ringing voice, "to stop the demolition at once. And the community must begin reconstruction work within one hour. The entire rock must be sealed with cement and the whole thing rebuilt. I repeat: within one hour! Our country is obliged to support heroic men of the people like Hatzis. The step taken by the City Planning Bureau was, to say the least, badly timed."

With this finale worthy of a Neapolitan operetta, he shook Tiger's hand twice and got back into his limousine. This was the same Prefect who on the day of the assassination had done nothing to protect Z., although warned of the danger by Matsas. The situation was different now. The disbanding of Autocratosaur's quasigovernmental organization had been decreed on his authority only a day before. His intervention on Hatzis's behalf, added to yesterday's deed, made the Prefect feel like a good Christian who has performed his Sunday act of charity.

"That was a premonition," thought Hatzis when they'd gone. "Now it's rabbit and partridge season on my mountain. I wonder if I shouldn't expect a hunting accident?"

Chapter 21

The Investigator is cornered. He is hemmed in on all sides. The pack is closing in on him. The Investigator is a door leading not to freedom but to prison. Since getting Mastodontosaur incarcerated in Yendi-Koule, the Investigator has become the target of the dinosaurs.

The dignitaries bustle about. The Minister is permanently settled in the "little palace." The Generalissimo; the Grand Judge of the Areopagus; the personal adviser of the Prime Minister. Interviews. Telephone calls. Tension. Layers of paint slapped on to hide the cracks. But at this stage it is difficult to conceal the truth. The Grand Judge of the Areopagus expresses anxiety: "Are you never going to finish the Z. affair? You promised to end the investigation in June and it's already August. You deceived me. What are you doing anyway? Don't you see that by examining witnesses incessantly you're likely to get confused?"

The Investigator knows all this. He is hunted. Doubly hunted, by those above him and by the masses who turn to him as their only salvation. The Investigator keeps vigil. He works eighteen hours out of twenty-four. He has already formed an opinion, but it's of no avail to utter it. He must allow the facts to speak for themselves.

"Why did you issue a warrant for the arrest of an officer of the police corps? Why did you place him in custody? Hadn't we agreed that officers would be jailed only if certain to be convicted? Yet the Public Prosecutor tells me the evidence at your disposal is not enough to convict Mastodontosaur, only enough to justify summoning him. However, I am not able to say any more to you about this matter over the telephone. What you do not seem to understand is that your activities are damaging the very structure of our society."

The Investigator is young, handsome, courageous. The hope of a cure for the rottenness. A dream moored to the dock. A door opened into the prison. Without water, without light. He rummages in the black hole. "I am performing my duty." He keeps working. He weaves the fabric for the merchants who will come to determine the price. But it must be knit firmly enough to endure the cold. With two needles, chopsticks, he counts each stitch, reels off the rice grain by grain. Each jerk of the needle is sagely calculated. Each stitch in relation to another stitch.

The Investigator has a large stethoscope. He is the moon probing the stadium at a football match played under floodlights. Thousands of spectators are involved in the contest. Who among them has bribed the players to throw the game? Who has staked a fortune on their losing? The Investigator studies the X-ray record of the crime, he makes a precise analysis of each suspicious shadow. There must be no doubt. How sweet the terrible responsibility! He reels with fatigue and determination. The Investigator distributes tickets to Yendi-Koule.

"The Investigator is accused of left-wing bias. A deputy of the ERE, known for his extreme right-wing opinions, has demanded that the Minister of the Interior inform Parliament of the personal activities and past record of the Investigator handling the affair at Salonika, Mr.———."

The Investigator declares: "The castle is well fortified." The Investigator is courageous. He is intelligent. Whenever he sees the need for silence, he says, "I have no statement to make." When the Generalissimo submits to him a list of witnesses to be questioned, the Investigator refuses it, on the pretext that he must gather his material at its source. One source leads to another. The earth is hollowed out beneath his feet, it collapses under him. Moles have tunneled everywhere, creating a subterranean labyrinth whose countless corridors converge at the very center of the affair. The Investigator is a helmeted deep-sea diver equipped with oxygen.

"The Grand Judge of the Areopagus has told the Investigator that in his opinion the guilty parties intended not to kill Z. but to cripple him. What is the meaning of these new warrants mentioned in the press? Well, issue them and let's be done with it!"

The Investigator is a climbing plant named "desire." He scales props. Ignores obstacles. He can even fill a room with foliage. The Investigator is an arbor with small green grapes hanging from its lattices, but by autumn they will be ripe for wine. The Investigator demolishes plastic flooring. He uncovers ancestral roots in buried corpses. The Investigator desecrates graves.

"He does not figure in the hegemony of the twelve gods of Olympus—any more than any investigator does. Nor is he listed among the saints of the Christian Church. Neither has his infallibility been recognized, that unique privilege being reserved for the Pope. The Investigator is a human being like the rest of us. He is a particular human being, who was born of particular parents, and whether he likes it or not he bears a given heritage in his blood and soul. He was perhaps moved by particular ideas in the course of his youth, and on his own individual nature depends his capacity to resist the weaknesses innate in man. Such is the Investigator—any investigator."

The Investigator doesn't have time for anxiety, agonies, metaphysical griefs. He is attached to the vessel as the rudder is attached to the keel. The Investigator is a gardener who uproots the weeds from the garden. The Investigator is a flower that blooms in solitude like those flowers of South America that make their appearance in the gloom of autumn and announce, even before winter comes, the eventual springtime.

Chapter 22

Winter is coming and I shall not see you; I want you to know how much I long for you. At least the nights will be shorter, and I shall have you more to myself. These summer days are endless. My black cotton absorbs the sun. It scorches me.

My love for you will not go to your children. My love for you will turn to smoke. It will rise as through a chimney at the point where our skies separate.

I am an empty stadium. The white boundary lines have faded. The little sandpit is unraked, where you landed when you jumped. Sand settles into odd depressions. The grains stick. I don't know when the next Balkan Games will take place.

Without you, I am so much untended sand. You, the champion broad-jumper, are missing. I keep your track clothes in memory of your body, your running shoes in memory of your feet.

Now that you are sailing further and further toward the horizon, following the curve of the earth, it will soon be that I can see nothing of you but a flag on the highest mast. Outside of that, I feel all right. I study your surgeon's instruments for the touch of your hands.

Another time I shall write you the little things about you I keep secret, never to be a part of other people's memories. I don't know how much longer I can bear this solitude. Perhaps I would do better to remember you through other people. A dangerous egoism takes form in solitude. You imagine that other people owe you something. But friction seals the wound, the scar forms over it, and what remains is the purest gold.

I am bored to death. I wait for day to close, for night to open its vast arms, in which I have my real existence. There is no possible compromise with death. That is the truth. A simple parting gives rise to expectation, uncertainty. Death is whatever had no time to happen.

This is why I suffer. Because I had still immense reserves of tenderness stored up for you. Because there were things still to be experienced. Even if we didn't always get on too well. You don't know how much comfort I find in our not having been the ideal couple, in the courage with which we disagreed, open, without deception.

All these things keep me alive. And if I am becoming a romantic, it is because I miss you. I truly wanted to see what kept us apart. I truly liked to suffer at your side. But the kite broke loose, and here I am, holding the string.

Chapter 23

A black limousine with a foreign license plate trailed in the wake of witnesses and reporters. A Taunus leaped up on the sidewalk in pursuit of a lawyer —who moved away in time—a Taunus with a foreign license plate. (Where were these license plates made? Were these numbers unrecorded at the central offices of the traffic police?) Two hands shot out of a little truck and gave Nikitas a "scientific" clout. Motor bikes circulated around the scene of the meeting on the evening of May 22. Ambulances bobbed up out of nowhere, picking up injured persons and disappearing into the night. There was Yango's kamikazi. And finally a Volkswagen driven by a policeman transported Z. to the hospital. All this had set up a train of thought in the young reporter's mind. As the investigation progressed, he came to the conclusion that, behind the persons involved in the case, there had been a motorized battalion at work that night, whose aim was to exterminate Z. and ensure the speedy evacuation of the assassins.

If things had gone awry for the culprits, if one by one the assassins had come out from behind the bushes—like children playing hide-and-seek, "Come out, come out, I see you"—it was thanks to Tiger's good work. But a conviction had taken root in the reporter's mind that the investigation should pursue the "motorized battalion angle." Otherwise many obscurities in the case would remain undispelled.

One of those sticky summer evenings in Salonika, while he was eating fried mussels at Stratis's down by the shore, he thought he'd hit on the solution to the puzzle. The General, before going to the meeting, had been at the Ministry of Northern Greece, attending the lecture given by the Assistant Minister on the subject of downy mildew. The Secretary General was also present. He had close connections with EKOF, an extreme right-wing student organization. (The reporter had just disclosed this fact in the press, with photographs to support it.) As for the General, he had close links with the mobsters, and both these men and the EKOF had participated in the counterdemonstration of May 22. The driver of the Volkswagen was the personal chauffeur of the Secretary General. Everything started from there. The lecture on downy mildew had been only a pretext. But he had to discover where the policeman had rented the Volkswagen. And so, playing the self-appointed private detective, a role he very much liked because it broadened the stifling limits of his own profession, he set out on this new adventure.

He went to the first-aid station and discovered with surprise that the license number of the Volkswagen had not been entered in its register of admissions. He made the rounds of all the car-rental agencies, inquiring about the Volkswagen and giving the relevant details, the date, the exact hour, all the data about the crash. They regarded him as an imbecile, of course, but he didn't care. He knew that one of the keys to the case was to be found in this "chance" circumstance. Finally, exhausted but not discouraged, he stumbled on the agency he was looking for. This time the man behind the desk paid careful attention as Andoniou told his story.

"Yes, of course I remember. But you told me over the

telephone that you had decided not to claim any damages."

Andoniou understood. He was silent, waiting to hear what would come next.

"Of course! Of course!" continued the proprietor. "You were hit by the policeman who was driving Z. to the hospital. Isn't that so?"

"Precisely."

"At first you asked for damages. And then, for some strange reason, you phoned me and told me you were withdrawing your claims. Are you coming back to your first position? You're perfectly right in doing so."

"What was the policeman's name?" Andoniou asked.

"I must have given it to you over the telephone."

"I lost it."

"Just a moment."

And he began to search through his records. He found the entry and gave him the name. Thus the reporter succeeded in verifying the testimony of one witness, that the policeman in question was the chauffeur of the Secretary General at the Administration Building.

"This policeman telephoned me about four in the afternoon, asking to rent a car. He wasn't the one who came for it; that was another guy whom I work with sometimes. I mean, the other guy rents them from me and then rents them again to third parties. His name is Meracles. The policeman got the car from Meracles at six and said he'd return it at nine that evening, but, because of the unfortunate incident, he returned it at ten."

"And who is this Meracles?"

"A poor devil trying to make a living. He doesn't have any capital. But they claim he has some pull at the Ministry of Northern Greece, and he manages fairly well. The best thing is for me to take you straight to him. He's the one directly involved, and he'll have to take care of your damages. Let's go. It's just a step away."

They left the agency. The proprietor talked with animation about the Z. affair: "What a case that is! Sometimes I think we're all involved in it without knowing it. That's the impression the newspapers give at least. Don't you agree? At least I have this impression. What do you think? What's your profession?"

"Reporter."

The proprietor froze right in the middle of the sidewalk. An old lady coming from the opposite direction bumped against him, spilling the bag of peaches she was carrying. They both stooped down to pick them up.

"Reporter? Then you must know better than I . . ."

"I don't know anything. I came for the express purpose of finding out."

"Oh, please!" the proprietor entreated. "Don't bring my name into it! I don't want to get involved. I have enough trouble making a living. I have a son, and a daughter in Geneva at the interpreters' school. And now that everybody's buying a car, it's harder and harder to rent them. I can't even meet the expenses of my own agency. We don't have the tourist activity they have in Athens . . ."

They had arrived at their destination. Meracles was in his office, on the phone. When he saw them, he signaled for them to sit down, thinking that the boss must be bringing him a new client. Covering the receiver with his hand, he asked if they would like coffee. They declined. Meracles finished his telephone conversation and addressed the boss: "What can we do for this gentleman?"

"This gentleman's a newspaper reporter and wants to talk with you," the boss said nervously.

Meracles was visibly irritated. Without looking at Andoniou, he asked, "What does he want?"

"There are a few points I would like to clarify," Andoniou began.

"I have an order from the Head of the Administration Office not to give out any information."

"From the Head of the Administration Office or from the Head of Security Police?"

"From the Head of the Security Police," said Meracles.

This information was all Andoniou needed. He left at once to make a deposition before the Public Prosecutor, and at the same time prepared the story for publication in his newspaper. Meracles denied it, claiming he had never said anything about the Head of Security Police.

In the trial that followed, he was condemned to seven months' imprisonment for perjury. It was brought out at the trial that whereas, prior to the crime, he had purchased a Skoda car on credit and was having difficulty meeting the payments, the day after the assassination he had paid cash for a new Vespa worth 15,000 drachmas. Where had he laid hands on the money in the course of one night? It also emerged that he had dealings with the Administration Office and that a certain policeman came frequently to his office—the same policeman, in fact, who was to declare when the Karamanlis government fell, and on the eve of the parliamentary elections, "If Karamanlis wins the elections, God help the Investigator!" But that was much later. For the moment—it was the end of summer over the Thermaic Gulf and the International Fair was about to open its gates as it does every year in September—the right-wing newspapers had begun to publish colorful accounts of how the Communists had killed Z., using Vango, a former member of ELAS, as their agent. In the chaos that reigned, the young reporter, having fulfilled his duty, went back to Athens for good.

Chapter 24

The General is free to go where he pleases. The General makes statements. The General takes mysterious trips. He has only one concern now, to stay out of the limelight and to die. He is pulling strings that connect with the infinite. A few strings break and the General curses. One of the broken strings is Nikitas. Another is Baronissimo, who declares in prison: "Why do they throw me in here now, when they're the ones who dragged me down?" Yango keeps his mouth shut. Vango's having a ball. Jimmy the Boxer is nowhere to be found. Then one day he gets caught trying to cross the frontier at the getaway point near Orestiada. He claims he's an itinerant boxer on tour. The General, former head of the Palace Guard of evzones, has powerful protectors. The problem, as the General sees it, can be reduced to one simple injunction: Conceal the guilty. He states that if the Chief of Police is relieved of his post, he will side unequivocally with him. The Chief of Police is relieved of his post, and the General doesn't stir from his hole. Without the General there would be utter chaos. Amid the charges hurled from all sides against the police force, he declares that he will assume full responsibility. But the General, by legal definition, is above responsibility. When the press accuses him of complicity in the crime, he retorts: "How are we supposed to arrest our own accomplices? How are we to take ourselves into custody?"

For the General, Salonika is a chessboard. Here is the Castle—the White Tower; here is the Bishop—the Ro-

tonda minaret; here is the Knight—the port riding horseback into the sea. All these pieces, reflected in the bay,
become double: two Castles, two Bishops, two Knights.
Although the Queen is missing, the pawns are numerous.
The General moves his men masterfully. But the opponent also plays well and has the advantage of external
support: the newspaper reporters. Every time the General loses a pawn, he explodes with rage. He is not accustomed to losing. All of a sudden he finds himself
without a line of defense. He goes to Athens in secret
and begs the authorities to take charge. His nerves have
given way. The General has an idea he is being pursued,
in these grievous days, by the Spirit of Evil. The Zionist
mafia and the Communist mafia join forces. The General
retires, "for reasons of age," just when he was counting
on becoming Generalissimo, the incumbent being due
for retirement. He has been accused in the report of the
Court of the Areopagus. The Investigator requests him
to prepare his defense. The General feels that his life
has lost its purpose.

Part 4
APOLOGIAS

Chapter 1

"I am beside myself. I am outraged, Mr. Investigator. Who could have imagined that I would attain the summit of departmental hierarchy—with the post of High Commander of the Royal Police within reach—only to be overtaken by so cruel a fate? That I, the General, should be accused of 'willfully aiding and abetting the perpetrators of this murder by my actions before, during, and after the crime.' And how did I 'aid and abet them'? 'By being present at the site of the crime and by promising assistance after it had been committed; by covering up the tracks of the criminals; by failing to sue and arrest them and by concealing the instruments of the crime from the Investigators'? And who is said to have done all this? I, I who have spent my whole life in the service of the Fatherland. And here I am, branded a murderer! No, no!"

That afternoon, he didn't remember precisely at what time, but he was sure it was that afternoon and not some other, because it was Wednesday and the shops were closed, and, forgetting it was Wednesday, he had set out for the shops to buy some underdrawers, but he hadn't found any, and that's why he remembered it was that afternoon, even though three months have passed and memory declines with age—well then, to get back to that afternoon, he had put on civilian clothes, because of course he couldn't very well go shopping for underdrawers in his General's uniform, and here he wished to add parenthetically that he was afflicted with hermorrhoids, so that the question of underdrawers—whether or not they chafed—was absolutely crucial to him. Consequently he couldn't very well tell his orderly to buy underdrawers for him, and his wife was busy with a Philanthropic Brotherood Tea—well, that same afternoon, at the Ministry of Northern Greece, a lecture was being given on methods of combating downy mildew. He himself was of farming stock (his father had been a farmer) and had a passion for agricultural problems. Having been invited to attend this lecture, reserved for the "higher echelons of the administration," he thought it would be interesting to learn about the most modern methods of fighting downy mildew. For he was still a farmer at heart. He maintained several small farms in the vicinity of Kavalla and his hobby was raising tobacco. Nature relaxed him. His responsibilities as General were crushing and his only relief was contact with the soil. As he grows older, a man returns to his roots, so closing the circle of his life like a great zero. He used the word "zero" because that was exactly what he felt like now. A product of the lowest though the most patriotic segment of the population, he had attained the Mount Everest of the hierarchy and now "the Communists, those termites who do everything in their power to undermine the foundations of our race," wanted to tumble him from his throne. But they would not succeed! He was innocent. He was not denying—on the contrary, he was proud of it—that he had made it his aim in life to combat Communism and Judaism, the two related diseases threatening our glorious Hellenic-Christian civilization. Alas, the masses failed to realize how closely related these two ills are. Well, he hadn't come to see the Investigator to expound his theories. He had brought the matter up only to show that it was the axis of his life, his compass so to speak, and because he wished to make it known that "by rubbing those twin stones together, I have produced heat and light."

The lecture on downy mildew had woken him up. At

noon he had squid with onions, a dish excellently prepared by his wife, but rather indigestible nevertheless,
which was why he'd gone to sleep afterwards, and
whenever he slept at noon he always woke up with his
head feeling like a boiler and had to drink at least two
or three cups of coffee to recover—that was why he'd
been confused and had gone down to the shopping district on a Wednesday afternoon to shop for underdrawers. But the lecture on downy mildew had brought out
the farmer in him, had brought back the days when he
had set traps and caught birds on the village stream in
Nea Karvali with his friend Zisis ("the poor fellow had
his throat cut by the Slavo-Communists"). So he'd
jumped up and spoken briefly of the Communist mildew
that was the scourge of Greece. What? The Investigator
already knew that. Who told him? Professional secrecy?
So there were spies in the auditorium? Or maybe he'd
learned it from that ex-Communist, now Salonika District Director of Rice Plantations? Oh well, on his way
down the stairs of the Ministry he'd stopped to chat
with the cleaning woman who was scrubbing the floor.
He knew her from long ago, when she had worked at
police headquarters. Her husband had been butchered
by the Red hyenas. She had asked a favor of him recently; the General never missed an opportunity to help
the simple people. Why did he go so often to the Ministry of Northern Greece? Because the Secretary General
was a friend of his. "This young man, inspired by the
unimpeachable ideals of the Hellenic-Christian Ideal,
lends an attentive ear to my theories about the sunspots
and—a point that cannot be sufficiently stressed—their
inverse polarity." After that, he had driven the Assistant
Minister to the Mikra Airport in his own car. They had
been delayed on the way and the Assistant Minister had
almost missed his plane, because they'd run over a
chicken. It couldn't be avoided. The road was slippery,
and if he'd put his brakes on suddenly, he might have
turned over and crashed into a parked tractor. The Assistant Minister of Agriculture, president of the Society

for the Protection of Animals, asked him to stop to see if they had in fact run over the chicken. He seemed upset and looked disapprovingly at the General. It didn't seem to occur to him that the chicken had run in front of the wheels and was at least partly to blame. Not naturally superstitious, the General was inclined to be so now. That chicken had been an omen! A few hours later, the General was to be accused of complicity in the death of a Red deputy. But let's take the events in their actual order:

When he got back to the city, he stopped at his office for his invitation to the Bolshoi Ballet. The invitation did not say what time the performance was to begin. He asked his orderly to phone the theater and learned that the performance was scheduled for a quarter to ten (which meant ten, he said to himself). It was then nine. He had a whole hour ahead of him. He phoned his wife to be ready at 9:30, he would drive by to pick her up. Then he phoned the Chief of Police to suggest that they all go together. The officer on duty informed him that the Chief was out. He had set out a short while before for the intersection of Ermou and Venizelou Streets, where a meeting of the Friends of Peace was being held. First word he'd heard about any such meeting. He decided to pick the Chief up right there.

Ah, yes. He'd been expecting that question! How was it possible that he, a fanatical anti-Communist, had agreed to attend the Russian ballet? Naturally, he would not have gone to see the ballerinas—thank God, he had no such vices! He would have gone to observe the troupe, study the physiognomies, colors, the movement, "which would of course be mostly on stage left." In short, he'd be doing his job! Because ever since the death of the Jew-Communist Stalin and the rise to power of the pure-blooded Russian Aryans, Russian propaganda methods had become subtler. Theater, cinema, satellites, astronauts were its new weapons. What's that? Stalin was like Hitler? He persecuted the Jews? The General didn't wish to offend, but he knew his history.

Stalin was a Jew! "In case you need proof, his name was Joseph."

So he parked his car outside the Modiano Market and asked for the Chief of Police. Recognizing the General despite his civilian clothes, a policeman froze to attention and informed him that the Chief was at the Kosmopolit Hotel. And there he found the Chief, engaged in vehement conversation. The Chief took courage from his presence and continued: "Mr. Spathopoulos, when you came to my office this noon, along with the other members of the Peace Committee, you told me you were an honorable man. What you are doing now is not an honorable thing. What are you trying to do? Create a sensation? Do you hear those loudspeakers? The racket they're making? They're saying you've been kidnapped. Couldn't you open the window and call to them that nobody has molested you and that you're not in danger. Or phone them at least." And Spathopoulos kept protesting that this was an intolerable state of affairs and that the jungle had broken loose out there. He himself had listened in silence. The mere sight of Comrade Spathopoulos gave him a bellyache. He felt the squid he had eaten that noon coming back to life inside him, squeezing his intestines with its tentacles. The Chief of Police offered to escort Spathopoulos to the meeting.

He had gone out with them and seen "a crowd of about 150 people, shouting their disapproval of the incendiary slogans issuing from a loudspeaker placed provocatively on the balcony of the Labor Union Club." They've gone back to those old megaphones from the Occupation, he reflected. Our home-grown Communism hasn't even learned to adapt itself like the foreign brand. The others send ballets to persuade us that life in the Red inferno is a dance, while ours—these cripples of our own race—are still using the old Occupation megaphones. In any case, he was sure of one thing now: it was out of the question to go to the ballet. Of course, even if he went, he was under no obligation to stay. But just as a doctor on a cruise can't help coming to the assistance of the man in the next cabin who suddenly falls ill, so he too put his professional conscience first; he was a green lighthouse in a Red sea of murderers. And so he went back to his office and phoned his wife that for reasons beyond his control he was obliged to call off their evening at the Bolshoi. Duty! Fatherland above all! And then he phoned the Secretary General and told him he had an extra invitation and if he wanted it he could send the Ministry clerk to pick it up. The Secretary General did indeed want it, though not for himself—he himself would not have gone, he had too much work to do —but for a friend, whose wife (a former ballerina) had moved heaven and earth to obtain a ticket and hadn't been able to, and who would now be thrilled. Then the General had gone back to the site of the incidents. It must have been ten, perhaps twenty, minutes past nine. He said at the very start that he had no sense of time.

Yes, of course he had arrived after the injury to Pirouchas. Did Pirouchas say he had seen him? If so, it was an hallucination of his own. Pirouchas was obsessed by the idea that the General had been pursuing him ever since the Occupation, when they had belonged to rival Resistance groups: Pirouchas to the Red EAM, he himself to the national camp. Ever since then, whenever there's a brawl and Pirouchas is there, whether he gets hurt or not, he imagines the General is behind it. Pirouchas needs a psychoanalyst. Still, the General was proud of having given him this "complex."

"Undoubtedly the loudspeakers were to blame. If your neighbor plays his radio too loud, you can sue him. If a loudspeaker on top of a car goes through your neighborhood advertising a movie, you blow your top—and now these blaring loudmouths right in the center of town! That's the difference between Communists and donkeys: when Communists get obstinate, they don't refuse to budge; they simply bray twice as loud. When it was suggested that they turn down the loudspeakers, they had turned them up."

He had never heard of Z. Not even from the newspapers. The General did not read the newspapers. On the whole, he was against the press, a deplorable institution, especially in Greece. Well, when the speeches and songs were over, he had seen a man approach the Chief of Police and point to some bruises on his forehead. The man was vociferating furiously. He shouted that the Friends of Peace had come as free citizens and would leave as free citizens. Such impudence had exasperated the General. To avoid uttering a curse that would have reduced him to the level of this fanatical riffraff, to remain a neutral observer, he had preferred to move off. Later he had heard that the impudent individual had been Z.

In his effort to get away from the scene of this exchange between the Chief of Police and Z., he found himself opposite the entrance to the auditorium where the meeting had been held. A detachment of police was seeing to it that the Friends of Peace left quietly and in small groups. He mingled with the demonstrators to note their impressions, to find out how much they had been influenced by Z.'s anarchism. Suddenly he had heard the roar of a motorcycle. He had turned his head and seen a man struck by the three-wheeler and falling to the ground. The vehicle had dragged him a yard or two and then with dizzying speed disappeared up Venizelou Street, which, as everyone knows, is one-way in the other direction. He had paid no attention to the incident but continued on his way, taking note of every word uttered by the Friends of Peace. But by the time he had reached Egnatia Street, the small groups were breaking up, so that nothing further could be gleaned. At the taxi stand he turned around and went back down the opposite sidewalk. There he met the Chief of Police, who was very upset and told him that someone had been injured. "We're sunk! I think it's Z.!"

His first thought was that it must have been a traffic accident. But even then they were involved, because the Communists, "who had probably arranged the accident to throw the guilt on us" (this had been his second thought), would be sure to exploit the incident one way or the other. The situation had to be faced with calm deliberation. He had taken the Chief of Police by the arm. They had gone to his car, parked outside the Modiano Market, and had made the rounds of the neighboring districts to see if there was any rioting. In the car they discussed ways and means of counteracting the Communist efforts to exploit the situation. The Chief of Police had seemed more and more agitated. The General had had to calm him down; it was his duty as a friend and superior in rank. In the end the ride had soothed the Chief. The General had finally convinced him that there was nothing to fear and that his own presence at the site of the incidents, though quite accidental, partly relieved the Chief of his responsibility. In any case, he would stand by him to the end. They reached police headquarters at a quarter to eleven. The Public Prosecutors arrived shortly afterward.

INVESTIGATOR: At what time, General, do you situate the arrival of the two Public Prosecutors at police headquarters?

GENERAL: I am unable to tell you even approximately for the simple reason that it was not my business to notify them. Moreover, three months have elapsed since then and I find it difficult to remember occurrences that seemed unimportant to me at the time. The affair was not within my jurisdiction and I was not responsible for notifying them.

INVESTIGATOR: Quite aside from questions of jurisdiction and responsibility, at what time did you first become aware of the presence of the Public Prosecutors at police headquarters?

GENERAL: I was indeed aware of their presence but reiterate that I cannot tell you even approximately when they arrived.

INVESTIGATOR: The Prosecutors asked you whether the culprit had been arrested and you replied: "No matter where he goes, he will be caught." In your estimation, how long after their arrival did they ask you that question?

GENERAL: For the reasons already stated, I am unable to give you even an approximate answer.

INVESTIGATOR: Why, in your opinion, did the Prosecutors go to police headquarters so late at night?

GENERAL: Undoubtedly to inquire into the circumstances of the accident incurred by Z. and to find out whether or not the culprits had been arrested.

INVESTIGATOR: If, as you say, the Prosecutors' purpose was to ascertain whether the culprits had been arrested, they must have addressed themselves immediately to you and to the Chief of Police. How then is it possible that you are unable to estimate the time that elapsed between their arrival and the moment they questioned you?

GENERAL: I cannot read prosecutors' minds. It is quite possible that like many persons at that particular time they suspected the police of organizing the crime or at least of having done nothing to prevent it. In that case their purpose in coming would have been to observe our first reactions and they would intentionally have waited some time before questioning us.

INVESTIGATOR: In your opinion, would the fact that the police failed to notify the Prosecutors immediately of the culprit's arrest justify them in suspecting the police of organizing the crime?

GENERAL: In my opinion, the suspicions of the police would have been partly justified if indeed the delay of the police in notifying the Prosecutors had seemed unjustified.

INVESTIGATOR: Express yourself more clearly. Was the delay justified or not?

GENERAL: It was justified.

INVESTIGATOR: Did the two Prosecutors have reason to believe that the police were implicated in the crime?

GENERAL: Only the Prosecutors are in a position to answer that question objectively. As for me, the mere thought that Public Prosecutors may have entertained such a suspicion would be inconceivably shocking.

INVESTIGATOR: When I say the police, I am referring not to the police force as a whole but to you in particular.

GENERAL: Question the Prosecutors.

INVESTIGATOR: Have you ever in the past observed a certain distrust of the Salonika police force on the part of the judicial authorities?

GENERAL: No such thought ever entered my head.

INVESTIGATOR: Did you that evening observe the presence at police headquarters of the Prosecutor of the Court of Appeals?

GENERAL: Certainly not. However, I remember well that about that time—I cannot tell you the exact date—I personally met the Prosecutor of the Court of Appeals in the office of the Chief of Police and that we had a conversation the tenor of which I have forgotten. I believe, however, that we discussed the circumstances of the accident incurred by Z. I do not exclude the possibility that this conversation took place on the night of May 22.

INVESTIGATOR: First you said "Certainly not." Now you say "I do not exclude." You are contradicting yourself.

GENERAL: Be that as it may, the Chief of Police announced in my absence that the guilty party had been arrested; he must have done so five or at most seven minutes after the question had been asked him in my presence.

INVESTIGATOR: Permit me to point out once again that "in my absence" and "in my presence" are two contradictory propositions. The question, then, was asked in your presence and the Chief of Police answered in your absence. How so? Was he afraid to answer in your hearing?

GENERAL: My answer had startled him. He did not wish to contradict me.

INVESTIGATOR: Can it be that he thought you were hiding a fact known to him and therefore preferred to keep silent?

GENERAL: Only the Chief of Police could tell you that.

INVESTIGATOR: It is possible that he as your subordinate, judging that you were trespassing on his prerogatives, preferred not to antagonize you. It is also possible that you had withdrawn his right to act in matters concerning the Security Police. Otherwise it seems incomprehensible that he knew the guilty party had been arrested, yet made no attempt to contradict you when he heard you say: "No matter where he goes, he will be caught."

GENERAL: The Chief of Police told me later that when he informed the Prosecutors of the arrest of the culprit, one of them, Mr. Panagakos, expressed keen dissatisfaction. He stood up and said angrily: "My friend, this is the second time you've pulled this on me!" Those were his exact words. He was referring to an incident in the 1961 election campaign. A policeman had committed manslaughter on the person of a Communist and the same Prosecutor had been informed of the crime only after an unjustified delay.

INVESTIGATOR: So he had reason to harbor suspicions. First a case of manslaughter, now this "traffic accident."

GENERAL: I would commit suicide if I did not regard this interview as a crude farce!

INVESTIGATOR: There has been so much talk lately about attempts at suicide by members of the police force that no one takes them seriously any more. Where did you go during those seven minutes?

GENERAL: I had diarrhea. I hadn't digested the squid I'd eaten for lunch.

The telephone rang. It was an urgent call for the Investigator. He adjourned the interview until late afternoon and left the office. The General followed him, inwardly cursing the Zionist movement and its adherents.

At the afternoon session he was faced with new trouble. His lawyer had been unable to come and that worried him. He was afraid of making a blunder. The Investigator gave the impression of wanting to finish him off as quickly as possible.

INVESTIGATOR: Who was in charge of the police personnel assigned to the meeting?

GENERAL: I cannot answer that question. As Inspector General of Police, I was not on duty that night. I am unable to tell you who was in charge.

INVESTIGATOR: I have here a copy of an order putting the Assistant Chief of Police in charge. But the Chief was also present at the meeting. Who then was actually in charge? The Chief or the Assistant Chief?

GENERAL: Insofar as the order was not rescinded by a new order from the Chief of Police himself, the Assistant Chief was responsible for maintaining order at the meeting, though this does not exclude the more general responsibility of the Chief as defined in police regulations, quite independent of his presence at the scene.

INVESTIGATOR: How could the order have been rescinded?

GENERAL: By a written or verbal order from the Chief of Police.

INESTIGATOR: In view of the fact that the Chief of Police had not assumed full responsibility for maintaining order at the meeting, how do you account for his presence from the beginning to the end of it?

GENERAL: Indoor meetings, and such was the case that evening, are as a rule entrusted to the supervision of the Security Police and of the neighborhood precinct. Ordinarily a small police detachment is used. But I happen to know that when his duties leave him time the Chief of Police likes to look in on these meetings to appraise the situation. That is what happened on the evening of May 22. This does not justify the conclusion that the Chief of Police assumed responsibility for the maintenance of order. It is perfectly natural that he should have stayed all through the meeting, especially as a counterdemonstration had started.

INVESTIGATOR: If the situation is as you seem to describe it and this kind of meeting is ordinarily the sole responsibility of the precinct police station, how do you account for the fact that, pursuant to Order No. 39/25/8712, police headquarters alerted the following for the night in question:

1. Two captains of gendarmerie and forty privates of the First District of gendarmerie;

2. The full strength of the Second Police Precinct;

3. One captain, two lieutenants, and twenty privates of the Third District of gendarmerie;

4. The entire First Company of the Fourth Battalion of gendarmes.

GENERAL: As you must know, the owner of the Catacomb Club had definitely refused to rent his hall to the Friends of Peace. In view of Z.'s impulsive nature, it was to be expected that he would hold the meeting in the open air in defiance of the government's prohibition. I presume that it was because of this eventuality, and in order to be able to break up any resultant demonstration, that such a large force was alerted.

There was a knock at the door. It was the General's lawyer. The General took heart. Until then he had sat as though riveted to his chair. Now he relaxed and loosened his belt. The lawyer tapped on his briefcase to indicate that it contained an imporant document. The General asked permission to take the glass of water that was on the desk, put in an Alka-Seltzer, and drank the effervescent liquid in one gulp.

INVESTIGATOR: Let us recapitulate. You go to the meeting to pick up the Chief of Police. Once there, you decide it is your duty to stay and to give up the Bolshoi Ballet. So far so good. But how is it that your sense of duty did not impel you to find out who was responsible for maintaining order on this occasion?

GENERAL: I saw the Chief of Police giving orders to several officers with a view to barring the counterdemonstrators from the scene. On the other hand, the Assistant Chief of Police was not inactive; he too gave the necessary orders to his subordinates.

INVESTIGATOR: How is it possible that you have made no attempt, up to the present time, to find out who was in charge that night!

GENERAL: If I had been on duty, I would be able to answer your question. I was present as a mere observer.

INVESTIGATOR: And as a mere observer what did you observe?

GENERAL: To my astonishment I heard the Assistant Chief of Police declare that he was no longer in charge since the Chief of Police was present—though the latter had not countermanded his order. I believe he was acting in good faith but had misinterpreted the regulations. Objectively speaking, the presence of the Chief of Police at the scene of the meeting did not signify automatically that he assumed full responsibility for the maintenance of order.

INVESTIGATOR: In short, the Chief of Police was not objectively responsible, and the Assistant Chief—subjectively—did not regard himself as responsible either. Consequently, on the night of May 22 the police personnel at the scene were without a responsible commander. I should like to know what you did in the face of such a situation.

GENERAL: It was not until much later that I found out, in the course of a chat with the Assistant Chief, that he had not considered himself in charge. Moreover, I wish to repeat, I was in a position to observe on the spot that the Assistant Chief was not inactive, nor was the Chief or any other member of the police force. At no time did I observe the slightest passivity on the part of the police. Consequently, there is no justification for your assertion that the police force was without a commander. All the officers present were on the move, trying to ward off disaster.

INVESTIGATOR: Z. was wounded the moment he arrived, Pirouchas was also attacked; more and more counterdemonstrators were gathering, throwing stones, shouting, attacking the pacifists. In view of your wide experience in this field, did all this not strike you as symptomatic of an extremely serious situation?

GENERAL: If the situation had struck me as extremely serious, it would have been my duty, in line with article 9 of the Police Code, to assume personal responsibility for the maintenance of order. But symptoms such as you have listed are usual in demonstrations of this kind. To characterize the situation as extremely serious, I should have had to know that Pirouchas was going to be gravely wounded and that Z.'s injuries were fatal. But how could this have been foreseen? I own that I have seldom seen Red Cross ambulances attacked. I remember only a single instance of that kind, during the Civil War. I add that if I myself had been at the corner of Spandoni Street and if I had seen the pickup van start up, I should not have got out of the way. How could anyone have guessed any criminal intent? Such methods of political assassination are inconceivable at a time when man is preparing to conquer the moon and the depths of the ocean.

INVESTIGATOR: I am of the same opinion.

GENERAL: Consequently, if I had assumed responsibility for preserving order, I should have done no more than the Chief of Police.

INVESTIGATOR: Many persons believe, on the contrary, that if you, with your uncontested authority and wide experience, had been at the head of the police force, the meeting would not have had a tragic outcome.

GENERAL: That is not so. Flattered as I am by your remark, I must tell you in deference to the truth that experience depends chiefly on years of service. The Chief of Police has served five years longer than I. His experience is therefore greater. He has always been regarded as a magnificent officer; that is just what he is, even if he lost a battle that night. Moreover, he has great authority.

INVESTIGATOR: Were the motorized units of the police mobilized on the occasion of the meeting?

GENERAL: I do not remember.

INVESTIGATOR: When Z. was run over, did any member of the police force start in pursuit of the guilty party?

GENERAL: It was reported to me that several started in pursuit of the van, but who they were and where they went I do not know.

INVESTIGATOR: Did you know Yango before the crime?

GENERAL: It is highly probable that I had seen him, and not just his picture on his papers. I had done the man a favor. In this connection I wish to point out that I have always taken a broad view of my duties: I have always tried to help those in need. I can go so far as to say that my name has become an object of wide popular affection. In doing favors I have not concerned myself with the political opinions of the beneficiaries. I have helped leftists in the hope of bringing them back to the right path; I have taken an interest in them, of which they were certainly not worthy, so proving that the state, one of whose most active forces I represent, looks with sympathy and understanding upon all its needy citizens.

INVESTIGATOR: Was Yango a member of the forces entrusted with the protection of General de Gaulle?

GENERAL: That is possible. We made use of all volunteers on condition that they were authentic anti-Communists.

INVESTIGATOR: And to reward them you treated them to a sumptuous dinner at the Aretsou Restaurant?

GENERAL: That is absolutely untrue; that dinner never took place. Yango boasted about it to make people think he was on friendly terms with a man holding a high position in our society and government.

INVESTIGATOR: And Autocratosaur?

GENERAL: Four years ago a National Resistance organization invited me to partake of an Epiphany cake with them. I thought it my duty to accept, because the gathering was held in Toumba, which, as you know, is a poor neighborhood where the Communists have a certain strength. Autocratosaur gained my sympathies by introducing himself as a captain in the National Resistance, of which I was a leader during the Occupation. Later he sent me a copy of his magazine *Expansion of the Hellenes!* It struck me as shamefully pro-German. I ordered an investigation into his past and found out that he had been a officer in the Hitlerite militia of Poulos, which I fought throughout the war. He called on me several times at my office. Good manners forbade me to send him away, but my attitude toward him became increasingly cool.

INVESTIGATOR: Did you notice that stones were thrown at the building during the meeting?

GENERAL: No. I did not hear of that for several days, perhaps more. I then learned that paving blocks had been used.

INVESTIGATOR: According to your statements, the loudspeakers were perfectly audible. When Z. asked for protection from the authorities, calling on you by name, what was your reaction?

GENERAL: I was never notified of any such request. Moreover, I am convinced that it was never made. Knowing how brave and proud Z. was, I do not believe he would ever have uttered such an appeal even if he knew his life was in danger.

INVESTIGATOR: In your opinion, were the slogans broadcast over the loudspeaker sufficiently seditious to provoke a counterdemonstration?

GENERAL: The slogans were more than seditious. However, the counterdemonstrators may have assembled by previous plan or at the instigation of others.

INVESTIGATOR: Who could those "others" have been?

GENERAL: I cannot answer that question. I have no way of knowing.

INVESTIGATOR: Could orders have been issued by the various sections of the Security Police?

GENERAL: I do not know. Those are administrative questions that do not concern me. But it strikes me as impossible.

INVESTIGATOR: How do you account for the fact that

press photographs show two plain-clothes men among the counterdemonstrators, shaking their fists at the Friends of Peace and threatening them?

GENERAL: In my opinion those policemen are guilty of a serious breach of regulations and acted on their own initiative. I cannot imagine that any of their superiors would have ordered them to behave in such a manner and to make themselves ridiculous.

INVESTIGATOR: Did you observe the presence of Mastodontosaur?

GENERAL: Yes, I saw him in plain clothes. But I don't recall having spoken to him.

INVESTIGATOR: Was he on duty?

GENERAL: I don't know.

INVESTIGATOR: In any case, his name is not on the list of officers mobilized for the demonstration. Why was he present?

GENERAL: He was free to go where he pleased if he deemed it proper to his functions.

INVESTIGATOR: What "functions"?

GENERAL: Information and the surveillance of persons.

INVESTIGATOR: One last question, General. I have fatigued you, but this interrogation was necessary. What is your explanation for all these events?

GENERAL: I am glad you have asked me that question. For many years I have taken an interest in astrological phenomena, and by studying the movements of the planets I have been able to predict events. A month before the events in question, taking the date of the reestablishment of the State of Israel as my point of departure, I noted certain troubling coincidences between a statement by Ben-Gurion about Christ and another statement by Khrushchev about the destruction of the Acropolis in case of nuclear conflict. These two facts between which I established a connection pointed to an offensive against Hellenic-Christian civilization. Under the influence of a conjunction of Aries and Saturn, and of planetary magnetism, a meeting was to take place in Salonika. I simply had to multiply the aforementioned date

by 7 and divide the product by the age of the Virgin
Mary and I saw the figure 22 rising from the depths of
the sea. Then I connected the midpoint of the moon
with the upper right-hand corner of the Great Bear to
obtain the fateful number 10. Q.E.D. The event I had
predicted did indeed occur at ten o'clock on the evening
of May 22.

And, radiating bliss, the General rose. His lawyer
sprang up with him, and they both left. Outside, reporters were waiting for them. The investigation had lasted
seven hours. They were hungry for news. But the General and his lawyer went past them without uttering a
word.

Night had slung its noose around the bay. Groups of
peasants brandished posters bearing slogans in favor of
the General. With a military gesture, he ordered them to
disperse. Fireworks burst in the sky from the direction
of the International Fair. At that very moment the most
famous Greek stars were emerging from the National
Theater, where the annual film festival sponsored by the
fair was being held. The General and his lawyer proceeded to the café, where the Chief of Police was waiting. When they were seated, the Chief asked what had
happened. The General ordered a double cognac. They
discussed their line of defense. Tomorrow was the
Chief's turn and their statements must coincide.

"Let's get out of here," said the General. "We
shouldn't be too conspicuous."

The flash of a camera lit up the interior of the café.
The Chief jumped to his feet and sprang toward the
photographer, but the photographer had already disappeared into the night. The Chief ran outside, looking for
him in the labyrinth of streets that twisted through the
deserted neighborhood. Now and then the camera
would flash, blinding the night with its glare and turning the silent buildings into visions of horror. The chief
searched frantically for the lightning, but never even
found the thunder. Breathless, he returned to the café.

All night long, the anguished General tossed in his bed. The face of the Investigator caused him to shake, as if he'd received an electric shock. He was obsessed by the dark glasses behind which the Investigator hid his eyes. The General knew that such glasses are worn only by those who have something to hide, who are cowardly and full of complexes. What infirmity was the Investigator concealing? What was his Achilles' heel? All night he felt torn by the hook he had swallowed. But he still did not suspect that in three days he'd be on his way to jail.

Chapter 2

The Chief of Police knew the one thing he lacked—in contrast to the General—was flexibility. The General was an eel; he himself, a squid. And the squid betrays itself by a film of ink. By the time he reached the Investigator, he had already developed an ulcer. For the first time he felt the absence of a faithful female friend. Such a sentiment had never before troubled his bachelor existence. But during the past days his loneliness had become intolerable. At last he appeared before the Investigator. Upon his arrival he was infuriated by a photographer who took a picture of him. Thinking it was the one who'd annoyed him the night before. he rushed at him, snatched his camera, and presented it to the Public Prosecutor, demanding that the film be confiscated because he'd been photographed without permission. "If I am judged and put in custody," he stressed, "then print whatever photographs you like. Till then, however, not a single one; do you hear that, not one!" The thought that he might be found guilty made him shudder. He felt like an executioner who, put to death one fine day by another executioner, suddenly realizes what tortures his own victims have gone through.

The charges against him were about the same as those against the General. Five typewritten pages. He denied them all. Before beginning to set forth the circumstances, according to his lights, he stated that "he had completed his thirty-sixth year of service in the Police Corps, during which time he had performed his duty faithfully and scrupulously; but his chief ground for satisfaction was not so much the highly favorable reports of his superiors on each occasion, as the recognition of his work by society as a whole." And he continued:

"Certainly, the unexpected incidents of the twenty-second of May filled me with bitterness, but the expressions of sympathy and consolation which I received from all sides more than compensated for this. Throughout my long years of service, I have always held key positions. I have had to confront many difficult situations, all of which I have dealt with successfully. I have faced massive political demonstrations or demonstrations of workers or students, and always by persuasion and by my own methodical measures I have managed to achieve the orderly disbanding of these meetings, without violence, 'without causing one nose to bleed.' It is doubtless thanks to these tactics dictated by my personal philosophy that I have been able to win the affection of all sections of society regardless of political convictions."

With this, he proceeded to come to the point. He related the circumstances as they had occurred: the refusal of Zoumbos to rent the meeting hall, the visit to his office of the Peace Committee and of Z. himself, the technical difficulty presented by the Catacomb auditorium, the phone calls from Matsas, the order for the reserve force, the news of a counterdemonstration—the point at which he had decided to go and see what was happening himself. It was about 8:30 when he arrived. Over the loudspeaker he could hear the "Communist-inspired" slogans: "Close down the death bases! Down with Polaris! Peace! Amnesty!" and the answering shouts from the counterdemonstrators: "Butchers, have your peace! Bulgars! EDA in Bulgaria!" He saw the pacifists, who from windows and balconies hurled insults at the people massed below: "Informers, sell-outs, collaborators!" He saw the people in the street answer with bricks and paving stones; he felt that "the situation did not appear dangerous enough to require violent measures for the disbanding of the counterdemonstrators." There was nothing in particular to distinguish it from other similar meetings. As a precaution, however, he called for reinforcements, because even though the situation seemed well in hand, there was no telling what turn it might take.

He heard the loudspeaker announce that Spathopoulos's whereabouts were unknown. He had gone at once to the Kosmopolit Hotel to ask Spathopoulos to put an end to the rumors of his disappearance. Then the General appeared at the entrance desk and said: "You're wasting your time trying to make him change his mind; that's how these people are." He himself had escorted Spathopoulos to the auditorium. He heard later that Spathopoulos had thanked him before beginning his speech and this had pleased him.

The Friends of Peace refused to turn off the loudspeakers. He reflected that if he used violence to shut them off, *they* might retaliate with increased violence. Above all, he did not want "one nose to bleed." And so he had let the loudspeakers blare away; he failed to hear Z.'s appeals, perhaps because at that moment he was attending to the evacuation of the demonstrators by bus— an evacuation which Z. had categorically refused. Then at his back he heard the noise of a motor. Turning round, he saw an individual "lying flat on the ground."

Concerning the Pirouchas affair, he could only say that he'd seen Pirouchas walking toward the ambulance with no help from anyone, while a group of counterdemonstrators prepared to attack him. At that moment a cordon of police surrounded the ambulance, thus facili-

tating his departure. He only learned later that Pirouchas had been badly hurt, "though it should be noted"
—the Chief's favorite expression—that at the time Pirouchas was in an area not under police control, a full four
blocks away.

To get back to "the individual lying flat on the
ground." He found himself at a point "located within the
area formed between the perceptible extension of the
left sidewalk of the descending line of Venizelou Street
and of the north sidewalk of Ermou Street, as well as
(by prolongation) its conjuction with Spandoni Street,
at the intersection of the said streets."

He saw a person jump on the pickup van. He thought
it must be a policeman in plain clothes and he crossed
the square fast to take down the license number of the
vehicle. But he didn't succeed, because it disappeared
up Venizelou Street, "the wrong way on a one-way
street." Then a group of policemen approached, some in
uniform, others in plain clothes, and he told them: "Go
after that pickup!" At the same instant he'd run into
someone he knew from the Security Police, "and in actual fact this person did set off in pursuit, though I did
not see him thereafter." He approached the site where
he had seen the person "flat on the ground," and saw the
"person" being put into a Volkswagen. He saw them fold
his arms on his chest so they could close the door. He
asked someone who the injured person was and he was
told it was Z., and "then I thought that it would have
been far better for this accident to have happened to any
other person whatsoever, because the uproar that would
follow, owing to the special function and mission of Z.
here, would be very great indeed; in a word, my first
thought (in view of all that had happened) was that it
had been an automobile accident; because, of course,
had there been any question of premeditated criminal
attack upon Z., I could not possibly have entertained the
thought that it would have been preferable for someone
else to have been struck, inasmuch as Z. had been walking in the midst of a group of his own followers."

And after these "thoughts" the Chief of Police began pacing up and down the sidewalk to forestall possible new disturbances, and then, "after approximately ten minutes," a policeman had told him that the driver of the pickup van had been apprehended and was already at the police station. He met the General, who had absolutely no knowledge of these events, and told him that Z. had been assaulted, without mentioning that the culprit had been arrested, "inasmuch as I thought he must know the circumstances, as this of course involved a fact relevant to the case." It must have been about 10:30 when they toured the surrounding areas in the General's car to see whether any more fires had been kindled. They spoke very little. They were both absolutely terrified at the thought of the "Communist exploitation of the unfortunate circumstance." And from there he had gone to his office and put through two long-distance telephone calls to Athens, "though it should be noted" that he did not talk, the General spoke in his place. He sent a police captain to summon the prosecutor from the theater. But the ballet was ending and the Captain, unable to make his way inside, waited at the exit, where he found not one but two prosecutors, put "the both of them" into the jeep, and brought them to police headquarters.

And then the misunderstanding had occurred. One prosecutor had asked for the culprit. "Before I had time to give an answer, the General interrupted me and answered: 'He has not been arrested, but he'll be caught no matter where he goes!' I experienced surprise and anxiety at the General's answer. Surprise, because I didn't see how the General could possibly not know of the arrest. Anxiety, because I reflected that perhaps the information I had received at the site of the meeting had not been correct. At which point I literally jumped out of my chair, went to the office of the orderly, and phoned the police station. The officer on duty answered that the culprit was indeed being held, and I, in a firm, strong, commanding tone, gave him the order, uttering the phrase 'Hold him there!' by which I meant that strict measures for guarding the culprit must be taken." And then he sent an officer to get the pickup van from where it had been abandoned, and had gone back to his office; though now the General was no longer there. He informed the prosecutors that the culprit was at the police station and that was when the second prosecutor got furiously wrought up and said: "Listen, are you hiding him from me? This is the second time you've pulled this on me!"

"I kept still, because I did not consider that I was morally obligated to give my explanation, it having been the General who said the culprit had not been arrested, and not I."

INVESTIGATOR: This is what strikes me as odd: the traffic policeman who arrested Yango did not know what he was guilty of, but at the police station, even before Yango was brought in, they knew that the alleged assassin of Z. had been arrested, and notified you at once.

CHIEF OF POLICE: News of such gravity spreads like wildfire from one section of the police to another. I can give you no more precise information.

INVESTIGATOR: Where had the anonymous policeman been who ten minutes after the assassination informed you that the culprit had been arrested on Karolou Deel Street, almost half a mile from the intersection where the accident had taken place? Either he was at the demonstration and could not have known that Yango had been arrested so far away or he was on Karolou Deel Street and could not have known any more than the traffic policeman or the fireman did—that the man who had just been arrested was the man who had run Z. over. Consequently, this anonymous policeman had been dispatched in haste by third parties who were in a position to link the two apparently unrelated facts—the murder and the arrest of the driver of the three-wheeler. Those third parties can only have been the officers in charge of the police station.

CHIEF OF POLICE: I do not know where that policeman could have obtained his information, but such rumors travel fast, you know.

INVESTIGATOR: They do indeed. So fast that at twelve-thirty the General still knew nothing . . .

CHIEF OF POLICE: It is very difficult for me to tell you anything about the source of the information in question; I have nothing concrete to offer you.

INVESTIGATOR: Then why did you send for the traffic policeman in the middle of the night? What did you wish to tell him?

CHIEF OF POLICE: I wanted to ask him if it was he or the people in the street who had arrested Yango. Newspapermen were beginning to phone their papers that Yango had been arrested by people in the street. And for reasons of police prestige I wished to . . .

INVESTIGATOR: I understand. Had you not been informed the previous noon that Z. was in danger of assassination?

CHIEF OF POLICE: No one informed me at any time that Z.'s life was in danger. The following day my orderly told me that the Public Prosecutor had phoned him in the matter, but supposing the warning not to be serious, he had forgotten to tell me about it. In any case, he had informed the Security Police, and they had taken appropriate measures at the airport.

INVESTIGATOR: Did you hear Z.'s appeal to you personally over the loudspeaker for your protection?

CHIEF OF POLICE: I heard no such appeal. If he had made it, I should have been very glad. That would have enabled me to take measures necessary to his security.

INVESTIGATOR: When after the meeting Z. came to tell you his life was in danger, did you not reply that he had nothing to fear?

CHIEF OF POLICE: I never said anything of the sort.

INVESTIGATOR: Had the counterdemonstration been planned?

CHIEF OF POLICE: I do not think so. Although most of the counterdemonstrators were illiterate, it does not seem impossible that the news of Z.'s arrival spread among them by word of mouth and that they decided among themselves to demonstrate their disapproval.

INVESTIGATOR: And what is your opinion about the crime?

CHIEF OF POLICE: A Communist machination. Vango is a former Communist resistant of the ELAS. He incited his *koumbaros* and friend Yango to run Z. over as part of an obvious plot to defame the Royal Police Force. I might add that they hurt no one but themselves.

Chapter 3

"Admittedly, when I arrived on the site with the Chief, the situation was not very pleasant. It had taken a rather nasty turn. The number of people in the area was increasing not from minute to minute but from second to second. This was in large measure abetted by the slogans over the loudspeakers and the arrogant retorts of the numerous persons assembled, constantly kindling and rousing tempers and provoking an influx of persons either because they had contrary views and wanted to show their disapprobation or else out of sheer curiosity, which we Greeks unfortunately have a surplus of."

He saw them passing by like this in front of him, a sad array of caterpillars crawling and dwindling over the pavement now that he, the Investigator, had sunk the knife in the sack and the oozing mass had spilled out, one glued to the other; without the protection of the moldering police station and the other departmental offices, without the files and the orders inside the faded dossiers, the procession headed by number one, the indomitable General; then number two, the Chief of Police; and then the others, a zigzag column, involuntarily forming on the pavement an enormous Z.

"Anyone who finds himself on the outside may discover among the wealth of minor incidents that some happened which ought not to have happened, and vice versa. But, in similar instances, the taking or not of a measure should not be judged objectively but subjectively, and as a case in itself, and beneath the prism of expediency. Because an untimely or psychologically unwarranted act, without due weighing of the circumstances, may produce the opposite result, as specifically foreseen by the Regulations of the Police Force, article 296. More specifically, regarding the act of arrest, I must state that the regulations, article 261, paragraph 5, prescribe that arrest must be avoided when it is a question of a minor offense or when disturbance of public order is threatened. At this point may I be allowed to state that no one would have held the police in the slightest degree responsible if the injury to Deputy Z. had not occurred. As far as the injury to Deputy Pirouchas goes, all I have to say is that I do not even know this deputy by sight. I recall that certain policemen did inform me that he had suffered a heart attack rather than an actual injury and that he had boarded an ambulance of the Greek Red Cross and been sent to the first-aid station."

He saw them passing in front of him against the black background of the Investigator's office, cut off, all alone, one by one, as he summoned them for the investigations, and their thoughts were black too and stuck to the background, and both—wall and thoughts—became one, as uniform as the uniforms enveloping them, rhyming, all made equal by the police regulations, and the Investigator holding the ruler in his hand saw that they were all the same size, regardless of rank, and his soul darkened.

"Within the framework of my own departmental jurisdiction . . . descending the stairs of the auditorium, I returned to my position outside the entrance, after reassuring Z. (he'd shown me his bruises) that there was no question of another such incident . . . Whereas Pirouchas moved by himself in the direction of the ambulance and indeed to its rear door; in a word, without having previously asked to be seated near the driver, whereas a Red Cross attendant (I do not recall that he was wearing his white uniform) had opened the double rear door of the ambulance and Pirouchas or one of his followers, during the instant he was mounting the ambulance, shouted: 'Down with the assassins!' . . . I relied on the thought that in any case the pickup and its driver would be arrested . . . After these events, one of my men reminded me that we should also consider the possibility of the Greek-Soviet League . . ."

He saw them passing by leaving on his desk their "I don't recall," "I don't know," "I am unable to express any opinion," "not . . ." "not . . ." "not . . " —all of them intact, basing themselves on negation, on the absence of memory—as though the camera had no film in it and its clicks and hummings were for the credulous; whereas he, the Investigator, kept bringing to light tremendously specific details, only to have these creatures efface them in their track of spittle, caterpillars, gastropods of the pine tree whose needles pierce like the worst pangs of conscience; only the caterpillars are privileged to slither onward without suffering, for they have no bones, no centers of resistance; leveled and indifferent creatures, changing uniforms twice a year. And ranking officers have two extra uniforms, one for coronations and one for funerals.

"Simultaneously with the arrival of these forces, by virtue of great effort and superhuman endeavors—using as always the logical methods which are, according to police tactics, conducive to handling situations, namely, first of all, to request; then, wherever this brings no result, to threaten; this must be followed by the minor precautionary tactics and finally by major precautionary tactics, taking care not to cause pain or enrage the crowd using said tactics, we succeeded in driving back the demonstrators to a distance of some hundred yards from the building, thereby creating a safety zone. The evacuation was general, and included persons as well as vehicles, even a pushcart . . . Yango was under guard in the office, as they reported to me (I cannot recall specifically who told me); this due to the electricity in the station lockup being out of order, and moreover, the lockup being full of *koulouria* trays, the kind abandoned by *koulouri* peddlers when they are chased for breaking Board of Health regulations . . ."

He saw them in X-rays in the darkness of the laboratory, fleshless bones, blood flowing in the veins of regulations, a heart beating in rhythm with the departmental telephone, a Buddha with a hundred hands branching out like a forest, arms leading from the same nerve center, obeying one single computer, this higher power that controls all, and is called . . . Here the Investigator preferred to remain silent.

"Nevertheless, before bringing to a close this, my present memorandum, may I be allowed to let my bitterness overflow, this bitterness which inundates my soul. Albeit I have served in the police force for thirty years and throughout this entire period never once been reproved, not even from a disciplinary standpoint, I was destined, O evil Fate! at the end of my career to suffer this cruel tribulation. But I am sustained by the conviction that justice, Mr. Investigator, will exonerate me, will prove me guiltless, as I have always been. Respectfully yours . . ."

"Concurring statements of the Investigator and the

Prosecutor were issued today shortly after twelve o'clock noon: warrants to place in custody pending trial four police-force officers; namely, the General, the Chief of Police, the Assistant Chief of Police, and one police captain. The persons jailed are charged with complicity in premeditated murder, in premeditated infliction of serious bodily injuries, in misuse of authority to a criminal degree, and with transgression of their duty."

Chapter 4

There is a rather peculiar procedure for incarcerating senior officers of the police force. First of all, the arrest warrants must go to the Assistant Ministry of the Interior; from there they must be transmitted to the High Commander of the Royal Police, and from there, if the accused are in some city other than Athens, to the local Chief of Police. Therefore, as they had been issued on a Saturday, with Sunday intervening, they had reached Athens on Monday and not been returned to Salonika before Wednesday.

In accordance with time-sanctioned usage, the accused went to the head office of the police department and "took cognizance." When the former Chief of Police saw someone else behind his desk, "impersonating" the Chief of Police, he thought for a moment that he was going mad. There was his own letter opener, the gift of an abbot on Mount Athos. The glass tabletop still bore his fingerprints. And when the new Chief of Police rose to take them to the door, he could see the shape of his own bottom in the armchair. All four requested to be locked up in Yendi-Koule, but this was refused by the

new Chief of Police, who said that only after the final
verdict had been delivered and only if the verdict were
nonacquittal, only then would he imprison them in a
military jail. For the time being, in accordance with the
regulations of the corps, he was obliged to send them to
the penitentiary of the Security Police. The rooms had
been done over for this purpose and were awaiting
them, all comforts provided.

Following this, the accused asked for a few hours to
visit their homes, to say goodbye to their families and
make their preparations. The General had a long face.
People in the Police Chief's office, who used to be scared
stiff of him, were now indifferent. Even the waiter from
the coffee bar paid no attention to the General, beyond,
of course, approaching him and whispering a few words
of consolation: "Don't worry, it will soon be over!" But
his glance told the General he no longer feared him. The
General went home. The phone rang. While he waited
for the warrants to be executed, the reporters had been
driving him crazy with their telephone calls. As though
they were doing it on purpose, to torture him. And here
was another one. He recognized the voice immediately.

"What do you think I'm taking with me? My pajamas,
my shaving things, and lots of books . . . Yes, I'm going
to write my book: *Towards the Consolidation of the
Hellenic-Christian Civilization* . . . What's the subject?
A reconsideration of the trial of Our Lord Jesus
Christ . . ."

"Do you believe you've been the victim of a judicial
error, like Dreyfus?" the reporter questioned him.

To be compared with a Communist Jew! He'd done it
on purpose, the swine! And he slammed down the receiver.

The Chief of Police headed for the church of Panayia
Dexia near the Arch of Galerius and there lit a candle
and prayed devoutly. He felt like weeping. And he did
weep, in the gloom of the church. He went next to the
Evangelistria Cemetery and prayed at the grave of his
predecessor, the former Chief of Police of Salonika, to

whom he owed everything, under whom he'd received his training as Assistant Chief of Police. When this man had died the year before last of a heart attack, he felt a great void in his own life. He had bought a few flowers, which he laid on the grave. Kneeling down, he began to speak:

"My dear Spiro, imagine what has been inflicted upon us in your old age! It's good you're not alive to see the state I'm in. I wish I had the strength to commit suicide, Spiro! This investigator, Spiro, how can I tell you about him! He got me all mixed up! I didn't want to squeal. Me responsible? When a full-blown General was there, supervising! I didn't know what was going to happen, my dear Spiro; I swear by your grave, I didn't know. And as soon as I got wind of it, I sent someone off to order the pickup to stay where it was. But the man wasn't in time and the pickup started off. And now here I am at your last dwelling place, weeping! Ah, Spiro, I owe you so much! The only thing you didn't teach me was how to protect myself from old foxes! Spiro, I can't bear it! Give me courage! He's to blame, he's to blame, he's to blame . . . the General!"

He was cut short by the sound of sobbing. He turned around and saw beside him a woman dressed in black, also speaking to her dead, also weeping.

The news had the effect of a bomb on Salonika. Newspaper extras, proclamations, street demonstrations. For the moment they seemed to eclipse the Hungarian Circus and the film festival. The sun seemed to have new meaning, thought the young reporter, who'd come back to Salonika for the festival. It had changed into the perceptible sun of justice. Since daybreak he'd been waiting outside the Investigator's office. But neither the Investigator nor the Prosecutor appeared before noon. Each was shut in his office, communicating with the other by phone. Around twelve o'clock they saw the General's lawyer enter and after a brief interval come back out.

"They're placing them in custody until the trial!" he said and quickly descended the stairs.

Along with the others, Andoniou was waiting to catch a glimpse of these heroic men—the Investigator and the Prosecutor—who in spite of pressures and threats had dared ferret at the very foundations of society. The Investigator came out first, sweeping them after him to the coffee bar. In spite of the exhausting pace of the past week, he did not look tired. He told them briefly the reasons why the four officers had been placed in custody pending trial and then, with a "Goodbye, gentlemen," slipped away. Andoniou was deeply impressed by the serene countenance of the Investigator. His face was relaxed. Occasionally he straightened the dark glasses he wore. The Prosecutor, plump and good-natured, said: "Since the Investigator's told you all about it, I don't have to say anything." Beneath this deceptive mask of kindheartedness was a soul of granite, decided the young reporter, who by now knew every last detail about the judges.

That afternoon leaflets were scattered on the streets:

"Indomitable General . . . Your struggles have been the struggles of our race, have been the struggles for the survival of the Greek nation. A few poor wooden stools; a mortgaged house; an only son, he too a police guardian of the Fatherland; along with the innumerable, lofty, honorary distinctions and medals awarded you by the Fatherland in its gratitude, are together with your prison cell the sole awards for your honor, manliness, and devotion to duty. The General gave everything. And now he is even giving his freedom. The body may be imprisoned, but the soul *never!* The students for National-Mindedness."

A little later, other leaflets took the place of the previous ones:

"Patriots and Democrats! The four officers, accomplices in the cowardly assassination of the First Martyr of Peace, Z., are now inmates of Yendi-Koule, keeping their counterparts company, the Yangos, the Vangos, the

Baronissimos, the Autocratosaurs, and the Mastodonto-saurs. The conception, organization, and execution of the plan for the dastardly assassination originated in a very high place. What high-ranking persons are con-cealed behind the General and Co.?"

The following day the *Macedonian Battle* reported: "Multiple bundles of leaflets were confiscated from EDA headquarters." It concluded: "Let the wretched not for-get that beyond the investigation—or any investigation, for that matter—public opinion is what counts. When the nationalist party triumphs in the forthcoming elections, we shall then decide . . ."

The night the festival prizes were awarded at the State Theater, the front-row seats reserved for the Gen-eral and the Chief of Police were vacant.

Part 5
ONE YEAR LATER

Chapter 1

I live beneath your phantom, Pirouchas reflected. Wherever I turn, I see your face. My hands grow rigid in the dry air of facts. They hang like stalactites above transcripts. I search the newspaper for something concerning you. Until lately, it was your trial. Now this too has been buried beneath new layers of journalistic cinder.

You have conquered me, all of me. Your eyes have inundated me. Now I know you too well to tell you that I didn't love you, that you set in motion, rather, my entire mechanism. Brain, heart, body, all placed at your disposal. I am a screen which looked big at first, then shrank as your image filled it. Now I understand that in order to contain you I should have needed cosmic proportions. Even so, I do contain you, however much you overflow the borders. These drops staining my street are what I leave behind me for others to find you by, to take you up, at whatever point I abandon you, and lift you to the heights. For, to tell the truth, I am growing weary.

At first I got well for you. Satellite that I am, I stole your light and for a spell shone with it. Then in the orbit of time we all obey, I began to wane. I grew thin. And now I am at that geographical juncture where the moon has disappeared. Will a new one rise? I don't know. I'm in the dark.

I measure by cigarettes the space that divides us. And rejoice that nothing I do can change you. Others, yes.

You, no. You have entered into me as the meteorite in the museum: a strange rock with dull colors that one day while I was out planting tobacco lit upon my field, brilliant as all chaos. It could have burned me like a bolt of lightning. It plowed a deep trough in the earth which still can be seen, especially when it rains and the waters gather there. Only you are missing. The specialists, the space experts and the diggers, came and removed you. They examined you beneath their lenses, classified you, put a little tag on you with the date of your landing on earth, and then glassed you up in the museum, like somebody's costume for a famous role, when the actress herself no longer exists. Only when you look closely at this costume, there in its cold vitrine, something about the sleeves suggests the movement of her hand. And all your corners, your excrescences, your granite surface, frozen in death like sculpture, bear witness to something of the flame that nourished you when you fell, the spurs of fire pricking your now invisible belly. Only the hewn marble is about to convey the stonecutter's shiver of intuition.

The more I let you slip away like this between my expert fingers—mine, "the surviving deputy"—the more you enter the region of dreams. Your own real face teeters between nightmare and waking, itself another nightmare since you no longer exist. In dreams you truly exist, because they do not. The degree of your involvement in the investigations, in the violent emotions I nourish for you—betrayal, jealousy, sick sensitivity, manic depression—bothers me not at all. But the moment I open my eyes and cannot find you, my dear emigrant, absence overwhelms me and I loathe whatever nails me to a bed in this provincial hospital.

And so I advance, casting off my burden. Each day-break reveals the increased distance between us. I no longer know how I shall reach you. Your face, for so many a lighthouse in the night, awakens in me the loneliness of the lighthouse keeper. At times I switch off your beacon and the ships crash against the rocks. I glut myself upon the shipwrecked bodies; dead men tell no tales. But what I'm saying is exaggerated. I am only he who worshipped your person and who remained behind, whistling like the wind, like a train, that is to say, romantically. But there's no place for romanticism in our age. Nowadays sounds are more abrupt than drawn out, more metallic than languishing, freaks of rhythm, no longer held to familiar scales and prescribed tonalities. Nowadays these sounds on the sonograph would form dots, tiny, disconnected lines, angles, intersections, depicting an asymmetrical structure, where nonetheless a swallow might perch and a paper kite become entangled, bequeathing us its skeleton. This skeleton I have become, swallow, bird of my heart.

To think of you in this way gives me the right or the pretext not to approach you in any real sense, not to mingle with the mob that surrounds your idol. Because there is no doubt that for the others you have become a photograph. Upon that likeness they project their own selves, whereas for me you are a pair of eyes only, eyes wet as the sea, eyes dry as a drained pool.

In my nightmares I see you needing me; even you have human needs. And then I want to come and help you, but it's as though I am bound by ropes I cannot break. And I wake up, drenched with sweat. And the thought that you are no more is a relief to me.

I say "relief." Don't let this seem too odd to you. At heart, I too mistrust change. I like my little lighthouse eyrie, gazing out to sea. I love this rock. I shall die here, not with you. You brought me only this infinitude. There are those of the vanguard and those of the rear who care for the fallen. I belong to the latter, however much you, the hero, may despise them. In order to be different now, I should have lived differently. But the one life granted us—for this one life granted us, I am all anxiousness.

Thoughts drop into the courtyard like ripe fruit. All this time without talking, my voice had grown ripe. But the spring snapped, the clock broke down. Every so often I wind it to the exact limit of its resistance, like faucets you mustn't twist beyond a certain point because the washers have been eaten away and they will start dripping again uncontrollably. That's how I am too.

All this, you'll already have noticed, does not concern you. It concerns only me and you don't care. I do care from the moment you create in me this need to tell you about it. You, no one else. From this moment there is a bond between us. I feel well, I feel ill, I have hope, I have none, in accord with you. That we cannot coexist is merely due to our belonging to different worlds: you to the world of the living dead and I to the world of the dead living.

And other times I see you in my sleep accusing me, telling me that you too are human and have need of me. That it is egotism, all my lonely suffering. And at this point I love you for certain little things that make or do not make our life. For a cigarette I lit you once, for some poems we listened to on records, for a blow you might have dealt but held back.

These few things I had to tell you before returning to the hospital ward. My abstinent heart pieces you together from an ocean of newsprint. Think how much ink you've consumed, how much film negative! Turn all that into blood and you would live eternally. But even so, you do live eternally, because that blood of yours has become light.

Chapter 2

He could no longer endure his city. He saw it small, confining, dangerous. Big ships are for big waters, he would tell himself and others. Ever since City Planning had stepped in to demolish his three little columns, he'd realized that the "hunting accident" wasn't far off. And so he made his decision, leaving wife, mother, children behind, and came down to Athens. Here in the anonymity of the big city he felt more secure. Here Hatzis was not in danger. Here his "own kind" were more powerful than the "others."

He had reached his own conclusions about the Z. case. Conclusions he discussed with everyone, since he considered himself an authority on the matter. Thanks to his leap onto a three-wheeled pickup truck, whole governments had collapsed. The police force had been turned inside out. The judges were at each other's throats. Society had purified its corpses, rejected its dead cells. He'd reached the conclusion that they would never have dared to assassinate Z. in Athens. Because the capital city (now that he lived here, he became more sure of this every day) had an expansiveness, a different layout, streets that did not lead to dead-ends, an atmosphere unshadowed by suspicion. All lay clear and distinct beneath a crystalline sky. The clouds did not cling to earth as in his own city, creating a curtain behind which plots could be hatched. And just as no atmospheric threat hung over upon the rock of the Acropolis, so no political threat dangled its sword above the heads of statues. In Salonika "the danger from the North" was a magnificent excuse for every sort of blackmail. "The Bulgars will butcher us!" "The Reds will descend on us!" "Arm yourselves!" "Destroy all!"

But Hatzis felt lost in Athens. The crowds circulating in and around Omonia Square, the tourists with their long beards and knapsacks, the inescapable advertisements, the furious rhythm of life (always in comparison with the heavy, indolent rhythm of his own city) made him from time to time regret Salonika. He felt nostalgia even for its dangers, its melancholy, for his mother, his wife, his children, his neighborhood.

Above all, his mother's letters upset him. Writing entirely about bills they didn't have the money to pay, she reproached him between the lines for having turned his back on the common fate of mortals and stepped into some unexploitable realm of immortality. Glory was all very well, halos were fine, she was proud of her son, but they had no bread at home. Had his head perhaps been turned? Why didn't all those people who were praising him give him a penny? And if they were, if pennies were getting to him "down there," then why didn't one or two reach them "up here"? Who was going to chop wood for the winter so they wouldn't freeze? His children had no shoes. The little girl was entering the third grade this year and didn't have the money to buy a school bag.

These badly written, bitter letters from the old woman (his wife, who worked as a cleaning woman, never wrote) made him feel guilty. But he didn't get discouraged. Left-wing as he was, he knew the meaning of history. And he felt that he had come into history lock, stock, and barrel, that he had made history.

The worst letter from his mother arrived when his photograph appeared in the newspapers along with the Prime Minister's! He and Nikitas, the furniture varnisher, had gone to visit him in his Prime Minister's office, as every citizen has the right to do. The kind and reverend old man with the clever eyes, with all the humor behind them, had asked him, Hatzis, to tell how he'd leapt onto the pickup. And Hatzis began relating the details, altered as they were by time and repetition, like a record whose fidelity, however often you change the needle, must in the end give way to scratches, static, and grooves skipped over. Yet the Prime Minister listened in wonder like a child carried away by a fairy tale. "Tiger, you're a fiend!" he told him when it was over. And then he took the *Black Book of the Fixed Elections of October 29, 1961* (when the very trees and the dead had voted) and inscribed it to him, with the phrase: "To the heroic Hatzis." The right-wing newspapers reported that the "old man" had said: "To you two the democracy owes a great deal. We must take particular care of you. From now on, you must take it easy. We'll find you comfortable jobs. You will work short hours, because you must acquire some education. Society needs you!" And so on. These newspapers were shown to his mother by well-wishers, and the illiterate old woman, seeing her son posing there with the Prime Minister, had written him this letter. The truth was that the "old man" had said nothing of the sort. Only that he was ready to help them whenever they needed help. And after that they'd left, because a crowd had gathered in the antechamber. The time allotted each visitor was measured by the second hand. On their way out they ran into a committee from Diavata that had come to protest the new expropriations made by Esso-Pappas. Other newspapers reported that Hatzis had gone to ask the Prime Minister for help and protection. At that point Hatzis dictated an open letter. "Heroes," the letter ended, "as the Prime Minister calls me in the Black Book, never ask for help and protection! Let the libelists take note!" The only thing he had done was sell his photograph to the newspapers, and this less for the money than for the glory.

Hatzis walked through the streets of the capital—streets constantly being dug up; did occasional construction work to make ends meet, rode up and down the escalators in Omonia Square and went as far as Piraeus to stare at the ships. Accustomed to the sea of Salonika, he suffered here without it. He was tempted by the smells of roast meat, freshly broiled *souvlakia,* the *kokoretsia* fragrant for miles around—Omonia Square was full of barbecue places: crusty roast pork, chops, grilled meatballs, fried potatoes. He was dazzled by shop windows, by the stream of cars, all this without a penny in his pocket. But he didn't mind. His task was not over yet, the Z. affair still lay over all Greece like a menace. At close range, he observed its developments and recorded them, as one by one they came to the surface, like mines disentangled from a dragnet.

Like an octopus from its lair, tentacles extended to en-
fold the lobster—thus Hatzis imagined the work of the
Investigator and the Prosecutor. The lobster was whatever or whoever hid in the recesses of the crime. Lobster
had always had the aura of wealth for him; he'd never
tasted it. Whereas sun-dried octopus was his favorite
mezes with ouzo. The lobster might well be armored:
breastplates and thorny knobs protected a tender,
vulnerable body inside. Once the octopus managed to
wrap itself around the lobster, it would suck its flesh
effortlessly. But how was that point to be reached, by
what play of tentacle? That was the question.

Up to a point he'd been optimistic. The evening the
newspaper extras came out, stating that the four police
officers had been placed in custody pending trial, he'd
gone and got drunk for joy. He went to the fair and saw
the fireworks bursting in the sky, writing his name. But
there you were, hardly fifteen days had passed when
these same officers, "by virtue of an intervening decision," were temporarily released from prison. The cage
was opened and the blackbirds allowed to fly away.
Then the Council convened to issue the final verdict on
the crimes of that night. On this three-man council were
the Investigator and two of the judges who had acquitted the four blackbirds. Two against one. Things looked
bad. Then Pirouchas and Z.'s widow had appealed to
have the two judges withdrawn. But the General also
made haste, now that he was free, to appeal for the
withdrawal of the Investigator, "on the grounds of preju-
dice against myself."

One day these appeals were all discussed together.
Hatzis was still in Salonika then. He'd gone to court.
They were all there. Yango and Vango, handcuffed to
each other, Baron, Autocratosaur, and the Commissioner. Vango, seeing a press photographer crouch to
snap his picture, rushed at him (Hatzis knew Vango
hated seeing himself in the papers), forgetting he was
chained to Yango. And Yango, with the sudden lurch of
his *koumbaros*, lost his balance and almost fell. But

Baron caught hold of him. Hatzis noticed that Baron had become much thinner; once a symbol of strength, he now looked helpless in his bulkiness, a big surface laid bare to the enemies' darts. Autocratosaur, though arrogant as ever, seemed drained, squeezed dry. Only the Commissioner was smiling, cheerful, greeting the plainclothesman at the door, who'd greeted him first. Since the bullies had invaded the courtroom, the question of the withdrawal appeals was discussed "behind closed doors."

As Hatzis later learned, the withdrawal appeal against the judges was based on ten points. First, these two judges—who had released the police officers and were now to pronounce the final verdict—had shown in the intervening decision "an ironical frame of mind toward the assassinated deputy Z." Second, they had taken a biased stand in everything that concerned the "peace movement." Third, their reactions to the eyewitnesses were highly skeptical, considering their testimonies as "aiming at the inculpation of the police." Fourth, they believed that Z.'s appeals for protection had been made for propaganda reasons, and half an hour later Z. had fallen to the ground, assassinated. Fifth, they had not said a single word about the injury to Pirouchas and about the attack on him in the ambulance. Sixth, they had excluded the possibility that the counterdemonstration had been planned, a view implicitly supported by quite a few of the accused themselves. Seventh, they had doubted the testimony of the two prosecutors that the police hid Yango in the police station. Eighth, they had refused to accept the testimony of one witness, on the pretext that his political views had not been examined first. Ninth, they had pronounced the odd opinion that "arrest or non-arrest of criminals falls within the discretional authority of the police." And tenth, one of the judges was a Mason, of lesser rank than the General in the Masonic hierarchy, and so could not possibly be objective toward his superior. In the end, despite all these factors, the withdrawal appeal was rejected, as was the other appeal, the General's for withdrawal of the Investigator.

And so they had proceeded to examine the accused, who, as always, maintained that it had been a "traffic accident" caused by intoxication. The others stated that they had not been at the site of the accident that night; and the policemen referred to their own original statements. Pirouchas insisted that the investigation be continued and that the court proceedings be returned to the Investigator, new factors having come up in the meantime, such as the Ministry report concerning the "Counteractions of the Communist Challenge by the National-Minded Organizations," which had been dispatched to the Secretary General twenty days before the crime. However, not even this proposal was immediately accepted. "And following this, the Prosecution walked out of court on the grounds that all three withdrawal appeals had been rejected, whereas the Penal Code clearly calls for the removal of any judge who so much as arouses suspicion among the litigants, in order that judicial impartiality be upheld. In this case, not only had suspicions been roused, but specific acts of partiality had been denounced; yet neither of the judges (out of whatever vestigial sense of dignity) considered himself offended."

They just went on and on, harping on the same old thing, reflected Hatzis. He had almost transformed himself into a self-taught lawyer, so avidly did he observe events at close hand. He read everything connected with the affair in the newspapers. He borrowed law manuals from a student and studied them on his own. At this time (Hatzis was still in Salonika, which had relapsed into its familiar lethargy now that fair and festival were over), the newspapers were full of the Hloros Report. This document dealt with the pressures brought to bear on the Investigator and the other judges by the Grand Judge of the Areopagus. "Just listen to Mr. So-and-so; he's very, very good." The report confirmed all the charges made in Parliament several months previously by the Assistant Judge of the Areopagus, concerning the "innate difficulties" and "the tragic difficulties involved in conducting the investigation." The contents of this report were known only to a very few people, who were now eager to make it public. In a panic, the right wing began accusing Hloros of going to Salonika expressly to influence the judges. The answer came like a sledgehammer: "I have never been adept," Hloros said, "at corrupting, confusing, or in any way influencing the opinion of persons inferior to me in rank. Others no doubt have this ability! Others no doubt particularly value this ability." Which made the Prosecution cry unanimously: "Mr. Hloros's report must be published!"

Ultimately the final verdict was pronounced, disappointing everyone, including of course Hatzis. That day he read every available paper. Each interpreted the verdict according to its own interests. The most optimistic commented that now the investigation must turn on "high-standing persons." Others seized on only one point of the verdict: "whether in actual fact Z.'s skull had been crushed with a club." Others rejoiced "that no order has been issued to return the accused to custody," which meant definitive acquittal of the Investigator's original charges. (However, "all persons already in custody were to remain there.") Others went further and blamed the Investigator, saying that, "throughout the investigation, testimony had been falsified and the truth corrupted." The fact was, this verdict created a judicial precedent favorable to the four accused, so that in the trial that would take place some day—if ever—they would be referred to the tribunal charged with "transgression of duty" rather than with "complicity in premeditated murder." The verdict proposed that the investigation be continued, but exclusively along these lines: 1) Whether Z. had been struck not only by the three-wheeled pickup truck but also with an iron bar. 2) Whether the counterdemonstration was spontaneous or organized. 3) Whether Pirouchas's injury had occurred in an area under police control or not. 4) That the responsibility for disturbance of law and order be defined. In other words, concluded Hatzis, the verdict granted the case a vague afterlife, dragged it out, thus weakening it, robbing it of its vital public interest, surrendered it to endless procedural delays, office to office, law court to law court, until something new, something more stirring came along and buried it altogether.

And Tiger was impatient. He wanted it to end. He wanted to present himself before the court and say all the things he'd told the Prime Minister; at long last, to see his act bear fruit. Just then the Hloros Report was finally published, falling like a stone on waters temporarily smooth as from the oil fishermen scatter mixed with sand, as Hatzis knew, in order to see deep into the spot where they harpoon the octopus. A few days later followed the memorandum of the Grand Judge of the Areopagus to the Minister of Justice, which unequivocally confirmed the Hloros Report. Without denying its accusations of him as a prejudiced intervenor, the Grand Judge merely interpreted them according to his lights. He denied neither his attempt to direct the Investigator "toward a new explanation of Z.'s death" nor his suggestion that the investigation be divided into four separate categories: the actual perpetrators; the behind-the-scenes perpetrators; the police; and the counterdemonstration. If the Grand Judge had had his way, Yango and Vango would have spent a few years in prison as the actual perpetrators; Autocratosaur and Mastodontosaur as the behind-the-scenes perpetrators; the police for transgression of duty (unrelated to the crime); and the counterdemonstrators (likewise unrelated to the crime) for disturbing that evening's peace. Thus no "high-standing person" would have been caught in the investigation's noose. Later they would pardon Yango and Vango, and since those two would never open their mouths, the whole case would be buried with ecclesiastic pomp. None of this was denied by the Grand Judge of the Areopagus. He simply interpreted it in his own way. But he made the blunder of going further still, and stated that it was untrue that Nikitas had been struck and the student had had his hair cropped by the police. He also mentioned an "unholy political exploitation" and castigated "the untrammeled publicity in the press of every piece of relevant information." Yet the reporters were the very ones who had helped the investigation, reflected Hatzis. Why would they not print what they had unearthed? With any other Investigator, the case would have been closed long before. But this Investigator was a hard nut to crack and he spoiled their game, just as he, Hatzis, had spoiled it at the very first, by jumping on the pickup. And so the whole thing had backfired. The young Investigator had raised himself high above his superiors, both in position and in experience. They were like the medals, Tiger thought, which generals wear into battle, medals which hide their cowardice, nothing else. The brave man goes forth from the battalion; it's the sergeant major or the lieutenant or the simple soldier who falls under fire, and the others share his glory. In the end, charged with having broken his judicial oath, the Grand Judge of the Areopagus was given a six-month suspension by the Minister of Justice. "An unprecedented crisis is lambasting our society," an old legal expert wrote. "The inexorable struggle surrounding one of the major crimes of the century. Who will win out? Justice or the collaborators? Gentlemen . . ."

At this point Hatzis had come to Athens. After the first tributes they paid him, they seemed to forget him altogether. The holidays were drawing near. The shops were laden like frigates. The streets were decorated with many-colored lights. The blind beggars with accordions multiplied. The mountaineers came down with Christmas trees to sell. The cold tightened its grip and Tiger wandered about, ever more of a stranger among strangers, ever poorer among the poor. His protectors began avoiding him. They didn't give any more money. They said they could find him work, if he liked, at a blacksmith's shop. But Hatzis could not go back to his old ways. He felt that he had been marked by history. And his protectors had heard it told too many times: how he'd jumped on the pickup, what had happened with Vango, the pistol, the club, Yango, the fireman's legs. Life was going on its way and he sat still at an intersection.

He frequented the square near the post office. There every morning he saw the plasterers and the house painters with their long brushes held high, waiting for a day's wages. They knew him and teased him and offered him coffee. Some gray winter mornings they were gloveless in the stinging cold. The hot-*salepi* vendor made them take a detour on their way from Omonia Square.

One such morning he met a woman coming out of an old hotel on Athinas Street. Some time had passed since he had left his city. He spoke to her.

"I can't get it out of my head I've seen you somewhere before," the whore said.

They went to bed. Afterwards she made him some coffee. "Where are you from?"

"The North," he said. "Big Mama Poverty."

"I've got lots of good customers from up there," she said. "At one point, when I was younger, I used to go up to the fair. I had my beat at Ladadika, back of the dock. Maybe that's where I ran into you and can't remember you from."

"Maybe you know me from somewhere else," he said. "I'm Hatzis, the one who jumped on the pickup and caught the assassins of Z."

"The doctor!" exclaimed the woman, tying her purple bathrobe. "The doctor who treated poor people free!"

She told him about an aunt of hers in Piraeus who every year, on the fifteenth of August, would make a pilgrimage to the Miraculous Virgin of Tinos. She had spent all her money on votive offerings and was never cured. In the end, Z. had cured her for nothing in two months. She had set his photograph among her ikons.

"But why did they kill him? Such a good man . . ."

That was all Tiger needed. He told her the whole

story, how he'd jumped on the pickup, what happened with Vango, the pistol, the club, Yango, the fireman's legs.

Athens seemed endless to Hatzis. A beautiful city, full of surprises. One day a rich lady who lived in Kolonaki invited him to her house. She was left wing, because her husband (who was also dirt-rich) was right wing, and she always wanted to antagonize him. She liked simple men of the people, who for all their poverty cared about ideals. Her chauffeur picked him up at his hole. Hatzis was seeing this district of Athens for the first time. A different sort of people. Lots of pastry shops. Where he got out, he saw a shop window full of baskets of tiny sleeping dogs. Dogs of the same breed greeted him at the lady's apartment when the maid opened the door. Hatzis was staggered. He'd never seen such a house before. High up on the sixth floor, he could see all Athens as on a platter. The hostess was wearing a purple dress. She shook his hand warmly. A strong scent of cologne made him dizzy. When they sat down to dinner, she asked him all about it.

Hatzis kept drinking water till he almost burst, to keep from talking. Before he left, the lady found a way to slip him an envelope. When he got outside, he opened it and saw that it contained some money. He sent this money home for the holidays and so for a little while was spared his mother's nagging.

Soon the time came when he was hungry again. He missed the hot *bougatsa*, the cheese pie, the *piroski*, the *souvlakia*, the pork-tripe soup. When it's cold, one has to eat. So he bought himself a kit, got some brushes, shoe polish, cut a piece of velvet off a seat in the Rosie-Clair Cinema, and set himself up outside the Municipal Hall. The other shoeshine men poked fun at him.

"The democracy sure needs you, man!"

"Bravo, Tiger! You're a hero! You don't accept help from anybody!"

"You made the snake come out of its hole and they stuck you in its place!"

"Hatzis, our hero, you chased out Karamanlis!"

Till one day someone in a dark overcoat came and said he wanted to talk to him. He took Hatzis to a restaurant and treated him to a meal.

"Well now," he said over a cigarette, "let's come to the point. I'll explain things simply to you, because you should know them. You're a Communist. And I'm a Communist. But the EDA party is rotten. It's a bourgeois party. Whenever it's a question of making someone a hero, they prefer to make a bourgeois the hero and not a man of the people like you. Z. was a bourgeois, he didn't care about Marxist dialectics. He was a good man and a humanitarian, but not the person to base the whole youth movement on. Do you understand? There's a great schism in the international Communist movement. I'm with the Chinese. The Russians, the more they move, the more bourgeois they grow. They're getting soft. They give in. They no longer believe in revolution. And they're right as far as their own situation goes. They've won their revolution. Now let other people fight things out tooth and nail. In Greece, though, things are the way they were in China. Poverty, hunger. Radical measures are needed, not all compromises and combines. I'm telling you all this just to say you should have become the hero and not Z. But you don't suit their purposes. You don't have the qualifications, the bourgeois-liberal background of Z. That's why they got rid of you. I know what went on behind the scenes and I'm telling you all this first-hand. We believe in the common people and in revolution. EDA believes that in a bourgeois regime you have to fight with bourgeois methods. We believe that in a bourgeois regime you have to use revolutionary methods. There's the difference. You're with the pro-Chinese, not the Khrushchevians. And look how you end up! Shining shoes! You! The Sing Nou Me of New China!"

"Don't you go insulting what's sacred to me," Hatzis replied. "I don't know much about politics. Z. I love. I believe in him. He's my leader."

The winter was hard on Hatzis, bitter. When spring came, things seemed to improve. Once in March he went up with a truck-driver friend to see his people in Salonika. He found his mother older, his children bigger, his wife a stranger, his neighborhood smaller. What was he doing down in Athens? There was nothing to fear any more up here. His house seemed like a prison. "Now that you got famous, son," his mother nagged, "why didn't you get rich too and take us out of our misery?" In vain he tried to explain that in his case these two things were unrelated. The old woman just couldn't understand. She wanted money. She thought her son had made good. She told him to give her greetings to the Prime Minister when he saw him again, and to remind him of the penury pension she'd been waiting for all these years. This was all so unpleasant that he eagerly went back to Athens.

With the Peace March, springtime took on meaning for Hatzis. As though by coincidence, Sunday (the day the march was to begin at Marathon to end in Athens) fell on May 22. The left-wing newspapers had been preparing it for some time: "The first spring following the death of Z. has returned to earth. Greece is celebrating the memory of the late great figure, the hero of peace. The hero of the entire world." Photographs of Z., journals, family albums. A festive atmosphere everywhere. The only thing that struck Hatzis as wrong was the Prime Minister's statement. Of course, he dared not forbid the march, but he was not in favor of it. He was trying to chill the people against it. He said the march was organized by the left wing and did not represent the vast majority of the Greek Friends of Peace, only the miserable minority of the left-wing Friends of Peace. Hatzis was bewildered. This man, at about the same time last year, as a member of the Opposition, had condemned the banning of the march, and now this year, when his party was in power, he was taking its failure as a foregone conclusion. And last year he had excoriated the crime and attacked the "government of blood." This

year couldn't he, if not honor it, at least hold his tongue
in awe of that blood? What was politics anyway, Hatzis
wondered. Did it hold nothing sacred? Or maybe there
was no difference at all between the bourgeois parties?
Sometimes the one rose, sometimes the other, like two
peasants sharing the same mule, and the mule—the common people—just went on carrying them one after the
other upon its back, understanding the change only from
the difference in weight. He didn't know much about it.
He was self-taught in such matters. He was a Communist, and though there were many weaknesses in his own
party, at least there was a dividing line. As for the others, whether you called them Mary or Katina, they were
both Athinas Street whores. These were Hatzis's reflections until daybreak Sunday, the day of the second Marathon Peace March.

In the dark of the night he mounted the bus from
Ameriki Square. He sat down next to the driver. When
he boarded the bus, everyone applauded. This bolstered
his morale. They drove with the lights on. The road, forty-two kilometers, was narrow; every time they met another car the driver slowed down to avoid a collision. At
the Tymvos Mound of Marathon there were few people
when he arrived. But later the place was teeming. By
sunrise the greetings, the speeches, the poems had
ended and the grand march set out.

Hatzis was at the head of the procession, along with
the officials. But at some point he stopped to survey its
full length. He was awe-struck. For two whole hours
people of every age passed in front of him, from all corners of the nation, carrying banners ("Immortal," "He
Lives"), photographs of the leader; singing, dancing.
The faces, however, were austere. Faces of seafarers, of
the first Christians. Then it was that Hatzis understood
the grandeur of the sacrifice. The man unjustly killed
rouses the conscience in lethargy. To a conscience already roused, he gives wings. He lends a steadying
hand, throws a rope from the sea wall. And Hatzis was
proud to have contributed something, himself, to the

moment. The march was no different than a religious procession, and Z. no different than the saints his mother believed in.

Young men, girls, old men, cripples passed in front of him; one had written on his crutch "No More War!" Manufacturers, builders, merchants, laborers. The bakers had written "Peace!" in loaves of bread. From Crete, from the Morea, from the Dodecanese, from Thrace and Macedonia. And when it started raining nobody stopped. They went on walking till the rain let up. At a crossroads, a marriage was celebrated; at another point, where some patriots had been executed by the Germans, a memorial service. And in Hatzis's eyes, misty with ecstasy, arms looked like olive branches, green foliage, downy skin; on towering legs the marchers grazed the dome of the sky. Last year Z. had walked alone. This year the road was all feet, a millepede. How did this miracle differ from Christ's feeding the starving multitudes by the Dead Sea with five loaves and seven fishes?

He remembered Z. coming down the stairs of the building where he had spoken, drawing the iron latch, looking out at the jungle that drew back from the shaft of light as in forests, where hunters wait for the stag to pass. Then Z. had crossed the street with his long strides (six of his to Hatzis's ten) and shouted: "Here they are again, they're coming! What are the police doing?" And with this last word on his lips, the pickup truck had placed a seal on him forever. He who had planted the trident in Hatzis's blue eyes. These saw again the dark case Z. was carrying, the striped suit, the tar of the road that became a matted wreath round his hair.

And night fell late that evening. The sun lingered over Salamis to survey the march in all its grandeur. In the city, people had come out on their balconies to cheer the marchers. They had put out their flags. That evening Hatzis slept peacefully.

But time passed and bit by bit the grandeur of the march faded within him. Once more he became a stranger in a strange city. A body washed up there, condemned to fast. The summer went by, and one autumn evening (when the weather turns honey-like in Attica), near the kerosene lamp of a corner chestnut vendor, he ran into Nikitas.

Chapter 3

Nikitas had come down to Athens too, about the same time as Hatzis, driven by the same need to seek safety. Since his release from the hospital, with a policeman to escort him everywhere to prevent further assault, no one had set foot in his shop. Finally he left, bag and baggage. Nikitas, unlike Hatzis, did not want to make his weight felt: he applied for a job in a varnishing shop and so earned his daily bread. He had gone with Hatzis to the Prime Minister; it had not changed his life. The only thing he was glad of was getting even with his sister. Now *he* was "in" and not she. Her party had fallen, and his own risen to power. But he bore her no grudge. When the Prime Minister asked him if he wanted anything, he requested only that his brother-in-law not lose his position.

His life changed in no way. After work he went back to his room or went to the movies. On Sundays he went to the football games. This year the PAOK was in second place. If the Olympiakos Team lost only one game, they'd have a chance for the Cup.

He took care to have nothing to do with the Z. case. Since ideologically he didn't belong to the party that had adopted the hero, he too sank into oblivion. He followed the newspapers, was annoyed by the lies of the

Grand Judge of the Areopagus and in the end approved of the six-month suspension imposed on him. Whenever any reporter discovered him, he said he had no comment, he was just waiting for the trial.

One day temptation appeared in the guise of the former Chief of Police. He saw him coming down the steps into the shop where he worked. He was startled. The bushy eyebrows brought back all the darkness of Salonika. He recalled the General, the hospital, the nightmares about their killing him, Yango. But, on a closer look, he saw that the Chief had changed. He might have been a defrocked cleric. The same face that beneath priestly regalia had exhaled an other-worldly air, now a layman's once more, might have belonged to any merchant in the marketplace. Stripped of his embroidered robes, he was without splendor. Are mitres and crowns capable of thus altering a person? Or was it that a year had passed, that everyone changes?

"How are you doing, Nikitas?" the Chief asked. "How are you getting along? You're here too? We've all become emigrants."

Nikitas offered him a chair.

"You'll ask me how I found you. I know Giorgios, your boss. I saw him the other day on the street and he told me you're working for him. 'Ah, Nikitas,' I said. 'He's a fine man. I'll drop around to see him.' And I've come. Let bygones be bygones, forgive and forget, as they say! Are you married?"

"No, not yet."

"Neither am I. Marriage is a fine thing, to be sure. But when you get on in years like me, it's not worth it any more. Either get married very, very young, or else . . . . You see, with my work, I didn't have time to think of myself. The Fatherland absorbed all of me. And what came of it all in the end?"

"You're not to blame, Chief, sir."

"I'm no longer Chief. They've assigned me somewhere —Holargos—in charge of a supplies warehouse, just to give me something to do. This case cost me my career, everything. I became the laughing stock of the country, and I wasn't to blame at all. Yes, I'm a victim!"

"That's what everybody says about you," said Nikitas.

"And you're a victim too," the former Chief said. "What reason did you have to get mixed up with that rabble? You know who I mean. The toughs and the Communists. You worked and minded your own business. You weren't interested in politics. Then, without meaning to, you found yourself involved."

"Now I've got disinvolved," Nikitas said. He didn't like the Chief's visit at all. "At the trial I'll say what I have to say and that's the end of it."

"Did you have any complaint against me personally? Did I ever molest you, before or after?"

"Before I didn't know you, and afterwards I didn't see you."

"I read that they promised to move heaven and earth for you. They were going to give you a position, they said, and money. Where's all this then? Giorgios tells me you barely manage."

"For them I don't exist."

"That's just what I mean. What did you gain?"

"I lost ten years of my life."

"There you are. The Communists are well off because they got a hero out of it. The center rose to power. The right lost its holdings, but they would have done so anyway, without what happened; eight years are a long time. In the end, no one suffered. Only you and me, and a few others."

"That's the way it is."

"Tell me, do you ever see Tiger?"

"No."

"If you happen to see him sometime, bring him to my office and we'll have a coffee. I have an interesting proposition for you. Here, take my phone number too." He jotted it down on a scrap of paper. "Before you come, phone me. There's one chance for us to get even once and for all, in a very simple way. You'll be compensated, and I, poor guy, I shall be vindicated!"

"What chance?"

"I'll tell you some other time. Now that I know you're here, I'll come and see you."

And he went off, leaving a big question mark in the air. And he did come another time, just as the shop was closing. He took Nikitas to Pancrati and treated him to an ice-cream special. This time he didn't mention the "chance." They talked only about the PAOK, which was headed full steam ahead for the Cup. He too was a PAOK fan, he said. And he gave him his phone number again, in case Nikitas had lost the first scrap of paper.

And here, speak of the devil, not a week had passed since their second meeting and Nikitas recognized Hatzis's bald head in the white light of the chestnut vendor's kerosene lamp. Nikitas approached him from behind and laid a hand on Hatzis's shoulder. Hatzis whirled round, a real tiger. They hadn't seen each other since the day they had gone to the Prime Minister together.

They went into a milk bar next door and ordered orangeade, Nikitas's uncarbonated, Hatzis's carbonated. There were two tables in all, but the noise of the huge electric icebox provided sufficient camouflage for their talk.

"I've been looking for you," Nikitas said. "But I didn't know where to find you. I went to the Post Office Square a couple of times, but you weren't there. It's about the Chief. He's been to see me twice. He gave me his phone number too. Here it is, I have it here." He rummaged inside his wallet and found the scrap of paper.

"What does he want with us?" asked Tiger.

"He wants to see us, so we can discuss a little job. How should I know what job he means? He seems very mysterious to me."

"You think he might have some photographer planted outside to start the rumor that we've been seeing him on the sly?"

"I don't know, Hatzis. But he's gone very soft."

"He's afraid, that's why."

"What can we lose by seeing him?"

"That's right. We can't lose anything," Hatzis said.

"I'll phone to say we'll come tomorrow."

"I don't mind going to see him once. Agh!"

"What's wrong?"

"My stomach! Those carbonated drinks!" groaned Hatzis.

The following evening, at a discreet hour, they went through the gate. The guard had been notified and they didn't have to say whom they wanted to see. He took them, not through the main corridor leading to the office, but through a side way, past some stairs, till they reached the ex-Chief of Police's room.

He was waiting with open arms. He was especially effusive over Hatzis. Someone else was there also, whom he introduced as a "person absolutely in my confidence."

"Here we are, we three, the victims of injustice in the case, the emigrants. We ought to establish a party."

"Exiles of the world, unite! That's how we'll call it," laughed Hatzis.

"Yes, yes!" agreed the Chief idiotically. "In union lies might! Would you like a cigarette?"

Nikitas did not smoke. Hatzis took one. The Chief lit it for him.

"How are we getting along?"

"We're not getting along at all well," answered Hatzis. "Gloom and doom are on us."

"Do you like Athens? Have you got used to it?"

"It's all right. Everywhere's all right so long as you've got money. If you haven't got any, everything looks black."

"That's it," said the Chief. "Nikitas and I had our little chat the other day. Now I want to hear your news."

"I don't have any new news," said Hatzis. "I've just got old news. I'm waiting for the trial, to have my say and find peace and quiet. But since I'm afraid I won't live that long, whatever I have to say I've recorded on tape. This way, even if they do kill me they won't gain anything by it. I've made my last will and testimony."

The Chief's eyebrows knit. "So you've settled your accounts? And what'll come of it?"

"Something doesn't always come of something, Chief, sir."

"I don't want you to call me Chief any more. I'm not the Chief. I'm not anything. Here they've handed me a tiny post as warehouse attendant. Well now, listen to what this is all about. I've invited you both here to ask you—I mean, to tell you. . . . For how much will you shut up? For how much will you change your statements? You two are the main witnesses for the Prosecution. If you take back what you told the Investigator, we'll all live happily ever after."

"What you're suggesting," Hatzis said, "is a serious offense. It sends us all to jail much more surely than Yango and Vango."

"I know that," answered the ex-Chief in a fake, melodramatic voice. "But for me personally the situation has reached a deadlock. I'll go out of my mind! And I thought of making this desperate overture because I know you're in need. I know they cheated you and that other people are reaping the fruits of your labors."

"That's how it is," said Hatzis, giving Nikitas a look.

Nikitas's huge Byzantine eyes had turned glassy.

"Give me that tape you made, Tiger, and you can have my soul. You'll become rich and I shall be reinstated. I wasn't to blame. By the Virgin of Dexia, I'm innocent! And the trial, whenever it takes place, will prove it. I'm not afraid. But my honor is at stake, you understand. You can't wipe out thirty-six years just like that."

"How much?" Hatzis was the first to ask.

"Two million drachmas. You can share it between you. You each get one."

Nikitas jumped out of his chair. "This table needs varnishing," he said. "Send it to the shop and I'll fix it for you."

"The question needs some consideration," said Hatzis. "We can't tell you anything right at this point. Isn't that so, Nikitas?"

Nikitas shook his head. Then, as though in league, they both looked at the stranger standing motionless, expressionless in the corner. The Chief was sweating and puffing where he sat.

"You'll get rich," he said to them. "You'll go live abroad. Who knows you, who's seen you? You'll be fine, just fine."

"Before we get abroad, we'll get to prison, for perjury!" said Hatzis. "We told the Investigator one set of things. How can we tell him different things now?"

"You'll say you were forced to say what you said then. You were pressured. After all, it's not an absolute lie," he added. "Isn't that so?"

"In two days we'll give you our final answer," said Hatzis.

"But take care these two days," the Chief threatened. "You'll be watched. This gentleman," and he pointed to the mute individual, "will be following you. Take care you don't doublecross me." He opened a drawer and took out a revolver. "I've never used this in my life. I've never made anybody's nose bleed. This will be the first and the last time. One bullet in the traitor and one in my own brow."

"No more suicides!" cried Hatzis. "You'll be the third police officer in a row—*not* to commit suicide!"

"Tiger, quit joking. Whoever squeals—he should know this from here on, because I like clean work—will end up like Oswald."

They went out through the back door, as stealthily as they had come in.

"There's something fishy in all this," Hatzis was the first to speak.

"What does he gain by setting a trap for us? He'd be the first to fall into it."

"If they catch us, who will they believe? You and me, or him? Between a varnisher or a blacksmith and a former Chief of Police, who will they choose? We ought to put one over on him first."

"I don't want any trouble," said Nikitas.

"Now, any way you look at it, he's going to be suspicious of us," said Hatzis. "The point is, who'll give the other away first?"

"Two million's no small sum," said Nikitas.

"The bad part is, it's a great deal," said Hatzis. "If the sum had been less, I might be more inclined to believe him. And if he's on the level, so much the worse. Think what a vested interest they have in our silence."

"Who have?" asked Nikitas.

"The people behind the Chief. How do you think he found the money, if he really does have it? On his own salary, five thousand drachs a month, he'd have to live as long as a dinosaur to collect two million."

"Everybody's getting his share," said Nikitas. "Why shouldn't we get ours too? You took Z. and made a martyr of him. The old man became Prime Minister and forgot him. What are we doing?"

"Nikitas, you don't understand the evolution of history. That's why you're talking like this. We two, when things change, will become historical figures. We'll be in the schoolbooks. Your face and my face will live forever. Why exist except to leave a good name for posterity? Marx said . . .'"

"Are you going to give me the catechism now, Hatzis? I'm just thinking out loud, just daydreaming."

The trouble was, Hatzis was daydreaming too. He could just see his mother in a big house, full of conveniences, automatic buttons, like in the movies. The gar-

bage, so they said, was whisked away by a machine inside the sink. A three-story icebox. And his mother with
all her medicines and two telephones. And his children
would have all kinds of toys. Bicycles, trains, dolls. In
the summer he'd take them to the country, to the sea-
shore. He'd rent a house . . . . His wife, who did other
people's laundry all week long, with her bad back and
her legs blue with varicose veins, would be able to shop
in all the stores of Europe: boxes, boxes, boxes . . .

"What'd you say?" Hatzis asked him.

"Pretend you bet on the lottery and lost by one number," Nikitas replied. "Take it that way, because otherwise it can drive you mad. I'd rather die, lose my blood
drop by drop, than act against my conscience. I just
wanted to test you."

"Me too," said Hatzis. "I just wanted to test you too. A
varnisher and a blacksmith who can't be bought! Long
live honesty!" And he burst into tears.

When he reached his underground hole, Z.'s eyes
magnetized him. Hatzis saw him staring with his
changeless gaze, stone-like, immortal. The site of the assassination, the roar of the motor, the hyenas howling—it
all came back. How could he have dreamed of betraying
him, this man whose words and glance, whose very foot-
prints he loved? This man whom he'd followed with a
dog's blind instinct. How could he? When he opened his
arms, he enveloped the whole world. When he smiled,
the rain let up. Hatzis sat down on the edge of his
wooden bed. The basement was damp, full of flying
cockroaches. He opened the drawer and his mother's letters spilled out. Of late, her obsession was that she had
some terrible illness and must go for a medical examina-
tion, but she didn't have the money. "So much the better," Hatzis said to himself. "Let her drop dead an hour
earlier." And he made all her letters into a packet and
burned them in the stove. Night. He heard only the foot-
steps creaking above his head. He was below, buried in

the ground. And even so, absolutely alive, because he could not be bought by anyone.

When Nikitas reached his own room, he felt precisely as he had the morning he read that Yango had killed the deputy and he had to go and testify. The nightmares of his mother and his sister came back. The ice bag on his head. The General: "You're one of our own boys; how could you do this!" "He fell and hurt himself. Ever since he was little, he liked fairy tales." "He was an epileptic." The whole web. But now his conscience had got into the habit of standing erect. It didn't get tired, as it had then. He wasn't left wing or center or anything. He was a furniture varnisher who enjoyed doing a good job, going to a movie and the football game on Sundays. These things cannot be bought for anything. His head ached. He took an aspirin before going to sleep.

Two days later they were back at the Chief's office. The same unknown man had materialized in the corner, like philodendron.

"Welcome, my friends! Welcome . . ."

"It's not enough," said the blacksmith.

"We each want two," said the varnisher.

"Have you gone mad?" exclaimed the Chief. "Where did you ever see so much money in your whole life?"

"Otherwise we're sorry. Can't be done," they both said in one breath.

"Come down a little, fellows," he pleaded. "You've gone too steep!"

"We're playing it all the way, Chief, sir. You think it's a small thing?"

"A last price?"

"We're not peddling wares or bargaining. We're selling you our lives," said Hatzis.

"One million two hundred? It's a deal?"

"It depends on what you want us to say," said Nikitas.

"You," he turned to Hatzis, "you'll say that you were

helped by the police to catch Yango. That Z. was lifted half dead into the Volkswagen and that, inside, the Communists finished him off. In the hospital where you were recuperating, a member of EDA came to see you and told you to say that Vango had a revolver on the pickup. If you say these few things, we'll be satisfied. You see, we're not asking to rob you of your glory. *You* jumped on the van, *you* fought the battle. But I don't think your own personal prestige is harmed if you say you were helped by a few policemen. As for the rest . . ."

"And how could I know the Communists finished off Z. inside the Volkswagen, since at that moment I was on the three-wheeler?"

"You'll say you heard them discussing it. And you," he turned to Nikitas, "you'll say that you did know Yango and did indeed use him for transport jobs. Only he didn't say to you that morning that he was going to do something crazy tonight, something really nutty, that it might come to killing a man."

"And where did I make that up? Out of thin air?"

"No. A Red came and told you to say it. And then you'll also say that the day the hearse with Z. was going from the AHEPAN Hospital to the railway station you fell of your own accord (as instructed by the Reds) and afterward said you'd been hit, to avoid going before the Prosecutor."

"There's already a court decision stating that they did strike me."

"You'll say what I'm telling you to say. Now pay attention: both of you together will state that when you visited the Prime Minister he said to you, word for word: 'Even if you hadn't done anything, as we'd planned with the Z. case, we'd have forced the government to fall.'"

"I can't say that," Nikitas said. "Who am I to tell lies on a full-fledged Prime Minister?"

"A perjury charge can be cleared for twenty thousand.

You're the ones who chased out Karamanlis; you're the ones who'll bring him back!"

"All right, we'll say what you tell us to say," replied Hatzis. "But what if one of the men now behind bars cracks and talks and the whole deal backfires?"

"None of those guys are going to crack. They're getting along fine."

"I read that Yango tried to commit suicide with Luminal."

"That was a trick," said the Chief, "so he could get out of prison and go back to his neighborhood for a bit. He missed his kamikazi."

"And if Mastodontosaur cracks?"

"He's made of steel. Well, are we agreed?"

"When's the money going to materialize?"

"As soon as you sign the statements I'll prepare for you."

"In cash?"

"No, in checks."

"Out of the question," said Nikitas. "Gold. Pure gold. In little sacks."

"Nowadays, jobs are done only with checks."

"And if they bounce?"

"You can pull a Tippit on me."

"Mr. Chief, we respect you. What's that you're saying?"

"And our passports for abroad?" asked Hatzis. "You'll arrange that for us?"

"I'll take care of it." He took out his pistol again and laid it on the table. "Take care. These are critical days. And don't forget, Hatzis, to bring the tape."

Suddenly he seemed terribly serious. Bushy eyebrows, fixed stare. The mute man in the corner opened his briefcase. "Day after tomorrow, at eight o'clock, here," he said.

Hatzis and Nikitas went off unseen. They jumped over the wall, because it was a police holiday and the front courtyard was all lit up.

In the two days before their third and final meeting, Hatzis bought a blank tape and made a telephone call.

On the appointed day Nikitas washed his hands well with turpentine so they wouldn't smell of varnish, dressed, shaved, and at 8:30 met Hatzis outside Papaspyro's Café. From there they got into a taxi and headed for Holargos.

The ex-Chief of Police and the unknown man were waiting. They had covered the windows with blue wrapping paper so they couldn't be seen from outside. Hatzis handed over the tape immediately. The Chief opened the drawer and was about to take out the statements when the door opened and in its frame he saw—was it true or a nightmare?—the new High Commander of the Royal Police who had succeeded the Generalissimo when the government fell, accompanied by his orderly. The former Chief shot up like a rod.

"Sir, I mean—"

The new High Commander entered the office like a whirlwind, paced about, and, seeing the others, who had risen, had his orderly take them into the other room. The orderly asked them politely to follow him. In the office now remained only the High Commander and the former Chief.

"And who are those people, Colonel?"

"Witnesses in the Z. case."

"What are they after?"

"They come and visit me."

"How many times have they come?"

"Three in all."

"What do they want?"

"That I haven't been able to ascertain. I'm feeling them out. They want something. I think, money."

"Are they blackmailing you?"

"That's not exactly the right word."

"Then what is?"

"It's that they move suspiciously. They want to see where they can get the most. They've had it from the left and the center. Now they're trying to get it from us too."

"And why didn't you report this to me at once?"

"I preferred to have something more concrete first."

"You should have brought it to my attention from the very start, if you intended to be proper vis-à-vis the department, and not expose yourself as you have now."

"It will be kept from the press."

"They will inform the reporters."

"Can't we lock them up on attempted blackmail?"

"On what evidence?"

"Unfortunately, I had the idiocy not to tape our discussions. What they said was incriminating enough."

"And why should the reporters, ill-disposed as they are toward you, not believe that *you* attempted to bribe *them*?"

"That is slander. Whoever dares to say so will pay dearly for it!"

"This is not a time for threats, Colonel. It's a question of formality, and I daresay essential. Look here: I drop in after hours with my orderly and catch you closeted with two persons whom you should not even say good day to, for the sake of the prestige of the Police Corps."

"I don't know what to say, sir."

"After the charges are filed, an investigation will follow. Good night!"

Cold sweat drenched the Chief. They had betrayed him, set a trap. But which of the two? Hatzis, surely Hatzis. Yet a smile spread over his face. He had the tape! Now, if only Hatzis could be removed, he wouldn't leave behind any dirty traces. The ex-Chief would destroy the tape.

The High Commander went into the next room, where the other three were. He told his orderly to search them. On Nikitas a note was found with the ex-Chief's phone number; on Hatzis, a letter from his mother; and in the third man's briefcase, a check for fifty thousand drachmas. He began with him.

"My name is Konstantinos Hristou, native of Kilkis, retired Police Major."

"Profession?"

"Head of the disbanded organization Guarantors of the Constitutional King of the Hellenes—Might of God —Divine Faith—Greek Immortality."

"Why disbanded?"

"It was recently disbanded on the grounds of illegal use of the royal emblem and usurping authority."

"And weren't you arrested?"

"I was arrested, but set free after being committed for trial."

"Why were you set free?"

"Owing to congenital idiocy."

The High Commander looked at him in amazement, then, smiling, turned to the other two.

"What did you want with the Colonel?"

"We—nothing. He wanted to tell us something."

And Hatzis pretended to explain the situation. Nikitas added that the second time the Chief had visited him at the varnishing shop he'd taken him for a ride to Pancrati and brought him an ice-cream special.

The following day the extreme right-wing newspaper reported: "In fact neither trembling nor stuttering, the ex-Chief received the High Commander. Several minutes after the High Commander returned to the ex-Chief's office, the High Commander addressed the Colonel thus: 'I have a bitter duty to perform. According to my information, you offered them two million drachmas to testify to certain things.'

"The ex-Chief answered coolly: 'You are in the presence of vicious liars. As it happened, retired Major Hristou was also present in my office. I kept him there to hear what those two were saying. They were the ones who made me the offer! I threw them out, saying that I was in the habit of fighting with the weapon of truth! I have nothing to add.'

"This insidious reportage, identical in all the center and left-wing newspapers, endeavors to represent the ex-Chief as an idiot. The unknown intriguers have surely underestimated not only the genius but the professional experience of this venerable officer of the Police Force."

That night the Chief waited in vain for even a whisper to emerge from the tape recorder. Hatzis's tape was virginal as untrodden snow.

Chapter 4

I am beginning to rise up from events, reflected the young reporter. I am emerging like deep-sea divers after a long plunge, short of breath, eyes stinging from the salt because I took care to keep them open in the depths, to see, to find what I needed to chart your submerged Atlantis. Finally, I brought back these photographs. Here and there, the development was imperfect. Things remained dark, the people shadowy. That doesn't matter to me.

What does matter to me is that I did not betray you. I did not forget you for a moment, though I was often without air. So many layers of water covering me, there in that utter dark, in that wet desert, you stirred my sleeping heart. The rest was the job of better or worse reporters. I am not of those. I belong to you, sweet martyr.

When I've finished, I shall forget you more easily. Above all else, I want to forget you. To be delivered from your beauty that weighs upon me. To migrate to a neutral plane, where you do not exist. For you weary me. I cannot rekindle dead fires. I prefer live ones, however much in comparison with you they are ashes.

Your face a terrestrial geography, I said once. Now I

say a celestial one, for the heavens are seamless. I call you springtime, because fall contains you. I call you sun, because you are made of mist.

All the same, I, Andoniou, must collect a few last details and add them to this unique collage of certain events following your assassination. I must tell you about the Hungarian doctor, Laslo Zoltan, who categorically stated that you were struck with an iron bar. Although he was not present at the autopsy (they had not invited him), he could nevertheless observe from the X-ray no serious injuries to your body, such as a heavy three-wheeler with two passengers might have caused if it had run over you. You had neither fractures nor breaks. Scratches only. What then caused your death? This riddle he solved by referring to the two small bloodclots he found on your skull and himself operated on. These clots, he said, could not have been caused by a fall on the ground. They were internal, each in a different place. So what had happened? He was prepared to testify under oath, he told the Investigator—assuming of course an invitation to do so. After so long an interval, he remembered you. "Z.," he said. "Ah, of course I remember him!" He pronounced your name with a foreign accent I found slightly annoying. One feels disturbed when a thing so familiar to oneself becomes a peculiar, distant phenomenon for another. You, who have nourished me so this year and a half I have lived writing about you, I cannot bear for others to remember you only dimly, remotely.

As though by coincidence or some diabolical conspiracy, that same week as Zoltan, I also got on the track of the "third man," the one who probably struck you with the iron bar. He too is from Kilkis and belongs to the attack squad of the local ERE "boss." He had come to Salonika on the day of the incidents, along with some other provincial toughs. Next day, when news of your mortal injury reached his home town, Kilkis, a rumor started that he was the one who killed Z. by striking him on the head with an iron bar. You know that rumors (especially in small, provincial places, where the very walls have ears) never circulate without reason. This rumor's gravity and the wrath it inspired now forced the third man to leave Kilkis and go to Nea Sanda, a village of Black Sea refugees near Salonika. And from there, with the aid of the same ERE boss, his papers were prepared for Germany. But he couldn't stick it out. His health suffered up there in the industrial smog and he came back. Upon his return, I found him and filed official charges. He went to the Investigator without a lawyer. As the investigation is secret, I don't yet know what was said.

Oh, why can't you yourself speak! Why? How much does a long-distance call from Necropolis cost? Speak. Reassure us. Talk to us. But the dead don't talk. This great accusation weighs upon them.

I'm talking like this to you because I could not keep you at a distance, writing my newspaper pieces as though you had never existed. That, no! I want you as the grapevine its trellis, that it may grow higher; as beauty its mirror, that it may grow more beautiful still. I want you because I want you. I have no explanation to offer. I want you, all the more for knowing there is no question of ever possessing you, you have gone beyond the limits, an incandescence.

Reporting keeps me from going down to the sidewalk and shouting out for you. Newspaper writing is my camouflage against becoming you. Even so it's good, it's useful. However much you differed from me by temperament, a man of action, therefore more just.

Meanwhile, these things become more and more tangled, what with our inability to free ourselves from your heritage. Five days ago a grenade exploded in the stove that heats the Salonika Security Department, destroying documents concerning you. At first they blamed the cleaning woman. But any such nonsense was quickly ruled out, and as usual a pile of question marks remains unanswered. How did such important documents come to be in a cupboard next to the stove? What sort of documents were they? Are there copies? Such things keep bobbing to the surface and there are left, unexamined forever, because no one can wrest the truth from those who don't want to tell it. And then this second "suicide" of Yango's! At first one heard he'd taken thirty-two Luminal tablets. But they pumped his stomach immediately after and he was forced to admit that he had taken at most four or five tranquilizers his doctor had given him because he suffered from insomnia—a quantity, furthermore, in exact accordance with the prescription. He had taken them, said Yango, because his request for transfer from prison to the reformatory had been ignored. And you, how are you feeling?

I am blackening my lungs with cigarettes. I'm smoking a lot. And drinking. I need you. Your face floating up in the night glimmers like stars that, weary of flashing erotically earthward, have retired to a corner of the sky, to spin their golden webs in peace.

I feel better as I finish this report. From now on I can relax my preoccupation with you, return to my everyday reality, so long forgotten for your sake. Return to port, having tasted the ocean. Return to life, having tasted your death. Of my own death I shall not be able to write.

Chapter 5

And so it went until—yes, until the Commissioner or Mastodontosaur cracked. He couldn't stand any more. After two years he was still in prison. Of the men in uniform, only he was still keeping company with the dregs: Yango, Vango, Baron, and Autocratosaur.

Why had the other officers been released? Once you're out, he thought to himself, you can stay out. There are ways. Your movements are free. But when you're in, you stay in. You can't do anything. Who cares about you?

He was the scapegoat. Why should he pay? From his very first days at the Police Training School, he had had a second-rate destiny. He was considered illiterate. They used him for hard labor. He'd married a cultivated girl, teacher at an English institute, to counteract the bane—to no avail. Nothing changed. They appointed him Commissioner in Ano Toumba, a district supposedly within the city but in actual fact resembling the most backward village. Instructed what to testify, he had obeyed readily. He felt a solidarity with the others. But they had cheated him, they had forgotten him in prison, and his resentment was mounting. One day he decided to compose a memorandum telling the truth. Until that moment, from the battlements of the police force, had come only silence and repression. The memorandum opened a crack in the wall. The waters rushed in, all but flooding the fortress. But within less than a month, July 1965, the Center government was deprived of power by an anti-Constitutional act of the King, and under the new puppet Cabinet primordial silence was restored. Nevertheless, the memorandum had said almost everything:

On the morning of that day the Commissioner, acting officer on duty, was also, according to regulations, officer in charge of victuals. With the canteen supervisor he went to the Modiano Market to buy fish: according to regulations, every Wednesday the police department eats fish. It was ten minutes to ten. The fishmonger told them the fish would be arriving from the Salamis market after 10:15. Fresh fish, codfish to be precise: according to regulations, the canteen provides no deep-freeze goods. At that point, leaving the canteen supervisor, he had thought of going to pay his telephone bill, which that month was higher than usual because his wife had called Crete twice, to speak to her family there. The

Telephone Company office was at Vasileos Irakleiou Street, alongside the Electra movie house. When he got there he saw a lot of people waiting and decided to leave so as not to miss the first pick of the fish. Just as he was going out the door, a voice behind him said, "Hello there, Mr. Commissioner."

He turned and saw Yango.

"How do you happen to be over this way?" Yango asked him, approaching.

"How do you?" he asked in return.

"My stand's here," he said. "I have the pickup. There it is." And he pointed to it.

"And I've come to pay my bill, but there's a line at the tellers' windows," the Commissioner said.

"Give it to me and I'll pay it for you," Yango offered.

Of course the Commissioner refused, saying it wasn't yet due and besides there were some questions about his wife's long-distance phone calls, this month's bill having struck him as exaggerated, there might be some confusion with another phone.

"Let me offer you a cup of coffee, Commissioner," Yango said then. "There's a coffee shop under the arcade."

"No, thank you," he answered. "Today I'm in charge of provisions and I'm waiting for the codfish to arrive from Salamis."

"I know," Yango said. "They say it comes at ten, but it's never there before eleven."

The Commissioner was impressed that he knew this.

"You've got plenty of time," Yango persisted. "Come on, let me offer you a drink of something."

"I already had my coffee this morning," the Commissioner had replied.

He had slept the night before in the main Security Department building because, as stated, he was duty officer. His watch lasted from Tuesday noon till Wednesday noon, the day of the incidents. Well then, Tuesday afternoon, Assistant Police Captain Mavroulis had telephoned all the branches of the Security Department with the order that the following day at 7:00 P.M. every patriotic citizen at their disposal be sent to the Catacomb Club for the purpose of harassing the Friends of Peace "in the usual fashion," with stones, shouts, shoving, and the like. Later that evening—Tuesday—Mavroulis stopped by in person to ask the Commissioner if he had carried out the order. He replied that he hadn't received any order, he hadn't been at his own station but here, as duty officer. Mavroulis told him to phone immediately then, and he did so in front of him. He phoned Ano Toumba and ordered the police there to notify five or six individuals, though not named, to come down to the counterdemonstration tomorrow. Then he also phoned his agent at Sykiés; he couldn't give his name now; no charges had been filed against him and it wasn't right to involve him. At any rate, he would give the message to his own group outside the Catacomb.

"Are we going to have a little party?" the agent had asked.

"Yes," he had answered. "Little party" was code for "trouble." By all this he wanted to say that the counterdemonstration was by no means spontaneous. It was pure make-believe that the crowd had gathered because of the slogans being broadcast over the loudspeakers.

To return to the following morning. He had refused Yango's invitation because it was a central location and the devil, as they say, has a lot of legs. If one of his superiors happened to pass by and see him drinking coffee with a character like Yango, he might draw conclusions. He said goodbye and went back to the fishmonger; the codfish hadn't arrived yet. He sent the canteen officer to mail a letter at the central post office, and as he was waiting for him to come back, another porter from Yango's stand appeared, also to invite him for coffee. These characters (he should explain here and now) thought it a great honor for a Commissioner to sit at the table with them. He refused this one too, explaining that he had just turned down Yango.

"Give us a chance there, Mr. Commissioner," the man persisted. "Do us the favor."

Finally he gave in. "You come with me and I'll treat you to a *bougatsa*," the Commissioner said. "I'll have some milk, because lately my stomach's been giving me trouble."

"Just a minute," the porter called and went off. "If I find Yango, shall I bring him along?" he shouted, stopping a little way off.

Knowing how easily hurt these underworld people are, he answered: "All right, bring him!" And so, shortly, there they all were, sitting in the pastry shop.

In the course of eating the *bougatsa*, Yango showed him the tip of a club he'd passed through his belt. He said he was carrying it because that evening he had some roughing up to do. The Commissioner advised him to be careful and not act rashly as his friend Odysseus had done once when he broke the leg of a man from Pylaia and it had cost him thirty thousand drachs. He should be careful not to strike anyone, because if charges were brought against him he'd be convicted. The Commissioner also advised him not to listen to Autocratosaur, because Autocratosaur was mad. By all this he wished to emphasize that Yango had known about the meeting before they ran into each other. Who had told him about the Friends of Peace? Who had given him the club? If the investigation were to turn in that direction, it might discover the thread within the labyrinth.

Finally, the fish had arrived. Mastodontosaur paid and left. He didn't see Yango again. Except that that afternoon he ran into him at the police station, going out with the other patriotic citizens from the slums who'd been rounded up there. How and why he did not know, but the order to collect outside the Catacomb had been canceled by Mavroulis and a new order issued for them to meet at the station. Mastodontosaur found them all there, gathered in the police station, that afternoon when (after finishing his shift) he passed by to see what was up. The "patriots" didn't all fit in the room and they spilled out in the corridor, as at court when an important trial is on. As he arrived, he heard Mavroulis winding up his speech with the words: "That's all we have to say. On our way out, go a few at a time to avoid attracting attention." He had not heard Mavroulis say: "Your target is Z.!" This he had learned later, from other colleagues. And so the "patriots" poured into the corridors, all on fire; Mavroulis had apparently kindled their blood. In their excitement they carried him along with them, though they didn't recognize him in civilian clothes. Among them was Yango. Mastodontosaur had left by another exit so as not to get in the way. As they poured out, he had gone over to the Catacomb. He saw a big poster announcing the change of site for the Friends of Peace meeting. There he met Leandros and Baron and someone else he didn't recognize. They came up to him and asked him where to go, meaning where to station themselves. He told them they weren't needed and to go back to their homes. This he said more for Baron's sake, who till then he'd considered a Red. He was afraid that if there were any incidents Baron might be beaten up as a Communist. Only later did he learn that Leandros had gone to Baron's house that same afternoon and taken him to the Ano Toumba station, where, as stated, Mastodontosaur had been away "on duty." How dare they accuse him of "conducting special activities in the course of the twenty-four hours preceding the meeting" and of "summoning people to the counterdemonstration," when during the entire twenty-four-hour period he'd been away from Ano Toumba? And whether or not he was lying wouldn't be difficult to ascertain from the Security Department files. No, over at the Catacomb he had not seen Yango tearing down the poster, or kicking a woman either. If he had, though, he wouldn't have stopped him, because that afternoon the officers had explicit orders not to make any arrests. This was part of the whole framework of the counterdemonstration.

He had gone to the counterdemonstration as ordered.

Besides, everybody was there. Only the officer on duty (the one who had taken the next shift at the Security Department) was missing. Now why his name hadn't been included when the Investigator had asked for the list of officers who had been at the site of the incidents, he did not know. Nor did he understand why they had concealed the presence of another police captain on the grounds of "a pressing need for secrecy." What game his superiors were playing, he couldn't say. His only gripe was that they had picked him to pay for it all!

Yes, the police at the rally had taken a passive role. The only active police officer was Mavroulis. He scurried this way and that, pointing out Communists, whom the bullies then beat up. He had also formed groups and assigned a Communist to each, for beating up afterwards. A few officers had said they left early, before the "accident." That was a big lie; according to regulations, no officer was permitted to leave before the last citizen, and then only on the order of the Head of Security. On this, the heads of the various branches might be better qualified to speak.

As soon as Z.'s speech was over, a very upset Chief of Police had ordered them to disperse the counterdemonstrators. And in actual fact they did begin. The Commissioner had helped push some of them back. He had talked with no one except the General's orderly, whom he had mistaken for the General because they resembled each other. The General was there, a short way off. No, he had not spoken to him. Nor had he seen Yango or Vango. Nor had he looked toward Spandoni Street to see if the pickup truck was there. Besides, why should he have looked, since he knew nothing about it? However, he had seen the many vicious acts of the bullies and the stones they threw, and had heard their curses. He also clearly heard Z. making appeals over the loudspeaker, saying his life was in danger.

At the moment of Z.'s mortal injury, the Commissioner had been in front of the auditorium. He heard the noise of a motor, saw a person standing upright in the van and another person fallen on the ground. He rushed in that direction. He asked what it was and heard from passers-by: "They've butchered our Z.! They've killed him!" He hadn't taken any action, because much closer than himself to the Volkswagen into which Z. was being lifted stood the General and the Chief of Police. The presence of superiors, according to regulations, canceled his own right to act.

Mastodontosaur had left the meeting by automobile around 10:30 and stopped by the station to make a routine report on what Communists from his district he'd seen at the meeting. In the station he ran into Yango again. "What are you doing here?" he asked. "I was speeding on my three-wheeler and I hit someone. They arrested me and carted me over here," Yango told him. Also present at the station were two lawyers he knew. He entered the office marked ASSISTANT COMMISSIONER to make his report. As he was finishing, in a hurry because his wife would be waiting for him outside the English institute, Yango came in and asked, "Mr. Commissioner, since my pickup's insured, will they hold me? And if they do hold me, will it be here or at the Traffic Department?" "I don't know," he replied dryly. Then he handed his report to the officer on duty and left quickly. The fact that he had stayed at the station all of ten minutes was corroborated by one of the two lawyers.

He went home, had something to eat, and went to bed. At 2:30 in the morning a policeman woke him. "Mr. Commissioner, you're wanted urgently on the phone!"

"Who wants me at this hour?" he asked drowsily.

"It's the Chief's office," the policeman said.

He got up and shuffled to his desk. "Commissioner of Ano Toumba speaking," he said into the phone. "What is it?"

"Come, come, Vassili! It's Mavroulis! You're late. I've been waiting for you for a long time!"

"What's up?"

"Listen. The Chief of Police wants Vango Preka from Ano Toumba by morning. Take some policeman who knows Ano Toumba, go find him, and bring him to the station. I've already tried but he wasn't home."

"Shall I arrest him?" Mastodontosaur had asked.

"No! The order is to find him and bring him in."

And in fact, along with the policeman who had awakened him, he did find Vango Preka and brought him in to the station as requested. The story about the "voluntary surrender" of Vango after reading the morning papers was untrue. Mavroulis had given him the order; not, as stated at the investigation, someone else. They all knew this; they were all lying; the General, the Chief of Police. Why they wanted to protect Mavroulis, he didn't know. Or who had given Mavroulis the order.

Next they sent him to the police station to tell Yango and Vango what to say. That they had been drinking at a tavern and blind drunk had run over Z., and so on. To his considerable surprise, he discovered that they both knew the story better than he did. Why he had been sent? To put them through a dress rehearsal before they "confessed" to the Prosecutor? A further surprise: he now learned that they had already talked with the Prosecutor, before daybreak! So why send him at all? He hadn't been able to understand then. Now he knew. To throw the blame on him! They had done everything, his colleagues had, to put the whole thing on his shoulders.

Three facts he learned much later supported this view. That Wednesday night, a superior officer had gone to the police station to ask the officer on duty whether he, the Commissioner, had been there. The officer on duty replied that Mavroulis had. "I'm not interested in Mavroulis. I want to know about Mastodontosaur!" This was one point. Another was that after he made his report and left the station, Mavroulis arrived, in a sweat. He was trying to hide Yango. When this proved impossible because they were seen by the officer on duty, who was apparently not in on it, Mavroulis had put Yango in the detention room and instructed him what to say, about being drunk and the rest. Last of all, Mastodonto-saur had learned from the Security Department barber that on that Wednesday afternoon, before addressing his toughs at the station, Mavroulis had stopped in the officers' lounge and told them, with a nod toward his assembled "patriots": "Today you'll see what happens!" A ranking officer, knowing the abnormal character of Mavroulis, warned him: "Watch out because someone might get killed and then we'll all be in trouble!" Mavroulis had not taken this well; words were exchanged. They would have been at each other's throats if the others hadn't pulled them apart.

One unshakable conclusion emerged: Mavroulis should be in prison and he, the Commissioner, should be out.

These few things he had wanted to say about his colleagues. Now if he might just say two words about the others who were in prison with him.

Yango he'd met only once, again thanks to Mavroulis. One evening Mavroulis had notified him that the Communists were descending on Toumba with leaflets, and to take care to set some ambushes outside their houses. Indeed, Mavroulis had reproved him for not knowing the situation. Mastodontosaur had gone to his agent's house and there met Yango, who had been alerted that night—except that not a single leaflet materialized. He had seen him next at the time of de Gaulle's visit. After that, at the pastry shop. And for the last time on that Thursday morning when Mavroulis had told him to escort an individual from Kalamaria who wanted to help Yango financially, this person, like Yango, having been embittered by the Communists. Who it was, Mavroulis could tell them.

Vango he knew as a type who sat down uninvited at a table of friends.

Baron he had thought was an active Communist. Once, in 1962, he had purchased two cardinals from him; "his pastime was catching songbirds."

And Autocratosaur he'd kicked out of his office, rough

and tough though he could be. He had come to gloat that his organization had protected General de Gaulle. The Commissioner told him if he ever set foot there again he'd break his legs for him. "I'll fix you!" Autocratosaur had howled. The two had always got along so badly that Autocratosaur, though he was in the Commissioner's precinct, went to another police station to see to the identity cards of the members of his organization. And fortunately so, because otherwise they'd have accused him of being behind Autocratosaur now, just as they had accused him of having organized the "colored-pin gang"—when in fact these pins had been given to the protectors of de Gaulle for the sole purpose of their recognizing one another.

"With good reason, the question arises: why have I delayed so long in bringing to light and justice this personal evidence? Alas, I should have followed Plomaris's path, who disassociated himself from the other accused officers, hired his own lawyer, even though they all said that if 'we went as a body, we'd be given general amnesty.' Plomaris said he was no guerrilla gangman, for the state to grant him amnesty, and went his own way. Had I done likewise, I would not be paying for it in this way now. For there is clear proof that the others have tried to throw the blame on me to vindicate themselves. Nevertheless, the first principle of justice is the just distribution of responsibilities.

"Most respectfully yours,
"MASTODONTOSAUR"

Chapter 6

Slowly but surely I am discovering my own face, his wife reflected, my own true face, hidden so long (ever since the day you died) beneath variously named masks. You, who are you? You have:

Two eyes
A nose
A mouth
A neck

From the neck I climb to your jaw and kiss it, all of it fitting into my mouth. From there to your lips, two strands of sand in the infinite. And from your teeth (now toothpicks for the rats, but adored once as the beacons on my coast, an avenue of lanterns, or, seen from an angle, a single whiteness flashing in the dark of your mouth as it swallowed glass upon glass of water) I reach the adored cheekbone, pure in corruption beneath the myrrh of a thousand kisses from the cemetery. I am not morbid. In my heart I celebrate you, as at a festival. I do not want to reach your eyes. I deny them once and for all. I deny them like the sleep that undoes me.

Now I know who you are. You are he who has gone and whom I shall love forever.

My feelings may not interest anyone. But they interest me. And with me, you do not exist. It's as simple as that. The irony is that without you I do not exist either. A freak of destiny killed you. I live by the same coincidence. Nothing separates us. I live in order to think about your death.

When I see young girls walking where you walked, I

come to understand your immortality. These girls, in the children they will bear tomorrow, will have been delivered as well of some trace of the emotion you aroused in them.

Inorganic matter wins out over organic. Texts, investigations, court proceedings, my God, how dead it all is! As if I were employed in the Public Registrar's Office. And you, how alive still! I have nothing else to tell you, I cannot think about you soberly. For me you are not part of reality. You are somewhere else, where cloud rests upon cloud in a net of starlight.

I feel sacrilegious, a trespasser, a violator. I should be behind bars. Perhaps an earthquake would cure me: to see buildings and people I believed in fallen, to see the world flat on its face, and so find myself cured—enough at least to know that dirge and lamentation belong to another order of human being. That action, everyday action, alone exists. That I who betray you every day am unworthy of you.

And yet, no! I cry it with all my heart. There is a corner for dreams, a corner where deteriorating can be arrested. And you and I . . .

With you, I come to my end. If I cease to suffer for you, I shall cease to exist. If I saw you before me suddenly, I would go to pieces, having learned by now to love you only from photographs.

I say, I shall leave you. And yet, deep down I do not believe it. I shall be occupied for some time more with certain details of your perfecting, the way photographers retouch the likenesses of the dead. But tell me—why don't you know me? Why do you never come some evening to the room with the broken clock? I loved you in my first springtime, when I did not know what fasting meant, or abstinence, or separation. You were my first love. There is no second.

Come to this cave with your great arms outspread, come. Take the whore, the widow, the soul, *Papilio crespontes, Vanessa atalanta:* me.

Chapter 7

His former colleagues, the police officers, betrayed Mastodontosaur. The Investigator summoned them one by one. The symptoms never varied: collective amnesia.

"I," stated Mavroulis, "it is not true that . . . in particular, it is not true . . . what the Commissioner of Ano Toumba maintains is absolutely fantastic . . . In large measure it is not true . . . nor is it true that . . . Besides, it was not possible for me to give the Commissioner an order; because I am six grades below him in the hierarchy."

"I," stated the second, "was not present at the aforementioned meeting of the Friends of Peace even for a moment. At that time our department was occupied with the case of the so-called Ogre. Thus, at approximately 6 P.M. on the aforementioned date 5.22.63, we had gone out with Captain Yevyenopoulos in search of individuals bearing the traits of the Ogre. We crossed Ayia Sofia Street, Ermou, Venizelou, Dragoumi, Nea Megalou Alexandrou Streets, as far as the Floka Pastry Shop opposite the Lambropoulos stores. Returning, we met Plomaris near the old Macedonian Research Building. 'Is there anything here for us? What is happening?' Yevyenopoulos asked. 'Nothing,' Plomaris answered. Whereupon we proceeded by bus to Seïch-Sou, where, as everyone knows, the famous Ogre committed his crimes. There we met Paralis; I asked him if he had any news of the Ogre. After a few minutes we proceeded to the Pendeli Taverna up over the Kavtanzogliou Stadium, and from there, after an hour, we went down to the center of the city and parted near Yevyenopoulos's house. Specifically, when Mastodontosaur named me as a witness, I said: 'How can I be a witness if we were not at the site of the incidents, except much earlier; that is, before the incidents took place!' "

"I," stated the third, "during the time of the incidents and preceding them was in my own district around the Administration Building for the purpose of surveying the movements of the Communists and guarding the Ministry of Northern Greece."

"I," stated Plomaris, "between four-thirty and five that afternoon went to my office for afternoon rollcall. The officer on duty informed me that, because of the Friends of Peace rally, I and my colleague Koukos had been ordered to be on duty, each with five policemen. Our job was not to survey the Reds but to watch out for malefactors in the vicinity of the rally, to prevent burglaries and other such breaches of the law. I was furious about this additional duty (I kept this to myself, needless to say); it seemed absurd to have a force of two officers and ten men for absolutely nothing at all. It was then that Mavroulis came by. As I said, I was in a state of irritation. 'You're dragging us to the rallies again!' I said to him. 'That's a job for the Security Department!' Mavroulis is a quick-tempered loudmouth. 'So it's only us who have to support the anti-Communist struggle?' he shouted. 'Why—you think the rest of us are Communists?' I retorted. That's what we said, and not as Mastodontosaur testified. A proof that we didn't go at each other is the fact that afterwards, if I recall correctly, I offered him a coffee."

"I," stated the fifth, "know nothing . . . I do not know who . . . it is not true that . . I do not know whether . . . Mastodontosaur was not hard on the Communists . . . He was indulgent, gave licenses to Communist vendors and made no objection to granting a passport to a Communist, Odyporidis Platonas, so that Platonas could go to Russia for treatment of a supposed heart ailment."

"I," stated the sixth, "since it was Wednesday and the market was closed, was out to prevent robberies and to search for the Ogre. I went to the police station after many days' absence on a personal matter—to interview the buyer of an apartment whose sale I was interested in. To be sure, we must have heard something about the incidents from the police captain. But it is absolutely false that I said 'I'm interested in Mastodontosaur, not in Mavroulis.' "

"As for me," stated the seventh, "that afternoon Captain Poulopoulos of the military reserve corps picked me up at my office and we went to visit the priest from the Phaneromeni Church, Kosta, who'd celebrated his name-day the previous day. We also visited an Eleni, who was also celebrating her name-day. Since my wife's name is Eleni too, I hadn't the chance to go out of my house for Konstantinos and Eleni. On my way past Ermou Street, I did in fact see Mastodontosaur, who greeted me, 'Good evening, Mr. Polychronis.' 'Good evening,' I replied and proceeded to take my bus. This is the truth and not that I said 'Let them get beat up!' It was still seven-thirty and no rally had even begun. In the end, we didn't find the priest at home (he was out at a baptism) or Mrs. Eleni either. She'd gone to the movies. But we stayed at her place till eleven-thirty, waiting for her to come back."

"I," stated the eighth, "learned that Yevyenopoulos was at the rally at least at the start, and had bought a belt with brass buckles from a stall in the vicinity."

"I," stated the ninth, "it is not true . . . nor is it true that I saw Mavroulis at the rally, spinning about like a top and pointing out Communists."

"I," stated the tenth, "when my attention was called to the change of site for the rally, was unable to go on. It was forbidden, and I was in civilian clothes. At this point I went to the Serraikon Restaurant, where I dined on rabbit and onion stew which the proprietor prepared especially for me."

Chapter 8

"The Investigator was awarded a fellow-ship in Paris. The Public Prosecutor died of a heart attack, so they said. Hatzis and Nikitas were placed in custody, charged with libel by the former Chief of Police. The police officials were transferred to peaceful provincial towns with lots of greenery and few worries. We are in the autumn of 1966. For three and a half years we have missed you terribly. For three and a half years King Constantine has been learning the mysteries of Japanese wrestling. He began with jujitsu, continued with judo, and for the past year now has been indoctrinated in the amazing secrets of karate. Here for a year now, ever since His Majesty's 'anti-Constitutional act,' I've been feeling deposed. I'm in the same room, facing the same house across from me. On the third-floor balcony, the old woman died who used to look through her binoculars. Now they're painting the house again. All day long, workmen sing. The hot wing of tiles is my only company. The trial about to begin will bring to light perhaps more, perhaps less. The result matters less than the procedure. It remains to be found who struck you with the iron bar, who ordered whoever ordered the one who ordered the one who ordered the next man, who gave the order that you be struck. Across the way, they're painting the balconies red. My teeth have discolored. I will no longer write you."

About the Author

VASSILIS VASSILIKOS was born in Kavala, Greece, in 1933 and is identified in the Cambridge *History of Greece* as the most promising writer of his generation. He published his first short novel at the age of twenty and in 1961 received The Award of the Group of Twelve for his trilogy of short novels, *The Plant, The Well, The Angel*. This award, given for the best fiction of the year, is the most respected literary prize in Greece and Vassilikos is the youngest writer ever to have won it. In 1959-60, as one of seven young European writers to receive Ford Foundation grants, he travelled throughout the United States. "Modern literature should reflect modern life," Vassilikos once said, "and the essence of modern life is conflict." His novel *Z*, based admittedly on the murder of the Greek physician and parliamentarian Gregory Lambrakis, is officially banned in Greece and Vassilikos now lives in exile in Paris. A best seller throughout Europe, *Z* has been adapted for film by Jorge Semprun, author of the screenplay for the Alan Resnais film "The War is Over," and Costa-Gavras who also directed the motion picture. The official entry for France at the 1969 Cannes Film Festival, "Z" was awarded the Jury Prize and will soon be released in America.

Now in paperback from Ballantine...

"Kevin Brownlow's superb mammoth history of the early film . . . a huge and hugely fascinating book . . . marvelous pictures . . . intriguing . . . enthralling . . . completely satisfying!"

—Richard Shickel, Life

"A must for movie buffs!"

—New York Times

Special large format paperbound edition— complete and unabridged—containing the full text and all of the photographs of the original $13.95 hardcover edition.

5⅜" by 8¼"   672 pages   283 pictures

Available at your local bookstore. Or order by mail by sending $4.00 to: Dept. CS, Ballantine Books, 36 West 20th Street, New York, N.Y. 10003